R

Father of lies

It was her mother's fault: if she had grown up with them, as by rights she should have done, they would be like cousins or brothers, no more, no less. As it was, they had come into her life as strangers, adult males, potential lovers . . .

When Georgie Payne knocks on the door of her grandfather's house, she has crossed the Atlantic alone to solve a mystery. Her mother, Olivia, had had no contact with her own father and mother for close on twenty years. What had happened to bring this about? The problem has dogged her for years. Now Georgie has come to claim her birthright.

To her surprise and delight, she quickly discovers two of her lost tribe: the slim, graceful, ambiguous Matthew, her mother's half brother, and big, blond, shaggy Luke, a sort of surly angel, her grandmother's son. Her two gorgeous uncles. And then there is the sardonic, enigmatic presence of her grandmother's husband, Nick Winter, a successful photographer.

The more she discovers, the greater the mystery grows, and the more entangled she becomes in the consequences of what happened long ago – with potentially tragic results. Georgie, whose claim to a right to her own history has broken the silence of decades, comes to realize that the past is not a foreign country after all.

In this absorbing, multi-layered story of a family fractured by deceit, Janet Inglis has faced the subject of society's last taboo with unflinching honesty. *Father of lies* is a powerful successor to her extraordinary first novel, *Daddy's girl*.

Also by Janet Inglis

Daddy's girl (1994)

FATHER OF LIES

Janet Inglis

Constable · London

First published in 1995 by Constable & Company Ltd
3 The Lanchesters, 162 Fulham Palace Road, London W6 9ER
Copyright © 1995 by Janet Inglis
The right of Janet Inglis to be identified as the author
of this work has been asserted by her in accordance
with the Copyright, Designs and Patents Act 1988
ISBN 0 09 474500 5
Set in Linotron Palatino 10.5pt by CentraCet Ltd, Cambridge
Printed in Great Britain by St Edmundsbury Press Ltd
Bury St Edmunds, Suffolk

A CIP catalogue record for this book
is available from the British Library

In those days there was no king in Israel;
every man did that which was right in his own eyes.

The Book of Judges

FIRST HALF

I have been a stranger in a strange land.

Underhill the sign read, a weathered wooden board nailed to the wooden gate, hand-carved letters infilled with black paint.

Georgie had no way of knowing if this was the right Underhill. The narrow lane had no name on her map. It was only a dirt track, or would have been if there were any dirt around here. Instead it was a shining white way, for when the thin topsoil was scraped away there was chalk underneath. The topsoil itself was chalky grey, not the rich black that she had always assumed to be the true colour of earth. This was an alien land, literally.

The bartender in the village had not mentioned the lane by name in his directions, which were what her father would have called of the Irish variety: go down the hill to the garage but don't turn there, then go along to the tea shop on the corner but don't go in there . . . The address in the phone book had no street name or house number. Not an address at all, as she would have reckoned it, but presumably the local post office knew what it meant: Underhill, Firleston, Glynde. Three improbable meaningless words. But she had found Glynde on a map, and then Firleston as well. Glynde even had a railway station, so that she could easily get herself and her bicycle within striking distance of Underhill.

The trouble was that any house around here could very well have called itself by that name. She had always imagined that when someone in a nursery rhyme or fairy tale was described as living under the hill, it meant a hobbit-house dug right into the hillside. But now she saw how it really worked.

The hill commemorated in Underhill was inescapable. It lowered over her like a tombstone marking the edge of the world, a giant dyke to hold back the sea, a frozen wave of rock threatening to overwhelm the inland plain. Not so much a hill as a geological phenomenon. Not a hill, anyway, but a long highland ridge formed from great knuckles of chalk, as if some prehistoric titan had gripped the earth in his death throes and left for unwitting memorial these green slopes and white perpendiculars. On her map the letters *South*

Downs trailed across the crowded contour lines. The knuckle to the west was labelled Beddingham Hill, the more dramatic rise eastwards had been given the romantic name of Firle Beacon.

This was geology with a vengeance, red in tooth and claw. From the brow of Firle Beacon, she guessed, anyone would be able to diagnose the ancient earth-history of Sussex. Very different from the dispositions she was used to, where the landscape took hundreds of miles to change its mind and its face.

She swung her leg over the bar of the bicycle and propped it against the stone wall. The wall itself was a lesson in geology, for the stones embedded in the mortar matrix were clearly flints. Chalk and flint were the opposite of chalk and cheese, it seemed; one lot went together and the other did not. Flints erupted from the chalky surface of the lane, making a bike ride even bumpier. The house beyond the wall was also built of flint, framed and pointed with some fancy decorative brickwork.

Georgie had read about cob and wattle and daub and tile and thatch and slate, the half-timbered houses of the Midlands and the dry-stone walls of the North, but in her New World insularity she had imagined that sort of thing must only exist in specially preserved areas like a real-life Disneyland. But this was just ordinary England, this quaintly constructed dwelling as unremarkable in its context as her parents' house in suburban Toronto. The thought of getting to see inside the old flint house intrigued her almost as much as her real errand.

She knew she was only trying to psych herself up, to collect her courage to the point of knocking on a stranger's door. What if it was the wrong stranger, what if she was about to make a fool of herself? She walked on a few steps past the gate, putting off the moment of truth.

Even in high summer, at four o'clock on a sunny Saturday, there was something faintly eerie about the stark beauty of this country-side. It was not uninhabited: she could see the sheep swarming aimlessly across the steep green slope, watch a pair of hikers creeping along the skyline, hear the distant sporadic murmur of modern transportation on the highway down below the trees. But she could also make out (and identify, since it was marked on the map) the swell of a neolithic long barrow high up the side of Firle Beacon. And the trees hereabouts, their stooped and slanted limbs were mute evidence that they knew in their knotted heartwood which way the wind blew, year in, year out.

She didn't know if it was a comfort or not, to be told by the map that just over the Downs lay coastal civilization, cities and towns with their toes in the sea and their backs to the hill, hundreds of thousands of people living totally modern lives, taking no notice of the wind from the sea. This time of year there would be thousands more on the beaches, holiday-makers like herself.

The past she had always thought of as vulnerable and easily destroyed. But right here it seemed much too deep and complex to succumb to human indifference and shallow mortal memories. The Old Country, her grandfather had called it, and now she understood that it was.

She touched the smooth face of a flint in the wall. It was hot, holding the heat of the sun. Its memory went no further back than noon, yet its history was almost as old as the earth. She shivered in the sunlight.

The shiver might have been her reaction to a sense of being observed. She glanced up at the windows of the house, where no curtains were drawn, no face visible. Not even – she turned to check – not even a curious sheep or cow in the field on the opposite side of the road. But when she looked back to the blind house, the watcher had revealed itself: a stocky black cat with great white whiskers, extensive eyebrows, and neat white cravat and slippers, perched upright on the wall. His owlish amber eyes stared at her with a slightly cross-eyed intensity.

He blinked benignly to assure her of friendly intentions. Georgie held out her hand and made inviting sounds with her teeth and tongue to indicate her own friendliness. The cat blinked again, this time as if offended by such childishness, such premature familiarity. He flicked his ears in disapproval, jumped down into the grass and stalked off.

As he disappeared, Georgie caught the sound of a car coming up from the village. She could hear it crunching over the chalk roadbed before it emerged from the trees and the screen of hedges lining the road. It slowed as it approached her and she could see the driver clearly, a woman of forty or so. Maybe the woman was lost, intending to stop to ask directions.

The car drove past her. It turned into a wide gap in the flint wall that surrounded Underhill.

It must be the wrong house then, Georgie thought. The woman was too young. Her mother's age.

She strolled past the entrance to the driveway, surreptitiously watching the driver get out of the car. A newish and expensive one – Georgie didn't know much about cars but she could tell that much. The woman was wearing a sleeveless navy dress which showed her slim figure to advantage. She opened the rear door of the car to retrieve several shopping bags. Georgie peeped guiltily over the wall as the woman walked away, taking her shopping around to the back

11

of the house. No doubt of it, she was too young. She ought to have been more like sixty than forty.

Georgie mooched back to the bicycle, brooding over her dilemma. She sat down at the roadside with her back to the warm wall, so that if the woman looked out a front window there would be no stranger lurking visibly.

To knock or not to knock? She had come all this way – not just all the way from London but all the way from Toronto, four thousand miles, half the width of the world – expressly to knock on the door of this house. And now she had lost her nerve.

She wouldn't have hesitated if the woman had been the right sort of age. She might even have accosted her in the yard . . . by saying what? Months, even years of speculation and imagining had not helped her to the magic formula.

Magic was the word, all right. In her day-dreams she had often knocked: not at the door of this flint cottage, unimagined and heretofore unimaginable, but on some anonymous and more familiar door, in an apartment block perhaps, or on a small suburban bungalow. She had knocked and the door had been opened to her, instantly recognized and welcomed. By strangers.

She looked down at her dusty legs and grimy boots, her ragged denim shorts cut from an old pair of jeans and smeared by now with chalk. She was all too aware of her sunburnt face and her hair inartistically deranged by the wind. Something else she hadn't considered till this moment was the impression she was likely to make.

She must look as if she had been sleeping under hedges. She shouldn't have worn the shorts anyway, women here didn't seem to wear them on the street. Experiences in London had taught her that she would inevitably sound to English ears like a broad, brash, flat-footed Yank. Supposing they actually did recognize this appalling apparition, would they even want to admit it?

And it might not be the right Underhill. She should have asked the man in the pub if there was more than one. She should have mentioned the name of the people she was looking for. Maybe she should go back to the village and ask, just to make sure . . .

But that was sheer chickenheartedness speaking. There was only one way to deal with this situation, and that meant knocking on the door.

She stood up, dusted off the seat of her shorts, and surveyed the house. She was standing right by the gate with the *Underhill* sign, which led directly to the front door. But the woman had gone around to the back. Maybe she should do the same, maybe they didn't really use the front door. She had a vague idea that country people did

12

things that way. Not that these people were farmers or anything like that. Not real country folks at all.

She pushed her bicycle into the drive and propped it against the garage. Brick-built, she noticed – these new-fangled building materials! She combed her fingers through her curly platinum-blonde hair in a vain attempt to civilize her appearance. She hadn't brought a comb or lipstick or anything. Some superstition had prompted her to leave all her belongings back at the bed-and-breakfast in London. Well, if they greeted her with open arms in spite of all, she would know they loved her for herself alone and not her yellow hair.

The back yard – garden, she corrected herself – was largely hidden from the lane by the house and the garage. It had a southern exposure, dominated by a view of the Downs at close quarters, but enjoying the sun all day long. Like every English garden she had seen so far, even the tiny cramped rectangles at the rear of the rows of little houses she had glimpsed from the train, it had an amazing abundance and variety of green growing things, blooming, trailing, winding up trellises and spilling over walls with a vigour and profusion that took her breath away.

Now you've got to knock, she told herself sternly. You can't walk into somebody's back yard without explaining yourself. She had gone too far to go away.

The back door was in two halves and the top half stood open. Shamelessly she examined the kitchen within. It had an immaculate old-fashioned farmhouse appearance which only money and modernization could have produced: red-tiled floor, scrubbed wooden table, an enormous fireplace with an enormous black cast-iron stove, natural pine cabinets, tiled countertops littered with just about every domestic convenience ever devised. No, she had never imagined anything like this.

The sound of a woman's voice offstage obliged Georgie to knock. It would be mortifying if someone came into the kitchen to find her gawping, unannounced and unknown.

She had to lean over the bottom half of the door to rap on the top half. Her first go at knocking was ineffectual and ineffective. She rapped harder. The loud sound in the quiet place startled even herself.

Someone came into the kitchen, not the woman. A tall man. The sunlight splashing through the window and the open door showed him up quite clearly. He was slim and erect, but his hair had gone grey, the steely grey that overtakes dark hair. He wore a white open-necked shirt with long sleeves, and light-coloured cotton trousers. He was strikingly handsome in a stern, gaunt, strait-laced English way. And he was the right age, in his sixties.

He stopped and stared at her without coming too close. His clear blue eyes were wary and reserved, like the rest of his face, like the way he held his body. He didn't say anything. Maybe he thought she should speak up first. She had turned up on his doorstep; it was her job to explain her presence.

She opened her mouth, still without any idea of what to say. She could start by introducing herself, at least. 'Sorry to turn up like this, without any warning. I'm Georgiana Payne.' She tried to speak slowly and softly in a vain attempt to avoid sounding like some awful American intruder, to avoid offending him as she had offended the cat on the wall. 'You are Dr Beckett, aren't you?'

As she babbled and he stared, she realized that he probably couldn't see her very well. The bright sunlight behind her would tend to dazzle him and keep her face in shadow. She moved away from the door.

He came forward until he was right in the open doorway, framed by brick and flint, his blue eyes blinking in the sunshine.

She pushed back her pale hair with a nervous hand. She had never been so nervous in her life. He still hadn't said his name was Beckett, but surely he'd have said if it wasn't? 'I'm sorry to come busting in on you like this,' she repeated inanely.

She saw his thin hands gripping the top of the lower half of the door, gripping so hard that the knuckles went white. His face had gone white too, in spite of a respectable tan. He leaned over the door, staring without speaking. She began to be alarmed. He was a pretty old guy, after all. She shouldn't have startled him like that. He could have had a heart attack or something. Maybe he was having one right now.

'Are you okay?' In her concern she forgot embarrassment. She came up to the door again and put her hand on his arm. It gave her a shock to feel the flesh and bone beneath his cotton shirt.

Flesh and bone, flesh and blood.

The contact had shocked him too. She felt him shrink away from her without moving, shrinking into himself. Maybe it had been a mistake, coming here.

But she couldn't go away now. She had to say something. She took her hand away, to let him recover himself.

'Are you okay?' she said again, and again she said, 'You are Professor Beckett, aren't you? Sorry, I don't know what to call you. It seems pretty nervy to breeze into your house and start calling you Grandpa.'

14

2

I am become a stranger to my brothers, and an alien to my mother's children.

She couldn't say it hadn't happened as she had imagined it, because she hadn't really been able to imagine it at all. Not beyond the meeting and greeting, the Recognition Scene.

For that, ideally and in the great tradition of folk tales, she should have brought some significant token – a locket, perhaps, which her mother had been given as a christening present and worn about her neck at all times. Or something she herself had been given by her grandparents, something unmistakable, unforgettable, a music box that played a favourite tune, a silver bracelet with a small charm, the sort of thing one might give a special baby. But she had no knowledge of such a thing, or any way of recognizing one if it existed.

Her mother, needless to say, had given her no help.

Maybe that was why she hadn't tried to imagine beyond the first encounter with her grandparents. In trying to guess what they might be like, she had to try to account for the fact that her mother had had no contact with her own father and mother for nearly twenty years.

It was stranger even than that might suggest. She had never talked about them, refused to discuss the subject when Georgie brought it up. Her father referred all queries to her mother. An emotional map that suggested *Here be dragons*.

For years she had hardly been aware of a lack of family on her mother's side. For one thing, she knew her mother was English, born and raised on the other side of the ocean. For another, she had no shortage of other relatives, grandparents, aunts, uncles, cousins, since her father came from a fertile family. She had always felt appropriately loved.

Until she grew old enough to work it out and wonder.

Her mother's answers were unhelpful, and meant to be so. England was a long way away and a long time ago. Ditto her childhood there. Some day maybe they would go back for a visit.

Some day never came.

When Georgie announced her intention to go to England, both her parents tried to discourage her. The more they tried to talk her out of it, or at least out of looking up her mother's family, the more determined she became, and the more convinced that some unspeakable Gothic secret was at the root of this mystery.

She had tried many times to reconstruct it. She knew that her mother had been only sixteen when she herself was born, and that her father was seven years older than her mother. She knew that she had been born in England. She knew that her father had worked in London and met her mother there. So maybe the family rift had happened over her mother's relationship with her father.

Most likely her mother's family had disapproved, perhaps kept them apart and prevented them from marrying until her mother was old enough to do as she pleased without parental permission.

That was all very romantic, and she couldn't understand why her mother would refuse to explain it. Nor, since the only fact she had prised out of her parents about her grandfather was that he was an academic and a historian, could she understand why a professor of history would object so vehemently to his daughter's marriage to a doctor.

It must have been her mother's age. She had been barely sixteen when Georgie was born, necessarily implying an illegal underage sexual relationship. Perhaps her grandparents had never forgiven her father for that. Georgie herself had been a bit shocked when she came to understand that. Her own virginity had been preserved to the ripe age of sixteen and a half. It was true that lots of her friends had been much younger, but, well, it was different for your *mother*. And presumably in those days people had been more old-fashioned about such things.

She had only within the past year worked all of this out. It must have been a consequence of growing up. Before that she had shied away from any knowledge of her parents' marriage as a sexual relationship. Even now, the idea that when her mother had been her own age, she herself had been nearly five years old – that knowledge was too much to take on board. She had only just graduated from university this spring, only begun to deal with adulthood and the horizons of life stretching formlessly before her. To be so bound and tied at twenty-one, married with two children, living half a world away from home . . . She couldn't begin to picture herself in her mother's place.

But neither could she imagine her mother doing anything so profoundly irrational and impractical as giving birth to a child at sixteen. She could only suppose that her mother must have been madly in love with her father if she had refused to terminate the pregnancy and insisted on keeping the baby afterwards. And she could certainly imagine that behaviour causing a lot of trouble on the home front. Especially now that she had seen her grandfather. He didn't look the type to subscribe to advanced views on sexual morality and the changing structure of the nuclear family.

After nearly dying of shock at the sight of her, he recovered enough to open the lower half of the door. 'I – ah – you'll have to forgive me, Georgie, I don't really know what to say. Except come in, of course.'

She went into the kitchen. Since he didn't back away, she took the liberty of hugging him and kissing him on the cheek – quite shyly, for they were strangers to each other and she didn't want to put him off by presuming an instant intimacy. He responded as well as he could, returning the hug and a peck in his stiff English fashion.

Then he put a little space between them, while keeping his hands on her arms. He was studying her face with wary disbelief, maybe half afraid she might turn out to be an impostor. 'I did recognize you, you know. I just couldn't take it in. You looked so much like Emma when I saw you standing out there.'

Georgie didn't know, and didn't care to ask for fear of revealing the embarrassing ignorance in which her mother had kept her, who on earth Emma might be. 'I really am sorry for turning up like this. I didn't have your address, you see. I had to try to track you down once I got over here.'

'Ross?' The woman from the car appeared in the doorway behind him. 'What's . . .'

At that point she obviously took in Georgie, not just her presence but her appearance. Flummoxed was a faintly comical word that described beautifully her faintly comical response: wide-eyed, literally open-mouthed, her hands flying up in stereotyped astonishment.

Georgie's grandfather let go of her and turned to the dumbfounded woman. 'It's Georgie.'

The woman managed to close her mouth. She agreed that Georgie was undoubtedly Georgie. 'You gave me such a start,' she explained unnecessarily. 'I thought at first you were Lia. But of course she'll be a good deal older now. I don't suppose you remember me. I'm Althea, Lia's stepmother.'

Stepmother. Georgie knew nothing of this. Perhaps the mysterious Emma to whom she bore such an unnerving resemblance was her grandmother. That explained one puzzle and started another: what had become of Emma? Again she couldn't ask, because it was clear that she was supposed to know.

Althea came up to Georgie and kissed her on both cheeks, Continental-style. Georgie detected a certain cool formality in the

17

greeting, like the French and the Germans coming to conference after an ambiguous war. Which suggested that her mother and Althea had not been the best of friends.

'Did you walk up from the station?'

'No, I have a bike.'

Georgie expected Althea to remark on her previous lurking presence at the gate, but Althea said briskly, 'You must be dying for a drink. It's such a hot day. Would you rather have wine or cider?'

'Just a glass of water for now, please. Maybe I'll have something else in a few minutes, when I've cooled off a bit.'

Althea filled a glass from a chilled bottle of mineral water rather than running water from the tap. Georgie wondered if there was something wrong with the tap water. Maybe it tasted funny. The mineral water certainly tasted funny. A bit like Seven-Up, but all fizz and no flavour.

She sipped politely and looked around. 'This sure is a wonderful kitchen.'

'It is good, isn't it?' Althea thawed a degree or two. 'The kitchen was the first thing I had done up when we moved down here.'

It seemed very odd to be chatting about kitchens when there was so much else to say. But obviously you couldn't just launch right into heavy questions like, What have you all been doing with yourselves for the last eighteen years? Still less the big question: What happened?

Her grandfather at any rate had something more serious than kitchen design on his mind. 'Matthew should be down here to meet Georgie.'

Althea glanced at the clock. 'You'd better ring him up right away, Ross. You know what he's like when it comes to catching trains. He couldn't find his way to Victoria if it wasn't on the tube map. And while you're on the phone, why don't you book us into the Beacon House for dinner? I hadn't planned on having two extra mouths to feed.'

While her grandfather got to grips with his telephone errands, Georgie fished delicately for enlightenment on the subject of Matthew, a name unknown to her. 'Where does Matthew live?' she asked Althea.

'He's staying up in London right now. We have a flat in the Barbican. He's been using that since he came down from Oxford.'

'Does he work in London?'

'Work?' Her grandfather caught that and snorted, an oddly plebeian sound to emerge from his fine-bridged nose. 'Chance would be a fine thing. Hello, Matthew? What's the matter, have you only just wakened up? Well, it certainly sounds like it. No, it is not, it's

18

four o'clock in the afternoon. The most extraordinary thing has happened. You must come down at once. Your sister's daughter is here. Lia's little girl, Georgie. Well, no, of course she's not little any more. You must come right down and . . . no, it bloody well will not wait till tomorrow. I don't care what you had fixed up for tonight, this is more important. Well, just explain the situation, I'm sure they'll understand. It isn't every day this sort of thing happens. We're eating out, so try to turn up looking as if you have a home, will you? If you take the six-twenty train we'll pick you up from the station. Six-twenty, have you got that? That gives you nearly two hours to get out of bed. Even you should be able to cope with a time-frame like that.'

While this conversation was going on, Althea busied herself preparing refreshments. Neither of them was looking at Georgie, and a good thing too. She didn't know what her expression must be like. Her mother had a brother, and Georgie hadn't even known of his existence.

They went to collect Matthew from Glynde station at ten to eight, as arranged. While they awaited the arrival of the train from London there was some tense speculation about whether or not he would actually be on it. Althea deplored her son's irresponsibility, while Georgie's grandfather seemed to be trying to devise a suitably outraged response to a no-show situation. Georgie wanted to say, Hey, guys, why not wait and see what happens? But then they were the ones who knew Matthew.

He did turn up, to everyone's relief, especially Georgie's. But he still managed to annoy his parents by wearing jeans and a T-shirt. 'I told you to dress respectably,' his father said in exasperation.

Matthew climbed into the back seat, next to Georgie. He glanced down at his T-shirt, which had the outline of a tie drawn on the front. 'What's wrong with this? It's a tie.'

'It's a cartoon drawing of a tie.'

'Distinctions between form and substance are old hat, Da. Conceptualism is the big thing now. I think, therefore it is.'

'In that case,' said his father, 'you won't mind eating the menu.'

The restaurant where they were having dinner turned out to be a wonderful country hotel, something right out of a holiday brochure. Her grandfather must have been in the habit of eating there because the people who ran it recognized and welcomed him and Althea. Georgie liked that. It gave her an absurd sense of coming home to a small-town community.

She could not, of course, have had dinner in such delightfully upscale circumstances while wearing her chalky denim shorts. Since she had nothing with her but the clothes she stood up in, Althea had undertaken to outfit her. It was fun, all part of the adventure so far, to be supplied with a stylishly slinky dress and appropriate shoes, and to make herself up at someone else's lavishly equipped dressing-table. Althea seemed to be enjoying it too.

For just one guilty second Georgie let herself think that it might have been fun to have Althea for a mother, someone who understood the meaning of luxury and didn't approach the world in a totally practical frame of mind. Her own mother didn't even have dresses like this, let alone all the feminine beauty kit, make-up and jewellery and perfume. Maybe her grandfather took more notice of Althea's appearance than her father did of her mother's. And of course Althea didn't spend a large part of the year living in the wilderness.

It was certainly going to be nice to have Althea for a grandmother. A granny the age of her mother. It seemed unbelievable.

Dinner was mostly cheerful and only a little bit fraught. There were obvious emotional shadows and dark places, and snares for the unwary, or at least for the ignorant. It wasn't the prodigal daughter who had come home but the prodigal's child. The daughter herself remained unforgiving and unforgiven.

Georgie wasn't sure if she wanted them to realize that she knew as little of them as they did of her. Less, even: her grandfather at least remembered her, whereas she had no recollection of him. Her ignorance was a reproach to her mother, compounding ancient sins. To avoid embarrassment for herself and potential pain for her grandfather, by mutual unspoken consent they talked of the present and the future rather than the past.

Her own present was easily explained. She had just graduated from the University of Toronto with a degree in anthropology, and wanted to do the Grand Tour before sinking into the mire of adult life and the grind of graduate school. 'Daddy wanted me to do medicine – well, he would, wouldn't he? – but I can't really cope with gore. So now my brother is being roped into maintaining the family tradition.'

Even that casual statement had pitfalls, she realized as she glanced around at their faces. Likely they hadn't known that her father's father was also a doctor. Maybe they didn't know she had a younger brother. 'Alex still has time to change his mind,' she added, explaining by subterfuge. 'He's four years younger than me, so he won't be going to university for another year yet. I think if he had his druthers he'd rather play professional hockey. He's crazy about that game but Daddy wouldn't stand for it.'

Althea asked brightly, 'Ice hockey, you mean?'

'What other kind is there? Oh, you mean that strange game with the curved sticks. Not the same thing at all. The whole point of hockey is that you get to skate. There's nothing much else to do in the winter. Some of the boys get so good at it, they're like centaurs – I mean – well, you know what I mean. What would you call someone with skate blades instead of feet? It's like flying, in a way. The puck is just an excuse.'

'An excuse for a punch-up, isn't it?' drawled Matthew.

Georgie looked at him with a faint stirring of dislike. He was the son of her grandfather's second marriage and he looked to be about her own age. That would make him her half-uncle, if such a creature existed. Easier to think of him as a cousin, since he was her contemporary. But she was not at all sure they were going to get on. 'Like watching a soccer game, you mean?'

'So what's wrong with spectator sports?'

He spoke with deliberate slowness, and his smile came slowly too, not like Althea's quick social smile or her grandfather's sudden flashes of amusement. It was not unattractive. And neither was he, for that matter, with black hair and his mother's brown eyes, and bone-deep beauty from both his parents. A remarkably handsome family they made.

Yet seeing them together as a family, *her* family hitherto unknown, she felt a vague and completely unjust sense of disappointment. Her father's family were all dark-haired, and so was her brother. Her mother had middling mousy hair. Georgie was the only blonde among them, not just borderline blonde but fair as fair could be. And now, once more surrounded by brunet(te)s, she realized that she must have been half hoping to find a tribe of tow-heads. Her blonde genes must have come from the other side, from her still-undiscovered grandmother. Farther up the Amazon, so to speak.

Georgie changed the subject, turning it back on Matthew. That was safe enough. Her mother couldn't be expected to know what her infant half-brother might be getting up to twenty years later. 'What do you do, Matthew? Are you a student?'

'I was. Right now I'm just catching my breath.'

'He means he's unemployed,' her grandfather added with an edge to his voice.

She felt obliged to defend a fellow ex-student. 'Well, give him a chance, eh? If you don't take a breather now you'll never get one.'

'It's my understanding that no one ever died from forgetting to breathe.'

'You're no one to talk, Ross,' Althea put in acidly. 'You've been leading the charmed life of a student all your so-called working life.'

Her grandfather was a historian. That was the clue that had

enabled Georgie to track him down, that and knowing that her mother's maiden name was Beckett. The only historian listed under the name of Beckett at an English university had been down in Sussex, in Brighton. Professor Ross Beckett, it had said in cold print, head of the history department. The phone book had done the rest for her. She was quite proud of herself.

And now that she had found him she didn't want unpleasantness, even if it didn't involve her directly. She said to Althea, 'Obviously you're not an academic or you wouldn't have that note of envy in your voice. What do you do all day?'

'I'm in the City. Capital markets.'

This turned out to mean that Althea was a banker. Not the sort of banker who refuses to give you a loan and writes you nasty letters about the state of your bank account, but the rarer and much superior kind who performs the large-scale sleight of hand that is called modern capitalism.

Georgie was profoundly impressed. She had never met a capitalist before. 'That must be really exciting.'

Matthew gave her a sardonically amused glance. 'You're joking, I presume.'

Althea's glance at her son was not so amused. 'I know you're too refined and sensitive to think of soiling your hands with commercial activity, Matty, but I do wonder why it doesn't seem to compromise your integrity to live off my immoral earnings.'

'We all have to make sacrifices, Ma. I know you only do it for me, and don't think I don't appreciate you having sold your soul to Mammon in order to maintain me in the style to which we've all become accustomed. I often think of you slaving away over a hot computer screen while I loll about in bed of a morning. It gives me a really warm feeling right here.' Matthew touched his chest ambiguously, somewhere between heart-warming and heartburn.

Althea decided to ignore him. 'How long are you over for, Georgie? Have you got a job to go back to?'

Meaning, maybe, You're not going to move in with us, are you? Georgie decided not to reassure her right away. 'I'll probably be going on to graduate school next year, but I haven't decided what or where. In the meantime I thought I'd travel around a while and maybe make a little money. My return ticket is open-ended, I can go back whenever I want to. I really just wanted to wander around and see what there is to see.'

Althea made the big sacrifice. 'Well, obviously you're welcome to stay with us for as long as you like.'

'I'd like to stay for a little while at least, if I may.' Georgie looked down at her plate, then up into her grandfather's face. 'You know, I have absolutely no recollection of you from before. How old was I when you saw me last?'

'You were three.'

'Three! No wonder I don't remember.'

The next question couldn't be asked, at least not yet: What happened? What had happened when she was three, to make her mother and her grandparents, whoever was at fault, throw away the next eighteen years?

3

Trust you not in any brother.

Georgie opened her eyes when she felt the hammock sway. It was a lovely lazy feeling, like being pushed on a swing, but it did wake her from her drowse.

Matthew was standing over her, looking down with the dark amusement she had already come to consider characteristic of him. 'Fancy a swim?'

She stretched her arms overhead and pushed her hair out of her eyes. The air was warm even in the shade, though it was not yet noon. Hardly what she had been led to expect of an English summer. 'Have you got a swimming pool? I didn't see it.'

'I had something more palatial in mind. The English Channel, for instance.'

'You mean the sea? The real true sea?' Georgie came awake at the thought. 'That would be really exciting. But how come you don't have a swimming pool? You've got acres of room for one.'

'My parents aren't terribly keen on water sports. Rather like the Wicked Witch of the West.' Matthew nudged the hammock with his knee, sending her swaying again. 'Swimming pools are a necessity of life in Toronto, are they? Do you skate on them?'

'I can tell you've never seen an ice rink. A swimming pool would be far too small. But everybody does put in a pool if they have room in their back yard. It's so hot and muggy in the summer, you need some way to cool off. Everybody leaves the city if they can. Alex and I used to go to stay with my grandparents. They have an island in the St Lawrence near Kingston and they spend every summer there, since my grandfather retired. All the men in my family are crazy about fishing. Including Alex, but I guess he doesn't have much choice.'

'I thought Canada was cold, not hot.'

'Only in the winter, idiot. In the summer it's much hotter than here – unbearably hot, and it doesn't cool off at night.'

'Well, I can't offer you a private island, or even a swimming pool. Can you bear to slum it by swimming in the Channel?'

'I'd love to go swimming, but my bathing suit is up in London.'

'I expect my mother can lend you one.' His amusement sharpened. 'Or we could go to the nude beach at Brighton.'

She didn't think she really wanted to go skinny-dipping with a man she had only just met, even if he was a relative, or half a relative. Not to mention the hundreds of strangers on the beach. 'Would your mother mind?'

'Our going to Brighton? She wouldn't give a damn one way or the other.'

She sat up, awkward in the volatile hammock. She felt like kicking him, but she knew it would only encourage him. 'Not Brighton, the bathing suit.'

'If she has one. I told you, she's not fond of getting wet in the pursuit of pleasure.'

His parents were on the patio – the terrace, as Althea called it – immersed in the Sunday papers. Althea looked dismayed and relieved by the request for bathing gear. 'I thought we'd show you some of the local sights and have lunch at a pub somewhere.'

'Along with half the population of south-east England,' Matthew observed drily. 'Da can take Georgie through the tourist routine in the middle of the week. You rest yourself up for the Monday morning rat race, Ma, while I entertain our long-lost relative.'

'Well, if Georgie won't think we're neglecting her . . .'

Georgie assured her she wouldn't dream of thinking any such thing.

She trailed upstairs after Althea in search of a bathing suit. The cat that Georgie had seen on the wall – or perhaps it would have been more correct and less anthropocentric to say the cat that had seen Georgie in the road – anyway, that fat black white-whiskered cat was asleep on a sunny corner of the bed. Althea shouted at him, startling Georgie more than the cat. The cat stirred, stretched, and stalked out of the room with his tail erect and twitching, making sure they knew he was leaving because he didn't like the company and not for any other reason, such as Althea's outrage.

Georgie was indignant on the cat's behalf. They had no cats at home but the dogs could do pretty much what they liked. Pet's privilege, she had always supposed. 'Isn't he allowed to sleep on the bed?'

'It's not supposed to be in the house at all.' Althea went to the bedroom door to make sure the cat had gone. 'It's not even our cat.'

'Whose cat is he?'

'I haven't the slightest idea. It just moved in. Like a squatter moving into an empty house.'

'I guess it was empty, from the cat's point of view,' Georgie suggested. 'Since you didn't already have a cat, I mean.'

'I don't like cats,' Althea said emphatically, perhaps hoping the cat would overhear. 'You can't train them like dogs. They just do what they please.'

'Moving in whether you invited them or not, you mean?'

Althea gave Georgie a careful look – checking for evidence of irony, Georgie supposed – and decided to give her the benefit of the doubt. 'Just that sort of thing. Now let's see what we can find for you to wear to the beach.'

She eventually dug out a bathing suit, but felt obliged to apologize for its deeply unfashionable appearance. 'Bikinis are right out this season, aren't they? But it's not worth my getting a new one when Ross has no interest in seaside holidays, and I've never been a frightfully good swimmer anyway. Try it on and see if it will do.'

It was a sort of adjustable minimalist bikini fastened with strings here and there, which the wearer tied tighter or looser to accommodate the size of her hips or bust. The bottom was a reasonable fit, the top not quite so satisfactory. Georgie looked at herself in the mirror and then down at her breasts, which looked surprisingly voluptuous overspilling the soft cotton cups. 'Am I likely to be banned from the beach?'

'You could always fake a German accent and take the top right off,' Althea suggested. 'Or wear a T-shirt over it. But a lot of girls go about like that deliberately, in a size too small.' She sounded faintly . . . not disapproving, more supercilious, as if having large breasts was the height of vulgarity, only exceeded by a propensity for displaying them in public.

Georgie didn't feel like apologizing for the way she was made. 'Maybe I should go up to London this afternoon to collect my luggage, instead of going swimming. Otherwise I'll be paying for two extra nights of bed and breakfast.'

'Ross will pay for that,' Althea said casually. Making Georgie feel really left-footed: an impecunious cheapskate.

She pulled her shorts and T-shirt on over the skimpy bathing suit. Then she collected the bag of towels, sun lotion, et cetera, that Althea had assembled for them, and climbed up into the vehicle that Matthew had backed out of the garage. It was some sort of high-class modern version of a Land Rover for people who wanted to look rough and ready without actually having to suffer.

They started down the chalky track, heading away from the village. It was rather like riding in a tractor, the air-conditioned kind that farmers back home used. 'I've never been in one of these before,' she said over the noise of the motor. 'Is it just country chic, or do you really need a four-wheel drive?'

'The lane gets pretty dire in winter. And everything goes to pieces when it snows. My mother's like an American postman, nothing is supposed to keep her away from her office.'

Georgie recalled her own mother complaining about the snow in Canada, maintaining that they arranged these things better back in England. 'How often does it snow?'

'About every second winter.' He grinned, maybe guessing her thoughts. 'Not what you'd call snow. It's gone in three or four days. But everything grinds to a halt while it's with us.'

One advantage of this rather ponderous vehicle, Georgie discovered, was that it made it possible to see over the hedges, and in this country that was a view worth having. The lane hugged the lowest slopes of the Downs, sometimes going over and sometimes around any particularly aggressive spurs of chalk. They crossed a little bridge over a little river in a cleft of the Downs, and began to climb the hill on the far side. The scenery was breath-taking: the winding river and valley below, the chalk escarpments above. Along the narrow road between these extremes they passed through ancient woodland, flinty hamlets, sunny uplands, sudden glimpses of the shining sea.

Matthew drove without a word.

'Aren't you going to give me a guided tour?'

'There's an Ordnance Survey map in there,' he pointed, 'under the torch.'

'Torch?' She had visions of reading by rushlight, link-boys in Drury Lane, flambeaux gleaming beyond the portcullis. Then she looked and understood. 'You mean the flashlight?'

'What did you think I meant? We're not making preparations for an assault on Dracula's castle. You'd better learn English, girl. Have you found the map?'

'Yes, but if I look at the map I can't enjoy the scenery.'

He shrugged. 'Suit yourself.'

'Thank you, I will.' He was not the most obliging host imaginable, she thought irritably. But perhaps she should be grateful for any show of hospitality, having arrived uninvited, unannounced, and perhaps as far as Matthew was concerned, unknown. 'Can I ask where we're going?'

'Birling Gap.'

She found that on the map and was none the wiser. 'What's there?'

'A beach. Wasn't that the idea? Unless you'd rather see a castle or an abbey or a palace or a battlefield or an Iron Age camp or a Roman villa or a stately home or a formal garden or Virginia Woolf's country cottage. Or perhaps you have more esoteric interests?'

'No, no,' she said hastily, bludgeoned into submission. 'The beach is fine. Just what I wanted.' But after a minute curiosity got the better of her. 'Do you really have all those things around here?'

'All within twenty miles of home.' He smiled his dark sardonic smile. 'You wouldn't count that as any distance at all, would you?'

'Well, no, we wouldn't. Twenty miles wouldn't get you anywhere in Canada. But everything seems much denser here.'

'Except the people.'

He was still smiling. She didn't want to start a fight, so she obligingly laughed.

They drove right up to what appeared to be the edge of the world. The grassy treeless ground sloped up sharply and stopped. Beyond was only a shining haze.

People disappeared over the rim, lemming-like. But some were coming up from the nether world, which was reassuring. Georgie grabbed the bag of necessities, scrambled down from the high vehicle, and followed Matthew towards nothingness.

The edge of the world, it turned out, had a rickety wooden staircase. That explained the coming and going. As they started down the cliff Georgie said, 'It looked like we were just about to throw ourselves off into the sea.'

'You're not allowed to pitch yourself into the sea from here. You have to go to Beachy Head.'

'What's that?'

He waved eastward. 'The other end of the Downs. Nature's very own suicide centre, the stylish way to end it all.'

She was puzzled and vaguely shocked by his words and his tone. 'What do you mean?'

'Just what I said. Every time I've been there, the Coast Guard has been hauling someone out of the water or scraping them off the rocks. Once they'd just got down to the bottom to collect a body when another bloke shot over the cliff on a motor bike.'

Her sense of shock was no longer vague. 'You're joking, aren't you?'

'No.'

The monosyllabic reply convinced her. She held tight to the handrail all the way down.

Birling Gap might not have been Brighton beach but it was certainly crowded. She remarked unfavourably on this.

Matthew shrugged. 'What did you expect? This is England, not the Canadian outback.'

'The outback's in Australia. Canada's wilderness is the Shield.'

'Whatever. We've got twice the population of Canada crammed into a land area you could drown in a couple of your Great Lakes. People are everywhere. It's a habit they have.'

And yet it seemed remote on the other side of the Downs, by Underhill. Remote and ancient. Despite the Land Rover and Althea's dishwasher, something ineradicably old remained. On a winter's day even Birling Gap would seem bleak and desolate. Perhaps the people of the Old World were less intrusive and expansive than their relatives on the other side of the ocean. Perhaps the settlers in the New World had absorbed too well the nomadic, transient, ahistorical culture of the tribes they displaced.

Matthew had already begun to strip down to his bathing trunks. He glanced at her impatiently. 'Come on, then. The water's not full up yet.'

Horribly aware now of the teeny-weeny bikini top, Georgie began to undress with some reluctance. She kicked off her sandals and hauled off her shorts, leaving the T-shirt for last. Because Matthew was so obviously sizing her up as her body was revealed, she deliberately did the same to him.

There was no denying he looked good. Above the neck he was more than good-looking, he was beautiful. Summer-brown skin, straight black hair and dark eyes, her grandfather's oddly aristocratic bone structure combined with Althea's sensually suggestive mouth, long dark lashes and authoritarian eyebrows. He also looked disconcertingly young, more like sixteen than twenty-one.

His body was slim, narrow-hipped with a flat backside. A sprinter, maybe, slight and quick rather than brawny. But the droop to his eyelids implied that he needed some sharp motivation to make him move fast. The suggestion of sinuous strength, alertness and languor, simultaneously aware and laid-back, was very appealing.

Physically he got top marks. Personally – well, he wanted watching, as her grandmother Payne would have said.

Evidently he thought she wanted watching too, because he didn't take his eyes off her, from the time she removed her T-shirt to reveal her inadequately clothed bosom, until her body was safely hidden in the sea.

Georgie struck out determinedly through the great rollers crashing in from the west. She was an excellent swimmer. She had worked her summers in high school as a life guard and swimming instructor at various holiday camps. Swimming seemed less pointless and more enjoyable than terrestrial forms of exercise. But this was the first time she had swum in salt water.

She licked her lips and all the old ballad clichés about the salt salt sea came back to her. She was swimming in the English Channel, between the Atlantic Ocean and the North Sea. She was borne up by the primeval waters that lapped the earth's shore, the waters that had been created before the evening and the morning were the second day.

She swam until weariness and hunger drove her back to land. Matthew had long since given up. She found him sprawled belly down on a bed of towels, toasting nicely.

The sea breeze on her wet skin, mild as it was, made her teeth chatter. But when she unzipped the bag her towel was not there.

She prodded Matthew's ribs firmly with her big toe. 'Are you hogging all the towels?'

He roused and stretched like a sleepy cat, and handed her one of the towels he had scrunched under him. 'You didn't show any sign of coming back.'

She examined the towel with a critical eye. 'It's all wet and sandy.'

'That's right, bitch bitch bitch. Here, I'll shake it out for you.' He gave it a cursory flap and returned it to her, slightly less sandy but no less damp. He watched her attempt to dry herself. 'Are you ready for lunch?'

'I'm starving. But first I have to warm up for a few minutes.'

She stretched herself out on the towel, lying on her back. She closed her eyes and waited for the heat of the sun to penetrate her Channel-chilled body. After a few minutes she opened her eyes, shading them with her hand. Matthew was sitting up right beside her, watching her with that irritating air of amused irony.

'Why don't you go and look for some pretty shells?'

'Am I bothering you?'

'Of course you are, and you're doing it deliberately.' She gave up and sat up, pulled on her T-shirt over the bikini top and began to comb the snarls out of her damp hair. Then she dusted the sand from her backside, pulled her denim shorts on over the damp bottom of the bathing suit, and strapped on her sandals. 'Okay, you win. Let's go for lunch.'

They had lunch in a pub in Alfriston, an unbelievably ancient building in an unbelievably Olde Worlde village nestled in the unbelievably picturesque valley of the Cuckmere. Afterwards they walked back up the village street to the car, with oak half-timbering to the left and leaded lights to the right and little gates in flintstone walls leading down to a water meadow or up to a cottage garden.

It was all so charming that Georgie had to protest. 'This is a bit over the top, isn't it?'

'It would be if it weren't real,' Matthew allowed. 'There's a truly grotesque Congregational chapel down the other end of the village, if you fancy a breath of bad taste. But honestly, this is just the way it all grew. Walt Disney never slept here.'

She began to be grateful for him. It was possible to be relatively at ease with him – at least when he wasn't ostentatiously sizing up her body in a bikini – at ease in a way that she hadn't yet achieved with her grandfather or Althea. It wasn't just the generation gap, or even the fact that her grandfather was obviously a reserved and formal sort of person. The trouble was mainly those eighteen absent years and the mystery that lay behind them. Matthew had had no hand in any of that; she didn't need to be wary of treading on his corns.

'You know,' she remarked companionably as they climbed into the Land Rover, 'I didn't even know you existed. I mean I guess I'd forgotten, and no one reminded me.'

'Ditto. Or do I mean vice versa? I vaguely knew that my father had a daughter by his first marriage and that she lived in Canada, but I never thought of her as my sister. It was all too remote, and the subject was never raised. Quite Victorian, really. As if her name was forbidden in my father's house.'

'What happened? What did she do?'

'Christ knows. I thought maybe you were the problem.'

'I couldn't have been. I was three when she left, he said so last night. If he'd been going to send her out into the snow on account of having an illegitimate baby at sixteen he'd have done it then, not waited for three years before expressing his moral indignation. Besides, there's my grandmother.'

'What about her?'

'She disappeared too. Out of my life, I mean. Do you know her?'

'I've never met the lady. As far as I know she remarried and lived happily ever after.'

'Where? Is she still in London?'

'Christ, I don't know.' He glanced at her, then back at the road ahead. They appeared to be climbing in a very roundabout way towards the crest of the Downs. 'Why don't you ask the old man?'

'I'm sort of scared to. There's so much I don't know,' she explained diffidently. 'I don't want to accidentally say something wrong.'

Matthew grinned without looking at her. 'I wouldn't worry about upsetting him. He disapproves of half the people in the world, and the other half he holds in total contempt. He's a hard man to please. Impossible, for me.'

30

She watched him, considering. 'Is he down on you just because you haven't got a job?'

He smiled again, with less amusement. 'That's the least of my crimes. To tell you the truth, I'm surprised he didn't send *me* out into the snow after I got sent down from Oxford.'

'Sent down?'

'Thrown out on my ear.'

'What was that for?'

'It's a long story.'

They had reached the very top by now. Georgie looked out the window and caught her breath in surprise to see all England laid at her feet. 'Wow, what a view!'

'Good isn't it?' He braked and pulled off the narrow road on to the grass. 'You want to get out? We can walk along the old road.'

For answer she jumped out and walked a few steps forward to the edge of the escarpment.

Not a bird's-eye view but a god's-eye view. The county of Sussex was spread out below like the magical landscape in *Through the Looking-Glass*: hedges and ditches and postage-stamp fields, some green and some gold, water-blue or chalk-white, or dirt-black if they were out of reach of the Downs; here and there a toy farmyard, a tiny church steeple, perfect little trees like in an architect's model. All of it stretching away to the east and north and west, till it vanished in a heat-haze of distance.

'It's good,' she agreed at last.

She turned the other way, towards the sea. She couldn't see the sea from here because the spine of the Downs was too broad. But she could see that a cart-track wound away along the crest of the hill, east and west, the exposed chalk clearly marking its route. There were hikers and Sunday strollers at odd intervals along it, out to enjoy the summer sun and the spectacular views.

Matthew started to move westwards along the track and Georgie followed him. They walked for a little while in silence. She too was enjoying the sun and the sights. In spite of the other occasional walkers, it seemed wonderfully still and remote, just the way the roof of the world should be. She felt oddly insubstantial, like a ghostly revenant.

'How far does this path carry on?'

'All the way from Eastbourne to Winchester. And it's not a path, it's one of the oldest roads in England.' He added in a singsong cadence, 'The first farmers preferred the chalk uplands to the clay Weald because their wooden ploughs could turn the light soil, and the beech with its shallow root system was easier to clear than the

31

thickset bloodyminded oak.' He reverted to his normal voice. 'That's my old man's spiel verbatim. If you get him up here he'll run through the whole thing for you – all about the spring line being evidence of climatic change, and the long-distance road network predating the Celts, and what it all proves about the society that built Stonehenge. I'll bet you can hardly wait.'

'It sounds extremely interesting,' Georgie the anthropologist said honestly, a little indignant that her grandfather's learning should be mocked in this manner. By way of retaliation she brought the conversation back to an earlier subject. 'What did you do to get thrown out of Oxford? Cheat on an exam?'

It was Matthew's turn to be indignant. 'Do I look like a cheat? I was just doing someone a favour.'

'They do say that no good deed goes unpunished. What happened?'

'A girl I knew wanted some dope and I got it for her.'

'And?'

'And she managed to get picked up and she grassed on me, the silly bitch.' He looked sideways at Georgie. 'You wouldn't do a thing like that, would you?'

'No, never,' she agreed amiably. 'I'm a gentleman, me. Do they throw people out of Oxford just for doing drugs? It sounds very old-fashioned.'

'It is very old-fashioned. That's their big thing, being old-fashioned. But the trouble was that I hadn't just given her the stuff, I made her pay me for it. Well, I couldn't afford to give it away, could I? We weren't all *that* chummy.'

'So they threw you out for drug dealing. No wonder your father's mad at you.'

'Oh, I don't think he was too cut up about that. I dare say half of his own students are zonked on something while he's lecturing to them and he probably knows it. No, my unforgivable sin was fucking up at Oxford. The only point of my being born was so that I could go to Oxford and graduate, so that he could go around throwing that little fact in his colleagues' faces for the rest of his life, to make up for himself having had to slum it at Manchester. He's an unbelievable snob, my old man. You'd think he'd been born in Belgravia instead of a back-to-back in Huddersfield.' Abruptly he caught her arm and drew her off the path, towards the north escarpment. 'Why don't we find somewhere comfortable to sit down and enjoy the view?'

Not too far off the path, they came across a grassy hump with a depression where its rounded top should have been, like a burst bubble. The northern edge of the dent had crumbled away, giving a

32

glimpse of the countryside below. The sunny sheltered hollow looked very inviting.

Georgie examined the short grass, mindful of the sheep that mowed it. The trouble with the countryside was that you never knew where it had been. 'Is it safe to sit here?'

'Sheepshit never killed anyone, girl. Sit on this if your arse is too refined.' Matthew pulled his T-shirt off over his head and tossed it at her, thereby shaming her into sitting down.

'You can have your shirt back, I don't need it.'

'It's okay, I don't want it.' He stretched himself out on the turf and closed his eyes.

'This must be man-made, this little hollow we're in.'

'It's a grave.'

She looked at him. He hadn't even opened his eyes. 'Are you serious?'

'It's a tumulus. Round barrow. Prehistoric grave-mound. Those old farmers I told you about, the ones who made the road.'

She looked around, feeling slightly spooked. As an anthropology student she had visited some Native Canadian burial grounds, but that wasn't quite the same thing as sunbathing inside somebody's tomb. 'Why is it hollow, then?

'Grave robbers, amateur archaeologists, who knows? The bones are probably in a museum somewhere. Or in the library of someone's stately home. Why don't you shut up and lie down? I thought you wanted to get away from the madding crowd.'

Georgie lay back with her arms across her face to block out the sun. It was surprisingly still. She could hear a skylark singing, and a distant airplane, the old-fashioned kind with a sleepy summerish drone, and local insects chirping out their lonelyhearts advertisements. Even the occasional voices of walkers on the old road above them seemed to blend appropriately with the other country sounds.

The hollow was a real sun-trap. When she got so hot she began to sweat, she sat up and pulled off her shirt and shorts, and lay down to get brown in the bikini.

She must have dozed off. What wakened her was someone touching her breast.

She opened her eyes and saw Matthew's dark face close to hers. His hand was still on her breast – over the bikini top, but that didn't cover much flesh. She was too drowsy and confused to be properly indignant. 'What are you doing?'

'Waking you up. I'd say you were done to perfection on this side. You might like to turn over before you burn.'

Georgie brushed his hand away and sat up. 'Funny way to wake someone up.'

'I thought it was remarkably effective. You came to just like that.' He snapped his fingers, no more than a couple of inches from the breast where his hand had just been.

This time she gave his hand a slap to knock it away. She struggled into her T-shirt, re-armouring herself, and looked at him, still faintly fuddled with the dregs of sleep, trying to decide what if anything he had had in mind. Matthew watched her with that small unreadable smile.

Was he just being funny, or did he mean it as a crude sort of proposition? He was certainly clever and confident enough to have come up with something much more subtle – almost anything would have been more subtle, come to think of it – and much more conducive to successful seduction, if that was what he had intended. Or maybe he just got a kick out of groping women. Whatever, she didn't want to have to spend her time at Underhill worrying about Matthew.

'Now let's get this straight,' she said briskly, fixing him with a significant stare. 'You were just innocently waking me up, is that right? Just being helpful, making sure I wouldn't get sunburned?'

He returned her look with a slight dark smile. 'Disappointed, are you?'

'Listen, Matt, whatever you had in mind, your technique needs some rethinking, I can tell you. A girl doesn't expect that sort of thing from her uncle.'

'Half-uncle. Hardly uncle.'

'I don't care if you're my third cousin twice removed, it's not kosher to take advantage of sleeping maidens. Even by way of waking them up. Didn't they teach you that at Oxford?'

'They must have sent me down before I got to that part of the curriculum.'

He held out his hand to help her up. She took it, as a sort of truce-treaty. He wasn't going to apologize, men never did, but she guessed she had made her point.

Though she still didn't know what his point had been. Who ever knew, with men?

4

If I be bereaved of my children, I am bereaved.

After collecting her luggage and settling her hotel bill in London (with the help of a substantial subsidy from her grandfather), Georgie had the rest of the week to enjoy her grandfather's company. Matthew disappeared up to London and Althea went in to the City every day, but her grandfather had the professorial privilege of a long free summer.

He asked her what she would like to do.

'Oh, don't feel you have to entertain me if you have other things to do.'

'Nothing that I'd enjoy more than entertaining you.'

He looked at her with a faint smile. Maybe he was just feeling good because it was another fine morning and they were sitting in the garden enjoying coffee after breakfast. Or maybe he was thinking that he had some catching up to do, having missed out on eighteen years' worth of entertaining his granddaughter.

She would have liked to ask him about that, but she didn't dare. He might not want to talk about it. And even if he did want to, he might prefer to wait till things had gotten a bit chummier between them.

'Well, if that's how you feel . . .' She gave him a broad suggestive grin and watched his own smile gradually widen. Funny thing to be doing, flirting with your own grandfather. Her mother had once accused her of being an incorrigible flirt. As far as Georgie was concerned it was just a way of making life easier. Why shouldn't she do it, if men didn't mind? 'Matt came up with a whole list of sights to see around here, everything from Roman villas to Virginia Woolf's house. Was he kidding me?'

'On that occasion, for a change, he was telling the truth. Is there something in the list that particularly caught your fancy?'

'The older the better, as far as I'm concerned.'

'The oldest things are up there.' He nodded towards the great chalk hill. 'Would you like to go for a walk?'

The past here was not a foreign country at all. It was in the fabric of the eighteenth-century house. It was just beyond the garden gate. In less than half an hour they had travelled five thousand years. Or so her grandfather asserted, as they stood by the long barrow high on Firle Beacon. The same one she had glimpsed that very first day, standing irresolute at her grandfather's door.

The ancient mound reminded Georgie of hobbits and barrow-wights, but her grandfather's imagination was made of sterner stuff. He told her all the things that Matthew had already warned her about, and a lot more besides. How the long barrows, like this one, were much older than the round ones, like the one that Georgie had sunbathed in, and how they had functioned as dynastic vaults rather than individual monuments. How the old chalk trackways had been the neolithic version of a motorway grid, with one prong rising from Dover to Reading and then north to East Anglia, while the other ran from Eastbourne all the way to Salisbury Plain; and how together they formed a remarkable long-distance communications system comparable to the great Roman roads, a system not otherwise seen again until the eighteenth-century vogue for turnpikes. Between the vanished barrow-builders and the Romans were the Celts, with travelling ambitions that extended only from farm to farm, their roads now reduced to footpaths and bridleways. After the Romans came the Saxons, whose country lanes could be seen down below, meandering through every hamlet and village like a drunk on a pub-crawl. But these upland chalk roads, the very first highways, had been intended for serious mobility rather than for visiting the neighbours.

The history lesson continued as they walked eastwards along the road under discussion. Show a piece of history to a historian and there's no stopping him, Georgie reflected. But she had to admit that her grandfather's enthusiasm was infectious. It even changed his face, making him look younger and more approachable. She wondered what his students made of him, wondered if they had ever seen him animated like this, taking such delight in the doings of dead men.

They had lunch in a pub in Alfriston, not the one where Matthew had taken Georgie but another one no less quaint and historical. After lunch they climbed back up to the crest of the Downs. This time they took a different path, from the south end of the village, which eventually offered a view of the sea.

'Why don't we just sit down and drink in this view for a few minutes,' Georgie suggested. For one thing she was a bit nervous about all the exertion her grandfather was undergoing. Her other grandfather was eighty-one and she couldn't help thinking of this one as equally old and potentially frail. For another thing, she was definitely feeling the effects of the cider she had consumed at lunch: drowsy and desperately in need of a pee.

In that last regard the point they had reached had something even better than a view. It had a copse of trees – thorn trees, according to her grandfather, much favoured by the fairies – skulking in a sheltered hollow. She racked her brain for some reasonably genteel way to explain matters to a respectable old Englishman and recalled her mother's use of the phrase *spend a penny*.

She came back from her mission to find her grandfather sitting on the turf with his arms resting on his knees, scanning the Channel. She dropped down beside him. In companionable silence they watched the small sailing dinghies darting to and fro below them like spastic butterflies.

If I lived so near to the sea, thought Georgie, I'd be down there doing that every day I could. But Matthew had said that his parents weren't interested in activities involving water. She wrenched off her boots and socks and lay back with her arms folded behind her head. She stretched out her bare legs and wiggled her toes to let the sea breeze blow between them. She watched her grandfather's long back and the rear of his grey head. She wondered what he would do if she sat up behind him and put her arms around him . . . No, that would only embarrass him.

'Do you often go for long walks like this?'

'When I have the time.'

'Yeah, I know, it's a tough life, the academic jungle,' she agreed sarcastically. 'My mother complains about it all the time.'

She saw his shoulders stiffen. She must have said something wrong, maybe by echoing Althea's dig at the restaurant on Saturday. Time to change the subject. 'You should get a dog. It's way more fun going for walks when you have a dog along.'

He turned his head, looking over his shoulder without shifting the rest of his body. 'You have a dog, I take it.'

'Yeah, we do, two of them. Well, a dog and a half.'

'Because of its size?'

'No, because the other half of him is wolf.'

Now his torso followed his head round to face her. 'A wolf? Where did you find a half-wolf?'

'It was an accident. His mother is a beautiful samoyed bitch that Mama took up North with her for company one summer. She came on heat and managed to escape – the dog, I mean, not my mother – and when she turned up a week later she was pregnant. That's why her son is called Booboo, because Mama didn't mean to let her out.'

'How did you know the father was a wolf?'

'Mama knew as soon as she saw the puppies. I mean, that's her thing, isn't it, wolves?'

He was staring at her as if she had been babbling in Chinese. She pushed herself up on her elbow, puzzled by his puzzlement. 'She's a biologist. Didn't you know? I thought that's what she'd always meant to be.'

He shook his head slowly, apparently too shocked to speak. What was so shocking about her mother's career?

'Well, Daddy calls her a lupinologist but he just made that up to be funny. She did her Ph.D. on timber wolves. Daddy and Alex and I went up to Algonquin Park with her last Christmas and it was really exciting. There are lots of wolves in the park but she said we might not see them at all because they're so shy. But we did see some on Christmas Eve. We could see their green eyes gleaming under the trees, and then they came out into the moonlight, looking all ghostly against the snow. There were five of them. It was really magic. They're so beautiful, I'm not surprised she's fascinated by them.'

She had gabbled on at some length to give her grandfather a chance to recover his self-possession, but it didn't seem to have helped. He was still looking stunned, more rather than less.

But at least he had his voice back. 'Lia has her doctorate?'

'That's right, she's officially Dr Payne, the same as my father. And my grandfather is a doctor too, so that's three Dr Paynes in the family. All delightfully confusing, eh? She got it three years ago. She's been teaching at the university for longer than that, because it takes ages to get a thesis written up and approved and all that crap. But I guess you know more about that than I do.'

She smiled at him. He was too distracted to return the smile. He got to his feet and walked a little way down the path, towards the sea. She followed him.

He was muttering half to himself. 'Wolves! I can't believe it. And I didn't know.'

Georgie came alongside him and laid a tentative hand between his shoulder blades. 'Are you okay? I mean, that's not bad, is it?'

'Bad? No. Naturally not.'

He stopped abruptly and turned towards her, so that the hand on his back became an arm around him and she was very close to him. She did what came naturally and put her other arm around him so that she was embracing him. And then he had his arms around her – no gentleman could have refused that embrace, and certainly no grandfather worthy of the title – and she started to giggle against his shoulder, for no reason that she knew of except as a release from tension, because her grandfather loved her enough to hug her. She had waited all her life to learn that. She could feel him laughing too; the laughter shook his tall thin body.

She took the opportunity of intimacy to kiss him the way she would have kissed her own grandfather. Own? No, other. She had two grandfathers now, though so far only one grandmother. Anyway, she kissed his cheek and chin, like it said in the old ballads, and to her delighted surprise he kissed her back.

'Do you love me after all?' she said lightly, flirting again in spite of good intentions.

He didn't freeze up, as she had half expected. Instead his face went kind of transparent and glowing. He answered rather primly, 'I suppose I must.'

That pleased Georgie more than she could have imagined, and surprised her too. Her grandfather was a man like any other, and responded to her advances like any other man. Only, she hoped, he meant it. And she wasn't going to let him get away with ambiguity. 'Oh, don't feel you have to.'

She gave him her best blue-eyed innocent look to take the sting out of her sarcasm. She could see him wavering between withdrawal and surrender. In the end he looked faintly amused. 'I meant to imply deduction, not obligation.'

Funny sort of love talk, but better than nothing. Best of all was his arms around her. She didn't believe in love unless it came with caresses. What was the use of loving words without the privilege of touching the otherwise untouchable? She felt a sense of triumph, not knowing why. Maybe her body, like the landscape surrounding her, had its own forgotten history; maybe the grown-up Georgie had won something from her grandfather that the baby Georgie had lost or never had.

They walked on wordlessly a while, an arm around each other, heading inland, for the path went full circle over the Downs and returned to Firleston.

Eventually, coming up from a dip that the map called Poverty Bottom, he broke the companionable silence. 'I talked all the way out. It's your turn to talk on the way back.'

'About what? I don't know anything.'

'You know everything I want to know. Tell me about your family, about your life in Canada.'

She talked all the way home, rambling shamelessly, telling him about her childhood, her time at university, her boyfriends, her brother, all her Payne relations. She didn't say much about her mother for fear of provoking another painful scene. But her grandfather listened attentively, asking questions, making comments, apparently absorbed in her prosaic narrative.

'Tell me about your brother.'

'Alex?' Just at first she was surprised. Then she realized that until last Saturday he hadn't known he even had a grandson. She reflected on her brother. 'Well, he's four years younger than me, but we get on pretty well. He's a really sweet kid, even though he's my brother. Mama spoils him a little because he's the baby, but Daddy comes down on him because he's the son and heir, so I guess it evens out for him. He's crazy about hockey, like I told you, but he'll probably end up being sensible and becoming a doctor. My godmother – our godmother – says he'd make a terrific doctor.'

'Your godmother?'

'Her name's Megan. She's a really amazing person. She's a nurse and she's married to a French doctor and they work for some medical charity that sends them to all sorts of awful places. They have four children and she takes them with her everywhere and teaches them herself. I've always envied those kids, it sounds like a great way to get an education. Every now and then she lands up in Toronto and comes to see us.'

'Megan Davies.'

'Yeah, that's right. Do you know her?'

'She was always Lia's best friend. I didn't know they'd kept in touch.'

Georgie realized she had stepped on another land mine: her mother had abandoned her family but not her best friend. Hastily she switched the subject back to her brother. 'I guess Alex will probably come and see you himself some day soon.'

'He can come whenever he likes. Tell him we'll be glad to see him.' His voice, dry, precise, a little sharp, became thicker and slower and softer. 'You can tell him how glad I was to see you.'

'I'll tell him all that,' Georgie assured him. She felt slightly embarrassed, as if she had been offered a glimpse of her grandfather's soul.

She began to talk about other things. The seasons in Toronto. Frost and snow. Summertimes spent in lazy days at the lake or on the river, baking on the dock or on the rocks, punctuated by plunges into the clear deep water. Doing absolutely nothing, because there was nothing to do. Lamplight and card games in the evenings when bloodsucking bugs were on the prowl beyond the window screens. At the cottage even the adults had nothing to do, and always seemed much younger for it. As she described those childhood summers to her grandfather, they sounded even to her like paradise.

By the time they reached the back gate of Underhill he knew almost everything there was to know about her life. But she was none the wiser as to what had happened eighteen years ago.

Her grandfather settled into one of the chairs on the terrace. He leaned back and closed his eyes. Suddenly he looked drained, like a man at the end of his resources. He looked old.

Georgie felt vaguely alarmed. 'Can I get you a drink, Grandpa?'

40

'Whisky would be nice. With ice.' He opened his eyes. Vivid blue they were. Her mother's eyes were grey. 'And call me Ross. You're grown up now. I've missed the grandfathering.'

'Okay.' She swallowed and deliberately added, 'Ross.'

She went into the house and wept into the cupboard where the drinks were kept. She understood precisely what he meant: he was drawing a line under his emotional losses. Whatever their relationship might have been when she was three, it had had no chance to develop. She had come back into his life as a stranger, and to call him by his kinship title was only rubbing salt into the wound.

With her own – other – grandfather she had spent a whole childhood, and that, rather than descent, was what made him a real grandparent. This man here, Ross Beckett, he was her mother's father but nothing to herself at all, except what they might make of it between them, meeting as adults unknown to each other. They might get on, they might come to love each other, but *grandpa* implied things that had never happened and could never happen now. Her mother had deprived them both of that.

She brought him his Scotch, with a Coke for herself. 'I brought along a photocopy of a paper Mama had published last spring. Would you like to see it?'

'Please.'

She went upstairs. The uninvited cat was on her bed. She stroked him but he refused to purr, pretending to be too deeply asleep, or else his purr was too soft for her to hear. His coat was surprisingly silky. One ear had a notch in it and the other had lost its tip entirely. A fighting man, obviously. From the depths of his catnap he twitched his ravaged ears and extravagant whiskers to tell her to go away.

She left him in peace and retrieved her mother's paper. The subject was pretty boring, something to do with seasonal changes in the diet of timber wolves, but her mother's name was there as the author, Olivia Payne Ph.D., assistant professor of zoology at the University of Toronto.

She brought it down to her grandfather and watched him browse through it. When he reached the end of the article he had also finished his glass of whisky. He asked her for another.

That one he drained in about thirty seconds. Then he put his head in his hand, half covering his face. 'Georgie, I'll tell you something. I don't know anything that happened after Lia went to Canada.'

She had thought as much but hadn't liked to say so. After all, it was half his daughter's life. Since he was being so frank, she took advantage of the opportunity. 'What happened? Why did she go away and cut you off?'

41

'I don't know.' He shook his head and glanced at his empty glass. 'Why don't you bring that whisky bottle out here?'

Georgie didn't think Althea would thank her for getting him drunk well before dinner, but maybe getting drunk with her grandfather was the only way she would find out anything. Except that he had just told her he didn't know anything.

She fetched the bottle of Scotch and watched him pour himself at least a triple. Without ice.

He needed the whole drink before he could speak again. In her experience people tended to dissolve under the influence of alcohol, but her grandfather seemed to dry out. He spoke flatly, without emotion. 'I don't know why she left. I don't know why she never came back.'

Georgie said hesitantly, aware of treading on ancient minefields, 'Would my grandmother know?'

'Emma doesn't know any more than I do.' His mouth twisted harshly. 'She didn't know then, she doesn't know now, I'm sure of it. One way or another she would have told me if she knew. She's not a subtle creature.'

Georgie had finished her Coke. She had never consumed Scotch before in her life but she knew it was time to keep him company, so she tipped a mouthful into her glass and took a heart-burning sip. 'What exactly happened?'

'She'd got a place at Imperial College. In London. She could have gone to Oxford or Cambridge but she didn't apply for them because of you.'

'What did I have to do with it?'

He glanced at her incomprehension, maybe recalled that she was a foreigner, and explained. 'They have a collegiate system that doesn't allow for the possibility of undergraduates having children. And in London she could live with us and leave you in the care of Althea's nanny, you and Matthew together.'

'That sounds perfect. So what happened?'

He shrugged painfully. An eloquent gesture from a man not much given to body language. 'I don't know. The day before her first day of term she told me she was going to Canada. Going to work as a nanny, for Christ's sake. She had a job with a family in Montreal and she was taking you with her. I couldn't get anything in the way of why out of her.'

Georgie had an answer of sorts, though it didn't explain the explanation. 'Maybe she went to be with my father.'

'Maybe she did.' He refilled his glass but did not drink it right away. He stared at it instead. 'I don't remember your father. Possibly I met him, but I don't remember.'

42

Georgie stared at him. 'Honest?'

He touched the wolf paper with his forefinger. 'Even if I'd seen that article, I wouldn't have known what it was. I'd never have recognized her married name.'

'So when I told you who I was, when I came to your door, I wasn't telling you anything useful.'

He looked at her and smiled, a stripped-down, minimal, basic, honest-to-god smile from the heart of him, sad and glad at once. 'Your face told me everything. Emma's face. Lia's face. Everything.'

But it struck her that he hadn't told her everything in return. 'And then what happened? She went to Canada, not to Mars. How did you lose track of her?'

There were limits to the intimacy he was capable of. He got up and stood behind his chair and leaned on the back of it, fixing his eyes on the hill that his house was under. 'I'm ashamed to say that I was so angry with her for throwing away her opportunity for education – throwing away her chances in life, I thought – that I didn't try to contact her. If she'd written I would have written back, but she only sent one postcard. One. My fault, maybe. I said some unforgivable things when she left.'

Georgie couldn't believe what she was hearing. 'You mean you threw away your daughter because she didn't want to go to university?'

'No, I don't think it was that. I would have come to terms with that eventually. People do, don't they? I'd already had to cope with – forgive me, Georgie – your existence. We survived that, we would have survived the loss of Imperial College. But she never even wrote to Emma. Emma sent letters to Montreal and they came back unopened, marked *Not at this address*. For some reason Lia didn't want to know us any more.'

Georgie felt a sudden, uncharacteristic, surge of anger. At her mother for depriving her of her family birthright. At her grandfather for letting his daughter go like that. 'Why didn't you go over there, go looking for her? She could have been murdered or something.'

'We'd have heard about that, I imagine, if it had happened,' he said drily. 'Emma did contact the police, but they told her that people vanish all the time, quite deliberately, and as long as they're of age there's nothing to be done about it. What good would it do to track her down if she wanted to be rid of us? She knew how to find us, at any rate, if she'd wanted to.'

He turned to face her at last, his hands still gripping the back of the chair. 'Does she know you're here with me?'

'I sent her a postcard yesterday. She knew I was going to come looking for you.'

'And what did she think about that?'

'She didn't like it,' Georgie admitted. 'Neither did my father. But they wouldn't say why.' She paused. 'Do you know where my grandmother lives?'

'I know where she used to live. I haven't had any contact with her since – well, since Lia disappeared. Lia was our only connection. Emma accused me of driving her away.'

No love lost there, apparently. 'You won't mind if I go to see her, will you?'

'I? Why should I mind? You have a right to your own history.'

5

Now nothing will be restrained from them, which they have imagined to do.

'Not much of a view, is it?'

'What do you mean? It's lovely.' Georgie turned from admiring the artificial lake and fountains to glance at Matthew in the doorway behind her. 'But maybe a little tame compared to the view from your back door down in Sussex.'

'Don't trouble to be kind. This is extremely unlovely architecture. Uncompromising concrete brutalism. *Barbican* means a fortress, and by God this is. People have been known to make several circuits of the outer walls before working out how to break in.'

'Oh, I don't know about that. It reminds me of Scarborough College, where my mother teaches.' She leaned out to admire the greenery draped from almost every balcony, including the one she was standing on, which gave the façades enclosing the lake, otherwise stonily barren, something of the air of a tropical cliff face. 'Or maybe the Hanging Gardens of Babylon.'

'Nebuchadnezzar would be turning in his grave if he heard that. I believe the vinery is there to disguise the disgusting stains. Concrete doesn't grow old gracefully, as you've probably noticed, and this place is definitely showing its age. The surface develops a patina reminiscent of public conveniences, though fortunately not the bouquet to go with it. Do you want a drink?'

'A glass of wine would be nice.'

'White or red?'

'Anything. Whatever you've got.'

He went back into the apartment – a flat, they called it here – which belonged to his parents. Some people lived in London and kept a country cottage; her grandfather lived in the country and kept a flat in London. Matthew had had the use of it since involuntarily leaving Oxford.

Althea had flown off to the Far East on a business trip and Georgie's grandfather had gone with her. Matthew had proposed that she come up and stay in the Barbican rather than live on her own away down in Sussex. Thinking to use her grandfather's absence as a chance to look up her grandmother in London, she had agreed.

Matthew returned with two glasses of Chianti. Georgie leaned against the rail of the balcony and sipped at her wine. It was a very narrow balcony, probably intended more for the convenience of window-cleaners than the enjoyment of the Barbican dwellers. 'What are you going to do now?'

'Drink my wine.'

'No, no, I mean,' she gestured towards the wide world, 'do with yourself and your life. You can't just sit around here for ever.'

'Why not?'

He spoke in apparent seriousness, so she answered him seriously. 'Don't be silly, you'd get bored. And you have to earn a living one way or another. Don't you have any idea what you'd like to do? What did you study at Oxford?'

'English Lit. I'm fully equipped for a career in being English.' Matthew came to stand beside her, carefully arranging himself against the balcony rail so as to imitate her own slightly pigeon-toed posture.

Making mock of me without a word, Georgie thought, with more amusement than annoyance. What a strange boy he was, especially to be the child of her grandfather and Althea. She looked at his black hair and dark eyes and summer-brown skin, nothing at all like her own. Maybe he was a gypsy changeling. Not her mother's brother at all.

'What about you?' Matthew demanded. 'What are you going to do now?'

'I came over here partly because I didn't really know what I wanted to do. Deferring decisions, I suppose. Or hoping for some flash of inspiration.'

'You've had no inkling?'

'Well, I'd thought of doing a thesis on the effect of twentieth-century civilization on Native Canadian societies. I don't mean European culture or imperialism or anything like that, because the first Europeans to contact them weren't really all that different from the Natives themselves. They had guns and Christianity and they called their leader a king rather than a chief. Big deal. The Natives could cope with that: new weapons, more gods, heap big heap big chief. Nothing new there. They were used to warfare and pushing each other around. The most successful tribes took over the best land and the losers got pushed up North to eke out whatever living they could. Which ironically worked to their advantage, because the white people wanted the best land too, of course, so it was the agricultural tribes and the buffalo hunters who suffered most, while the ones up on the Shield were largely left alone. Not that that saved them in the end.'

Georgie paused to think how best to describe what she wanted to say next. It wasn't something that any of her professors had ever mentioned, but it seemed to her to be a very relevant thing.

Matthew said impatiently, 'So what *was* new?'

'The same things that were new to everybody. Not new gods but no gods. Not new work but no work. Not feast and famine as the year turns, but relative plenty all year round. Their culture wasn't made to cope with that kind of thing. Neither is ours, for that matter. My grandmother says she can't even cope with strawberries all year round. She says it takes all the fun out of eating them.'

'Whyever? It sounds like paradise to me.'

'Does it? Life on welfare? No effort, no reward?' She turned away from the lake to face him. 'It's not paradise for them, it's hell. What do you do, without a good reason for getting out of bed in the morning? If God doesn't exist, who cares what happens to you? Why shouldn't you just do whatever takes your fancy?'

She found herself staring at, glaring at Matthew as if he were personally answerable for this state of affairs. He shrugged, unconcerned. 'Well, why not?'

'Well, for one thing, because most human beings left to their own devices apparently have a very circumscribed range of activities that take their fancy. Mostly they seem to involve getting blind drunk, shooting your friends, beating up your wife and screwing your children.'

Matthew registered some slight disapproval at last. 'Children?'

'Yeah, that's right. But it's not just the parents, it's the kids themselves. They see things, hear things, imitate things, because their parents don't give a damn any more. Because who cares? So you get settlements where the only virgins are small children under school age. And they're all addicted to glue and gasoline.'

'Are you making this up?'

'What do you think?'

'No, no, of course not. But it sounds fascinating, for all sorts of reasons. Why don't you want to investigate this phenomenon? Deculturalization or whatever it is.'

'Demoralization, you mean.' Georgie stared glumly at the lake. 'It's too awful to think about for long. And it's catching: I'd find myself not caring whether I got out of bed in the morning. It would be like documenting the end of the world.'

'I see what you mean.' Matthew considered what she meant for a while, the hissing and splashing of fountains standing in for silence. 'So what did you think you might do instead?'

'Well, I've had . . . not an inspiration, but at least a thought, a possibility.'

Georgie paused, suddenly self-conscious. The idea was still so new to her that she wasn't sure how she herself felt about it. Matthew poked her with his elbow, startling her so that she nearly dropped her wineglass into the lake below. 'Don't keep me in suspense, girl.'

She backed away from him, turned away from him, holding the wineglass with both hands. 'Well, your father showed me around Sussex last week. We must have covered about five thousand years of history in a few days. He talked about everything with such interest and enthusiasm, he made it seem so real and . . . and commonplace, in a funny way. Not commonplace as in boring, but as in ordinary, everyday. Like the past wasn't somewhere else, dead and gone, but right here, right now, in the midst of the present.'

'That's because there isn't any "right now" for him,' Matthew observed with a touch of contempt. 'His head is always somewhere else, somewhere in the past. It's easier to cope with a script that's already been written than one that you have to make up as you go along. Don't tell me you want to be a historian?'

Georgie turned to face him, more confident now. 'No, it's the archaeological aspects that interest me.'

'You want to think very carefully about that,' he said with surprising severity. 'I knew some of those blokes at Oxford and I got the impression that coal-mining would have offered a more comfortable and rewarding way of spending one's time. Do you want another glass of wine?'

'Yes, please.'

She gave him her glass and followed him into the flat. She sat down on the sofa that Matthew had said made into a bed, testing it for comfort. 'How does this open out?'

His answer came from the kitchen. 'Why bother with that contraption, when you can have half of the real bed?'

Georgie considered that. She had on occasion – usually after a party and in a drunken state – shared a bed, fully clothed, with a boy she wasn't actually sleeping with. But somehow she didn't think

47

that was what Matthew had in mind. So she considered what he almost certainly did have in mind.

The fact that he was her mother's half-brother didn't really bother her at all. Genetically a half-uncle was no closer than a second cousin; and nobody, except possibly a medieval baron desperate to annul his marriage, would have claimed that sexual intercourse between second cousins was intrinsically wrong.

Socially and emotionally, Matthew was a stranger she had known for just over a week. Nobody nowadays thought anything much about going to bed with someone you have only known for a week. And you didn't need to be Romeo-and-Juliet-ish about each other either. Lots of her friends went home from parties with a fanciable man they had only just met that night, and maybe never would meet again. It wasn't like the old days when people used to start off holding hands, and progress through kissing and necking and petting to what her grandmother called 'going all the way'. Nowadays there was no reason not to have sex with someone right away, if you felt like it. There were no taboos any more.

While she was reflecting on all this, Matthew came back with the refilled wineglasses. He handed Georgie hers and sat down at the other end of the sofa. 'Is it the Teutonic approach you don't fancy, or me?'

'The Teutonic approach?'

'Well, actually, I think an offer to share one's bed would be regarded as oblique and romantic by the Germans. Apparently they prefer a more direct approach, something along the lines of Why don't we take all our clothes off and screw for a while?'

He said this in a matter-of-fact tone, with only a hint of amusement. Nothing to suggest he was consumed with desire for her, or anything like that. 'What makes you think that sort of courting technique ever gets results?'

He shrugged. 'I presume the Germans get laid as often as the rest of the human race.'

'Possibly so, but I don't think it would get you very far in Canada, for instance.'

'Is courting necessary in Canada? I've always assumed that sex must be obligatory there. How else do you survive the winter?'

'It's not obligatory, it's impossible. On account of all the clothing we have to wear to bed.'

They looked at each other, laughing. If he had set down his glass and come and kissed her right then, she might have ended up sharing his bed. He was a beautiful boy, slim and brown and graceful, and she had always been attracted to men who made her

48

laugh. But he didn't make any move to touch her at all. So he was just trying it on, after all.

She didn't even know if she was disappointed or not.

With the assistance of a street atlas and the London subway system, Georgie tracked down the address her grandfather had given her. It turned out to be a turn-of-the-century row house, or terraced house as they were called here, according to Matthew. It was half-way up a hill, in the middle of a line of identical houses.

Not quite identical: the one she wanted had an extra window in the roof. There was no front yard at all. The front steps came right down to the sidewalk. The front door and windows needed painting, she noticed.

As at Underhill, she dithered for a while on the street. At least this time she knew it was the right house and the right person, and she had dressed herself up for the occasion in a skirt and blouse instead of tatty denim cut-offs. Finally she worked up the nerve to ring the door bell.

Nobody answered, even though she rang three or four times. She was just turning to leave when the door opened.

The woman who stood in the doorway was quite young, probably not a lot older than Georgie. She was holding a baby on one hip. A small boy with a semi-shaven head peered around her leg at Georgie.

Everything was wrong – the age of the woman, the children, the general feel of the place. Her grandfather had told her that his ex-wife was a successful jewellery designer, and this woman didn't look as if she knew anyone who designed jewellery, even unsuccessfully.

The woman was staring at Georgie. 'Yeah?'

'Oh, I – I'm looking for Emma Hardy.' Hardy was her grand-mother's maiden name, and the name under which she sold her jewellery, according to Althea. But she recalled that her grandfather had said she had married again, to a man named Winter. 'Or she might be Mrs Winter.'

'No one of that name here. Try next door.' The woman started to close her own door.

Georgie said urgently, 'Wait!'

The woman stopped with the door half shut. She shifted the baby impatiently. 'Yeah?'

'I'm sorry to bother you but this is really important. I know this is the right address and that she did live here once. Maybe she left a forwarding address when she moved?'

'Last people here were named Brown. Never heard of any Hardys or Winters.'

This time the door was firmly shut in her face.

By the time Georgie got back to the flat in the Barbican it had started to rain. It was already lunch time and Matthew had only just got up. She must have looked like rain herself because when he saw her he said, 'Did she send you away with a flea in your ear?'

'What's that mean?'

'I thought they spoke English in Toronto. It means, did she tell you to piss off?'

'Well, she wasn't there. They'd never heard of her.'

'What are you going to do now? Give up?'

'I sure am not. I'll ring up every Hardy and Winter in London if I have to.'

'She might not live in London. Some people don't.'

'Listen, Matt, you're no help at all. How would you feel if you'd lost your grandmother?'

'As it happens, I've often wished the old trout would get lost.'

Georgie tried to calculate relationships. 'Is that the one who's related to me?'

'No, the other side, my mother's mother. Your lot are dead.'

She wondered if her mother knew. No, of course she wouldn't know. She wondered if her mother would care when she heard. Her grandfather's parents were total stangers to her but they must have been real people to her mother, maybe as close and dear as her own father's parents were to Georgie herself.

In the event she saved herself dozens of fruitless phone calls because Matthew had a clever idea which actually worked. At his suggestion she looked for and found an E. Hardy listed at the same address as an N. J. Winter.

She looked it up in her atlas of London. It was in Chelsea, Matthew said. She rang to see if anyone was home but only got an answering machine. There was no way she could squeeze eighteen years into a short taped message, even if she had known for sure that she was leaving it for the right person, so she hung up without leaving a message.

She tried again about eight o'clock. This time a man's voice answered, very curtly. She decided to hang up without speaking. She wasn't up to announcing her existence to someone she hadn't even seen. But at least she knew someone was home.

It had been raining on and off all afternoon and the evening was cool as well as damp. Matthew lent her an old raincoat, a man's coat by the length of the arms, though it only came to her knees. She put that on over her respectable blouse and skirt and went off to Chelsea.

The houses on the street she wanted were terraced, like the house she had gone to that morning, but these looked to be Georgian rather than Edwardian, if her guidebook was to be believed, and they were four storeys high. And probably several times the price, she reckoned, comparing the expensive cars parked in the street, and the general air of neat prosperity, to the elderly Fords and shabby peeling façades along the terrace at her grandmother's previous address. That neigbourhood might have gone downmarket since she had lived there, but she had definitely come upmarket when she moved to this place.

At nine o'clock the evening light had already almost faded from the overcast sky. The house she wanted had a crack of light visible between drawn curtains. That encouraged her and made her more nervous.

She had walked into her grandfather's house in all innocence, never expecting anything but the welcome that he gave her, the welcome that she had imagined must be her due. Yet she was still no nearer to solving the mystery of those missing years, of her mother's abrupt departure and determination to cut herself off from her family. And her welcome was not unqualified, as she had discovered from Althea.

'I'm in two minds about the possibility of Lia turning up here,' Althea had warned her on an occasion when her grandfather was not around. 'It's all very well to kiss and make up, but how could she do that to Ross when he'd been so good to her? He paid for her schooling and saw you were properly taken care of. Some fathers would have washed their hands of her. And then to throw it all up in his face and go off like that, no explanation and no word, never from that day to this . . . It shattered him, really it did. If she were to come waltzing in here tomorrow like nothing had ever happened – well, there are some things that just can't be forgiven, aren't there?'

Maybe her grandmother would think so too. Maybe her mother was right after all. Maybe she shouldn't have come. She looked back to the sunny certainties of her life at home in Canada. Looking back to the last remnants of her childhood, perhaps.

Well, she had come not only to find her lost family but to solve a mystery. Her grandmother might know what her grandfather did not. She fluffed up her pale hair against the damp twilit air and walked up the steps to the front door.

A sound system was playing quite loudly. Loud enough to drown the sound of her knocking with its own bass thumps, she assumed when she got no response. She hammered with the knocker, then banged directly on the door, and finally leaned over the railing to rap on the curtained window.

There was no change in the volume of the indecipherable music, but when she straightened up to face the door again it opened abruptly. A man stood glowering at her.

A young man, a boy about her own age, she guessed. Well over six feet tall, with shoulders like a linebacker and longish unkempt hair almost as fair as her own. Astonishingly attractive, at first impression. A sort of surly angel.

For some reason his sudden presence rendered her speechless. Perhaps it was his size, perhaps the evident dislike with which he was glaring at her. She stared back at him open-mouthed, unable to utter a word.

'He's not in,' said the young man tersely. He shut the door in her face.

As soon as the door had slammed she regained her powers of speech and movement. Thank you very much, pal, she muttered to herself. She thumped vigorously on the door with both fists and kicked it for good measure.

The door opened again almost immediately. This time Georgie had the impression that if she had been a different sex the man in the doorway might well have started thumping her in return. The look in his light blue eyes was positively poisonous.

She said quickly, 'Does Emma Hardy live here?'

The question seemed to astonish him, as if she had asked after Santa Claus's whereabouts, but his hostility did not diminish. He stared at her for quite a while before he answered.

'She's dead.'

And he shut the door again.

6

I sat down under his shadow with great delight.

Georgie stared at the door, hardly knowing what to think. Maybe this was the wrong house and he had just said that to get rid of her.

Surely no one would do that. Not even someone as deliberately bad-mannered as this man. But if it was true, why would he say it like that? He hadn't even asked what Emma Hardy was to her, or she to Emma Hardy.

She had a sudden conviction, like a blow to the heart, that what he had said was true. She had come too late. Her grandmother was dead. And her mother didn't even know.

She sat down on the wet steps and began to cry. For the death of a stranger.

She didn't hear when the door opened for the third time. What she did hear was the young man's voice saying roughly, 'What's the matter with you? What do you want?'

She couldn't stop crying enough to answer him. She stood up and blew her nose and turned around to face him. Eventually she managed to say, 'I want Emma.' She wept some more and blew her nose again. 'She's my grandmother.'

She couldn't see very well with her eyes full of tears, so she didn't know how he was looking at her now. He must have looked at her one way or another for quite a long time before he said gruffly, 'You'd better come in.'

She followed him blindly into the living-room. He turned the music off and told her to sit down. She sat on the nearest chair, then realized it was some sort of antique and that her raincoat was wet and maybe muddy from sitting on the doorstep. She stood up again in confusion.

'My coat – I've made a mess of your chair – '

'Bugger the chair. Give me your coat, I'll get you a drink. Whisky or brandy?'

She must have asked for brandy, because that was what he brought her after he had taken her coat away. When she had swallowed a large mouthful to stiffen her sinews she was able to ask, 'Is it true? She's really dead?'

'She died six months ago. Brain haemorrhage. An aneurysm to be precise, if that means anything to you.'

Georgie nodded wordlessly. She was not a doctor's daughter for nothing. 'She must have gone suddenly, then.'

'Three days in a coma. Then they switched her off.'

He spoke with brittle bitterness. She was able for the first time to wonder what her grandmother had been to him. 'I'm sorry,' she sighed. Sorry for unknown Emma's death, for this boy's evident grief, for having turned up like this on his doorstep. 'I'm Georgiana Payne. I'm – '

'You're Lia's daughter,' he said with a sudden wide surprising smile. 'I should have guessed when I saw you.'

She looked at him in astonishment. He had the advantage of her there. 'You know about me?'

'Only vaguely. That you existed. That she existed.' He waved his hand, a hand of a suitable size for catching and throwing a football. The coach at her high school would have loved to have the likes of him on the team. 'There are old photos buried somewhere in the house.'

She drank the rest of the brandy and found herself able to smile at him. 'Well, I'm afraid I didn't even know that you existed. Are you – '

He anticipated her again. 'Luke. Emma was my mother.' He returned her smile. 'That makes me half an uncle or some such unlikely thing.'

Georgie stared at him as if he had only just materialized before her. Another unsuspected mother's-brother. A second semi-uncle. More stranger-kin.

But this one was definitely of her own lost tribe: very fair hair, blue eyes with sandy-silver brows and lashes. Just like hers. Unlike Matthew, this one looked as if he belonged to her. Which meant, of course, that he didn't look at all like her own family back in Canada.

As he stood smiling down at her, she felt two distinct and contradictory responses. On the one hand she felt drawn to him in a peculiar and powerful way, like an orphan who suddenly finds herself no longer alone in the world. On the other hand, because he looked so utterly unlike all the other people who had been close to her till now, he seemed completely alien. As if, having been brought up on earth, she had met a man from Sirius and discovered that she herself was not after all an earthling but a Sirian, a race of which she knew nothing at all.

'Let's call it cousins,' she suggested.

'Yeah, okay, why not? What's in a name, as somebody once said. Listen, I'm sorry I slammed the door in your face. I thought you were somebody else.'

Someone he didn't know, thought Georgie, but someone he nevertheless disliked. She wondered aloud, 'Who did you think I was?'

He made a gesture with one of those big hands, like brushing away a nuisance or a thing of no importance. 'Oh, just another one of his goddamn women. Models, they call themselves.' He grunted contemptuously. 'Trollops, more like. They haven't even got the grace . . . Well, never mind that. Can I get you another drink? A proper one this time?'

'Are you having one?'

'If you are.'

They looked at each other and laughed, for some reason. Georgie said, 'I'll have a glass of wine, if that's okay.'

'Yeah, sure. My mother always drank wine. We should have a bottle or two left. Unless he's been pouring it down the throats of those . . .' He was going out of the room as he spoke and consequently his final words were indistinct, but she thought he had made use of an expression so spectacularly vulgar and obscene that she had never actually heard it cross the lips of anyone personally known to her. Certainly none of her Payne relations would ever have uttered it. Evidently the Hardy-Winters, despite their Georgian Chelsea house filled with antiques, took a fairly broad view of the boundaries of language permissible within their elegant drawing-room. Another instance of their alienness.

While he was gone she took the opportunity to look around. The room she was in had been beautifully and expensively decorated in period style. The attention to detail made her quite certain that it was a woman's taste reflected here. Her grandmother, presumably.

But the paintings on the walls – real drawings and paintings, she noticed, not reproductions – suggested another influence, a different taste. The person who had furnished the room with antiques would surely have hung Old Masters, but these were definitely modern paintings, dry and classical in the approved Georgian manner, but mostly abstract. Oddly enough, they suited their surroundings; one way or another, it was all tasteful and restrained.

Yet Luke had cheerfully, openly, bluntly, used that amazing phrase, neither tasteful nor restrained. Presumably he hadn't picked up that sort of language from her grandmother. From his father, maybe – the *he*, she assumed, whose women were liable to turn up on the doorstep. Up to now she hadn't given any thought or speculation to the subject of her grandmother's second husband. He was a complete unknown, just as Althea had been.

Apparently the unmentionable ladies of unspeakable habits had not yet consumed the contents of her grandmother's wine cellar, for Luke soon returned with two bottles of wine, as well as a corkscrew and two wineglasses, all of which he set down with a casual clatter on a fragile-looking occasional table.

'I think the white's supposed to be chilled, and the red's supposed to be warmed to room temperature and allowed to breathe, whatever that means, but what the hell, let's just have a drink. What's your preference?'

Georgie smiled back at him. 'What the hell, I'll have the red to start with.'

'Sounds good to me.' He filled both glasses from the bottle of red wine. 'You know anything about wine? Bouquet and all that crap?'

'Are you kidding? I think most of the wine produced in Canada is made in Moose Jaw.'

'Now you're kidding me.'

'No, honestly.' She giggled and he started to laugh. 'There really is such a place, and they really do make wine there. No vineyards for thousands of miles, but plenty of plonk. They give it names like Baby Duck and Gimli Goose to entice people into buying it.'

'Sounds like the Russians. My father claims that vodka is the nearest thing to lab alcohol you can buy in a wine shop. It's all to do with the climate, I suppose. Is Canada really as cold as they say?'

'Colder, I'd imagine. My mother still hasn't recovered from the shock of the Canadian winter.'

'Does she stay indoors?'

'No, she goes up North and stays outdoors. My father says she's never grasped the difference between forty above and forty below.'

He looked at her a little more seriously. 'What does she go up North for?'

'Timber wolves. She studies wolves. She's a biologist.'

'What, really?'

'Yeah, really. She teaches at the university when she's not up North hanging around with wolves.'

'What about you? Why are you over here?'

Georgie went into her standard explanation. 'Well, I've just got my BA and I haven't really decided what I want to do next, so I thought I'd do some travelling and think about it.'

'What did you read?'

'Read?' She looked at him, trying to work this one out. 'What do you mean, read?'

'At university. What was your subject?'

'Anthropology. But I didn't necessarily want to be an anthropologist, it's just that I had to major in something or other. What about you, what do you do?'

'I've just finished too. Art college.'

He didn't look or sound much like Georgie's idea of an artist – much too large and muscular, for starters – but maybe he had a sweet sensitive soul tucked away inside that big athletic body. 'So are you really going to be an artist?'

'Why not?'

He sounded challenging, almost surly. Perhaps other people had been more openly sceptical that she had dared to be. 'No reason. I guess an artistic bent must run in your family.'

That didn't please him either. She began to wonder why on earth he wanted to pursue a career as an artist when he seemed so defensive about it. 'What does that mean, an artistic bent in my family?'

'Well, my family too, I guess. Emma made jewellery, didn't she? That's quite an arty thing to do.'

'Oh yeah.' He sounded surprised and relieved. 'I suppose it is, sort of.'

What else had he thought her comment was referring to? Cautiously Georgie enquired, 'What sort of art do you do?'

'Mixed media.'

That sounded more like TV than painting. She didn't ask him to elaborate, because he spoke as if she ought to have known what he meant. 'Can I see it some time?'

She must have touched a sore nerve again. Her interest did not appear to please him. 'I haven't got a studio right now. I had to clear out of the one I had at college and I haven't found a new space yet.'

'Can I see it anyway? You must have had to store your stuff somewhere. Is it in this house?'

'Upstairs. But they're constructs, they need to be deployed to get the right effect. It's the artist's intention that makes art out of objects. Otherwise it just looks like a heap of old rubbish.'

Meaning it was a heap of old rubbish, Georgie deduced. 'Didn't you have to do any proper art at college? Drawings and paintings and things like that?'

'Nobody does that crap any more. Representational art was killed off by photography, and abstract art is a blind alley. And photography isn't art,' he added belligerently, as if daring her to contradict him.

'I wouldn't dream of claiming that it was,' Georgie said to pacify him. 'But you can only photograph things that are actually there. An artist can make pictures of things that aren't there. All those Christs and Madonnas in the National Gallery, for instance.' She looked at Luke: fair-haired, blue-eyed, beautiful Luke. 'Angels and so forth.'

She was treading on alien territory here, so she spoke with some diffidence. Which didn't save her from his scorn. 'That's all been done too. To death, in fact. Surrealism and all that shit. You can't keep covering the same ground over and over again for ever, that's how traditions get debased and decadent. Anyway, restricting the concept of art to traditional areas like drawing and painting and sculpture is deliberately élitist.'

Georgie had to think for a minute to work that out. 'You mean because the only people who can draw are the people who are able to draw. Is that what you mean?'

'Well, you have to admit that enlarging our idea of what art is also makes it more democratic.' His sudden smile had a mischievous edge. 'Look how well the concept has worked for pop music. Everyone's a potential star.'

She was astonished, reflecting for a moment by way of catching her breath, how far they seemed to have come together, already arguing in the friendly, familiar manner of old intimates. It was almost like a conversation with the other side of herself. And that was just what he looked like: the other side of herself. The genes from Sirius, the past she had forgotten.

Perhaps Luke had been thinking much the same sort of thoughts. He said abruptly, 'Speaking of art and non-art, shall I dig out those old photos I mentioned?'

They spent the next hour looking at family photographs. It was a missing link in her life as far as Georgie was concerned. There were pictures of herself as a baby and her mother as a (very) young woman. The infant Luke was in many of them as well, a sturdy tow-headed child clearly father to the man. And her grandmother appeared, over and over – a strikingly beautiful blonde woman, fine-featured and slim. That was where it had come from, her Sirian blood.

She realized with a shock that when these pictures had been taken her grandmother must have been about the same age that her mother was now. And now her grandmother was dead.

Resolutely Georgie pushed that thought aside. Some things didn't bear thinking on. 'It's the strangest thing,' she remarked. 'I don't remember any of this.'

'Why should you? You were just a baby. I don't remember either.'

'Do you know why it happened?' She could safely ask him. Like Matthew, he carried no baggage from back then. 'Why did my mother go away like that?'

'I don't know.' Luke was sitting cross-legged on the carpet, frowning at a photo of two small blond naked children splashing each other in a pool. Presumably him and her. They looked like twins. 'How would I know? I was only three, same as you.'

'I thought maybe your mother might have dropped a hint sometime.'

'Not her. I think she took it as a personal affront, and the less said about it the better.'

She had curled up beside him on the carpet, leaning over to look at the picture in his hand. He was so close she could smell him. She wanted to put her face against his shirt. Better still, her face against his skin, to touch and smell and taste her lost inheritance. The craving was so strong, she began to be afraid he would sense it somehow. Deliberately she turned her attention to the photographs scattered across the rug.

'These are amazingly good photos. Not your average family album shots. Who took them?'

'Not your average family photographer.' He looked down at her, half smiling, half expectant, waiting for the light to dawn. She couldn't imagine what it was she was supposed to have guessed. He said, 'My old man is Nick Winter.'

The name meant nothing to her.

Seeing her blank look, he gave a shout of laughter. 'Wonderful!

58

Wait till I tell him I've found a female between fifteen and twenty-five who's never heard of him.'

She speculated wildly. The father of Luke must surely be too old to be a pop star, or at any rate one of interest to girls and young women. Maybe he featured in some British TV series. Maybe . . . She gave up. 'Enlighten me.'

'Wait right there.'

He leapt to his feet, nearly spilling his wineglass on the obviously valuable and probably irreplaceable carpet. Georgie rescued the wine, or the carpet. Luke went out of the room without even noticing. It was a large room, but his departure made it seem much larger. And emptier.

He returned almost immediately with a stack of magazines, which he dropped into her lap. Glossy fashion journals of a type she rarely read, though some of her friends did. She opened one, without a clue as to what she was supposed to be looking for.

Logic came to her rescue. There were only four sorts of people involved in these magazines: journalists, models, couturiers, and photographers. And they had just been discussing photographs. After that, the answer fairly jumped off the pages at her. *Cover photo by Nick Winter. Photographs by Nick Winter.* For anyone who regularly read this sort of thing it would have been difficult to avoid seeing his name, even if it didn't turn up in the articles, which it did in at least one feature.

'Right. I see. Excuse my ignorance.' She set aside the magazines and turned towards Luke. 'So what's it like having a famous father? Good for picking up girls, is it?'

'It's bloody awful,' he said with surprising vehemence. 'They suck up to me in the hopes of getting to meet him. They all have these crazy fantasies about modelling. They think maybe he'll take a fancy to them and make them rich and famous. I never bring them home any more because I know what's going to happen if I do.'

'Why, what happens?'

'They spend the whole time sucking up to him, in the most disgusting way. And what's even more disgusting is the way he laps it up.'

'And has he actually made any of them rich and famous?'

Luke shrugged. 'Not that I ever heard of. The last one I brought back, I thought it would be okay because she was an anarchist who believed that the whole fashion industry exemplified capitalism at its most corrupt and effete. She said it fed on planned obsolescence and consumerism gone mad. She really believed it, too. She used to wear her clothes until they fell apart. One pair of jeans, one pair of shoes. She wore the same outfit everywhere. Fashion-proof, like.'

They were well into the second bottle of wine by now. Luke hunched over his drawn-up knees, brooding. He looked like a sulky god, Georgie thought, big and blond and beautiful, trailing havoc and earthquake in his unconsidered wake. The ways in which he was like and unlike her were becoming clearer. And he was a man, of course, which inevitably made him alien. An unknown self. The need to touch him was even stronger now; she had a notion that the shape of his body must be instinctively familiar to her. She sat on her hands to avoid temptation. She made herself ask about this girlfriend of his, the thought of whom inexplicably enraged and appalled her.

'So what happened with this girl?'

'Well, she started off in fine style. She told him his profession was corrupt and frivolous. She told him he should be using his talent with a camera to expose evil in the world instead of helping to gloss it over and distract people from their real situation. She went on like that for quite a while. She was wonderfully rude to him. My mother kept trying in a genteel way to shut her up or change the subject.'

'And what did your father do?'

'He let her rave on for a bit. Eventually he pointed out, quote unquote, that no one is obliged to read the bloody magazines or buy the fucking clothes. And then he said he'd noticed that she had interesting hands – some shit about the length of her fingers relative to the size of her palm – and he needed a pair of hands for a spread in one of the Sunday papers and would she mind . . .'

'So did she?'

He smiled sourly. 'What do you think?' The smile disappeared. 'She was a real airhead. She kept asking me when it was going to be in the paper.'

Georgie began to have a suspicion that she was not going to like her grandmother's husband – or widower, as he was now. But she could see another side to the story. 'He was probably just getting back at her for all the rude things she'd been saying to him. It's bad manners to come into someone's house as a guest and then start denouncing them for capitalist immorality.'

'At least it made a change,' Luke remarked sardonically. 'The others all start throwing themselves at him as soon as they walk in the front door.'

'Good-lookers, are they, all your girls?'

She thought she must have spoken with embarrassingly revealing sharpness, but Luke just looked at her blankly. 'Well, yeah. Of course. Why not?'

'No reason. It's just – they must have thought they were in with a chance or they wouldn't have bothered trying.'

'So what? You want me to go around with ugly women?'

'I don't care who you go around with,' she said completely untruthfully. 'But if you took them out because you really like them rather than because they look good on your arm, maybe they might be more interested in you than in your famous father.'

'How do you know – ' He started to protest, then changed his mind. 'Yeah, okay, fair cop. I never thought of it like that before. In fact I never . . .' His fingertip was tracing the abstract patterns in the rug, an activity that appeared to absorb him. 'I never told anyone about it before. Because – well, you know.' He shrugged to disclaim responsibility for his own revelations.

She licked her lips. 'So why are you – why tell me?'

He shrugged again. Great broad shoulders he had; she watched them rise and ripple and subside. 'You're a stranger, aren't you? You don't know me. You'd never even heard of him. And also,' he glanced up at her with a slight smile, 'you're the opposite of a stranger. Whatever that might be.'

'Yeah, I know,' said Georgie. And she did, she knew exactly what he meant. She changed the subject – sort of. 'Have you got any recent photos of your mother?'

Again he got up and went away, and came back with another photograph. This was a real posed studio shot, the sort that models put in their portfolios. 'He took that last Christmas. About a month before . . .'

He stopped and turned away and made a big thing out of sharing out the last of the wine.

Georgie studied the picture of her grandmother. Compared to the earlier photos she was still beautiful, though obviously twenty years older. Not twenty totally blissful years either, to judge by the changes in her face. Now she looked thin rather than slim, thin and worn and fragile, as if her physical self had eroded along with her earlier happiness. How much of a part had the disappearance of her daughter and granddaughter played in that? Georgie stared into her grandmother's dead blue eyes and felt personally guilty for the shadow she saw there.

She set down the photograph and stood up to stretch her legs, to give both herself and Luke a chance to recover from the image of dead Emma. One of the paintings on the wall caught her eye. She went over to it. 'Hey, is this really a Mondrian?'

'Yeah.' Luke scrambled up to stand beside her. 'My old man's taste. So old-fashioned it's already classic, I guess.'

'What does your father think about your own work?'

'Let me see.' He frowned, trying to recall. 'Pointless. Misguided. A waste of my time and his money. I might have felt really bad, if he hadn't said the same sort of thing about my tutors' work.'

'When did he say all this?'

'At my degree show. He also said the whole thing reminded him of nursery school, with everybody colouring in a fucking clown one day and doing potato prints the next.'

Georgie was scandalized. This sort of frank criticism, even if true, seemed to her to be outright dereliction of parental duty. 'Didn't he have anything nice to say about it?'

'Well, yeah, he did. He said at least I had the sense not to spout a load of pretentious crap about it, unlike my tutors.'

'Is this show still around? Can I go and see it?'

'You mean you still want to, after hearing that? But you can't, it's already come down.'

'Oh, that is too bad,' she said earnestly. 'I'd really have liked to see it.'

Luke hesitated. 'Well, I have got some photos.'

'Go and get them, for heaven's sake. This is no time for false modesty.'

The photos were not very helpful. You had to have been there, Georgie supposed. She squinted at an image of what Luke explained was a Victorian chimney-pot with a Victorian manhole cover on top, in the vain hope of achieving some aesthetic enlightenment.

But aesthetics was not what it was all about. 'That's supposed to encapsulate the idea of Victorian society as exploitative of human resources,' he explained, with a touch of conscious self-irony. 'My tutor really raved about that one.'

'I like the chimney-pot,' Georgie murmured vaguely. 'Did your father take these pictures?'

Luke said huffily, 'It wasn't my idea.'

'I just meant, he must have liked your stuff if he went to the trouble of photographing it.'

'My tutor persuaded him to.'

Georgie laid all the exhibition photos out on the carpet and looked at them. The works thus immortalized were not only Luke's but all his fellow graduates'. Luke's style appeared to be more . . . she groped mentally for a word that wouldn't suggest any sort of inferiority, because inferior was precisely what she didn't mean . . . more *minimalist* than most of the others. They were really just large-scale *objets d'art* in eccentric configurations. But at least his *objets* themselves were quite interesting and attractive, which was more than could be said of the rest: a stack of rotten window frames, a

62

sandbox in the semblance of a computer (or perhaps it was meant to be the other way around), a dressmaker's dummy sitting on a three-legged milking stool with a lampshade where its head would have been. The humour (where intentional) was heavy-handed.

But now, seeing them all together, she noticed another sort of intentional humour at work. Presumably the photos had been taken at the time the exhibition opened, since there were plenty of people wandering around in them. The students' friends and relatives, she supposed, being unable to imagine who else would turn out to see such stuff. But the people were doing odd things. Or rather, they were doing perfectly ordinary but seldom photographed things, and they were doing them against the bizarre background of the exhibits. A woman with her eyes shut – just blinking, presumably – facing the window frames. A man discreetly scratching his buttock beside the dressmaker's dummy. A woman peering into Luke's manhole-covered chimney-pot, holding a Kleenex to her nose. The funniest one was of a person doing nothing in particular, just looking at one of the exhibits, but caught at an unguarded moment with his face blank and mouth slightly agape, no hint of thought or intelligence to disturb his expression of total witlessness.

'Did your – ah – your professor see these photos?'

'Yeah, why?'

'Didn't he notice – '

'She.' Luke looked amused. 'Why do you think my father let himself get talked into it?'

'Well, didn't she notice what these people are doing?'

Luke squatted down to examine the photos again. Obviously he and his tutor had simply focused their attention on the exhibits, because that was what the photos were supposed to be about. This time he concentrated on the incidental human background, and started to laugh. 'No, I guess she didn't notice. Neither did I. What a bastard.' But he kept on looking and laughing.

Georgie watched him, aching to touch him, any bit of him at all, his hair, his elbow, the tip of his little finger. All equally impossible, on two contradictory counts: because he was her uncle, and because he was a stranger.

She glanced at the carriage-clock on the mantel. 'Gosh, it's after mid-night. I've got to get back. Matt will think I've turned into a pumpkin.'

'Matt?'

'He's the same as you, my half-uncle or cousin or whatever. My grandfather's son.'

'Do they live in London?'

'No, Sussex. But they have an apartment – sorry, a flat – in the Barbican and I'm staying there. So is Matt.'

He stood up again. This time he did it remarkably gracefully, considering his size and the amount of alcohol he had consumed. 'I'm too drunk to drive you home, but I'll call a taxi for you. Listen, have you got a phone number for that flat? My father will want to see you. It looks like he won't be home till the small hours tonight. If at all,' he added in a muttered aside. 'But I'm sure he'll want to see you. Eighteen years, Jesus Christ.'

'I don't remember him at all,' Georgie said dubiously, thinking perhaps it was just as well.

'But he'll remember you.'

'If you say so. Here's the phone number.'

When the taxi came he fetched her coat and came down the front steps with her. They were both what her grandfather Payne would have called three sheets to the wind.

'I'm really glad you came, Georgie. I'll see you again soon.'

'Soon,' she repeated. Soon was not soon enough, whenever it was.

He handed her a scrap of paper. She looked, expecting a note of some sort. But it was a drawing, a quick cartoon-like sketch of someone recognizably herself, holding an enormous glass of wine. He had caught her in a few lines. And in a few minutes, since she hadn't noticed him doing it.

'What's this?'

'Souvenir.' He smiled shyly, slyly. 'Real art.'

'Hey, it's terrific. I'm impressed. Thanks.' She stretched herself up to kiss him quickly on the corners of his mouth, less than one per cent of what she wanted. 'Kissing cousins,' she explained. The wine slurred the words. She hoped he would think she was only drunk, not crazy.

7

If I be wicked, woe unto me.

'How did you make out? Did you find her?'

'Yes and no. She's dead.'

Matthew nearly scalded himself with the boiling water he was pouring into the teapot. 'What? Really?'

'Yes. Six months ago.' To her surprise Georgie began to cry. 'I waited eighteen years and missed her by six months.'

He set down the kettle and came over to the table where she was sitting. He put his arms around her and stroked her hair while she wept. That was the first time he had touched her, except for that day on the Downs. But he didn't seem at all self-conscious about holding her, and this time there was nothing remotely sexual about his embrace. It made her feel much better, being cuddled like that. Better about Emma, and also about Matthew. It made her think maybe he loved her. Like his father.

When she had regained her composure he brought her tea to the table and she sipped at that to console herself.

'Who did you see?'

'Her son. Luke. Another one of my mother's brothers who I didn't even know existed.' After a moment of bitterness she added in a vast understatement, 'He was really nice. We got on famously.'

'Nicer than me, was he?'

'Oh, much. I was there all evening and he made no attempt whatsoever to proposition me, in the German style or any other way.'

'Nor he shouldn't have, being your uncle and all.'

'Not all that much of an uncle. I worked it out. I mean, kinship is all about genetics, isn't it? In his case that's all it can be, because I didn't know he existed until last night. So look: a parent and a child, or a brother and sister, share on average half of their genomes. A grandparent and grandchild, or a half-brother and half-sister, or cousins, or an uncle and niece, have one-quarter in common. Second cousins have only one-eighth, twelve and a half per cent, and so do you and I. Does that sound remotely like incest to you? If you were one-eighth related to the Queen, you wouldn't be holding your breath waiting for your coronation.'

Matthew was looking at her in a funny way. 'You've given this a lot of thought, I see.'

'Well, I just thought I'd work it all out. Just out of curiosity. It's such a strange idea, being related to people I've only just met. You can't conjure up the appropriate feelings out of nothing, can you?' She held up her empty mug. 'Could you pour me some more tea, please, Matty?'

Matthew obliged. 'So what about your grandmother's husband? Is he still around?'

'Of course. But he wasn't home. I gather he's been playing the part of a merry widower and Luke definitely doesn't approve.'

'I disapprove of his disapproval,' Matthew said firmly. 'It's better than sitting home and brooding, isn't it? Your uncle Luke sounds like a puritanical prig to me. Why shouldn't the old boy let himself be consoled by a brigade of willing widows?'

'Um . . . I don't think it's like that. Apparently he's a big-time fashion photographer and the consolers are all gorgeous young women hoping he'll make them rich and famous.'

'That sounds even better to me. Young Luke is obviously animated by envy.'

'Don't be a pig, Matt. It's disgusting, the idea of an old man going with young girls.'

'Well, if your Luke is lucky maybe his old man will screw himself into a heart attack before too long.'

'Not before I have a chance to meet him, I hope.'

He wasn't a bad sort, Matthew. A little strange, maybe, but, well, who wasn't? They could share a flat without getting on each other's nerves, and he hadn't pressed the offer to share his bed as well. He was funny and astute and sometimes even kind. And he had an air of aloneness about him that attracted her in a vaguely maternal way.

Georgie always felt some degree of responsibility for her boy-friends. Maybe it gave her an illusion of being in control. Maybe she only picked the ones that made her feel a little motherly. Matthew was not her boyfriend, but she found herself beginning to wonder about him. To worry about him.

He had no job but plenty of money. Well, he lived rent-free in his parents' flat and collected the dole, which he professed to find scandalously inadequate, so maybe the money wasn't such a mystery. Though he did seem to have a *lot* of it. Maybe Althea was slipping him something on the side. Without her grandfather knowing, of course; she couldn't see him subsidizing his son's idleness.

Matthew certainly wasn't making any effort to find a job. He claimed to be taking the summer off. When she asked him what he wanted to do, he was vague. Something to do with TV, maybe. His idea of job-hunting appeared to be simply waiting for some plum to drop into his lap. To Georgie, who had worked every summer from the age of fourteen and part-time throughout university, this laid-back attitude seemed nothing short of scandalous.

What he did with his time was another mystery. He never got up till noon. Sometimes in the afternoon he would take her sightseeing. Sometimes in the evening they would go to a play or a film, or just to a pub or out to eat. Sometimes he did nothing but watch TV twelve hours straight. Sometimes he just disappeared without explanation, mostly in the late evening.

'Hey, Matt, do you have a life? Are you going to let me in on it?'

'What, take you home to Mother, you mean?'

They were sitting in the Wallpaper Room at the Tate. At least, that was how Georgie thought of it. All the walls in the room were hung with huge monochromatic Rothko canvases. Some of them had two colours, one in the top half and the other in the bottom, just for the sake of variety, Georgie supposed. Not much to see really, is there, she whispered. People say they find it very restful, Matthew explained. Restful, repeated Georgie thoughtfully, I thought this guy killed himself. Well, yeah, he did, Matthew agreed. Out of boredom, I should think.

'I've already met your mother, idiot. Do you have any friends? People who aren't actually obliged by ties of kinship to spend time in your company?'

Matthew considered this carefully. 'Does this mean you want me to take you to a party?'

'Sure, if you know of one to go to.'

He did, the very next night. One of those rambling aimless affairs in a large house, where no one, not even the party-giver, appeared to know everyone else, though most people seemed to know Matthew.

At any rate they all looked quite normal. Only one person wore an ear-ring not in her ear (in her eyebrow, as a matter of fact) and no one tried to convert Georgie to a new improved brand of religion.

They settled down in a room where the entertainments on offer were dope-smoking and dancing to amazingly archaic music. 'Sophie's old man has the biggest collection of rubbish Fifties music anywhere in London,' Matthew informed Georgie as he passed her a joint.

A girl with very short dark hair and an even shorter skirt came over and plunked herself down on Matthew's lap in a proprietary way. 'I heard that, Matthew Beckett. This isn't rubbish, it's Art.' She sang along with Art for a moment, then rolled her eyes in Georgie's direction. 'Who's your little friend?'

'My cousin from Canada.'

The girl, presumably Sophie, gave Georgie a shameless sizing-up to decide whether she believed him or not. Georgie couldn't say anything in her own defence because she was concentrating on inhaling without coughing. She had never quite gotten the hang of smoking dope while looking cool.

'What's her name?'

'Georgie. And she may look dumb, but she isn't deaf.'

Sophie giggled, unabashed. 'Hey, Georgie, you don't mind if I borrow your cousin for a bit, do you? He's a super dancer.'

Super, perhaps, but definitely reluctant. Sophie had to haul him to his feet.

Georgie turned to her neighbour on the other side to offer him the joint. He took a drag and passed it back because there was no one beyond him. With Matthew and Sophie out of sight, Georgie had to share the rest of it with him. Eventually, when she could just about feel the smoke coming out of her ears and eyeballs, she generously let him finish it off.

She couldn't remember his name. Not surprising, since she could hardly remember her own name by this time. He asked her to dance and she saw no reason to refuse. It was a slow song, a black man singing in a wobbly voice about being the great pretender. Dancing slowly turned out to mean putting your arms around each other, like people in old films. Georgie began to wonder why this sort of dance had ever gone out of fashion. Because it could only be done in couples, presumably of opposite sex, she supposed. There wasn't really anything you could say that of nowadays, not even getting pregnant.

'Are you really Canadian?'

'Don't I sound like it?'

'I suppose you do.'

Over his shoulder she noticed Matthew standing by the door. Sophie was leaning up against him, looking distinctly drunk or stoned or both. Matthew was talking to another man. She could see his lips moving and the other man's mouth replying but she couldn't hear a word they were saying. She put her head on her partner's shoulder in a dreamy sort of way, watching the man in the doorway give Matthew money and Matthew give him something in return. The rest of his dope, she supposed. He had brought far too much to smoke.

Time went by in the eccentric manner of the stoned mind. Time went by in the music too: Time goes by, a man was singing in an even more tremulous voice than the great pretender. The boy she was dancing with asked her if she wanted to go upstairs. While she was giving this proposition her aimless consideration, Matthew came over and told him to push off, and started to dance with her himself.

'Did you come over because you heard what he said?'

'What did he say?'

'He asked me if I wanted to go upstairs.'

'German, is he?'

Georgie giggled against his shoulder. She wanted to go on dancing like that for ever, with time going by and Matthew holding her. It felt really good, having Matthew hold her.

Sophie came up and put her hand on Matthew's arm. 'Come and dance with me for a while.'

'Clear off, Soph. I'm busy.'

'I thought she was your cousin.'

'Well, I'm looking after her. I'll see you later.' But as soon as Sophie had gone away he said to Georgie, 'Let's go.'

'Go where?'

'Anywhere else but here. Home, for a change.'

'Is Sophie your girl?'

'When she's drunk she seems to think she is.'

There was no one at all in sight at the tube station, no staff, no customers, no one to even notice whether or not you had a ticket. The dim underground lighting made the dingy walls even more depressing. The electronic signboard said *Next Train 5 Minutes*.

'Five minutes,' Matthew read out loud, in a tone that suggested five minutes was a semi-eternity. 'What'll we do to amuse ourselves?'

'Why don't we just stand around and be patient? It's only five minutes.'

'Not five minutes, five London Underground minutes. They're three times as long as the normal kind. Listen, if you can sing that song about time going by, we could dance while we're waiting.'

He put his arms around her waist and she put her arms around his neck and hummed the tune, and they danced. Or pretended to dance, since they seemed to be sticking to the same spot, just sort of shifting their weight from one foot to the other. Well, if it was just an excuse for him to hold her, that was fine with her. Time goes by, and time can do so much.

Next Train 4 Minutes.

She wondered how different it would be to be held by Luke. He'd be a lot bigger, for one thing. She'd have had her face against his chest instead of on his shoulder. He would have smelled different, more familiar somehow. And without ever having touched his hair, she knew just how it would feel: springy, untameable, vigorous, like a natural extension of the vitality of his body.

Matthew's hair was not like that at all. He had lovely silky hair. She slid her hand up into it.

He looked at her. She thought he was going to kiss her, and she would have liked that. But he didn't kiss her. Instead he said very softly, 'Why don't you take your clothes off?'

She was shocked, but in a muffled way, as if her brain had been insulated from the effect of his words. 'What are you talking about? I can't do that.'

'Sure you can. You do it every night, don't you?'

'Not in a tube station I don't.'

'If you put your raincoat back on, no one will know.'

'You'll know.'

'Well, of course. That's the point of it.'

Next Train 3 Minutes.

They had drawn away from each other. Georgie stared at him, trying to work this out, handicapped by the anti-intellectual effects of alcohol and marijuana. 'Why would I want to go home wearing nothing but a raincoat?'

'Because it's a turn-on.'

'For you, maybe.'

'For you too, maybe.' He gave her a slanting, significant look from beneath his silky lashes. 'I dare you.'

It did sound sexy, come to think of it, but also kinky. The idea alarmed her. Screwing was one thing and raincoats were another.

2 Minutes.

She licked her lips, considering the proposal as abstractly as she could. 'We haven't got time. And I never said I'd screw you.'

For Matthew too, it appeared, screwing and raincoats were separate things. 'Who said anything about screwing? You can sit on the opposite side of the carriage if you want. Pretend you don't know me. It'd be even better that way.'

Georgie tried to visualize that. Sitting opposite each other like strangers, except she would be naked underneath the raincoat and he would know it. The idea gave her a very unfamiliar thrill. She had never considered such a thing before: sex as an act of the imagination.

Matthew came up to her and put his arms around her. She buried her face in his neck. *Next Train 1 Minute.* 'Too late now,' she whispered.

'Chicken.'

She pinched his arm for that. 'Hey, Matt, you know what you should be doing for a living? Writing screenplays for horror films.'

She was seriously disturbed by the scenario Matthew had presented to her. It suggested – and her own reaction confirmed – that sex was not just a simple and natural activity between two people, as she had always supposed, but a strong and far from simple impulse in every individual. Of course, she knew all about the Freudian view of the sex drive, but she had taken that to mean that people naturally liked to do it. All of a sudden the definitions of *people, natural, like* and *it* were far from understood.

The train roared into the station and they got into the last carriage, the only passengers. Georgie sat on Matthew's lap, feeling in need of some comfort.

'There's no shortage of seats in this carriage, girl,' he pointed out. But he put his arms around her all the same.

She laid her head on his shoulder, as if they had still been dancing. Closed her eyes and let him hold her steady while the train rocked from side to side. 'Do you screw that Sophie?'

'I did for a while. Up at Oxford. Why, are you jealous?'

'Should I be?'

'No,' he said, against the roar of the tunnel. 'No.'

She woke up. Something had gone bump in the night. Right in the room where she was sleeping, as far as she could tell in her drowsy state.

She dithered, trying to decide if it was a burglar, in which case she would pretend to be asleep, or Matthew, in which case she ought to turn on the light before he bumped into something breakable. The odds being in favour of Matthew, she turned on the lamp beside the sofa.

A good guess. Matthew stood at the foot of the sofa-bed, blinking in the sudden light, looking distinctly disoriented, as if he had just been pushed out of a flying saucer and found himself on a strange planet.

For all Georgie knew, that was precisely what had happened. As soon as they had arrived back at the flat, Matthew had gone out again, for purposes unspecified. And only now returned, evidently.

She didn't want to ask the obvious question, *Where've you been*, because it was none of her business. Instead she wondered out loud what time it was.

'Too late,' Matthew told her. He sat down on the bed. Dropped down, as if his legs had stopped working. He only just missed landing on her foot. 'Why don't you get me a drink?'

His pupils looked to her to be unusually large and dark. That might have been from trying to see in darkness, or it might not. 'A drink of water, you mean?'

'No, I don't mean. Pour me a shot of my father's whisky. Pretty please.'

'Matty, you're already plastered. Or flying on something.'

'So what?'

He sounded so truculent that she only answered mildly. 'Well, it seems like a waste of good Scotch.'

'So what?' he repeated, less agressively this time.

'So go to bed and let me get back to sleep.'

'What for? You don't have to get up in the morning until you feel like it.' He turned away from her, leaning across her right shin. She couldn't see what he was doing, but she found out soon enough – when her right foot was exposed to the air and the attentions of Matthew's mischievous fingers.

'Hey, cut that out. What are you doing?'

'Waking you up.'

71

She tried to pull her foot away, but the weight of his body had pinned it down. Then she tried to push him off with her other foot, but the blanket got in the way. 'Stop it, Matt, I hate being tickled.'

'I know.'

She couldn't reach him because she couldn't bend her knee. It was torture, pure and simple, and like all torture victims she said whatever was necessary to make him stop. 'Okay, okay, let me go and I'll get you a drink.'

He rolled off and she climbed out of bed, pulling her night-gown down to her knees. When she went into the kitchen he followed her, and watched her pour the Scotch.

'More, more. Don't be so miserly.'

'Pour it yourself, then.'

But she didn't give him the bottle, only the glass. He swallowed the contents in one mouthful. She found that scary, for some reason. He scared her even more the way his dark eyes looked at her, above the hand with which he was wiping his mouth. She moved away uneasily towards the safety of her bed, still holding the bottle of Glenwhatsit.

Matthew came after her, came up behind her and put his arms around her waist. Just for a moment she wondered if she might need the bottle to defend herself. But he wasn't being rough or amorous, as far as she could tell. He buried his face in her hair. She set the bottle down on the coffee table beside her, and put her hands over his to prevent them from straying.

'Matty, what have you been up to?'

'What do you think?'

What she thought made her feel slightly shocked. 'What did you do, drop me here and go back to the party?' Back to Sophie, she meant.

'That's too far to go. I just picked up someone in a bar.'

That shocked her in a different way. 'You shouldn't screw strange women. You never know where they've been.'

His arms tightened around her. He was speaking very softly. If his mouth hadn't been right beside her ear she might not have caught it, what he was saying.

'Women? What women?'

She stiffened involuntarily. She would have pulled away from him, but he was holding her too tight. 'A man?' She tried to turn her head, to look at him. He wouldn't let her move. 'You had sex with a stranger?' She felt astonishment, disgust, bewilderment, even betrayal. 'Why'd you do that?'

'I've done it lots of times.'

'You'll get Aids! Maybe you've already got it!'

72

'No, I haven't. I don't do any of that shit. I don't do anything at all, I just stand there and let them suck my cock.'

He released her. She turned around to stare at him. He looked the same as ever, a beautiful sunbrown boy, midnight hair and midnight eyes, that slight sardonic twist to the corner of his mouth. She had never imagined him as gay. Bisexual maybe. Omnivorous, more likely. She didn't know why he had told her this. She didn't know what to say.

'Disgusting, isn't it?' He slurred his words, as if they were too hard for him to say. 'Kiss me, Georgie.'

She hesitated, more bewildered than before. Then she saw his mouth twist, and something within her made a leap of understanding, so fast and far that she couldn't quite catch up with it. But it made her come right up to him and kiss his crooked mouth with a lover's kiss.

He responded to that like a starving man suddenly presented with meat and drink. When she tried to draw away, he kissed her again, deep heavy kisses, pushing himself against her. Between kisses he told her that he wanted to fuck her. She ignored that at first, but he said it several times, more and more insistent.

'Matty, we can't.'

'Why not? Because I'm queer?'

'Don't be silly. And you're not. But you are my uncle.'

'Second cousin, you said. Like second cousins.' He was staring at her with an odd sort of glitter in his eyes, like a man with a fatal fever. 'Don't you want me, Georgie?'

She realized that when it came right down to it, she couldn't refuse to let him make love to her. Because if she did it would be like throwing him out of the human race.

While she dithered over this dilemma, he pushed her down on to the bed and pulled up her night-gown. She started to shake. She didn't know what he would do if she shoved him off her. Not try to rape her, at any rate. It was her acceptance of him that he wanted most to win, rather than a merely mechanical hetero conjunction. And as for words, they would mean nothing at all. It was so much easier to lie than to lie with, so much harder to give your body than empty assurances.

'Okay.' She was shaking so much she could hardly say it. 'Okay, Matty.' She wrapped her arms and legs around him, in case despair had made him deaf. At least it helped to stop her shaking.

His urgent and uncharacteristic desperation made him so vulnerable that she dared not do or say anything with however faint a flavour of rejection, such as suggesting he put on a condom. She didn't have one anyway, and didn't know if he did. And she couldn't claim fear of pregnancy, because he knew she was on the pill. A sensible precaution while travelling, she had thought, in case of who knew what unforeseen circumstances. This was about as unforeseen as you could get.

Matthew said her name over and over. Do you love me, he said. She had never seen him in such a state before; he had always been so cool and self-contained. It alarmed and frightened her, as if he were dangerously ill or wounded and she had to save him from fatality. It was the strangest sexual encounter she had ever had. Scarcely sexual at all, even though they were going through the usual motions. There was nothing she could do except tell him that she loved him, which was true, but not in a sexual sense, but he didn't mean it that way anyway. She didn't even know if he had heard her in his hectic condition.

Coming seemed to calm him, or at least exhaust him. It calmed her too; she stopped trembling. She had gone to bed before now with men she didn't desperately desire – most of them, in fact – and couldn't quite understand why letting Matthew make love to her should have shaken her so much. Unless it was that what he wanted from her was something more complex and terrifying than sexual conjugation.

He must have realized at some point that he had frightened her, because now he made soothing sounds. At least, sounds that were meant to reassure, though in fact they came out in staccato, as if he too was shaking inside. 'Okay. It's okay. Okay, Georgie.'

Georgie forgot her own alarm. She held him in her arms and stroked his silky black hair. And asked all the questions that shock had prevented her from thinking of before. She wasn't shaking now.

'Matty, how long have you been doing that, picking up men?'

'Let me see. Eight years.'

'You were *thirteen*?' She was trying to be broadminded, but she couldn't keep the scandalized note out of her voice completely. Never mind, knowing Matthew he would probably find it gratifying.

'Yeah, that's right. We used to live in Highgate and somebody picked me up on Hampstead Heath. I thought it was – well, all right. And dead easy.' He added drily, 'Boys peak early, it seems. If you're gay, it's downhill from fifteen onwards.'

'Are you really gay?'

'What do you think?'

'I don't think you'd have screwed me just now if you were.' That had been part of the purpose of doing it, she knew very well; but that didn't mean it wasn't true, what she had said. 'The men – the pick-ups, I mean – they're not really lovers, are they?'

'What would you call them?'

74

'Chocolate.'

That took him by surprise and made him laugh. 'What's that mean?'

'Well, you know sometimes you get a craving for chocolate, so you have a sort of chocolate orgy, and the craving goes away. But you're not, you know, developing a relationship with a Mars bar.'

'That sounds about right. I guess it is a craving. A kind of addiction.'

'What's the big attraction?'

'Well, the ones I pick up, they're all the same. Respectable-looking, stiff-upper-lip middle-aged types, the kind you wouldn't think even had a dick. Maybe they don't, I never see it. But they all remind me of my father.'

'So what?'

'So instead of freezing me out or talking to me as if I had no brain, they make up to me. And then they go down on their knees for me. I like that, I really do. And I particularly like thinking about how horrified my old man would be if he knew. Make what you like out of that, Dr Freud.'

It was as if he was daring her to reject him by throwing in her face all the dreadful disgusting secrets he had been keeping about himself. And she understood now that it was important, not irrelevant, that she should be not a stranger or acquaintance but his sister's child, a blood relation, a member of his family. She felt more like his mother than his lover. And she did understand how the son of her grandfather and Althea would have despised himself for such feelings and behaviour.

Matthew started to stroke her breast. An incontrovertibly hetero thing to do. 'Why am I telling you all this?'

She answered without hesitation, without thinking. 'Because you want to make sure I love you. And I do, I do. I don't care about all those men.'

'Don't you? Really?' His hand tightened on her breast for a moment, quite painfully. Then she felt him relax again. 'You're not afraid of my father, are you?'

'Afraid?' The idea astonished her. 'Of course not. He's a sweet old man. And sad because he's lost his daughter.'

And his son, she thought but did not say. His son who loved and was afraid of him.

8

I rose up to open to my beloved.

Luke phoned up while Georgie was at the Tower of London, admiring the crown jewels or replicas thereof. He left a message with Matthew to the effect that his father had proposed taking Georgie out to dinner that evening, if it was okay with her and if she had nothing better to do, and could she let him know what about it.

She phoned him back. 'You're coming too, aren't you?'

'Naturally. I wouldn't pass up a free meal at my old man's expense, especially not where he's booking us in.' He told her where they were going, a name which of course meant nothing to her. 'That's just over in the King's Road. If you come round here first we'll have a drink before we go.'

Matthew was impressed when she told him where she would be having dinner. 'Well, at least they're not taking you out for a pizza.'

'Is it classy? What should I wear? I didn't bring anything fancy with me. I wasn't expecting to be out on the town with a celebrity.'

'You can raid my mother's wardrobe. She keeps some clothes here in case of emergencies.'

'Would she mind?'

'She's in Tokyo, isn't she? And I won't tell.'

Georgie tried on some of the dresses in Althea's closet. The usual problem with Althea's clothes on Georgie's body presented itself: bottom okay, bust too tight. She had to settle for a sleeveless black silk jersey dress with a low-cut bodice which allowed her to overflow a bit at the top. She also 'borrowed' Althea's perfume and put on a pair of Althea's sandals. Althea's feet were a size smaller than hers, but since the shoes only consisted of a high-heeled platform with a network of fine straps, it didn't matter.

'How do I look?' she asked Matthew.

'Ravishing. You always look ravishing.'

'That wasn't what I meant. I want to know if I look right for where I'm going.'

'Well, they won't refuse to let you in.'

It was uphill work, getting the right answers out of Matthew. 'I mean, Luke and his dad won't want to disown me?'

'On the contrary, I should think.'

'I'm all nervous. Give me a hug to calm me down.'

'Hugging me is supposed to have quite the opposite effect,' Matthew protested, but he did as requested. It was the first time he had touched her since the night she had . . . consoled him. Neither of them had said a word about that, or about the contents of his confession. Maybe he regretted having told her. But he hadn't tried to take it back, by pretending he'd just been drunk or something like that.

By the time she mounted the steps of the house in SW3 the effects of Matthew's cuddle had worn off and Georgie was feeling almost as nervous as the first time she had gone there. Nervous about seeing Luke again, and also, of course, meeting his formidable father. She wondered if he would be anything like her grandfather, since they had been married to the same woman.

The sight of Luke's smile when he opened the door reassured her.

His outfit, studiedly informal, had clearly come off a designer peg and probably cost more than her father's entire expenditure on clothing for the past year. His shaggy blond hair was as neat as it was ever likely to be. And he must have shaved that evening, because she caught a whiff of expensive aftershave as she moved towards him.

She laid her fingertips lightly on either side of his shoulders, hardly touching him just because she wanted to touch him so much. She felt his hands hovering at her elbows. Didn't he want . . . or didn't he dare? She looked into his face.

His smile widened. 'You look fantastic,' he told her in an undertone.

She reached herself up to give him a formal double-barrelled greeting, a peck to the left and a peck to the right, standard salute in these parts. He must have aimed for her right cheek while she was headed for his left, because what actually happened was that their mouths met. More of a collision than a kiss.

Fortified by the sight and smell and tentative taste of Luke, Georgie went into the living-room – sorry, drawing-room – to meet her grandmother's husband, her mother's stepfather, the famous photographer Nick Winter.

He was standing with his back to her, his attention apparently attracted by something on the mantelpiece. That gave her a moment to study him.

Here was another member of her lost blond tribe: thick fair hair cut short, just beginning to turn ashen with age. Broad back and shoulders, like Luke expensively and fashionably clad. Shorter than Luke but still a tall man, six foot maybe. Not remotely fat, but not at all thin like her grandfather Beckett: strong, solid, muscular.

She was still sizing him up when he turned. His eyes widened in surprise or pleasure, then narrowed almost immediately to suggest the opposite. For a man who meant nothing to her, she had certainly evoked a strong reaction in him. But swiftly controlled: if she hadn't been so curious, staring at him, she might have missed it altogether. He was smiling now, welcoming her, with no sign of . . . what had it been?

Anger. Her body had recognized it instinctively, braced itself and pushed up her pulse rate, all in the demi-second that the look had lasted. She felt quite breathless. Why should a virtual stranger be roused to rage by the mere sight of her?

She had no time to consider the question. He was speaking, offering her a greeting. 'Georgie, hi.'

He was younger than she had expected. He didn't look any older than her own father, who would be forty-five come Christmas. She was disconcerted and unaccountably dismayed. She had expected to find an old man, her grandfather's contemporary rather than her father's.

But he was Luke's father, no question, the same light blue eyes and wide mouth. In Luke's face that mouth looked generous, if slightly petulant, but on his father the hint of generosity must have hardened long ago.

Georgie had been wondering on the way over whether it was her duty to kiss him as she had her grandfather, even though this man was no relation to her. But the question had resolved itself when he looked at her. She saw at once that he was not the sort of man to subject to social kisses, even from his dead wife's long-lost grand-daughter. Maybe especially from her, given that inexplicable flash of anger. And while she had been staring at his face he had been staring at her breasts, so generously revealed above the too-tight bodice of Althea's dress.

She needed a couple of seconds to take this on board. It was so far from anything she had expected, even given Luke's mutterings about models. Her grandmother's husband was sizing up her tits.

There was nothing coy about it either. In the few seconds it had taken him to greet her, he had assessed her physically and selected her bust as the most obviously interesting thing about her, just as if she were a hopeful model instead of his step-granddaughter.

She was used to men staring at her breasts, in fact she had come to expect and enjoy it. What else were well-developed mammary glands for, her father always said with a doctor's authority; babies certainly didn't care about the size. But this was on the one hand remarkably blatant, as if by being born female she had automatically entered herself for some competition in which all males were authorized judges, and on the other hand entirely dispassionate, as if she were someone in the street, nó relation whatever. Maybe it came of being a fashion photographer. Maybe he couldn't get out of the habit even with his stepdaughter's child. And after all her grandmother was dead, he was a single man now. Though she was pretty sure that he would have been looking at her just like that even if her grandmother had been alive and sitting in this room.

Anyway it was all over now, she had been looked over and given a rating, or whatever went on in his mind when he looked at women like that. He had already turned half away from her by the time Luke had followed her into the room. 'Champagne all right with you, Georgie? I thought the occasion called for it – family reunion and so forth.'

'Champagne is fine,' she said breezily, as if she drank it regularly.

He uncorked the bottle with practised confidence. Maybe he did drink it regularly. He filled three glasses, handed one to her and one to Luke, and raised his own. 'Cheers.'

She joined in the toast, then settled herself carefully on an elegant and delicate antique chair, reflecting that whatever had driven her mother to leave home so thoroughly, it couldn't have been an attempt to escape from the clutches of poverty.

Nick sat down with his champagne, on the sofa, not on one of the delicate chairs. Luke stayed on his feet, draping himself over the mantelpiece, which Georgie realized upon closer examination was probably a work of art in its own right. She sipped at the champagne and wondered what you said in the way of small talk to somebody you hadn't seen for eighteen years, and didn't remember at all. She couldn't compliment him on his kitchen, as she had done with Althea, and she was reluctant to express her admiration for this beautifully decorated room, because the decorator had almost certainly been his dead wife. It might be an unhappy reminder. So she sipped champagne and waited for him to speak.

Nick was in the process of lighting a cigarette. He inhaled, then exhaled through his nose, dragon-like. He said abruptly, 'How's Lia?'

Taken by surprise, Georgie could only answer inanely, 'She's fine.' After a moment she added, more in the spirit of the question, 'She's teaching at the University of Toronto.'

'Is she, by Christ.'

Unlike her grandfather, he seemed to find this information more amusing than amazing. Georgie was stung into elaborating. 'She's got her Ph.D. She's Dr Payne now.'

He was still smiling, but his eyes had narrowed in a way that made her feel definitely uncomfortable. She must have unwittingly trodden on a sore toe. There were minefields in this house too, it seemed, even with her grandmother dead and gone. Perhaps the death of Emma had left her husband with scores still to settle on her behalf.

Nick got up and took the champagne bottle to top up her glass, then Luke's and his own. After that he sat back on the sofa again. 'So Lia's a professor just like her old man. Must run in the blood. What about you?'

'What about me?'

'What are you doing? How come you're over here?'

'I've just finished university. I came over for the summer. Naturally I . . . I wanted to look up my mother's family.'

'Naturally.'

The cool irony of his tone was like a slap in her face. And an unjust reproach: she had been barely three when her mother took her away. Until a few days ago she had had no idea that this man even existed.

At least . . . Looking at him now, listening to his voice, she began to feel a very faint tug at her memory, as if buried away somewhere under eighteen years of debris, like the trapped survivor of an earthquake, there might still breathe some real recollection of him. She must have known him. There were pictures to prove it.

She decided to be blunt. 'I don't know why my mother left England, or why she never came home again. But it's nothing to do with me, I was only a baby. I just wanted to meet you all.'

He gave her an oddly speculative glance and then another broad smile. 'Sure you did, sugar. Why shouldn't you?'

Georgie had an idea that he might know of some reason why she shouldn't. But she couldn't ask, not yet at any rate. She drank champagne, shy of speaking for fear she might innocently trigger off another of his oddly vehement reactions. For a man who obviously kept a cool face to the world, he seemed extraordinarily touchy. Unless it was something to do with her . . .

He interrupted her thoughts. 'So Lia has no plans for coming back?'

Georgie shook her head. 'I've tried for years to get her to come over and she wouldn't. In fact she – she wasn't terribly pleased with me for coming over myself,' she added in a burst of frankness. 'I gather from my – from Ross and Althea, that she didn't leave on terribly good terms with everyone here.'

'You gather bloody right,' Nick said tersely. He glanced over at his son, who was scowling into mid-air. 'Well, I'd say it's about time to get going, I'm hungry. Wake up, Luke.'

Luke went out into the street first. Georgie followed him, with

Nick right behind, so close that the hand with the cigarette landed on her bare shoulder, to steer or usher or invite, at any rate to make clear his role as host. It was just a casual touch, a courtesy touch, but she wasn't sure she liked it. For one thing she didn't think she liked him. But to shrug it off would have been childishly churlish, so she ignored it.

As they stepped out the door she asked, without having intended to, 'Why did you call me sugar just now?'

'Don't you remember?'

Her blank look must have answered him, but she shook her head.

He smiled amiably enough. But his eyes were cool, his amusement a private joke. 'Never mind, sweetheart, you will.'

The restaurant was, as Matthew had warned her, very upmarket in a trendy rather than stuffy way. The *maître d'* knew Luke's father, just the way the man at the country hotel near Glynde had known her grandfather. Behind Nick's back as she followed him to the table, Georgie looked sideways at Luke. 'Come here often, do you?'

'Not me,' said Luke. 'Him.'

The menu was in French and the waiter had an absurdly overdone accent. The inevitable ethnicity of restaurants struck her as a suitable subject for conversation, and also a way of postponing possibly disastrous personal enquiries. 'Why are there no English restaurants?'

'There are,' Luke assured her. 'They're called caffs.'

'Greasy spoons, you mean? Those aren't English, they're just grotesque. I mean places that serve real English dishes like roast beef and Yorkshire pudding, or . . .' She hesitated, trying to think of some other typically English item.

Luke anticipated her. 'Fish and chips.'

'Bangers and mash,' said Nick. 'Faggots.'

'Toad in the hole.'

'Jellied ells.'

'Fried bread.'

'Chip butties.'

They were both laughing by now, whether at her foreigner's ignorance or their implausible menu she wasn't sure. 'That all sounds disgusting. What on earth is a chip butty?'

Nick explained. 'Two slices of bread with chips in between.'

'White bread,' added Luke. 'With margarine if you feel really decadent.'

'Chips? You mean French fries? Oh, yuk! Does anybody over the age of five really eat such a thing?'

81

'I grew up on them,' said Nick. 'My mother's speciality.'

'I think I prefer peanut butter,' Georgie said firmly. 'And the eels are right out, jellied or not.' She began to study the menu.

Luke was doing the same. 'This is more like it. The French really know how to eat. What about some snails, Georgie? Or maybe frogs' legs?'

'How about horsemeat?' Nick suggested more brutally.

Georgie looked from one to the other, half smiling. She didn't mind their teasing. In fact it made her feel more at ease, because it reminded her of her father and Alex, or even of sitting down to dinner in Sussex, between her grandfather and Matthew. There was, when she thought of it, something faintly disquieting about having a man on either side of her, even her blood relations. Men were inescapably alien. In a way they meant safety, in a way the opposite. It was like taking a walk with a pair of pet tigers. And in this case the tigers were strangers to her, whether blood-kin or not.

The younger tiger said to the older one, 'Your mother made chip butties? I didn't know you had a mother.'

'How d'you think I got here? Even Jesus Christ had a mother.'

'You know what I mean. I always thought you'd misspent your youth in foster homes.'

Georgie glanced from one to the other again, this time alert and unsmiling. Evidently her mother wasn't the only one with a mysterious past and lost relatives. Luke wasn't asking out of idle curiosity; there was a note of real resentment in his voice.

And of irritation in Nick's voice when he answered curtly, 'The fucking cuisine was the same everywhere.'

The waiter returned at that point with their meal. On a full stomach Georgie's tigers became much more amiable. They were almost mellow by the time coffee and cognac had arrived.

Nick offered Georgie a cigarette. She declined but Luke did not. As father and son lit up, she was reminded of a boyfriend she had had in high school. He used to smoke and her father had made him go outside to do it, even in midwinter. She never knew, when they broke up, if it was because he had preferred tobacco to her.

As if he had been reading her mind Nick said, 'What does your old man do for his living, Georgie?'

'He's a doctor. A paediatrician. And my grandfather was a cardiologist, but he's retired now.'

'A family of quacks, eh? Now there's a frightening thought.' He flicked the ash from the end of his cigarette with a practised and automatic gesture. 'And Lia's a doctor of a more harmless sort. What's her line?'

'She's a biologist. She studies wolves.'

82

'Wolves, Jesus.'

His open amusement annoyed her. 'What's so funny about that? It's a perfectly respectable field of scientific enquiry.'

'Sure it is, sugar,' he said in a way that made her feel about as old as she must have been when he last saw her, and also gave her a strong desire to kick him. 'It just struck me as kind of funny for a stunner like Lia.'

It shocked her that her grandmother's husband should refer to her mother in that way. Even though it was probably true. She remembered her father saying to her when she was all dressed up to go to her first school dance at the age of twelve, You're going to be a knock-out just like your mama. But it was one thing for her father to say that about his wife, and quite another for this man to talk like that about his stepdaughter. To remind him of his place in the order of things she said, 'Was my grandmother a stunner too?'

A low blow, with her grandmother only six months dead. As soon as it was out she regretted it. She had no right to suppose that just because he had stared at her breasts it meant he had no finer feelings at all.

If he did have any, he didn't parade them for her. He looked into the shallows of his cognac for a minute, then back at her with a faint, faintly mocking smile. 'Well, I married her, didn't I?'

'I hope she appreciated the honour,' Georgie replied sarcastically. But it was no use, he had already taken the sting from her response with his own irony. She drank the last of her coffee and set the cup down with meaningful resolution. 'I should be getting back.'

As they came out into evening on the King's Road, Georgie arranged Althea's soft lacy shawl around her shoulders and took the opportunity to do something she had been itching to do for the last half-hour. An unanticipated side-effect of wearing a dress too small across the bust had become apparent: her breasts had begun to go numb, a sensation milder than but not unlike having her foot go to sleep. As she adjusted the shawl she managed to slip her hand down inside the bodice of the dress – there was no room for a bra under that dress – and give her breasts a quick rub to restore their circulation. She did her best to be discreet; it was after all in the same category as scratching your crotch. It wasn't until she caught Nick eyeing her oddly, while Luke stood at the kerb attempting to hail a taxi, that she realized her attempt at discretion hadn't been entirely successful.

If he hadn't been who he was, she might have passed it off with a joke, or even – especially under the influence of the cognac – explained what the problem was. But she wasn't going to discuss her female anatomy with her grandmother's husband, not even if he was a famous photographer who had doubtless seen more tits than she had had hot dinners. And enjoyed the sight every time, she suspected.

When the taxi stopped in the street of Georgian houses, Nick opened the door and got out, but Luke only shifted himself from the folding seat to the space beside Georgie where his father had been sitting.

'Don't you live here?'

'I'm taking you home, like a gentleman should.'

'But then you'll have to come all the way back.'

'A daring feat of endurance.'

'Oh well, okay.' She made a show of being reluctant to inconvenience him, but in secret she was delighted at the chance to be alone with Luke again. She turned to Nick, who was standing by the open cab door. 'Luke's coming with me, he says. Good-night, Nick. Thanks for dinner.'

He ducked his head just enough to look at her face to face. 'My pleasure. See you again soon, all right, sugar?'

The meeting of hands that took place wasn't quite a handshake because it wasn't the proper hands, her right meeting his left instead of two rights encountering briefly. And if it was a handclasp it was a very odd one. He only held her hand for a few seconds but he ran the ball of his thumb across the palm of her hand, which gave her a strange shivery feeling, not at all unpleasant. Then he was gone and the cabby pulled away.

She stared at her open hand for a moment, trying to work out exactly what he had done to produce that surprisingly pleasurable sensation. Some kind of Masonic recognition signal, maybe? If it was, Masons had the means to make themselves very popular with the opposite sex.

She wished she could remember why he called her sugar.

She said to Luke, 'How old is your father?'

'Let me see, fifty-three, no, fifty-four. Old enough to know better.'

'Better than what?'

'Better than to drool over your cleavage, for one thing, the dirty old sod.'

Georgie didn't need Luke to defend her bust for her. 'But you're the one who's related to me. He's no real relation at all.'

'No relation at all,' Luke repeated with surprising vehemence. 'Would you believe that tonight was the first time I've ever heard him refer to his mother?'

'What in your whole life?' That really did astonish Georgie. 'Where did he grow up, Timbuktu?'

'Some hell hole in South London. Can't you tell he's a prole by the way he talks?'

'I haven't gotten on to English accents yet. Leave me out of your class struggles.'

That wasn't strictly true. She had noticed that her grandfather and Althea and Matthew and Luke sounded pretty much like her mother, with what she would therefore have regarded as a proper English accent, whereas the little man who sold the evening paper outside Moorgate station spoke some incomprehensible Cockney dialect. Nick didn't sound like the little man, but he didn't sound like her grandfather either, and it wasn't just because of his vocabulary. Though she did feel obliged to admire the unselfconscious eclecticism of a man who could casually juxtapose the words *f***ing* and *cuisine*.

From that thought she went on to wonder what sort of woman her grandmother could have been, to marry someone like Nick. She could imagine plenty of women who might want to be married to Nick, and plenty of women who might be happy to marry her grandfather, but there didn't seem to be any common ground. Unless, having enjoyed an unsatisfactory relationship with Georgie's grandfather, her grandmother had decided to try someone as unlike him as possible. If that had been her aim, she had certainly succeeded.

She said to Luke, 'What was your mother like?'

He shrugged. 'What's your mother like?'

'I asked you first.'

He had to think about that for a while. 'After meeting my father you probably won't believe this, but she was quite a buttoned-up sort of person, shy and reserved and rather prudish.'

Georgie thought about her own mother. 'Snap so far.'

'Well, what else can I say? She was always kind of out of it, worrying about the wrong things. She was good at worrying. She let my father front-end for her a lot of the time. I think she was afraid of him.'

'Why?'

'How do I know? She never pushed him, that's all. He always got what he wanted. Still does, come to think of it. I wish I had the knack.'

You wait, thought Georgie, you will. Men always did. She had seen that happen in her own parents' marriage, where her mother was the practical one who made the decisions – all the decisions that her father didn't want to make. Yet it was her father who got his way when push came to shove. Even with her boyfriends it had happened. There was a kind of ruthlessness at the heart of a man that made them ready to press their point beyond all reason. Ready to bring down civilization rather than give an inch.

She brought her mind back to the man under discussion. 'Did he screw around while your mother was alive?'

'Christ, how would I know? I wouldn't be surprised if he laid a few of those bimbos I used to bring home. It would've served them right. But I couldn't say for sure, because I dumped them as soon as they gave their game away.' He added, trying to be just, 'If he did sleep around, he was a hell of a lot more discreet about it then. But he would be, wouldn't he?'

He stared out of the window, stone-faced, while Georgie watched him, wanting to touch him, console him, heal whatever hurt him inside. She knew him in a strange psychic way, knew things about him that maybe he didn't know himself. All because of the colour of his hair.

She could see how he had loved and pitied his mother, admired and despised his father. She had never had to cope with such heavy domestic baggage. She loved and admired both her parents in different ways, while being well aware of their foibles and personal shortcomings.

But then she hadn't been landed with a father like Nick, who would have made heavy going for any child, son or daughter, though in different ways. A son, to such a man, was maybe inevitably a potential sexual rival. A daughter, if he'd had one, would have been . . . potentially a woman like any other, with all that implied. A living breathing example of the mythic Freudian Father.

Luke turned back to her. His face had come to life again. 'Why don't we go somewhere for a drink? You don't really have to get home, do you?'

'No, of course not. Matt won't be back till the small hours, and anyway he doesn't care.'

'Let's do that, then.' He tapped on the cabby's window to indicate the change of plan. 'There's a pub just down here by Covent Garden that's okay, music and clientèle not too gross. They won't throw us out for an hour or so.'

The pub was indeed okay. Georgie thought pubs were the jewels of Britain. The British took them for granted and even complained about them, presumably because they had never had to make do with a Canadian bar. Or Canadian beer, for that matter, of which the best that could be said was that it was not American beer.

She remarked on this to Luke when he ordered a pint of something that had to be drawn from a hand pump. He expressed surprise. 'You really like our beer? Shall I order the same for you, then?'

86

'Ah . . . can I just maybe share yours?'

He grinned. 'So you don't actually like it enough to drink it. What is it that appeals? The quaint names, the laborious process of pulling a pint?'

'No, no, I really do like it, but right now I only want a few sips. I'm full up from dinner. You don't mind, do you, if I have some of yours?'

'Mind? I'm honoured.'

They had no trouble finding a table, because most of the people who should have been in the pub were actually standing out on the sidewalk. Pavement, she corrected herself.

Luke had apparently decided to start the conversation all over again, as if the earlier part of the evening hadn't happened. He took a healthy swig of his beer and wiped the foam from his lips with the back of his hand and looked at Georgie expectantly. 'So what have you been up to since the last time I saw you, all of five days ago?'

Georgie tried to remember. The only thing that came to mind was what she had done on Saturday night. Saving Matthew. She wasn't sorry she'd done it, but she didn't think she wanted to tell Luke about it. He was very unlikely to understand.

In fact, now that she thought about it, she didn't think she wanted Luke to know about any of the men she had gone to bed with. But not because he was likely to be bothered by the knowledge, or because her virginity was of any interest or significance to anyone, or because she imagined that he was any less experienced than her. Maybe because he might think that he was of no more importance than the rest. She hadn't loved any of them, and she had known it at the time. She had done it . . . out of curiosity. For fun. Because it was done. To be nice to someone. She had fancied whoever it was. It gave her a sense of power, to please a man so easily. Why not? Sex was as natural as eating and sleeping, everyone said, and practice makes perfect, doesn't it?

Now all of a sudden she wished . . . she didn't know what she wished. Just that when you had gone all the way, as her grandmother termed it, for casual reasons, with people you didn't really love, when the real thing came along you had nothing left to express it with. Something to do with strawberries all year round, maybe. If you drank champagne every night, what would you do for a real celebration?

The real thing. She had never entertained such an absurdly romantic, old-fashioned idea before. She had learned about the marriage market in her anthropological studies: how people choose their partners, at least subconsciously, according to rules about class and culture and their own perceived value in the market – how rich or beautiful or powerful they happen to be. But now this mythical notion of true love had come into her head, just now when she looked at Luke and saw him smiling at her.

'Well, I was at the Tower of London today,' she recalled at last. 'And on Friday we went to the Tate.'

'What did you see there that you liked?'

'Oh, I like Turner. I've always liked Turner.'

'Everybody likes bloody Turner,' Luke said sharply, letting the vehemence of his opinions override his social obligation to be polite. 'He's so easy to like. Vague and woolly, pretty colours. Undemanding.'

'Not a classical taste, I'll admit.' Georgie chose her words carefully, on the one hand not wanting to get involved in an argument on a subject she knew nothing about, and on the other hand not wanting Luke to dismiss her as a complete philistine.

'And hardly modern art. He's rather less contemporary than Queen Victoria.'

'Oh. Ah. Modern art,' murmured Georgie, wishing he hadn't brought that up. 'I don't suppose the Impressionists count as modern either, do they?'

'Not even if you're Rip Van Winkle. You like them too, do you?'

'Yeah, why not? Vague and woolly, pretty colours. Except for the one – I forget his name – the one who couldn't draw. He painted all the apples.'

'Cézanne.' To her surprise she had made him laugh. 'That's right, the father of modern art. The first man to make his intellect and imagination triumph over a lack of ordinary artistic skills. He had ideas and meant to express them. He's where it all came from afterwards.'

'But I thought art was supposed to be, well, you know, art. Not mathematics or philosophy or politics, I mean. Appealing primarily to the senses. Possibly even moving.'

'You are a right little romantic, aren't you?'

He drank more beer and pushed the pint glass over to her. She took a sip and swallowed, and pushed it back.

'You've got a moustache.' Reaching across the table, he ran his fingertip across her upper lip to remove the foam, then licked the remains of the froth off his own finger. A kiss at third hand, maybe. His casual touch aroused her own desire to touch him, to know him physically. To know for real what she knew already in her head, that he was the other half of herself.

Georgie found herself staring at his mouth. Generous and petulant, she had termed it earlier. Now she thought it sensuous, half-hungry . . . inviting.

88

When she saw him looking back at her, she felt obliged to say something. Nothing about his mouth, preferably. 'It's disappointing, going to famous art galleries.'

'The art's disappointing, you mean, after all the reproductions?'

'Oh, no. But there's so much of it all at once, and so many people around, and the gallery's really there to say to everyone, Hey, pay attention, this is serious stuff and you're supposed to respond seriously to it. Almost like an exam in aesthetic sensitivity.'

'Well, you're right, of course. The whole concept of art galleries is élitist. The best one I've ever been to was a sculpture gallery in Holland. I went there years and years ago, when I was just a kid, with my parents. Imagine, my old man engaged in an overtly cultural activity.'

'Don't sneer like that. I'm pretty sure my father has never been inside an art gallery in his life. And you know perfectly well – even if photography isn't art,' she put in carefully, ' – your dad must have some real talent and aesthetic sense to do the work he does so successfully. Not to mention that complete philistines don't spend a fortune on original Mondrians and drawings by Picasso.'

'Maybe not,' Luke allowed grudgingly. 'Anyway, let me tell you about this place in Holland. There was a building with paintings inside it – lots of terrific Van Goghs, in fact – and outside there was a garden with lots of sculpture on display, and outside that there was a park, also with lots of sculpture sitting around in it, and outside *that* there was a whole forest dotted with sculpture. I'm calling it sculpture but I don't just mean statues, you know. A lot of it, especially in the woods, consisted of huge three-dimensional constructs.'

'That sounds amazing.'

'It was. You could spend all day there, it was like a treasure hunt. And the art was all meant to be touched and climbed on. Some of the pieces had moving parts you could fiddle with.'

'So you were moving the works of art, instead of them moving you.'

He laughed. 'I guess it worked both ways. Do you want to finish this off?'

He gave her the remains of his pint and watched her while she drank it down. She did it quickly because he made her nervous, watching her like that.

'You've got a moustache again,' he pointed out.

'Aren't you going to wipe it off for me?'

This time he leaned forward and took her jaw in his hand. He ran the broad ball of his thumb over her upper lip, then laid the thumb across her mouth, inviting her to lick the froth for herself. She slid her tongue along his thumb, tasting the bitter beer and the salt of his skin. Tasting Luke.

He put the tip of his thumb inside her mouth. She bit it, half joking and half experimental.

He took his hand away. 'They're about to call time. Let's go.'

He hardly spoke in the taxi on the way to the Barbican. She thought she must have put him off. Maybe she bit him too hard. Though he did insist on getting out with her, and going up the staircase to the highwalk to see her to the door at the foot of the block her grandfather's flat was in.

'Don't you want to come up for coffee?' It came out in a timid little voice because she was so nervous. She licked her lips and thought of his thumb. She looked at his hand on the door, holding it open for her. She had a sudden strong desire to grab his hand and kiss it.

That would really put him off. He would think she was crazy.

'Is what's his name, your uncle Matthew, up there now?'

'Him? Are you kidding? Life begins at midnight where he's concerned.'

'Well, then, I – ' He stopped and simply stood there, looking down at her. It was too dark to see the colour of his eyes. Blue, she knew from memory. 'Well, no, I won't. I'll see you again soon, okay?'

'Okay.' Georgie surreptitiously touched her front teeth to see if any of them had just been kicked in. 'Thank your dad again for me, will you?'

'Yeah, sure.'

She went upstairs with her stomach in a knot. What had she done wrong? Maybe biting somebody's thumb was the local way of inviting them to participate in some unspeakably vile perversion.

When she got into the flat the first thing she did was to take off Althea's dress. Another half-hour and her breasts might well have developed gangrene and fallen off, she thought, as she coaxed them back to life. Rubbing them made her miss Luke again. She wished it were his hands on her breasts instead of her own. The thought, along with the stimulation, made her feel as if she were melting somewhere down below. She hadn't felt like that the other night with Matthew. Nor had any of her boyfriends ever made her feel like that. Lovers, she supposed they should be called, though she hadn't loved any of them.

She had just got into bed when the phone rang.

'Georgie?'

'Luke! Where are you?'

'Downstairs. Around the corner, I mean.'

'What's wrong?'

'Nothing's wrong.'

'I mean, why are you still here?'

'I've just been . . . ah . . . wandering around.' At this point he actually stammered, and her pulse stuttered along with his tongue. 'C-c-can I come up?'

'Of course. Why didn't you just ring the buzzer?'

'I couldn't remember which flat was yours.'

'Idiot. Come up at once and I'll let you in.'

She spent the next few minutes rearranging the bed into a sofa and reinserting herself into Althea's dress. She didn't want him to know that she had already gone to bed, or to imagine that he might in any remote way be inconveniencing her. Because he wasn't, of course: just the opposite. By the time she opened the door for him she was all out of breath and flustered. Too flustered to do more than stare at him as he came in.

He was out of breath too. Maybe he had run up the stairs. He looked like a man coming down with the flu, his fair complexion flushed, a hectic heat in his eyes. Even with his mouth half open he looked incomprehensibly beautiful.

They stared at each other like two strangers colliding, coming around a corner and finding themselves accidentally, intimately, entangled.

Georgie found just enough air in her lungs to say 'Coffee?'

Luke said Yeah. Or maybe it was just his way of breathing.

She went into the kitchen to switch on the kettle. He came after, lounging against the counter while she loitered by the kettle, deliberately keeping their eyes from each other.

His hand rested on the counter top, half-way between them. Through the corners of her eyes she stared at the coarse hair, silver-blond. Sun-bleached hair and sun-browned skin. It struck some chord within her, as if she had dreamt of it long ago. She could not keep herself from reaching out to touch.

Her hand on his was much too small to cover it. She felt some fleeting surprise, as if the contrast should have been greater, the contrast of size and colour between their hands. Not that it mattered, because he felt just right.

She wanted to explain herself, to tell him how she had been longing to touch him from the moment she saw him, however crazy that might sound. But she didn't have to say a word. He came up behind her and put his arm around her, reaching right across her from shoulder to shoulder. She settled herself against him with a sigh that took all the breath from her body. She didn't have to say anything, because she knew now that he already knew it all.

She turned within his arm to face him, to take pleasure in the sight of him. She began to explore him, timidly at first, touching and stroking his clothes as if they were part of him, sliding her hands under his jacket to feel his shirt over his skin, wanting to know everything, to study him through the sensuous learning habits of a child or an animal. He was touching her too, in exactly the same way, not yet erotic, more primitive and powerful than that. Something to do with survival.

They took off each other's clothing, slowly and lovingly, trying the other's body as it was revealed, as if they had never seen such sights before. And from Georgie's point of view that was true. It was like undressing the obverse side of herself. Not that Luke was made in any way like her; he was a man, very much a man. It was just that everything surprised and delighted her with its rightness and perfection, as if she had already some hidden knowledge of him.

His body was every bit as divine as the head that topped it: beautifully proportioned, naturally athletic and well-muscled, no artificial top-heavy beefcake. Like Esau he was a hairy man, but the abundant curly hair on his chest and limbs was so fair that it only made him seem more god-like. And it went without saying that he turned out to be as well-built in the most important place as he was everywhere else.

By some means or other they transported themselves to the bedroom. As he stretched out beside her on the bed, Georgie made herself say it. Just for the record, not because it was true in any serious sense. 'Luke, you're my uncle.'

'Christ, I know it. That's why I went away. But I couldn't stay away. Does it bother you?'

'Mm-m,' was the best response she could manage, not for the sake of ambiguity but because he was kissing her and doing things to her with his hands. But she could tell by the heavy thickness of his voice that he wasn't going to stop now, any more than she wanted him to stop. And anyway she had allowed Matthew to do this, though for quite different reasons, and no thunderbolts had struck her down. Whereas she was doing this with Luke for the most natural reason in the world, the only real reason to do it, because she was besotted with him.

To his credit he did pause, just before entering her. 'Do we need anything? I haven't got anything with me.'

'I'm okay,' she whispered. 'It's all right. It's all right.'

More than all right. He came into her, the full glorious length of him, and it felt wonderful, like coming home. Intensely sexual, but also a way of knowledge. They were learning each other.

There was no room for the corner of detachment that she usually kept in her soul. She had never been so moved in her life. Among the inarticulate sighs and cries that his lovemaking wrenched out of her, she said things she hadn't meant to say. Oh Luke, I love you. Love me, Luke. And she heard him say it. I love you.

She didn't come. She had never had an orgasm in her life. But this time it seemed entirely irrelevant.

She was very glad he didn't ask about it afterwards. It would have been dreadful if he had, because she had made it a rule to drop any man who asked nosy questions that were none of his business. She had read in a survey somewhere that ten per cent of women occasionally faked an orgasm, twenty-five per cent of them often faked it, and sixty-five per cent of the female population pretended every time. Cheering and chilling statistics. Cheering because if they were faking it they weren't getting it, and so she wasn't such a frigid freak as she had hitherto been led to suppose. Chilling because all those women were sacrificing their natural enjoyment on the altar of the great male ego. As far as Georgie was concerned her sexual pleasure was her own affair. She wasn't some kind of performing seal. If she wanted anything in particular she would ask for it.

At the moment she had absolutely no complaints, about anything whatsoever in the world. They lay entwined, exchanging languorous nuzzles and caresses to reassure each other that what had just happened was making love rather than merely having sex. The first time, in a funny way, that she had ever made love.

At last she felt obliged to rouse herself to practicality. She repeated the offer she had made at the front door. 'Coffee?'

'That would be good.'

She slid out from under him and went into the living-room, living/dining/kitchen room to be precise. At the door she stopped dead and said Oh! very loudly. Because Matthew had come back.

He was sprawled in an armchair, looking across the room at her with a rather alarming smile on his face. 'Evening, Georgie. Am I interrupting something?'

Her exclamation had brought Luke out of the bedroom. He was standing right behind her, six foot three and stark naked, like a visitation from the locker room after a football game, and scarcely more self-conscious about his nudity.

Matthew moved his attention from Georgie to Luke. Georgie turned to Luke and he put his arm around her, so that her back was to Matthew and her body came between Luke's body and Matthew's eyes. That was for Luke's benefit, not her own or Matthew's.

'I thought you were out for the night,' she muttered into Luke's chest-hair, addressing Matthew.

'I got bored and decided to come home. No problems with boredom around here, I see. Shall I go away again for a while?'

'Just sit tight for a minute.' Luke's voice came out as a growl. He wasn't pleased but it was all his own fault. He pushed Georgie back towards the bedroom and followed her, collecting his clothing on the way and slamming the door behind him. He was swearing under his breath.

Georgie went up to him and put her arms around him. 'Don't be mad. He had every right to come home.'

He consented to hug her in return. After a moment the temptation of her bare breasts pressed against his chest got to be too much and he started to stroke her. 'I'm just pissed off because I wanted another go.'

She giggled and lifted her face to kiss his mouth. 'We can do it again.'

'When?'

'Tomorrow, if you're free. But we'd better get dressed right now.'

She pulled on her jeans and a T-shirt and went back out to the living-room. She had decided to be totally cool with Matthew. 'We were just about to have coffee,' she told him. 'Do you want some?'

'Why not?'

He stood up when Luke came into the room after her, barefoot and buttoning up his shirt. 'This is Luke, this is Matt,' Georgie explained unnecessarily, playing no favourites.

They shook hands quite solemnly like proper Englishmen, just as if Luke hadn't been standing stark naked in front of Matthew five minutes earlier. Georgie watched them do it. Luke was shaggy and fair, Matthew smooth and dark. Luke was big and broad-shouldered, Matthew much shorter and slighter. Her two gorgeous uncles. It was all her mother's fault: if she had grown up with them as by rights she should have done, they would be like cousins or brothers, no more and no less. As it was . . .

As it was, they had come into her life as strangers, adult males, potential lovers like any other unknown man walking the earth. She was amazed to find herself speculating about what would happen if she proposed that they should all remove their clothes and go to bed together. She could easily imagine Matthew agreeing to it. But Luke – no, Luke was straight and square. He would go away in a rage, and she would have lost him.

He did go away eventually, but in a relatively good temper and without the offer of an orgy. She stepped outside the flat into the corridor to say good-night to him. It was quite a passionate, extended sort of good-night and he promised to phone her in the morning. Unlike all the other men she had had this conversation with, she didn't for a moment doubt what he said.

'Sorry about that,' she said straight off, as soon as she was back inside the flat. She thought she ought to apologize to Matthew. It was her grandfather's flat, after all; she had no automatic right to be bringing strangers home, especially for immoral purposes. And besides, Matthew might feel . . . well, he might be jealous.

'So you should be.' Matthew looked at her with a sly, sidelong, faintly flirtatious sweep of his lashes. They were long and dark, the kind a girl would kill for. 'Do I get mine now?'

'You sure do not. What do you think I am?'

'As a gentleman, I wouldn't want to answer that.'

'Don't be rude. And sexist. Why shouldn't I go to bed with someone I fancy?' She put it like that because she felt sensitive and faintly ridiculous about the feelings that Luke aroused in her. Crazy romantic notions about true love.

'The very question I put to you just now. I particularly fancy the idea of going down on you right now.'

She didn't know if he was serious or not. With Matthew it was hard to tell. Since he knew she had just been making love with Luke, it was a very . . . um . . . odd thing to say. Maybe he was only trying to shock her. In which case he had certainly succeeded. 'Cut that out, Matt, or I'll tell Luke on you. He's a lot bigger than you are.'

'I noticed that,' said Matthew.

9

Thou hast ravished my heart, my sister, my spouse.

She woke up the next morning and checked herself for emotional breakage.

Georgie was in love with Luke. She had never been in love before, but she knew it when she felt it. A new sun had been installed in heaven, shining in a wonderful new way. Black-and-white vision had yielded to the rainbow.

She got out of bed, full of impatience to see him again. Only she knew it wasn't going to be as simple as that.

She couldn't just go out with him. He was her mother's brother. Half-brother, hardly brother, more like a second cousin, that was all true, but it was the *brother* bit that counted. Screwing him wasn't legally incest, but a lot of people might still see it that way.

Her mother, for instance. Or her grandfather.

So she couldn't, say, go and sleep at Luke's house. It wasn't his house anyway, it was his father's. And that was another problem. The thought of Nick knowing that Luke was screwing her, maybe even being in the same house while they did it, made her feel quite as uncomfortable, though in a very different way, as the idea of her grandfather knowing about it.

She was brooding over this while she waited for Luke to ring. Matthew had risen remarkably early for him and was rummaging around in the kitchen. 'Do you fancy bacon and eggs for breakfast?'

'Sure, if you're going to be the cook.'

'That was the idea. How did it go last night?'

'You know how it went. You had a ringside seat.'

'Aside from that, I mean. I thought the point of the evening was to meet your grandmother's husband. Shagging your grandmother's son was just an optional extra.'

'Don't be crude.' What with the kettle humming and the bacon starting to sizzle, it was difficult to hear him, and with the balcony doors open she didn't want to shout in case the neighbours over-heard, so she wandered into the kitchen corner of the room and poured herself more coffee.

'So what about the old man?' Matthew persisted. 'Did he bring along one of his models?'

'No, I had the benefit of his undivided attention. I should say, my tits had the benefit.'

That made Matthew laugh. 'His wife's granddaughter! Is nothing sacred these days? So he really is a dirty old man, just like your Uncle Luke claimed.'

Uncle Luke was a dirty dig, but she let it pass. 'To be fair, I think he was just checking me out as a matter of habit because I'm female. But anyway he's not really old. Well, let's see, Luke said he was fifty-four, so strictly speaking I guess he's old enough to be my grandfather, but he seemed more like my father's age than my grandfather's. I mean, he's thirty years younger than my Grandpa Payne. And your father really is an old man, he's got grey hair and all.'

'A sure indication of one foot in the grave,' Matthew agreed drily. He pushed the bacon aside, cracked eggs into the frying pan, and removed the toast from the toaster.

'Here, let me have that.' Georgie snatched the hot toast away from him. 'I want to butter mine while it's hot. You'll stick it in the toast rack and let it get cold.'

'Let it stay crisp,' Matthew corrected. 'If you butter it too soon it goes soggy.'

'You guys have never gotten the hang of toast, it seems to me.' Georgie, having won possession of the toast, was having her way with it, buttering briskly. 'A toast rack is a really perverse device. Hot buttered toast is what it's all about. A toast rack is designed to cool it off, and then the butter won't melt either. Cold toast is disgusting.'

There wasn't much that Matthew could answer to that. He was just serving out the eggs and bacon when the phone rang.

'Hi,' said Luke's voice, sort of growling and shaggy like Luke himself. 'How are you, Georgie?'

'I'm okay.' But she felt quite faint. She really truly was in love. With her mother's little brother. Or rather, her mother's big beautiful blond brother. 'How about you? Did you get home okay?'

They carried on in this unproductive but peculiarly satisfying vein for some time, till they finally got around to arranging to meet at the pub in Covent Garden that evening, with a view to going on to entertainment elsewhere.

When she came back to the table her toast was cold. And soggy.

For some reason she felt obliged to tell Matthew her plans for the evening. She didn't know why, because he was always disappearing without a word of warning or explanation. And why shouldn't he? She wasn't his girl. 'I'm going to a movie with Luke tonight.'

'A film,' he amended firmly. 'You're in Rome now, not Hollywood. And will you be wanting the use of the bedroom afterwards?'

She glanced at him, hoping it didn't show how much she would be wanting it. 'Would you really not mind?'

'Only if I can watch.'

She recognized the joke punch-line but it didn't mean he wasn't serious. 'You're a prevert, Matt Beckett.'

'I am not. Rapists and child molesters are perverts. Anything that goes on between consenting parties is merely exploring alternative expressions of human sexuality.'

'Oh, I like that,' Georgie said admiringly. 'You do talk fancy, mister. But did you mean it about tonight?'

'Sure, why not?' After a moment he added, 'I'll be wanting a favour in return, of course.'

She looked at him consideringly over the top of her coffee mug. 'No raincoats.'

'Of course not. Nothing vulgar or juvenile.'

She had to leave it at that. She wanted the bed too much to try to drive a firmer bargain. She understood that there were households in which Matthew might sit yawning at the television while Luke and Georgie in the bedroom ran through the Kama Sutra, but in practice she knew that Luke would never have stood for it.

Georgie waited till half-way through the movie before whispering to Luke that Matthew had promised to be out of the flat from ten till midnight. If the film had been more enthralling that would have been a mistake, because Luke insisted on leaving immediately so as not to waste anything of the two magic hours.

· Once inside the flat he put the deadbolt on the front door, so there would be no chance of being interrupted again. They made love for two hours straight, until they were both so sore they hardly dared to move, and only just restored themselves to respectability on the very stroke of midnight from the church across the lake.

Luke unlocked the deadbolt while Georgie put the kettle on for tea. Then he came back into the kitchen and explored the fridge for something to eat. 'Christ, that doesn't half work up an appetite. Doesn't your Uncle Matt think this is a bit, you know, off? Mating with your mother's brother, I mean?'

She liked the way he said that, *mating*. It sounded profound and biological, like grand cosmic forces beyond human control, rather than something casually recreational or socially obligatory, which was what sexual relations had so often seemed to her to be. The fact that she was his sister's daughter scarcely counted in such a context. She was his mate.

'Why should he care? He knows how much this uncle bit really means. I told you, it's more like cousins. Less than cousins, even. I worked it out. First cousins on average have twenty-five per cent of their genes in common, but you and I only have twelve and a half per cent of them the same, like second cousins. And even first cousins are allowed to get married.'

Luke's reply was muffled on account of his head being inside the fridge. 'I'll have to take your word on all that. I managed to avoid all biology lessons in school.' Emerging triumphant with a wedge of cold pepperoni pizza, he added, 'If it's no big deal genetically, why do they have laws against it?'

Georgie hadn't spent three years studying anthropology without learning a thing or two on this subject. 'There are always laws against incest, however it's defined in different societies, and they're nothing to do with genetics. In some places you're forbidden to marry your cousins, and in other places your cousins are the only people you're allowed to marry. In the Old Testament, for instance, all the patriarchs married their cousins. Abraham even married his half-sister and everyone seemed to approve, including God. In fact that would have been genetically the same thing as marrying his cousin. Only nobody knew there were such things as genes, until about a hundred years ago.'

'So what are all the laws for?'

'Who knows? Some people say it's a social thing, because marrying a non-relative doubles the size of your kinship group. Or else

98

economic, from the days when a family was a production unit as well as a consumer unit.'

Luke gave her a look that reminded her of his father. 'These are human beings we're talking about, are they?'

'That's just jargon,' Georgie said breezily. 'It means that every business used to be a family business, and every family was a sort of business on its own, so the more the merrier.'

'What's that got to do with incest?'

'Well, if you were my brother and I married you, our parents would only have the two of us to support them in their old age, whereas if we each married somebody else, they'd have the benefit of our spouses as well, and two lots of children instead of one.'

Luke was chewing thoughtfully on a mouthful of pizza. After swallowing it he said, 'I'm not sure about the mathematics of that proposition, but never mind. If it's to your advantage not to marry your sister, why would they have to pass laws against it?'

'Well, exactly. It's just a theory, and not terribly convincing, I don't think. The fact about incest is that it's basically just a taboo and nobody knows why.'

'But there must be some reason.'

'My mother says it's to do with evolution. What kind of tea do you want, Earl Grey or Lapsang Souchong?'

'I don't know. Isn't Lapsang Souchong the kind that tastes like mud?'

'I guess that answers my question.' Georgie deposited four spoonfuls of Earl Grey into the teapot and splashed boiling water over it. 'The thing is, my mother says, the whole concept of incest is all to do with gene pools and breeding populations, but also with tribal social structures. All animals have tribes, she says. It's the tribal thing that makes us programmed to be attracted to people who look like us. And who looks more like you than your immediate family? But that would lead to intensive inbreeding, which is bad for the gene pool. So she says the incest taboo is a way of keeping it in the tribe without making the tribe too small for maximum evolutionary potential.'

'I thought the saying went that opposites attract.'

'Well, the saying is wrong. In fact, it's a well-known phenomenon that when people who've been adopted go back to find their biological families, they're very likely to be sexually attracted to relatives of the opposite sex. They actually warn people about it as one of the hazards to watch out for. Apparently it's a particular problem for women meeting their long-lost sons, because if the son looks like his father, it's like she's found her old lover again, only instead of being fat and bald after all those years, he's still young and beautiful.'

99

'That's kind of touching,' Luke allowed. 'I could sympathize with that situation.'

'I thought it sounded really sad and romantic,' Georgie agreed. 'I mean, it must be really weird for people like that, because in spite of being parent and child, they're actually complete strangers. Only nowadays I suppose it's much more likely to be fathers and daughters meeting up, because hardly any women give up babies for adoption any more, but fathers are always disappearing. Half of them lose track of their kids within two years of divorce, did you know? And of course a huge number of people don't bother to get married in the first place.'

She reflected on the underlying paradox, while lining up mugs and spoons and milk for tea, and finally answered her own unspoken question aloud. 'I think the real reason why most people haven't the remotest interest in screwing their parents or siblings is because they've grown up with them and that seems to pretty well kill any attraction. It's as if only strangers are sexy. My mother says that even wolves don't make it with their litter-mates, though they don't mind doing it with siblings from other litters, older or younger ones.'

Luke finished off the last crumb of pizza crust. He licked his thumb to remove a smear of tomato sauce. Georgie remembered that thumb caressing her mouth. Luke too was considering the thumb, frowning at it, when he asked, 'So what would your mother think about us? Would she be logical and scientific and count our common chromosomes, or would she be just like everybody else and cry taboo?'

Georgie didn't need to speculate on how her mother's scientific detachment would fly out the window at the first sign of personal involvement. She said defiantly, 'Who cares what she thinks? She didn't even tell me you existed. We could have met by accident and never even known we were related. Besides,' she added with brutal practicality, 'she's on the other side of the world.'

Georgie was less concerned right now with her mother's hypothetical horror than with the payment that Matthew was going to demand for his co-operation tonight. She felt like the hapless heroine of some fairy tale, rescued from her predicament by a sinister stranger, in return for a promise of unspecified reward at some unspecified future time. But like the girl in the fairy tale she couldn't tell her prince what the problem was. Well, whatever Matthew wanted, it wasn't going to kill her to go along with it.

Matthew came in soon after that. He greeted them quite affably, just as if he didn't know perfectly well what Luke had been doing with Georgie half an hour before. Or if he did, he didn't care.

100

He offered Luke a glass of Scotch. Like his father – her grandfather, that was – he didn't call it Scotch, just whisky, as if bourbon and rye had never been invented.

Luke accepted the invitation. Despite the conversation earlier, he didn't seem at all self-conscious now about Matthew knowing what was going on. Nor was he in any hurry to leave.

Maybe they were curious about each other. And it was a curious situation: each of them the brother of her mother, but never having met till now; having only the link of a broken marriage, with not one drop of common blood between them. Now they had her in common.

Nick had asked her last night what her father did for his living, but that form of the question was old-fashioned, Georgie discovered. Matthew asked Luke what he did with his time. Luke said he had just finished his stint at art college and was trying to decide what his next move should be. Matthew poked Georgie in the ribs with his elbow, as she happened to be sitting next to him, and said *Pho-to-graphy* in a Monty Python voice.

'Bugger that,' Luke said bluntly. 'I'm not following in anyone's footsteps. What about you?'

'Christ knows. I'm still regrouping after being chucked out of Oxford a month before finals. Well, I was only going to get a third anyway. Maybe I'll take up photography.'

Luke took it as a joke and laughed. But Georgie had a sudden dreadful premonition of what Matt's favour was going to be.

As soon as Luke had gone she locked the door for the night and turned to Matthew. 'No photography.'

He laughed. 'Oh, I see, the lady's looking for respectability. No evidence, no blackmail. You have an evil mind, Georgie. Let's leave the dirty pictures to your grandmother's husband.'

She looked bewildered in her turn. 'What do you mean?'

'I was taking the high-minded view of my father that the whole fashion business is an obscenity. It's remarkably easy to hold firm views on a subject one knows bugger-all about.'

She couldn't tell if he really hadn't meant anything by his remarks when Luke was here, or whether he had been deliberately torment-ing her. He was smiling that slight sardonic smile so familiar to her now. She had thought she knew what lay behind that smile, and now she found that he was a stranger after all. Maybe a dangerous stranger.

She turned away, moved away. 'What do you want, then? for your quid pro quo?'

He followed her and caught her arm. 'Georgie, that was only a joke. You don't have to do anything you don't want to do.'

101

She looked at him and licked her dry lips. 'Can Luke come back tomorrow night?'

'Sure, why not?'

'No favours required in return?'

He smiled again, broadly this time. 'Well, you could always tell me about it afterwards.'

10

Where is the place of understanding?
Man knows not the price thereof.

The weekend went by like that. Matthew absented himself for several hours each night so that Georgie and Luke could have the flat to themselves. On subsequent nights they were not so physically desperate; they spent time talking, unbaring their souls, callow and quivering, to assured acceptance and approval. Of course they could have done as much downstairs on a bench by the lake, but it was easier somehow when they were naked and touchable.

Then Matthew came home, and he and Luke talked more and more like old friends. Maybe they were old friends, in a way: brothers who were not brothers, who had no other brothers. Who had maybe been waiting all their lives to meet each other. Just as she and Luke were lovers who had unbeknownst been living for the day of their first encounter.

Only she knew very well the oddest thing of all, that if they had known each other all along, none of this would have happened. In that sense, her mother would have only herself to blame. But it had happened now, and nothing could retrieve it. She couldn't take back the way she felt about Luke.

On Monday Matthew announced that he was going to want the flat that night and she would have to take her paramour elsewhere.

Georgie was curious. 'Are you entertaining Sophie?'

He gave her a mysterious little smile. 'She's not the only girl I know.'

'Just so long as it is a girl,' she said sternly.

She phoned Luke to tell him what was happening, or rather not happening. 'Maybe I could come over there and cook dinner for you tonight. How about that? And your dad, if he doesn't mind chancing my cooking.'

'I don't think he's going to be home.'

'All the more for the rest of us, in that case.'

She went shopping at the supermarket behind the Barbican and turned up on Luke's doorstep with her purchases about six o'clock. It gave her an absurd sense of anticipation and satisfaction, the idea of cooking dinner for herself and Luke. Her pleasure was only slightly diminished when he opened the door for her with the announcement, 'I rang to warn you but you'd already gone out. My father is going to honour us with his presence after all.'

'Doesn't matter, it's only moussaka, with feta salad. Infinitely expandable.'

'Greek food? I thought you might be intending to produce a proper English meal.'

'I wouldn't presume. Where do you keep your kitchen?'

The kitchen was small and efficient, but clearly sadly neglected since her grandmother's death. It was probable, she reflected, that no one had made a proper meal here, English or otherwise, in the last six months. All the usual herbs and spices, plus some unusual ones, were sitting neatly in a wooden rack, gathering dust. Which made her wonder how the rest of the house avoided gathering dust. She couldn't imagine either Nick or Luke wielding a vacuum cleaner.

'Who keeps house for you?'

'We used to have a woman who did things in the kitchen – I wouldn't go so far as to call her a cook – but she disappeared when my mother died. Now we just have a sort of daily who comes in and supposedly tidies up and hoovers. I think my father had to pay her extra to get her to stay on, because we're both such hopeless slobs.'

Georgie received this dismaying admission from her beloved in diplomatic silence. She unpacked her groceries and set them out on the countertop. 'Where's Nick?'

'He said he'd be home about seven thirty. I shouldn't have told him you were coming. I think he wasn't planning on coming home at all tonight, but he changed his mind when he heard about you.'

'The man's a masochist,' said Georgie, but she felt obscurely pleased. She enjoyed cooking. She did it at home for her father and Alex, when her mother was away with the wolves. And she had made dinner for her grandfather and Althea while she was staying down in Sussex, to save Althea having to do it when she got home after a long day in the capital markets, doing whatever it was her employers paid her to do. But this would be even more satisfactory, with only two non-cooking men and no Althea to make silent culinary comparisons.

Luke came up behind her and put his arms around her, taking her breasts into his broad hands. 'Do you want to come upstairs?'

'Of course I do but I don't think we should. It would be disastrous

103

if your dad came home early.' She turned around within his arms to face him. 'And I mean really disastrous. Calamitous.'

He knew very well what she meant, so he didn't argue, except to mutter, 'I don't suppose he'd bloody well care.'

'But he might tell my mother.' She didn't want to think about that, or about the future at all. She buried her face against his chest and let him hold her.

'He's going to be away for the rest of the week. From tomorrow we can have the house to ourselves.'

'That would be blissful.' She hoped Matthew wouldn't mind. Well, why should he? He wasn't her lover. But she had an idea that he was jealous of Luke, all the same. Maybe his getting chummy with Luke was a way of coping with that.

Luke's father arrived home more or less as advertised. To her surprise he was dressed very casually, in a worn denim shirt and faded jeans which made him look even less like fifty-four. She had gotten used to the sight of Englishmen, even very young ones, going to and from their workplaces in what at home would have been regarded as absurdly formal clothes, so she had expected him to be wearing a suit and tie. But of course he didn't work in an office, he worked for himself. He could do what he liked.

This time he really did seem pleased to see Georgie, without any sign of the ambivalent undercurrents she had caught at their first meeting. He greeted her casually – again no social kisses, or any other kind, for that matter – and offered to fix her a drink.

'Luke's already poured me a glass of wine, but it could do with topping up.'

Nick found the wine bottle, refilled the glass and handed it back to her. 'It's very sporting of you to come and cook for us.'

'No trouble. We're having your old favourite, chip butties, but I've put ketchup in them, Canadian style.'

He laughed. 'Well, if you want a job, I need a cook. Are you planning to stay over here for a while?'

'I'd love to, but they won't let me stay for more than three months. I'm an alien.'

'No you're not, you're British,' Luke said suddenly. 'You were born here. You can stay as long as you like. For ever.'

Her heart lifted. Not so much at his words, welcome as they were, but at the knowledge that he was thinking the same thing as her. 'I never thought of that. What do I have to do to make it official?'

'Just get a copy of your birth certificate.'

'Oh, I've got that with me. I always carry it around for ID.' She rummaged around in her purse and produced the plastic card that officially stated her name and the date and place of her birth.

Luke looked down his nose at it. 'You call that a birth certificate?'

'I guess it isn't exactly,' Georgie allowed. 'It's what the Canadian government gives you if you weren't born in Canada. But it's all I needed for my Canadian passport.'

'Well, they won't accept any of that plastic rubbish here. You'll have to go down to St Catherine's House and get a real one. Then you can get yourself a British passport, and *voilà*, you're one of us. You can do it tomorrow if you like. And with a British passport you can live anywhere in Europe.'

She put up her hand to cover her mouth, to hide her sudden excitement. She had been having idiotic thoughts all weekend, not daring to mention them to Luke in case it wasn't what he had in mind. She couldn't stay here for more than three months, and he couldn't stay in Canada for more than three months, unless they were legally married. And they couldn't get married because he was her mother's brother. She had looked it up in the reference library at the Barbican that morning. In the Marriages (Prohibited Degrees of Relationship) Act it stated clearly and sternly that a man may not marry his sister's daughter, and in a footnote it added for good measure that half-blood counted for as much as whole. Luke was officially taboo.

But now that didn't matter. She was British.

The dinner went swimmingly. Afterwards they carried their coffee through the french doors. French windows, Althea had called them, and when Nick invited Georgie to go out through the window, a number of hitherto preposterous events in English novels suddenly became clear to her. At any rate, whatever the architectural terminology, the dining-room opened on to the garden and they went out there to enjoy the evening.

The garden was postage-stamp size but it had high walls covered with climbing and blooming things to make it beautifully private and green. Georgie guessed that the green fingers were hired ones.

It was odd, the idea of living in an expensive house in an upmarket part of town, but having no garage or swimming pool. The English had different priorities, she supposed. 'If this was at home, we'd be having a barbecue. It keeps the mosquitoes away.'

'That solves a mystery,' Nick commented. 'I've always wondered why anyone would want to stand around choking on smoke and chewing a slab of half-burnt half-raw meat.'

'Oh, well, they're really just an excuse to eat out in the yard. It's nice to be outdoors in the summer, isn't it?'

'That's right, make a virtue of necessity. What else have Canadians got going for them except their Great Outdoors?'

'Well, at least we have an outdoors. And a summer.'

'And a winter too, so I hear.' Nick lit himself a cigarette and tossed the packet over to Luke, along with the lighter. 'Is your old man the outdoor type, Georgie?'

Georgie had to think about that. Think about her father. She wasn't sure what an Englishman's idea of the outdoor type might be, especially in a Canadian context. Her father liked swimming and sailing, hiking and canoeing. He loved fishing. He even seemed to enjoy cleaning and cooking the fish that he caught. She remembered watching him do it, remembered him pointing out to her how the fish was put together, and in what ways it was like and unlike people or dogs, for example. She remembered thinking that for him as a doctor it must work the other way around as well: he could look at a human body and anatomize it as dispassionately as the fish.

Her mother, eccentrically for a biologist, always refused to clean her father's fish. She said she preferred her animals alive.

Georgie returned her mind to Nick's question. 'Well, he likes that sort of thing, I guess, but he's not a fanatic about it. Only about fishing, but I think that's partly an excuse for being out and about at sunrise. I used to go with him sometimes, when I could make myself get out of bed. There'd be mist rising off the water, turning gold as the sun came up, and the whole world so still you could hear a heron fishing a mile away. It was magical.' She looked at Nick, half smiling, moved by her own memory. 'You should try it some time.'

'Maybe I will.'

He was looking at her in an odd way, as if she had been describing something sad rather than magical. Sad for him, or for her? The thought and the look make a pain inside her: a fleeting physical awareness of the soul's inescapable isolation. Surreptitiously she touched Luke's arm, as if he were a talisman to take away the ache.

To distract herself she said, 'I like your garden.'

The look, whatever it was, had passed from Nick's face; the shutters had come down. 'I like it too. I'm going to miss the garden, this time of year.'

'Miss it?'

'Yeah. Didn't Luke tell you? I'm selling the house. It's too much trouble without Em to look after it. And it was her idea in the first place. She wanted it, she did it up. I wouldn't have chosen any of this.' He waved his hand, taking in the house and its contents, the neighbourhood, maybe the implied conventions of their married life together.

Georgie was shocked, for no reason that she knew of. Maybe it was the thought that if she had come a year later she might never have found them. There would have been no Hardy in the telephone book. 'Where will you move to?'

106

'My accountant has a list of suitable countries.'

'Suitable for what?'

'Taxes, what else? Luckily they're mostly in warmish parts of the world.'

She glanced at Luke. 'What's Luke going to do?'

'I'm buggered if I know.' Nick also glanced at his son and repeated the question with that hint of irony that Georgie was already coming to count as characteristic of him. 'What's Luke going to do?'

Luke shrugged. 'Find my own place, I guess.' He swept his hair out of his eyes and looked at his father defiantly, contemptuously. 'I wouldn't want to cramp the old man's style.'

'No fucking fear, mate. But what do you reckon to use for money?'

'She left me some, you know that.'

'That won't go far.'

'Far enough to get me out of here.'

'You don't need money to leave home,' Nick observed drily. 'A sleeping bag and a cardboard box do nicely for some. Or maybe a good line with the ladies.'

'Ladies,' said Luke with a sneer. 'Is that what you call them?'

'You've just learned a new word and you're itching to try it out, I suppose. Be careful you don't shock Georgie. She's a well-brought-up young gel.'

As Nick said Georgie's name he turned his head to smile at her. There was something so cool and knowing in his blue eyes, something so hard-edged about the seemingly genial smile, that her heart stopped for a second.

He knows, she thought.

How could he possibly know?

It was time to break up the conversation anyway. The tigers were taking dangerous swipes at each other. She stood up. 'I think I'd better go in and clear the table while I can still move.'

'I'll help you,' Luke said gallantly.

She carried the plates into the kitchen and clued Luke in on how to load up and start up the dishwasher. Obviously her grandmother had totally neglected her obligations to any future daughter-in-law. Then she went back out into the garden to collect the coffee cups. Nick was still sitting there in the semi-darkness, city darkness, nursing a shot of whisky and smoking a cigarette. She could see the smouldering tip, and his face reflected in the glow when he took a drag. The shadows made him look . . . not old, but older – older and wiser, older and sadder, eroded by life. Like the trees around her grandfather's house, that grew askew because the unrelenting sea-wind bent and sheared them from their earliest days.

Without any idea of what she was going to do before she did it, she perched herself on the arm of his chair, stretched her arm across the back of it behind his broad shoulders, and leaned down to say what she was going to say into his ear. If he could divine secrets, pluck them out of people's heads, then maybe he knew the answer to her mystery. 'Do you know why my mother went away?'

He leaned back to look up at her, so that the back of his head rested on her arm. She liked that. It felt pleasantly but not threateningly intimate, and made it easier for her to have said what she had said. Made it okay.

He didn't answer right away. After a moment she lowered her gaze and found herself staring at his mouth. Luke's mouth. If she were to kiss it he would taste of whisky and tobacco.

He spoke quietly, like her. 'Why don't you ask Lia?'

'I have. She evades.'

'Well, I guess it's her secret, sugar.'

He said *sugar* with some acerbity, as if she had said something stupid or improper. Or maybe just to warn her off. Well, she had a warning of her own for him. 'You mean you don't give away other people's secrets?'

'Not even if I know them.'

'Georgie,' said Luke from the french window, 'what the hell are you doing out there?'

She leaped to her feet. 'I'm just collecting the coffee cups.' She did that hastily and ducked inside.

Luke followed her into the kitchen, fuming. 'What was that all about?'

She stuffed the cups and saucers into the corners of the dishwasher rack and straightened to look at him. She knew he was put out about finding her *tête-à-tête* in the garden with his father. She wanted to say, If you carry on like that he'll know for sure, if he doesn't already. 'I'll tell you later, okay?'

She had more to think about just then than Luke's jealousy, or his acrimonious relationship with his father, or even whether or not, or how, Nick had worked out that his son was her lover. She was suddenly pretty sure that he was privy to another secret: that he really did know, or had guessed, what had happened eighteen years ago. How to get it out of him was another problem.

The strangest thing was that he seemed to think she should know the answer herself, and even that she was somehow at fault in the matter. That made no sense. How could she have had any bearing or influence on events back then? She had only been a baby.

11

Have you not known? Have you not heard?
Has it not been told you from the beginning?

Four divine days and nights she spent with Luke in the Chelsea house, and most of that time in bed. They sat up at night, smoking dope or getting drunk, and talking, talking about themselves, their separate pasts. And about the future.

The future was trickier than the past.

'Nobody needs to know what's going on, do they?' Luke said hopefully. 'People live platonically with strangers all the time, for the sake of convenience. Everybody will just think we're flatmates. Like you and Matt.'

Not quite like that, thought Georgie. 'They might cotton on after a while. Anyone can see through a brick wall in time. Your father's already guessed.'

He stared at her, taken aback. 'What do you mean? How do you know?'

'I can just tell, that's all. He was looking at me funny.'

'He looks at every woman funny. You keep away from him, he's a bastard.'

'How can I keep away from him if I'm going to live with you?'

'We can do what your mother did, go to Canada and never come back.'

'They won't let you stay in Canada if we're not married. I can live here but you can't live there. Anyway, we'd have my parents to deal with over there. And I can tell you it won't take my mother much longer than your father to add up two and two, and she will definitely make a fuss.'

'Well, I vote we let them think what they bloody well please and just deny everything.'

Babies, thought Georgie. How are you going to deny anything when we come to have a baby? But he wouldn't have seen that far ahead yet. Men didn't. To her intense irritation and dismay, she had found her mind moving on to babies as soon as they were alone in the house. Thinking how lovely it would be, if . . . when . . .

The idea of having Luke's baby excited her sexually. So much for educating women, she thought resentfully. After all that, we're still slaves to the most basic biological instincts.

On the other hand, a baby might change everything for them. Everything, everyone, would have to bend to accommodate a child. What could her mother do, however much she disapproved, when confronted by Georgie saying This is Luke and he's the father of my baby? It was the baby that would matter most then, not some pernickety legalistic consideration about the fringes of what formally constituted incest. And it was only a sin, not a crime, to screw your mother's brother. She couldn't ever marry him, but that wasn't the end of the world. As she had observed the other day, heaps of people didn't bother to get married anyway.

She looked at Luke lying beside her. It would be wonderful to have a little Luke inside her, a baby bearing the genes for that unkempt blond hair, that long strong body, the pale blue eyes and deliciously sexy mouth . . . She bent over to kiss his mouth, wishing they could be making a baby right now. Pure fantasy, of course.

On Saturday morning she went down to Sussex with Matthew. Her grandfather and Althea were flying back from Singapore that day and Matthew had obligingly offered to collect them from the airport, probably to give him an excuse to drive his mother's classy car. Georgie was just going along for the ride, because she was supposed to be staying down there for the next week anyway.

When she stood in the arrival hall at the airport with Matthew and saw her grandfather come through and raise his hand in a character- istically minimal greeting, she felt quite stupidly sentimental. It was all so homey and familiar now. They were her proper family which her mother had unjustly deprived her of. She hugged her grand- father and Althea and felt like crying.

They all went home to Underhill-by-Firleston and Georgie made dinner for them, pressing Matthew into service as the scullery boy. Between flurries of activity, she leaned out the open upper half of the kitchen door to chat with her grandfather and his wife where they sat on the terrace, drinking gin and tonic in the mild summer evening. Across the lawn, unbeknownst to Althea, the persistent cat was curled up in the hammock. The moon rose roundly over Firle Beacon.

Too perfect to be true.

Georgie got up late on Monday morning. After a leisurely bath, she came downstairs to what she took to be an empty house. Althea would have gone up to London as usual. And the car was gone, so her grandfather must have driven into Brighton as he had threatened, to do some research for his latest paper. Academics, she knew, were always working on a paper, even if it took fifteen years to get written. It was their credentials, the work-in-progress.

Before leaving, her grandfather had tidily put the mail on the little table by the front door, the mailman being the only person who ever made use of the front door. The forbidden cat was perched on the table, on top of the mail, his forepaws neatly tucked under his white bib like a hen brooding over a clutch of eggs. It seemed unkind to depose him when he was so happily settled. Instead she lured him into the kitchen for a saucer of milk. Althea would have objected if she had known, but she didn't, and Georgie and the cat swore each other to secrecy.

With the cat out of the way, she picked up the mail. She wanted to see if her mother had written back in response to her own postcard, sent just after she had first discovered her family down here. She was disappointed but not surprised to see nothing in her mother's familiar handwriting. Peculiarly disjointed, she had always thought it, but now she had discovered that everybody in England wrote like that.

Her mother would be up North till the end of August. Her father would have forwarded the card, no doubt, but it had to travel by canoe and dog sled or some such thing, and of course there was no mailman to slip it through her cabin door. And it went without saying that her father didn't write letters.

There was a letter for her, though, postmarked London. She had it half-way open before she realized what it was: her birth-certificate. She had gone to St Whatsis House with Luke and found her name and date of birth in the registry list, and paid the fee for it to be sent to her down here. Then they had gone around to the post office to pick up a passport application form, and to Victoria station to have her photo taken in one of those machines. Canadian passports wouldn't allow the machine photographs, but Luke assured her that the British Home Office was more understanding.

She took the birth certificate out of the envelope and looked at it. A funny old-fashioned thing, all handwritten. There was even a space for the father's occupation . . .

She stopped and looked again more carefully. There was her mother's name, her maiden name that was, Olivia Jane Beckett. Under *Name and Surname of Father* it said Unknown. And so of course the *Occupation of Father* was also marked Unknown.

Father Unknown.

She couldn't take it in. Not Thomas Henry Payne, *Occupation* Physician. Not even John Smith, *Occupation* Milkman.

No father at all.

111

Maybe, because she was under age when she got pregnant, her mother had been trying to protect her father. Maybe that was why no one here seemed to know anything about her father, not even his name or the fact that he was a doctor. She thought about those two implausible suppositions for ten seconds, struggling, and finally conceded defeat.

Her father wasn't named on the birth certificate because he wasn't her father.

She had found her mother's family, at the price of losing her father's.

She went and sat down in the big deep armchair by the fireplace where her grandfather usually sat. She felt some small scrap of comfort from sitting in his place. He was still her grandfather, confirmed as her mother's father. He at least really and truly belonged to her. Letting the chair enfold her was like being hugged by him, in an accepting and unselfconscious way that he himself could never have managed.

But her own father, the man she had always called Daddy, he was a stranger. No relation. Her mother's husband.

She had acquired a lot of these non-relatives. Her grandfather's wife. Her grandmother's husband. Now her mother's husband. Who, she wondered, was her real father's wife?

And semi-relatives. Two half-uncles. Now a half-brother. Alex was only half her blood. His father wasn't her father.

Who was her father?

She thought for some reason of her mother's little samoyed bitch, returning home from a sexual spree, well pleased and hopelessly pregnant. Father unknown. Father a stranger. A wolf from the wilderness. A god come down to earth in disguise. Lies, lies.

Why had her mother never told her?

Lots of people had fathers who weren't their real fathers, but who loved them all the same. Why had her father never told her?

If she had known all along, it wouldn't have mattered. Well, wouldn't have mattered so much. There was no way it couldn't matter in the end, to think that your mother didn't even know which man had started a baby in her.

How could she not know? Or did she know but not want to say? Why not?

Georgie sat there for an unknown length of time in a fair approximation of a cataleptic trance, going over and over the same ground again. No father, only half a brother, no Grandpa and Grandma Payne, no aunts and uncles and cousins. No family back home at all. Except her mother who didn't belong there.

And worse – she had just realized this – they must all know, all

112

the aunts and uncles and grandparents at least. They all knew she wasn't really one of them.

She couldn't bear it. She wanted her mother. No, she hated her mother, her mother had deprived and deceived her. She wanted her father, but he wasn't her father. She felt empty, hollow, sick. She wanted Luke.

She put her arms around her own body and hugged herself, for want of another's love.

Somebody was talking to her. Matthew's voice. He shouldn't have been here, he was supposed to go up to London today.

But Matthew, he was real, he was her mother's brother. She hadn't known he existed until three weeks ago. Her life till then had been filled up with fake relatives, people she didn't belong to.

'Georgie, are you okay? You look like you're going to be sick.'

'I'm okay,' she said automatically. 'I'm cold.'

'It's always cold in here in the summer. Come outside, it's nice and warm in the sun.' She watched him bend down to pick up a piece of paper from the rug. 'Is this yours? Oh, it's your birth certificate. You told me about that.'

He trailed off and frowned. 'Father unknown?' He began to laugh. 'Your mother must have been the town bike if she couldn't work out who the guilty man was.'

She thought of her mother and the samoyed. Her mother, a schoolgirl of fifteen. Her mother, still so much younger than she herself was now, in the photos that Luke's father had taken. Her mother at thirty-five, celebrating the achievement of her doctorate.

The town bike, Ph.D.

Her eyes must have been open, because she could still see, but she could feel the warmth of tears running down her face. She couldn't move to wipe them away.

'Georgie, don't cry, I was only joking. It was just a joke. A stupid joke, I take it back.'

He sat on the arm of the chair and put his arms around her and pulled her towards him. He wasn't Luke, but he was human and warm. She leaned against him, weeping helplessly, pointlessly, silently. Not sobbing.

Matthew began to sound alarmed. 'For God's sake, girl, do stop. I'm sorry if I impugned your mother's honour. I'll lie down and let you walk on me as atonement, if it makes you feel better.'

She didn't exactly stop weeping, but she did start to laugh at his suggestion. 'Would you enjoy that, Matt? Shall I wear stilettos to do it?' When she had finished laughing she found she was still weeping. She turned her face in to him, so his T-shirt absorbed her tears.

Matthew didn't seem to mind. He held her and stroked her hair.

'He's not there,' she said at last.

'Who?'

'My father.'

It took him a minute to work this out. 'You mean you didn't know that your mother's husband isn't your biological father?'

She shook her head without taking her face away from the safety of his shirt. 'Nobody is.'

'I don't think we're dealing with parthenogenesis here.'

He propped her back quite gently in the depths of the chair and went into the kitchen. Georgie sniffled and tried to dry her eyes with her shirt-tail, an inelegant and probably unhygienic operation. Matthew came back with a double shot of whisky. 'Knock this back, it'll sort you out.'

She swallowed a large mouthful. That brought tears of a different sort to her eyes, but it certainly stopped the snivelling. He also handed her a box of tissues to use instead of the shirt-tail. She recovered herself enough to thank him.

'Now let's get this straight,' he said briskly. 'You really thought that the same man had put your mother in the club at fifteen and married her at nineteen?'

'Well, why not?' Georgie gave him a defiant look. 'In this country you can't get married without the consent of both your parents until you're eighteen. I looked it up.'

'Then why wait another year? But I suppose it makes some sense. She would have had to finish school, for instance. Only my father doesn't know your father, and he would have if he'd been lurking loyally all that time.'

'I know. I couldn't work that out.' She brooded, then burst out, 'The main reason I've always assumed he was my father is that nobody ever even hinted that he wasn't! Why didn't they tell me? It's not the end of the world. At least it wouldn't be if I'd known it all along. It's just – finding out like this . . .'

She felt the tears coming back, and took a gulp of whisky to burn them away. With her throat seared, she could only whisper a repetition of the question. 'Why didn't they tell me?'

'Aside from all the usual reasons, whatever they are, it might be because they figured you'd want to know who your real father is.'

She hadn't gotten that far yet. She was still too shocked by the sudden snatching away of basic biological certainties. But of course he was right. And now that she thought of it, she did want to know. 'Well, they were right. And it seems to me I have a right to know.'

114

She picked up the fateful certificate and looked again at the offending entry. She couldn't believe that her mother really didn't know who her father was. If she hadn't known, she wouldn't have carried the baby to term. If she had found herself pregnant by an anonymous rapist, or – totally impossible, knowing her mother – as a result of some drunken orgy, there was no way that Georgie would have lived to be born. Her mother was a practical and determined person, the kind who made up her mind what she wanted to do and then did it, which was how she had gotten her Ph.D. It simply beggared belief to suggest that she hadn't been the same way even as a girl of fifteen, that she would have consented to be the unwilling victim of a trick played by fate. If her mother had had her and kept her, it meant that her father was not unknown.

She flapped the paper at Matthew. 'Do you think this was for my benefit? To prevent me from finding out what they didn't want me to know?'

'Who knows? No, wait, it couldn't have been, if she didn't know your father – I mean your putative father – back then. It's more likely she didn't want your father – your real father – to have any legal claim on you.'

That was another possibility she hadn't thought of. There must be dozens more. But she was already tired of pointless speculation. She wanted real answers.

She felt like flying home on the next plane and travelling by whatever means to the cabin where her mother was spending the summer, to break down her cabin door if necessary and demand the truth. And a necessarily inadequate apology, for having lied by omission.

But she had other reasons for not going back yet. And she might have an oracle nearer to hand: her grandfather would surely know who her father really was.

She jumped up, impatient. 'Let's go for a swim or something. I'm fed up with sitting around.'

It was nearly the end of the week before Georgie found what she judged to be the right opportunity to speak to her grandfather.

First she had to wait till Matthew went back up to London, which he seemed in no hurry to do. She had to do it during the day, when Althea wasn't around. When she had her grandfather's undivided attention, which meant while he was not working on his paper. When he was relaxed and in a good mood.

On Thursday she went with him to Brighton, and the stars came together when they had lunch at a little restaurant deep in the Lanes.

115

After they had ordered dessert – a sure sign of relaxation and good humour if he was actually eating dessert, she had noticed – she started in an unthreatening roundabout way. 'I hadn't realized before, but I'm eligible for a British passport. I was under the impression I could only stay for three months, but with a British passport I can stay as long as I like. Luke said all I needed was to get a copy of my birth certificate and a passport application form.'

'Luke?'

'You know. Emma's son.'

'Oh yes.'

Not promising. She could tell he didn't approve of Luke, even without knowing him. 'I don't suppose you'd recognize him. He'll have grown up a lot. He's six foot three and built like a running back.'

Her grandfather did not take this to be a complimentary discription. 'And brains to match, no doubt. Emma wouldn't have taken on board the genetic consequences of cross-breeding with a Neanderthal.'

'You didn't take to her husband?'

'Have you met him?'

'Yeah.' In Nick's, or at least Luke's, defence she added, 'I understand he's famous in certain circles.'

'So Althea tells me. It only confirms my general opinion of the tastes and capabilities of the people who orchestrate popular culture. That man is almost a definition of the lowest common denominator.'

Georgie was taken aback by this pronouncement, and by the depth of hostility that evidently ran under it. It seemed a pretty harsh judgement, even against Nick. It also suggested that her grandfather would not be best pleased if she announced that she was going to be living with Luke, even if supposedly on a flat-sharing basis. As for having to tell him, as she hoped she would some day, that she was carrying Luke's baby . . . she could just imagine what he would have to say about her introducing Neanderthal genes into the family. Maybe the whole thing was going to be even more complicated than she had thought.

'Luke seems to be a normal specimen of *Homo sapiens*,' she assured him. 'But I didn't want to talk about him, I wanted to ask you something else. Have you ever seen a copy of my birth certificate?'

'Not that I recall. You can get one from St Catherine's House.'

'I know. I did.'

She took the certificate out of her purse – her bag, as they called it over here – and gave it to him. Since it was clearly expected of him, he unfolded it and glanced at it, without commenting.

She took a deep breath and said, 'Who's my father?'

116

Her grandfather looked carefully at her and then at the paper again. He held it at arm's length, rather than go to the trouble of putting on his reading glasses. Finally he said, 'I see,' and added, 'I've never seen this before. Lia must have filled in the forms while she was in hospital.'

'Do you mean you didn't know that officially I have no father?'

Just for a fleeting moment he looked at if he would much rather have been somewhere else, almost anywhere else. Then his thin handsome features fell into their habitual lines: the expression of a man standing in an arctic blizzard who was quite comfortable really, only he could have done with a cup of tea perhaps to warm him up a trifle.

Maybe, if he had truly been in such a situation, he might have been justified in saying what he said next, but not otherwise. 'Well, it's not of any importance, is it?'

Georgie stared, disbelieving. 'Who's *your* father?'

Now, she was pleased to see, he definitely wanted to be somewhere else. He cleared his throat. 'I – ah – take your point, but it's not the same thing. If your parents hadn't established a relationship, your father's only hypothetical anyway.'

'Well then, let me rephrase my question. Who is my hypothetical father?'

She knew that he knew, by the way he was obviously squirming inwardly. Like her mother, he didn't want her to know her father. Was she the child of a criminal, a lunatic, what? For a minute she thought her grandfather was going to lie and say he didn't know.

But he didn't say that. 'He was just a boy Lia was going out with. He wasn't very bright and she had no intention of marrying or living with him, even if she hadn't been far too young.' He looked at her, slightly smiling, taking his revenge for her having put him on the spot. 'You were just the consequence of his stupidity.'

Georgie wasn't totally surprised to hear all this. But she didn't let it rest there. 'Why didn't she, you know, get an abortion?'

He was never going to finish his dessert now. She had taken away his appetite entirely. She felt faintly guilty. And faintly vindicated.

'To tell you the truth, I don't know. We wanted her to do that, both Emma and I – you understand Lia was only fifteen at the time – but she wouldn't have it. So if it's any consolation, I can tell you that she must have wanted you very much indeed.'

She took that at face value and was somewhat consoled, as well as gratified, to hear that her mother at fifteen had been just the sort of person she was now at thirty-seven, and had been as long as Georgie could remember: persistent, practical, reserved and rather secretive. The influence of Scorpio rising, maybe.

But Georgie herself could be persistent. 'Do you have any idea where my father is now?'

Her grandfather gave her a speculative look. 'Althea tells me he's the managing director of a large construction company that's quoted on the Stock Exchange, so I should think he'd be quite easy to track down. But he's also very likely a married man, with children of that marriage. Do you really want to disrupt his life just for your own personal satisfaction?'

She hadn't thought about that. She hadn't envisaged her father's life beyond the point of her conception. But of course her grandfather was right. The world had moved on. Her mother's life had moved on, her father's would have too. Funny – terrifying, even – how quickly she had learned to think of this unknown man as her father.

Though in the back of her mind, in the heart of her heart, she still regarded Thomas Henry Payne MD as her father. Maybe, if he was lucky, she would to the end of his life. He didn't deserve it, she thought resentfully. Not because he wasn't her father, but because he hadn't told her.

To her grandfather she said, 'I don't intend to disrupt his life. His family don't need to know. If I go to see him at his office, it'll just be business between the two of us, won't it?'

He looked at her sidelong, surprised. 'Maybe it will. But what do you want of him?'

'I don't know.' She spoke slowly, thinking aloud. 'Just to see him, maybe. Just to see what he's like, and satisfy my . . . curiosity. He might be curious too. Maybe he's wondered about me. Can you get Althea to find out where I can find him?'

'If you want.'

'I do want.' She added vehemently, because he didn't seem to understand, 'It's important. Very.'

The waiter came and hovered. Her grandfather said, 'More coffee, Georgie?' in a brisk way that made it clear he was not going to talk about her father any more.

12

Who made thee a judge over us?

On Monday Georgie did herself up as smartly and respectably as she had the means to do, and took the train to London, to the address that Althea had given her.

She asked for her father by name.

The receptionist said he was on holiday until the following Monday.

After having psyched herself up for nothing she felt slightly adrift. She mooched around the National Gallery for a couple of hours, mostly among the gilded Italian altarpieces out of a sense of touristical duty. Then she went to meet Luke for dinner.

She hadn't seen him for over a week. He knew nothing of her catastrophic discovery. Too bad, now that she came to think of it, that it hadn't turned out to be her mother who was no relation. Because then Luke would be just a man she had met this summer. Not taboo.

She decided to break the news by passing him the birth certificate. He glanced at it and passed it back. 'That's great.'

'Great? What do you mean, that's great?'

'Now you can get your passport.'

'Forget the passport, for heaven's sake. Just read that certificate.'

He looked again, more carefully this time. And responded almost exactly as Matthew had. It made her feel even more like a total cretin. 'You mean you really thought your father in Toronto was your real father?'

'You mean you knew he wasn't?'

'Well, I did wonder, when I realized that my father didn't know anything about him. And then he said something.' He paused, looking uncomfortable.

'Well?' she prodded impatiently. 'What did he say? And why didn't you tell me?'

'It was after you'd gone down to Sussex. I wasn't going to ring you up to tell you your mother had lied to you about your parentage.' Again he hesitated. 'But you were right about something else. He does know about us.'

'I told you, didn't I? But how do you know?'

'Well, when he got back he asked me if I'd had a good time while the cat was away. And then he asked if you'd had a good time too. Just, like, letting me know he knew, the bastard.'

'Warning you, you mean?'

'No, I don't think he cares. Why should he? It's not like you're his granddaughter. He's got no reason to look out for your morals.'

'But you're his son. What about your morals?'

'I think he thinks that morals is a word that only comes in the feminine gender.'

Georgie wouldn't have been surprised. 'But what did he tell you about my father?'

'He said, and I quote, I think your sister has been telling her

119

daughter porky pies about Daddy.' He added drily, 'You can make what you like out of that, because I didn't ask.'

She flushed. She could just hear Nick saying it, and the thought made her squirm with embarrassment. 'God, it makes me feel like such a fool, all of them knowing something I didn't. Something so important to me.' She brooded bitterly. 'I'll never forgive my parents. I mean my mother and – oh, God, I don't know what to call him now! I don't know if he's even my adoptive father. I'll never, never forgive them for not telling me from the first.'

'It is pretty unforgivable, I have to agree. But if that's the only thing you have to hold against your parents, you're better off than plenty of others.'

Georgie didn't feel particularly grateful merely because her parents, or whatever they were, hadn't behaved as badly towards her as they might have done if they'd been really trying. In fact what her mother had done, she realized now, was to turn her into an orphan.

The people that she loved as father, brother, grandparents, uncles, aunts, cousins, the whole emotional family baggage that had given her a sense of security and belonging – they were all fakes. Even her so-called brother Alex was only half-blood to her. She had loved them all under false pretences. Her whole family life was a complete fraud.

And on the other side of the ocean, the people who really were her blood relatives were utter strangers to her. She could never now love her mother's father with the sort of love that properly belonged to a grandfather. As he had so painfully pointed out himself, to call him Grandpa was a sham in itself. As for Matthew and Luke, she had never even dreamed of their existence. Whatever she felt for these people – and after a few short weeks she had come to love them all, in widely different ways – they could never be more than notional kinsfolk.

So in effect she had no family at all. Except her mother, whose fault it all was.

After dinner they went back to the Barbican flat. Matthew wasn't there. Which was just as well, because by the time they got inside, Georgie was so desperate with desire for Luke after ten days' absence that she nearly tore off his clothes and raped him on the doormat. They made it to the sofa in the first instance, then moved on to the bedroom for seconds.

The relief she felt under her wholehearted pleasure made her realize how unsure she had been of him. In her head she had been

120

thinking love, commitment, children, in her heart she had only Luke, Luke, Luke. But somewhere in her gut lurked the old inescapable feminine fear: what if he doesn't love me any more?

For now that was assuaged. But she couldn't help wondering at what point the fear would lift. Obviously her mother no longer wondered about her father – sorry, the man she was married to. Her grandmother Payne must have long since ceased to doubt her grandfather. (Or whatever they were, now that her father was no longer her father.) And Althea was clearly confident of her grandfather Beckett.

When would she be sure of Luke?

Maybe never. She had a different example in that family, one she couldn't check, could only suspect. Had her grandmother, Emma Hardy, ever been sure of Nick? She couldn't tell from what Luke had said if his father had been promiscuous all along, or only (or at least obviously) since her grandmother's death. She did know that he took notice of women in a way that her father – oh damn! that man, Tom Payne, whatever he was to her – and her grandfather did not, at least as far as she knew. But that might be only because of Nick's profession, which must require a constant eye for potential talent.

They got dressed, so as not to be taken by surprise again, and migrated back to the living-room. Georgie took the liberty of offering Luke some of her grandfather's single malt Scotch whisky, and poured herself a glass of wine. They stood out on the narrow balcony, looking down at the lake and the fountains, while they discussed practicalities.

'Has your dad sold the house yet?'

'He's had a couple of offers but he turned them down, said they weren't high enough. Not that it makes any real difference to him, fifty thousand quid more or less.'

Georgie translated that into dollars. It worked out to quite a lot of money. 'Is he really that rich?'

'Rich enough to make it worthwhile paying his taxes somewhere else, apparently.'

'So why doesn't he buy you a condo, I mean a flat? He doesn't strike me as the miserly type.'

Luke swallowed a mouthful of whisky and considered his father's character. 'He's not, really. He just doesn't want to be taken for a ride. And then there's all this school of hard knocks stuff – when I was your age I'd been on my own for seven years, blah blah. As if that was some kind of argument for throwing kids out on the street at fourteen.'

Georgie was appalled. 'Is that what happened to him?'

121

'I don't know, something like that. Or maybe his parents got run over by a bus. They might just as well be dead as far as I'm concerned, I've never set eyes on either of them. I guess he must have done something like what your mother did, walking out on everyone. But he's never talked about it much. Just, you know, when something really gets him going.'

Georgie considered this image of Nick, alone in the world at fourteen. She couldn't somehow see him as an abandoned child. He was more likely to have walked out than to have been thrown out. Men in general had a deep-rooted need to be (or to imagine themselves to be) in control of their life and surroundings, and Nick had it in spades. Leaving home would have been a way of asserting control over his life.

'So what does he want you to do, become a bank manager or an insurance salesman?'

'Oh, Christ.' Luke began to laugh. He turned away from the lake and leaned back against the parapet. 'I think he'd throw me out on the spot if I did something like that. He used to needle my mother about being a card-carrying member of the respectable classes. She was slumming a bit when she married him, and he never let her forget it.'

Georgie would have expected him to say, And she never let him forget it. The fact that it had been the other way around, and she could readily believe that, made an interesting comment on Luke's father and his relationship with her grandmother.

'So what do you want to do for a living? Make art?'

'Why not?' He shrugged, looking faintly defensive. 'Somebody has to, don't they? Civilization is all about art.'

Georgie quite liked the idea of the fate of civilization resting on Luke's broad shoulders. On the other hand, that might suggest that civilization wasn't what it was cracked up to be. 'I thought civilization was about people behaving properly to each other. In a civilized manner.'

He looked at her and laughed again. 'My mother would have approved of you. She was big on manners.'

'Mothers always are. But I didn't really mean politeness, I meant tolerance and kindness and things like that.'

'Sterling qualities, no doubt, but bugger all to do with high culture. The Neanderthals might have been models of tolerance and kindness for all we know. Probably were, in fact. It would explain why they became extinct.' He slapped the concrete facing of the wall. 'This is what constitutes civilization, this stuff right here. Mud huts don't go with Mozart.'

'You mean artefacts.'

'I mean art. This is not just a mountain of steel and glass and concrete, it's the aesthetic expression of an informed imagination. The man who designed it might have been a narrow-minded brute in his personal life, but that would have no bearing on his contributions to civilization.'

'You mean if Hitler had been a great artist, Auschwitz would have been okay?'

He shrugged. 'No, but it wouldn't have had any bearing on his art.'

'How could it not?' she protested. 'How can a moral monster be a great artist? His art would be monstrous.'

'It couldn't be monstrous, if that means non-human. Everything done and felt and thought by human beings is necessarily human. To call someone a moral monster is just an attempt to deny that he's like you in any way. But of course he has to be, doesn't he? What's that famous line – I am a member of the human race, and nothing human is alien to me. That goes for the bad things as well as the good ones. Everybody wants to borrow glory from Raphael and disown the Marquis de Sade, but that's biologically and existentially dishonest.'

Georgie looked at Luke, her lover, her beloved. The evening had deepened into darkness, but light came to them from here and there, catching the contours of his features as he spoke, sculpting with shadows the bones and planes of his face. If men had made the gods in their own image, then Luke looked now like the image of a god, with the quintessential, monumental, elemental beauty of a man.

She gazed up at him, half in awe, half in besotted adulation, listening to him with half an ear and answering with half her mind. 'So okay, everything that humans experience has to be allowed as human. But your Neanderthals probably had a few criminals and crazies in the tribe. Where do art and civilization come in?'

'Action and experience don't constitute art. It's an act of will. The transformation of ordinary objects and events into a significant, communicable experience.'

'And morality has nothing to do with it?'

'How could it?' he asked impatiently. 'There's no such thing as an invalid event or experience. They just exist.'

A god who didn't believe in God. 'But some experiences are better than others.'

'More comfortable, you mean.'

'Well, maybe I do, and so what? Don't tell me you don't care about comfort, or I'll tell your father he can sling you out on the street without a qualm when he moves to Monte Carlo or wherever. And I can also tell you you're not likely to make much of a living out of transforming objects into significant experiences.'

123

He smiled without taking offence. 'Too true. But I can keep going for a while on the dole and the money my mother left me, as long as I've got somewhere to live.'

'The dole? The state is paying you to produce these aesthetic experiences?'

'Paying me for doing nothing, if I like. It's none of their business how I spend my time.'

'Why not? They're paying you, aren't they?'

'Look, it's not a job. It's not even a living, come to think of it. They just don't want me to die of starvation in the street.'

'Fat chance. Anyway, your father's rich.'

'That's none of their business either. And it's probably his taxes being recycled into my benefit cheque. He worked it out once, how many deadbeats and freeloaders must be living off him.'

'Would he approve more if they were artists?'

Luke snorted. 'Are you kidding? He put the national opera and the ballet at the top of his list of freeloaders.'

Georgie laughed. She was beginning to get the flavour of Luke's father, and he was definitely an acquired taste. She was also beginning to suspect that Luke's relationship with his father was not as unhappy as he liked to make out. It was already clear to her that he didn't really think his father any sort of fool. Beneath his overt scorn, he wished as much as any son to win his father's approval.

Well, at least he had the advantage of knowing who his father was.

'I guess I'll just have to be boring and get a job.' She leaned against Luke's shoulder, facing outwards to the lake while he had his back to it. 'We will do it, won't we? Even if we have to lose ourselves in Paris or Amsterdam, where nobody knows who we are.' More exotic places to get lost in, at any rate, than Toronto where her mother had gone to earth. For reasons that she still hadn't uncovered.

'A fate worse than death, having to live in Paris.' Without turning, he ran his hand over her backside. 'Having to live in Paris with you.'

Matthew, when he came home and Luke had gone home, demanded a report on Georgie's expedition to find her father.

'He was on vacation,' Georgie confessed. 'I've got to go back again next week.' To meet another sham-relation – this one the one that should have been dearest, was technically nearest, and who would yet be the uttermost stranger of them all. 'I told Luke about it. And guess what? He already knew.'

'Well, I told you, it's obvious.'

'Don't rub it in,' Georgie said gloomily. 'Anyway, he hadn't guessed off his own bat. His father dropped a big hint.'

She recalled what else Nick had been dropping hints about. She told Matthew about that too. 'He also let on to Luke that he knows about – well, about him and me.'

'And is he shocked and horrified, and proposing to report you to the authorities?'

'No, actually Luke said he didn't think his dad cared much one way or the other. He thinks he was just being nasty. Anyway, there's nothing to report. Uncle and niece don't officially constitute incest.'

'You've checked this out very carefully, I notice.'

'Now you're being nasty. But yeah, I have. It's important, you see. Because I – well, I'm in love with Luke.'

Matthew looked at her sardonically. 'Lucky Luke. What's he done to deserve that?'

'Love isn't something you have to earn. It just happens, that's all.' She fiddled with one of the buttons on her shirt. 'His father's moving to Monte Carlo or Bermuda or something, and we're going to live together.'

'You're going to live with his father?'

She had a brief flash of feeling, gone before she could catch or identify it, when she understood what he meant, or was pretending to mean. The idea of living with Nick was – well, different from the thought of living with Luke. Much scarier, for one thing. 'No, dopey. His father is moving elsewhere. Luke and I are going to live together here. Or maybe in Paris.'

'Why Paris?'

She walked away, across the room. 'Well, it's – some people might think it's a bit odd, that's all. Him being my mother's half-brother and all.'

'Whereas in Paris no one will notice, of course. That sort of thing goes on there all the time.'

'Well, it might, for all anyone knows. There are no laws forbidding any sort of incest in France. It's not a crime at all. Anyway,' she added vehemently, turning on him, 'you know perfectly well it's not really incest, Matty. Aside from the business of the second-cousin genetic relationship, the fact is that we've had no relationship of any sort until this summer. How can anything between Luke and me be seriously called incest? For that matter, since my "real" father is officially unknown, I could have already gone to bed with my brother without knowing it. With my own father, even. I could have unknown brothers all over the place, even if I knew my father's name – after all, you don't often ask for proof of someone's ancestry

125

before you sleep with them. And if my father happened to be a sperm donor, I could be related to half the population of London. How can that kind of thing be incest?'

Matthew shrugged. 'Don't ask me. I don't make the rules.'

'That's the whole trouble,' said Georgie. 'It seems to me there aren't any rules, because the old ones don't make sense any more.'

Unlike Matthew, her grandfather pointedly did not ask about the search for her father, when she was down at Underhill the following weekend.

But Althea did, when Georgie's grandfather wasn't around. 'How did you get on?'

'I didn't get to see him,' Georgie explained. 'He was on vacation but he'll be back tomorrow.' She watched Althea at work on the kitchen table, arranging flowers in a couple of vases. Althea went at that the way she did everything: briskly, efficiently, and with satisfactory results. Georgie was hopeless at artistic things like flower arranging. 'Did you know him? What's he like?'

'I always found him rather charming and sweet. He was just a boy then, of course, and not frightfully intellectually inclined. Ross thought he wasn't good enough for Lia, but the man never walked this earth who'd have been a suitable match for Ross's daughter, so she just had to settle for what was available. If she'd been a few years older she probably would have married him, and Ross would have got over the disappointment in time. After all, he got over the shock of your arrival.'

'And the shock of my departure?'

Althea raised her eyes from the flowers to give Georgie a significant look. 'That's not something he'll ever get over, even if Lia came back. I don't know that I want her to come back. Ross might forgive her because he's her father, but he's my husband and I'll never be able to forgive her for what she did to him by going off like that. I've always felt it altered his attitude to Matty, the knowledge that your own child can kick you in the teeth.'

Matthew, as Georgie had so recently discovered, had invented a way of kicking his father in the teeth over and over again, without having to suffer the consequences. On the other hand, she had also just found out that her own parents, or rather her mother and her mother's husband, had in effect been kicking her in the teeth every day for the past eighteen years, by lying in their own teeth. For that she didn't think she would find herself any more forgiving than Althea.

13

I have said to corruption, You are my father;
to the worm, You are my mother.

Confronting her father on Monday morning seemed too cruel and gruelling, especially when he was just back from his vacation. Georgie washed and dried her curly hair, and brushed and fluffed it till it shone around her head like a halo. Then she dressed herself as Althea had advised, in a white cotton blouse and a short flared navy skirt, nice and simple, cool and summery, but not totally informal. But she didn't set off on her mission till after lunch.

She had had a whole extra week in which to get extra nervous.

Maybe her new-found father would know, and more importantly would tell her, the answer to the other old enduring mystery: why her mother had gone abroad. But for now, one mystery, one solution, was enough. She had lost a false father and wanted to meet the real one. Real at least in the sense that he had made her.

She found the address again, rather a classy one in the West End. Surprisingly classy for a construction company, she thought, though of course the people who ran such companies didn't go around with mud on their steel-toed boots. She took the elevator – no, they called it a lift here – up to the second floor. The button in the lift said it was the first floor, but really it was the second. She went through the door marked *Cahill Brothers plc* and up to the reception desk, where a different receptionist was sitting, not the one who had sent her away last week with the news that he was on holiday. That had been a young woman, this one was middle-aged. Maybe she had been on vacation last week too.

'I want to see Mr Cahill, please.'

'Which Mr Cahill? Mr John Cahill, Mr Charles Cahill, or Mr Barry Cahill?'

Georgie was slightly taken aback by this sudden abundance of Cahills. A family firm in fact as well as name, evidently. 'I want Charlie.'

'Mr Charles Cahill,' the woman amended reprovingly. 'Your name, please?'

'Georgiana Payne.'

The receptionist punched the phone buttons and said in her best artificial voice, 'Miss Georgiana Payne is here to see Mr Cahill.'

Georgie felt hopeful. She hadn't gotten this far the previous time.

A pause on reception. The woman said into the phone, 'That's right, Mr Charles Cahill.' She frowned at whatever the other voice was saying. Then she frowned at Georgie. 'Do you have an appointment?'

'No, it's . . .' Georgie floundered. She should have been prepared for this. She wasn't used to dealing with high-powered businessmen and their secretaries and receptionists. 'It's not really business. But it's very important,' she added firmly.

'What did you want to see him about?'

'I'd rather not say.' Not to this person, at any rate. 'If I could just have a few minutes . . .'

The woman told the phone, 'Miss Payne says it's important.' Another pause, more unintelligible noises from the other end of the line. 'Yes, of course. Certainly.' She put the phone down and gave Georgie a disapproving look. 'I'm afraid it's impossible to see Mr Cahill today without an appointment. He's just come back from holiday, and he has a very full diary this week. If you wish to make an appointment you'll have to ring his secretary.'

By way of dismissal, she transferred her attention to someone else who had just come through the door behind Georgie. Georgie moved away from the desk, to let the guardian dragon grill the next trespasser on her sacred ground.

She didn't know what to do now. There was no point phoning his secretary, who would just demand to know what it was about. And she didn't want to phone him directly, in case he made some excuse, or pretended not to know who she was. And it wasn't fair anyway; she couldn't just dump her paternity on him over the telephone. Maybe she could persuade Althea to phone up on her behalf . . .

While she dithered, a man pushed through the *Cahill Brothers* door beside her and started to walk past the reception desk with the absent-minded stride of someone who did this every day. The receptionist interrupted her interrogation rites to speak to him. 'Oh, Mr Cahill, Mr Brandon's arrived. I've sent him along to Mrs Standish.'

Georgie seized her opportunity. Forgetting that there were three Cahills, and that therefore the odds were against this being the right man, she ran up to him and touched his arm. 'Mr Cahill? Charlie . . .?'

He turned at her touch. She stared at him, tongue-tied a moment, not even aware that her hand was still resting on his sleeve. He was tall and fairly slim, dark hair, blue eyes, like her grandfather and her father. No, this man was her father; the other man was only Tom Payne. He was handsome in an open, easy way that suggested a good-natured soul. For a man who was no relation, he looked remarkably like Tom Payne. Maybe her mother had done it on purpose. Or maybe she just preferred them like that.

He was staring back at her, looking at least as astonished as she felt. She remembered then that she still didn't know if he was the right Cahill. 'Are you Charlie?'

'Who are you?'

'I'm Georgiana Payne. I'm – '

'Oh yes.' He seemed to have recovered himself quite abruptly. He cut off her explanation before she had even begun it, and put his arm around her in a sort of ushering way to steer her towards the door he had just come through. 'Let's go downstairs, Georgie.'

As he virtually pushed her through the door that led to the lift, Georgie could hear the dragon's plaintive, outraged cry. 'Mr Cahill, what shall I tell Mrs Standish about Mr Brandon? Mr Cahill!'

Mr Cahill shut the door on her distress. He punched the button to call the lift. He didn't look surprised or confused any more. He looked rather grim, but also as if he wanted to laugh.

Georgie stepped into the lift. 'You are Charlie, aren't you?'

'That's my name.'

'Do you know who I am?'

'You're Lia's little girl.' He looked at her and shook his head and smiled, but it was a slightly rueful smile. 'Not so little now.'

'I'll be twenty-one at the end of this month.'

'I remember. I knew you as soon as I saw you. You have your mother's face.' The door opened on the ground floor and he let her get out first. 'There's a pub just a few doors down. Let's go and have a drink.'

To celebrate, or to drown his sorrows, she wondered. At least he hadn't pretended he didn't know her, or why she was there. He installed her at a table in the corner of the pub and fetched two glasses of wine.

He seemed to be prepared to do the talking, so she let him. 'Your accent threw me off at first. But I'd heard that Lia went to Canada, so it's only natural you'd sound like a Canadian. Where is Lia now?'

'Still in Canada.' She searched his face, to see what he knew. 'She didn't want me to come back here.'

He shrugged. 'Funny girl, Lia. I never really knew what was in her head.' It was his turn to look at her carefully. 'Who put you on to me? Not her.'

'No, not her. It was my grandfather. And Althea.' She sipped her wine, watching him. It had all been so easy, too easy in a way. And all he had done so far was talk about her mother. He hadn't actually said . . .'Do you know why I came to see you?'

He leaned back on the leather seat and tapped the knuckle of his forefinger on his front teeth in a contemplative way. It was a gesture that her fa – no, Tom Payne – habitually used. He really did look remarkably like Tom Payne. Perhaps it wasn't surprising that her fathers should look alike. And that both of them should resemble her grandfather Beckett. He said, 'Why don't you tell me about it?'

She fixed her gaze on her hands, clasped around her wineglass. She couldn't look at him while she spoke. It was too humiliating, what she had to say. 'Well, believe it or not, until a few days ago I thought I was the child of my father and mother, Thomas and Olivia Payne. I thought I had a younger brother, Alex, and a Grandpa and Grandma Payne, and aunts and uncles and cousins, all Paynes, all in Canada. I knew that somewhere in England I had some grand-parents called Beckett, because that was my mother's maiden name, but I'd never seen them or heard from them. So I came over here to find them.'

She drained the wineglass, to fortify herself. The worst was yet to come. 'When I got here and tracked them down, I discovered that my grandmother was dead. And that my mother had two half-brothers I'd never even heard of. And then I found . . . I found this.'

She took the birth certificate from her purse and opened it out in front of him.

He glanced at it, evidently seeing no surprises there. 'You mean Lia never told you this Payne person isn't your natural father?'

This Payne person. That was what he was, all he was, all he deserved. She felt his betrayal more sharply because the man whose place he had usurped was sitting at her elbow. 'Not a word, not a hint. I showed this to my grandfather and he said . . . he told me you were the man I wanted to see.'

Charlie Cahill was definitely looking grim now. Grim and angry. For the first time since accosting him, Georgie felt nervous. He said in a flat voice, 'I think the ball is definitely in your mother's court over this one. Why don't you ask her about it?'

'I can't. She's up North. Thousands and thousands of miles away. Whereas you and I are here.'

He thought about that for a bit, looking more thundery than ever. Then he appeared to make up his mind, and gave her an unpromis-ing smile. 'Right. Okay. Next time you're talking to Lia, you tell her she set herself up for this. Your grandfather thinks I'm your father. I thought so too, once upon a time. But I'm not.'

Her first reaction was that he was trying to wriggle out of it. And she couldn't blame him, all things considered. She said stiffly, 'Look, I'm not trying to make trouble for you. I know you've got a family and a life of your own. I'll go away again, if you want me to. I just wanted to – you know – see you, meet you.'

He touched her hand, just briefly. It startled her. The first time he had touched her, the man who had begotten her. And he was denying that. 'Yeah, I know, I understand. I'm just telling you what Lia told me. I'm not your father.'

She stared at him. She had never felt more in danger of fainting, not even when she first saw the birth certificate. That had only told her what, as Matthew had pointed out, she might have worked out for herself, from dates and discrepancies. But this time she had been told directly, definitely, who her father was. And he was telling her what her mother had said.

'After you were born, I wanted to see you. Her father wouldn't let her see me but I said you were my kid, I had the right. I said I'd go to court if I had to, I was that determined. And she showed me this.' He brought his open hand down hard and flat on the birth certificate. 'I was so mad when I saw it, I can't tell you, I could have killed her. It was like she'd signed me out of your life. I told her they could do blood tests to prove my rights. And she said,' his forefinger tapped the paper, 'she said, Charlie, all the tests will do is confirm what it says here.'

Georgie uttered something between a croak and a whisper, something that was meant to be Then who is my father?

He must have guessed what her question was. He didn't look angry any more, he looked drained and sad. Insofar as Georgie could feel anything, she felt sorry for him. 'Damned if I know who your father is. I asked her that, but she wouldn't say. I asked her why she'd lied to me, and she said she hadn't. She said she'd never told me you were my child. And I suppose she hadn't. I just didn't think it could be anyone else. I thought she was a virgin, the first time.'

He took his hand off the birth certificate and passed it over his face. 'Jesus, what a mug I was. For all I know, she'd been entertaining the local football team.'

My mother the town bike. What had she been up to, a schoolgirl of fifteen? And why should she tell Georgie when she hadn't told anyone else? Maybe Charlie was right, maybe her father was an entire football team. She wanted to die, or at least burst into tears. But she just sat frozen.

Charlie looked at her and touched her hand again. 'I'm sorry, Georgie. I shouldn't have said that. I thought you were mine and she took you away from me. Believe me, I'd love to be able to tell you, yeah, I'm your father and welcome home and let's live happily ever after. But it's not the truth.'

Georgie pushed away her glass. She picked up the birth certificate and put it back in her purse and stood up, clutching the purse. 'I'm sorry to have troubled you. I do appreciate your telling me the truth. It's more than my mother's done.'

Charlie stood up too. She walked towards the door and he followed her. 'Hey, don't take it too hard. She was just a kid, a little girl really. Fifteen, Jesus, who knows anything at fifteen?'

They were standing on the sidewalk now. She was blinking in the bright sunlight. She said flatly, politely, 'Thank you for the drink, Mr Cahill. I'm glad to have met you, even if it was all a mistake.'

He was watching her a little anxiously. 'Are you all right? Can I get you a taxi?'

'No, no, I'm okay. I'm meeting someone. Not too far from here.'

'Are you sure you're okay?'

'Yes, yes.' She blinked again and managed to smile at him, at the man who looked like Tom Payne, and like Tom Payne was not her father. 'You'd better go back and see to your Mr Brandon.'

14

Who has put wisdom in the inward parts, or given understanding to the heart?

She walked for a long time. Wandered, rather, without knowing where she was going. Anything to keep moving with some pretence of purpose, anything to keep the distractions of the world flowing by. Anything, rather than sit down and cry.

Who was her father? What was her mother?

Did even her mother know who her father was? Did her father even know she existed?

Did it matter to anyone? Even to her?

Pointless questions, unanswerable at least for now. She went on walking. Down Piccadilly to Hyde Park Corner. Along Knightsbridge to Sloane Street. Down to Sloane Square and the King's Road, like a lost dog coming home, to the house where Luke lived. So she must have been moving with a purpose after all.

She knocked with the knocker and no one came. Maybe he was up at the top of the house. Maybe he was out in the garden. How would she call him, if he was in the garden? They had no back lanes in this country. She knocked harder, more desperately.

Someone came at last. Luke's father opened the door, looking irritated and rather rumpled, as if he might have been asleep. Dozing in the garden, maybe.

Georgie stared at him, temporarily flummoxed. She had had her mind so set on Luke that for a moment she couldn't cope with not-Luke. 'Where's Luke?'

He must have been asleep. 'How the fuck should I know?' He rubbed his eye with the heel of his hand and looked at her again. This time her confusion and dismay seemed to reach him. 'Sorry, Georgie. Come on in.'

She didn't. 'Isn't Luke home?'

'Don't think so. He'd better not be, since he didn't answer the fucking door. Was he expecting you?'

'No, not now. I was just – well, it doesn't matter. Never mind. Sorry to have disturbed you.'

She turned away to go down the steps. The expectation of Luke that must have sustained her all the way from Mayfair to Chelsea had vanished, leaving nothing in its place. She couldn't think of a single reason to go anywhere at all, not even home to bed – where was home? No reason not to lie down and die, right where she was.

She stumbled. And grabbed the railing to keep from falling down the front steps. Her body, if only from force of habit, wasn't quite ready to lie down and die.

Nick caught her and steadied her. 'You all right?'

'Yeah.' She took a breath. 'I'm okay.'

'You don't look okay. You better come in.'

She shook her head, trying to shake off the dizziness, the sense of unreality. 'No, I'm okay. I've got to go.'

'Where are you going? I'll give you a lift.'

She couldn't answer him. She couldn't think of anywhere to go. She couldn't even think of a plausible lie. She was completely empty: of thought, of feeling, of the unfailing sense of routine that gets the world out of bed in the morning and moves it through the day. She might have collapsed if he hadn't been holding her up. Maybe it was her awareness of him, the physical pressure of his body against hers, that simple sense of connectedness to another living creature, that kept her from dropping down dead.

He was holding her now, not just holding her up but holding her in his arms, embracing her. It felt as good as anything could have felt just then. It saved her from being totally frozen. She was not at absolute zero but four degrees above it, the body heat of the universe.

'Whats the trouble, sugar?'

She shook her head again, this time without speaking. Speech was a higher function of the brain. She wasn't warm enough yet for that.

133

'Okay, if you won't come in, I'll come out.' He shut the door behind him, keeping his arm around her. 'Let's go down to the pub. I'll buy you a drink.'

He manoeuvred her down the steps, on to solid ground. She wasn't trying to be unhelpful, she just couldn't seem to make her body work right – too rigid to collapse, too rigid to move properly. He steered her down the street as if she were a shopping trolley with a wonky wheel. She thought it would have been easier for him to pick her up and carry her.

That thought reminded her of something, but she couldn't work out what it was. Her brain, like the rest of her, was still in deep freeze.

There were plenty of people in the pub, all apparently having a wonderful time. It was enough to make Georgie want to jump in the Thames, if she could have made herself move so far. Fortunately they were crowded against the bar, or grouped near the door. Nick sat her down in the darkest, most obscure corner of the place, and provided her with a double brandy.

She sipped at the brandy and felt it slowly begin to thaw her inside. Maybe that wasn't a good idea. Maybe there was nothing but ice inside her, to give her shape and form. Maybe the brandy would melt her away altogether, like a snowman in March.

He let her drink it all, without speaking. Then he got her another one and a pint of beer for himself, and he sat down on the bench beside her and said, 'Okay, sugar, are you going to tell me?'

She couldn't not. She had no one else to tell. Besides, she had an odd idea that Nick might be the one person in the world who wouldn't be shocked and appalled by whatever it was her mother might have done. Maybe that was only because he was what Luke had called him, a shameless old sod, but at any rate what she needed right now was someone immune to a sense of scandal.

She brought out the birth certificate. That piece of paper was beginning to feel like a brand, the mark of Cain on her forehead, or the scarlet letter that Hawthorne's heroine had pinned to her breast. She handed it to Nick. 'Did you know about this?'

He unfolded it and looked at it. He looked at it for a surprisingly long time. How long did it take to read one seven-letter word? Then he looked at her in a funny way, not remotely surprised or discomfited as her grandfather had been. A funny sort of assessing way, as if he were trying to take her temperature by looking at her. 'Did you just find out?'

'I found out two weeks ago. When I saw that.' She remembered what Luke had said his father had said. She burst out bitterly, 'I suppose you think I'm a chump for not having guessed before. It just never crossed my mind. And if it had, I would have assumed that it couldn't be, because my parents – I mean my mother would have told me. Maybe you think I'm a boob for that as well, for believing that my mother wouldn't lie to me.'

'Did she lie to you?'

'Well, she didn't have to, did she? If you grow up calling somebody Daddy, you just assume he's your father if no one ever says otherwise. But it's deception all the same.'

She took another swallow of brandy. Her anger was probably doing as much as the drink to restore her to a human state. He gave her back the certificate. While she was stowing it away she heard him say, 'I guess she had her reasons.'

'I guess she did,' Georgie agreed, resenting his defence of her mother. 'And I'm just beginning to guess what they might have been.'

He didn't reply to that, he just watched her and waited. After a minute she said, 'My grandfather told me that my real father was a man named Charlie Cahill. Did you know him?'

'I knew Charlie, yeah.'

So odd to think of all these people knowing, and not knowing. Knowing vital things about her life that she hadn't known. Not knowing that some of those things weren't true. Maybe only her mother knew the truth. Her mother, the liar.

She held the glass of brandy in both hands. 'I went to see him this afternoon.'

'How did that go?'

'I thought at first it was going to be okay. He recognized me right off, even though he hadn't seen me since . . . well, I don't think he'd ever seen me. He said I look like my mother.'

Nick said drily, 'Perceptive bloke, our Charlie.'

Something in his tone made Georgie's skin prickle. As she started to speak, she had a flash of something only half comprehended, a sudden speculation that he already knew what she was about to tell him. But she told him anyway. 'He also said, as politely as possible, that he's not my father.'

He didn't seem surprised, which confirmed her suspicion. Maybe her grandmother had known something her grandfather had not. 'That saying about the wise child knowing its father cuts both ways, I reckon. How did he know that?'

'My mother told him. He wanted to be able to see me and she wouldn't let him and he said he'd take her to court. So she told him.'

Georgie remembered Charlie's voice, the echoes of grief and anger for a loss and a betrayal twenty years gone. Her own loss and betrayal were only two weeks, only two hours old. She felt that

135

dizzy emptiness inside her again, felt her internal temperature dropping fast, freezing her up. She closed her eyes and covered her face with her hands.

Nick put his arm around her, as he had on the doorstep. She was comforted enough to cry.

To cry on her own, alone in a foreign country, would have been the beginning of desolation, with nothing but exhaustion at the end. To cry in somebody's arms meant at least some creature comfort, some possibility of breaking her fall before she hit bottom. She clung to him and wept for a while, quietly and undramatically so as not to distract the merrymakers at the other end of the pub.

Nick was stroking her hair while he held her. Unlike most men, he didn't seem to be embarrassed or distressed by her tears. 'Georgie, you'd never set eyes on the bugger before. You can't be all that broken up to find out he's not your father.'

'It's not him,' she whispered, when the sobs had died down. 'But if it isn't him . . .'

'Well, he wouldn't know, would he?' he pointed out reasonably. 'Under the circumstances, he's the last person Lia would have confided her big secret to.'

'Maybe she doesn't have a big secret,' Georgie said bitterly. 'Maybe that's the big secret. Matt made a horrible joke about the town bike, and Charlie suggested a football team.'

He said sardonically, 'You reckon?'

'No, not really,' she admitted. She was relieved that he had dismissed the possibility so readily. She would have dismissed it out of hand, except that . . . if her mother could have deceived her all her life on such a fundamental matter, she began to think she didn't really know her mother at all.

She kicked off her sandals and curled herself up on the bench beside Nick. He still had his arm around her, and she cuddled up to him quite unselfconsciously. After all, on the one hand he was her grandmother's husband, her mother's stepfather, and on the other hand he was her lover's father, sort of a father-in-common-law. The fact that these two relationships were irreconcilable didn't concern her just now. It didn't even bother her when he shifted his arm so that his hand rested on her bottom rather than her shoulder. Something – possibly the two double brandies she had just poured into an empty stomach, on top of the wine that Charlie Cahill had given her – suggested it was more comforting that way. It certainly warmed her up faster when he stroked her bottom instead of her shoulder.

She propped her arm on his shoulder and said in his ear, 'Who's my father?'

136

He didn't like the question. Or maybe it was the answer he didn't like. 'You'll have to ask Lia.'

'Is that another secret you're not giving away?'

He looked at her, amused. 'Not even if I knew it.'

He really did look a lot like Luke. Or the other way around, because Nick had begotten Luke. He wasn't as tall as Luke, and he was thicker by thirty years, like a tree would be – not fat, just bigger around. His face had weathered the way men's faces do, crinkling around the eyes and mouth, and the skin was a little baggy in places. She could see it all in detail, with his face so close to hers.

Luke, without the handicap of thirty extra years of wear and tear, would undoubtedly have won the beauty contest, and no doubt too that he had the more beautiful soul, but she had to allow that his father was amazingly attractive, even sexy, for a man of that age. No, she took that back: he was sexy, full stop.

She whispered to his cheek this time, rather than his ear. 'How come you know all my mother's secrets?'

Another unpopular question, provoking a flash of that inexplicable anger he had shown so briefly when he first set eyes on her. Before he could answer, she changed the question. 'Why don't you like me?'

Georgie felt him stiffen. He turned his head to stare at her. For a change, she had astonished him. 'What d'you mean, I don't like you?'

'You didn't like me the first time you saw me. You're mad at me now.' The fact that he had taken pity on her in her catatonic state of shock didn't prove he liked her. Most people would stop to help an injured dog, even if they didn't like dogs. Recalling Althea's bitter resentment, she asked, 'Is it because you didn't like my mother?'

She said this in a stupidly childish way, as she realized when the words came out of her mouth. She was doomed to be stupid this afternoon, she supposed, because her brain didn't dare to wake up and feel. Like dreading the return of sensation after having a wisdom tooth pulled. So she sat numbly, saying stupid things, knowing they were stupid, but not being able to stop herself. 'Why didn't you like my mother? Was it because she went away? Or because my grandmother didn't like her?'

She was uttering heresy, she knew, the notion that parents and children might dislike each other. A personal impossibility for her, at any rate. How could she dislike someone she didn't even know? Father unknown, mother a mystery. She herself was only Georgiana X, parentage unproven. Nobody at all. She began to cry again.

'Hey, sugar, you're going too fast for me.' His voice was half-way between a growl and a whisper. He pulled her on to his lap and held her like a child, stroking her all over.

She went quiet at last, not calmed, only exhausted. Every cell of her body was still quivering, but her muscles couldn't get themselves together any more; they just lay there, trembling ineffectually. She had even run out of tears. A sort of Sahara of the soul.

Since there was nothing else to do, nothing at least that she was capable of doing, she burrowed her face into the angle between his neck and his shoulder. They were pretty substantial, that neck and that shoulder. Not even her own thoughts could assail her there.

She took a deep breath. Nick smelled like Luke, but smokier. Cured versus uncured bacon, perhaps. Then she did a childish thing: she stuck out the tip of her tongue to touch the side of his neck. He tasted like Luke too, but drier and saltier, *manzanilla* rather than *fino*. A tantalizing taste and smell, at least in her present still stupid condition. Threatening to reach memories that the normal chatter of consciousness kept hidden from her.

She stroked the fabric of his shirt with her thumb, in a curiously babyish way. Rough denim, worn smooth by hard usage – rather like the man himself. She wanted to unbutton the shirt, to see if she had guessed right about what was underneath. The word *furry* came into her head. More childishness. She could feel the coarse hair flattened under her thumb, under the denim. She unclenched her hand to move her fingertips over the pectoral landscape of muscle and bone. No fat detectable there.

That was her adult mind commenting. She must be reviving in spite of herself. She didn't want to leave that childish world of sensation and security. Another word came into her head, a grown-up word this time. *Exile*.

The pub seemed to have gotten much noisier all of a sudden. It was filling up, as the afternoon's idle roisterers were replaced or reinforced by the arrival of those who had finished their work for the day. When a group settled themselves loudly at the next table but one, Georgie reluctantly sat up and slid off Nick's lap. 'Hey, I should be going. I'm supposed to be cooking dinner for Matt and Luke tonight.'

'All one big happy family, are we?'

She glanced at Nick and away again. She was getting paranoid. The way he said that, she had thought for a second that he knew about that time with Matthew, as well as Luke. But there was no way he could know about that. 'Well, I guess we are at that,' she agreed. 'They're both my uncles, but no relation whatsoever to each other. Funny arrangement, isn't it?'

'It's a funny world. Getting funnier all the time.'

She stood up and had to put her hand on the table to steady herself. She felt quite light-headed. He took her by the arm to steer her towards the door. 'Are you going back to the Barbican? I'll give you a lift.'

'There's no point, this time of day. It's faster just to take the tube.'

She managed to miss her footing in the street outside the pub. I'm drunk, she thought in annoyance. Fortunately Nick still had a hand on her, and saved her not only from falling on her face but also from being run over by a bus. 'Georgie, you're bloody well not safe on your own. I'll take you home.'

'No, really, I'm going to take the tube.'

'Then I'll come with you to make sure you get there.'

Again, but for different reasons, he had to manoeuvre her down the street. He put his arm around her and she leaned into him. 'Do you want to come for dinner too?'

'I do, but I can't. I have other commitments.'

Georgie felt unjustly resentful. To her own surprise she said, 'Is she a stunner like my mother?'

'Who?'

He must have known perfectly well what she meant. He was just trying to annoy her by making her spell it out. 'The girl you're going to fuck tonight.'

She must have spoken more loudly than she intended, because a middle-aged woman coming towards them gave her a shocked and disapproving look. Georgie felt like showing the old bat her birth certificate. Father unknown, mother the town bike. What else would you expect from the kid?

She had almost forgotten the question she had asked, the one that had shocked the unknown woman. Which was just as well, because Nick didn't answer it. Instead he asked her a question. 'Why don't you and I have dinner by ourselves?'

She considered. She was tempted. She didn't really feel like cooking. On the other hand she was, as Nick himself had pointed out, a well-brought-up young girl. 'No, I can't, I've got a date with Luke and Matt. Matty wouldn't mind, but Luke sure would.'

They had reached the tube station. Nick put money into a ticket machine. When it wouldn't give him a ticket he swore and thumped it twice, till it gave him both a ticket and his money back.

Georgie leaned on him and giggled. 'You've mugged it. Robbery with violence.'

He bought another ticket, this time without curses or thumps. Armed with that, he guided her through the turnstile and down the steps. 'Do you mind if Luke minds?'

'Yeah, I do. I'm in love with him,' she confided, turning to him as they reached the platform and sliding her arm around his waist. To steady herself, she supposed. Or maybe just because it felt good. Because Nick felt good. Comforting and exciting at the same time, that was how he felt.

'Lucky Luke,' said Nick, just as Matthew had done.

The train at the platform was going to the wrong place, Georgie noticed. Ealing Broadway, wherever that was. She laid her head on Nick's shoulder and he put his arm around her shoulder, to wait for the right train in comfort.

'Do you mind about Luke and me?'

'Yeah, I do.'

'Because of our being related, you mean?'

'Bugger that. I'm just jealous.'

He was kidding her, she supposed, but it warmed her anyway. 'Does that mean you don't really dislike me?'

'Don't be daft. Does it feel like I don't like you?'

Maybe *like* was the wrong word, implying casually friendly feelings. There was nothing casual about the emotional vibes she had received from Nick, from that very first glimpse of surprise and fury down to the confusing but powerful sensations she was getting at this very moment. She was letting herself feel them for the first time right now, without Luke around to distract her. Heavy stuff they seemed to her, love and desire and hate. Much too heavy for her to have provoked them from a man she hardly knew.

'Is it my mother you don't like?'

'For Christ's sake, I haven't seen her for nearly twenty years, and I'm not likely to bump into her in the next twenty, am I? How the hell would I know whether I like her or not? I hadn't thought about her for ages, until you turned up.' He withdrew the security of his arm. 'Here comes your train.'

Now he really was mad at her. She stood alone on the station platform, suffering obscure but painful withdrawal symptoms, like emotional cramps. He had withdrawn from her.

A Circle Line train arrived. Fifty million people got off and on. Nick managed to put her aboard at the last minute. Then he climbed on himself, squeezing in right next to her just as the doors snapped shut behind him.

When the train lurched away from the station, it made Georgie lurch too, and to her vague surprise she found herself back in Nick's arms. Well, it did save space, she supposed, with the train so jam-packed. 'I thought you weren't going to come.'

'I couldn't leave you alone, sugar.'

His voice was rough and smoky, like the smell of tobacco on his clothes. The sound and smell of him stirred extraordinary feelings in her, a longing that wanted satisfaction, a confused and diffident desire. These feelings were dim and rusty at first, quickly growing stronger within the obligatory intimacy of an overcrowded train. He leaned back against the panel next to the door and drew away from the press of strangers' bodies to press her against his own body, which was not, inexplicably, a stranger's at all but seemed very familiar to her.

He must have forgiven her, because he kissed her. A stirring rather than a soothing kiss, making her want to respond with her body as well as her mouth. When he put his hand on her bottom to pull her up against him, she thought she must have dreamed of him doing it before. It was almost as if she had been teleported into somebody else's body, one that recognized and welcomed his touch. What he was doing to her should have been alarming, but instead it was thrilling, like feeling the rush through the veins after shooting up. An irresistible fate impended; there was nothing she could do but enjoy the experience.

After the doors had closed at the next station, and all the other bodies had conspired to confine their own two bodies into the corner between the panel and the door, fate in the form of Nick put his right hand up under Georgie's flared cotton skirt and down inside her panties. And that was truly the sexiest, most exciting thing that had ever happened to her: being sexually molested by her grandmother's husband on the London Underground.

She wanted to move against his hand when he stroked her, but his left hand held her hard against him, keeping her quite still. On purpose, she realized, so that the fat man behind her whose briefcase was bumping against her thigh wouldn't notice any unusual activity. She wanted to laugh, or would have if she hadn't already been in the grip of emotions that overrode laughter.

She looked up at Nick's face. He wasn't looking at her just then, he was glancing over her head at the fat man and his equally fat friend, but she could see by his expression that he was in the same state, torn between desire and hilarity. Or rather, not torn at all; it was no contest.

She recalled Matthew's warning about London Underground minutes being equal to three of the normal kind. Georgie discovered now that it was true. And also, when she came to look back on it afterwards, also just the opposite. She had never experienced such intense sexual excitement. Perversely under the circumstances, it was as if she had been isolated from all distractions, even distracting thoughts, in order to concentrate on what Nick's hand was doing to

141

her. She didn't even notice when the train stopped and started. Fate or the Devil must have arranged for the doors not to have to open on their side of the train for a long way.

Reaching the point where she thought she must either expire or explode, she made a pathetic noise between a groan and a whimper. He growled to shush her and covered her mouth with his to stifle any sound. Which was just as well, because right then everything seemed to speed up, getting out of control. As if she had been running downhill, and now her legs had gotten ahead of her somehow so that she had to run impossibly fast to keep from falling head over heels, and then suddenly she did fall. For one heart-stopping moment it felt like flying into emptiness. And that moment of taking off, of irretrievably losing control of herself, was the most unbearably poignant and piercing microsecond of pleasure since the beginning of time.

She didn't crash to earth, she floated down in blissful waves and landed on the Circle Line, still jammed up against Nick. For the third time that day he held her up to keep her from collapsing. He took his hand out from under her skirt in order to hold her up, and again that was Somebody's intervention, because at that point the train pulled into another station and this time the doors opened up right beside them.

Georgie thought she would happily have forgotten all about Luke and Matt and dinner, in order to spend the rest of the day riding around on tube trains while Nick did that to her, but he had other ideas. When they reached Moorgate station he hustled her off the train, then propped her up against a pillar while the other passengers surged past on either side of them. He was looking down at her.

No, not at her. Into her, through her, past her. Maybe looking into the blank spot inside her, the empty bit that had no name but ached at unexpected times, not just in the middle of the night but in the middle of a party, in the middle of making love, a black hole in the middle of her that said she was nothing and no one, her own personal *memento mori*. If he saw that place he wouldn't want her.

But he did want her. Whatever or whoever he thought she was.

Another train arrived and disgorged. This time they were swept along the platform with the new crowd of commuters. Georgie was being swept along by Nick. The force of his will, or his desire, was the psychological equivalent of the single-minded crowd in the station. It carried her with him, not only physically but emotionally, making her want what he wanted. Compelling desire in a man is a powerful aphrodisiac to a woman, she found to her surprise.

As they came around the corner to the turnstiles by the exit, he pulled her aside, into a doorway marked *Emergency Stairs*. She clattered down the spiral staircase after him, holding his hand and the railing all the way down because going round and round at that speed was making her dizzy. It reminded her of the dark waterless wells in *The Time Machine*, the ones that led down to the underworld of the Morlocks.

When they had reached about the depth of a diamond mine Nick stopped on a landing, so suddenly that she bumped right into him and found herself in his arms again.

This time was for real. He kissed her violently and felt her up with what would previously have been an alarmingly authoritarian urgency. He unbuttoned her blouse, in his haste almost tearing the buttons off, pushing blouse and bra aside to give his full attention to her breasts.

He was avid and rough. She felt like a maiden being sacrificed to some dubious ancient god, the sort who persuaded people to worship him by terrorizing them. Yet she did it herself, the sexual equivalent of falling down to worship him: unzipped his jeans and knelt down to take him into her mouth.

He let her do that for a minute, with evident pleasure. Then he hauled her upright against the wall. She felt his cock come into her like something she had been waiting for all her life. As if she had often imagined it as a moment of fulfilment, though she hadn't even known of his existence.

This was even more exciting than the tube train, because more purely sensual. The urgency with which he took her seemed to intensify her sensations, focusing her mind on her body . . . if she even had a mind any more. She could hear herself emitting squeaks and grunts as if she were someone else, those noises coming from another throat, perhaps a mouse upon the rack. From absolute zero an hour ago he had brought her to melting point.

She sensed a shudder in his loins, the onset of his orgasm. He uttered a sound, a word. A name, she thought.

Not hers.

It wasn't her he wanted, after all. She was standing in for someone else. Then she realized what he had said was not a woman's name, only a word, two words.

Oh kitten. Oh Christ.

In the violence of his coming he lifted her up against him, like a child, for the last few frenzied thrusts. To her vast surprise that triggered another climax in her, as if he had picked her up and thrown her over the edge of ecstasy.

When she came down this time she was in a different place.

She had remembered, at last.

15

The preacher sought to find out acceptable words;
and that which was written was words of truth.

It's hot and Georgie is bored. Hot even here inside the church, where the sunshine can't come.

Her mama has gone mad on churches since coming to the villa. Or maybe it's her grandma who is mad on churches. Every day they go somewhere and look at a boring church, at least one, sometimes two. The churches are all dark and gloomy. There's nothing to see but a few gloomy pictures on the wall, and you can't get close enough to see them properly. Sometimes there aren't even pictures.

The pictures are all the same anyway, a lot of people standing about with funny flat golden hats. Haloes, her mama calls them. Georgie has never seen anybody walking about with a halo. Her mama says they're meant to show that the people in the picture are holy.

What's holy, Georgie wants to know.

Very very good, her mama says.

Can I get a halo, says Georgie, if I'm very very extra good?

Chance would be a fine thing, her mama says, laughing.

Yesterday they went to see tombs.

Her mama said that tombs are a sort of graveyard, but they're nothing like that. Tombs are like little houses, with little streets running between them. It's spooky at first, and she holds tight to her mama's hand. But after a while, when she discovers there are no dead people in the tombs, she ventures to go exploring with Luke.

That has its hazards, because Luke keeps running ahead and hiding, so as to jump out at her and make a noise like a dead person. At least he says that's the noise dead people make. He says he's seen some dead people on TV once, when his mummy was out and his daddy let him stay up and watch television until midnight. He says midnight but Georgie doesn't quite believe him. Midnight means the middle of the night and there is no way a little kid like Luke would get to stay up as late as that.

144

She and Luke play in one of the tombs, pretending it's their house, because it's just about the right size for a play house, until her mama comes calling them. Luke tells Georgie to stay quiet so her mama won't find them. They hide in a corner of the little tomb house, scrunched up to make themselves smaller. When her mama comes near, Georgie starts to giggle and Luke puts his hand over her mouth to stop her. Her mama goes away without finding them, and then they both begin to giggle.

They are still laughing about it when Luke's daddy comes and finds them. He is really mad. He shouts at them for going off by themselves. Georgie is so scared she bursts into tears. Luke sticks his tongue out at his daddy and gets smacked for it. But he doesn't cry, not then, not till nobody but Georgie is watching.

'I hate him,' Luke tells her, wiping the tears away with his grubby fists and making his face grubby as well. 'When I grow up I'll hit him back.'

'You shouldn't stick your tongue out,' Georgie says severely. 'Grandma says it's rude.'

Luke sticks his tongue out at her.

Yesterday was a really exciting day, because after the tombs they went down a well.

Her mama says there are two staircases, one for going down and one for coming back up, like escalators, only the staircases go round and round inside the well. Her grandma doesn't go down the well, but Georgie and her mama and Luke and his daddy all do. Luke goes ahead and gets to the bottom of the well first. Georgie holds on to her mama's hand all the way down.

At the bottom there is only a pool of water, very dark. Her mama says that's the well.

'What's it for?' Georgie wants to know.

'So they could get water without going outside the city walls.'

'It looks yukky. Why did they put it down here?'

'Because the water's down here. They can't move the water level.'

'Why not?'

'It's too hard to explain.' Her mama's favourite phrase.

On the way back Georgie grows too tired to climb. Her mama picks her up and carries her. Then Luke's daddy looks back and says, 'Give her to me, Lia.'

Georgie's mama passes her to Luke's daddy. Georgie is scared of him. He's big and rough and unpredictable. Sometimes if she and Luke do things that might be naughty he just laughs. Other times he yells at them, and sometimes he even smacks Luke. Georgie is scared that one day he will smack her too. Once or twice he's threatened her with it: 'D'you want a smack too?' And she shakes her head, not daring to answer aloud. Her grandpa never ever hits her or Matty.

Luke's daddy carries her up the rest of the stairs while Luke holds her mama's hand. She can look down at him over his daddy's shoulder, and watch him climbing slowly, pretending he's not tired, till she and Luke's daddy get too far ahead to see him because of the stairs going round and round. Then she looks out the windows as they go by them.

It's kind of spooky in the well when she can't see her mama any more. She puts her arms around Luke's daddy's neck. He smells all smoky and sweaty. It's not a disagreeable smell, just different. Her grandpa doesn't smell like that.

Luke's daddy always smells smoky. Her mama says it's because of the cigarettes. Luke says he smoked one of his daddy's cigarettes when he found it sitting in the ashtray, but Georgie doesn't believe him. Luke is always telling her things she doesn't believe. Not like Matty, who is always accusing *her* of making things up, when she hasn't.

They get to the top. He doesn't put her down right away. Her mama and Luke are still climbing up the stairs, unseen.

'Where's Grandma?'

'She's over there, sugar pie. Sitting on a bench and admiring the view.'

She looks at him. He often talks to her like that. 'Why do you call me sugar pie?'

'It's in the rhyme, isn't it? Georgie Porgy pudding and pie kissed the boys and made them cry.'

'It's *girls*,' protests Georgie, outraged by this assault on tradition. 'She kissed the *girls* and made them cry.'

'No, she didn't. The boys kiss the girls and the girls kiss the boys, that's the way it works.'

He says this with the unanswerable authority of a grown-up. To win the argument one way or another she says, 'I don't want to be called pie. Or pudding,' she adds quickly, in case the idea has occurred to him.

'How about sugar, can I call you that?'

'Why?'

'Because that's what little girls are made of.'

Georgie looks down at herself doubtfully. 'I am not. I'm made of skin and bones.'

'Christ, the mind of the infant scientist. It's just a joke, okay?'
A grown-up joke, obviously, since she doesn't get it. 'Okay.'

But today there are no tombs or wells, just a boring church. She tugs at her mama's skirt. 'Mama, can I light a candle?'

She does that in every church. It's the only fun thing to do in these gloomy places.

Her mama goes over to the altar with her, and helps her put the money in and light the candle. Sometimes the candles have little bulbs that light up as soon as you put the money in, which is not so much fun. But these are real candles with a real flame.

'Who are you praying for this time?'

Her grandma told her that the candles are prayers for people, so each time Georgie insists on making it clear to God who the candle is for. She has just about run out of people by now, on account of all the churches she's been dragged into. 'Great-grandma Hardy?'

'You did her yesterday. How about Nick? You haven't given him a prayer yet.'

Nick is the name of Luke's daddy. She thinks he might not like being prayed for. She also thinks he probably doesn't need any help from God, he is already so big and strong and full of alarming confidence. But she dutifully lights her candle on his behalf.

They go downstairs. Aside from the candles, this is the only good thing about churches: sometimes they have spooky underground places, or bell towers, or stairs where you can climb up and look down on everybody else in the church, or even outside the church.

She comes up to a glass box with a light in it. There is something in the box, a man lying down and sleeping. He is all dressed up in red clothes, with a little red hat on his head. Except that when she gets close it looks more like a monkey than a man.

She presses her face against the glass. What's a monkey doing in a church?

Luke pushes in beside her. He's been up ahead with his daddy. 'Do you know what that is?'

'A monkey.'

'No.' He pokes her to indicate his scorn. 'It's a dead body.'

'It is not.'

'It is so.'

'How do you know?'

'Daddy told me.'

'Who is it, then?'

'Some fucking wop saint.'

147

'You're not supposed to say that,' Georgie says automatically. Luke has a whole fund of words he's not allowed to say. That is, his mummy, who is Georgie's grandma, tells him not to say them. He learns them from his daddy, who for some mysterious grown-up reason is allowed to say whatever he likes.

She examines the body. Despite her denial, she believes Luke. At least she believes his daddy. She's noticed before now that the things his daddy says almost always prove to be true, whereas the things that other grown-ups claim, including her grandpa and her own mama, are not necessarily so.

She can't see much of the body on account of its being all dressed up. She looks at its hands, brown and withered and bony like a very very old person's hands. Like a skeleton's hand, if a skeleton had skin. That thought makes her shiver.

She looks at the head of the body, partly hidden by the hat. At the sunken cheeks and bony nose. At the eyes.

There are no eyes.

There can't be no eyes. She's seen people asleep, even old people like her Great-grandma Hardy, and they all have round eye-shapes under their eyelids. They have eyes, only covered with skin like the rest of their body, when they're asleep. But this body has sunken hollows under its eyelids.

Which means it has no eyes.

The thought, the image, is so horrible that she starts to scream.

Her mama comes running and snatches her up. 'Georgie, what's the matter?'

Georgie continues to screech hysterically, even after she's been removed from the vicinity of the body. The whole church seems contaminated by those eyeless sockets. She can't even begin to explain.

Her mama tries unsuccessfully to muffle her shrieks against her shoulder. 'Oh God,' she says to Georgie's grandma, 'I'll have to take her out of here.'

'Give her to Nick,' says her grandma. 'He's just about to take Luke outside anyway.'

Georgie, still wailing, is handed over to Luke's daddy. He seems to be immune to the embarrassment roused in her mama and grandma by her screaming in church. He carries her out tucked in one arm, holding Luke's hand with the other.

When they come outside into the stifling sunlight and heat he sits down on the steps of the church and settles Georgie on his lap. 'Hey, sugar, you stop that now. What's the matter?'

'It's got no eyes,' she explains tearfully.

148

'What's got no eyes?'

'The dead body,' Luke tells him, man to man. 'She's scared of the dead body.'

'I am not,' Georgie says indignantly. 'Only it's got no eyes.'

'Of course it's got no eyes,' Luke's daddy says in a totally matter-of-fact way, as if they were discussing the number of wheels on a car. 'It's only a mummy.'

Georgie stares at him, stupefied. 'A mummy?'

He understands her confusion and is amused by it. 'Not somebody's ma. A real mummy. The Egyptians used to make them. They're just skeletons with skin overtop the bones.'

What Georgie gets out of this explanation is that Egyptian mummies are something made up, rather than ordinary dead bodies. The idea of artifice calms her. She lets Luke's daddy dry her eyes and blow her nose.

Then she follows Luke over to the fountain in the middle of the piazza.

Fountains are as common as churches in this country, but more interesting. Luke has already taken off his shoes and climbed in to wade around and fish for coins. Georgie copies him, remembering to hold up her dress so it won't get wet.

Her mama or her grandma would have forbidden them to get in, but both children understand very well how things work with Luke's daddy. He lets them do all sort of things that are absolute no-nos with the two women, but if they cross the invisible line with him all hell breaks loose. There's no plaintive *Luke, please don't do that* or *Georgie, do come back here*. There's either complete indifference, or else *What the fuck d'you think you're doing*, followed (if ignored) by a smack for Luke and the threat of a smack for Georgie. So they paddle happily, keeping one ear out for a bellow.

Georgie begins to be aware of other problems. In the church she vaguely wanted to pee. Now, with the sound of the fountain, her need rapidly becomes unendurable. Surrounded by water as she is, maybe no one will notice. It will be like peeing in the ocean when you're at the seaside.

Luke is standing in front of her and notices immediately. 'Georgie's peeing her pants,' he announces to the world.

Most of the people within earshot speak no English and take no notice, but Luke's daddy stops fiddling with his camera and looks at her. She stands transfixed, the stream of warm pee running down her leg into the colder fountain. In her mortification she stoops down till her bottom touches the surface of the fountain, so that no one can see what's happening, not even Luke.

149

'Jesus Christ,' says Luke's daddy. 'Get over here, Georgie.'

She doesn't want to go. She's afraid of him. She crouches lower, forgetting to hold her dress up to keep it dry.

'Jesus,' he says with more vehemence, 'get over here before I come and get you.'

She has a vision of him striding unscathed across the water, like Jesus in the book Gran Beckett gave her. She wades reluctantly over to the edge.

He snatches her out of the water and shakes her, scaring the breath out of her. 'Look at you, you stupid little tart. You're soaked. What's your mother going to say?' He plunks her down on the rim of the fountain, her legs dangling over the outer edge, and squeezes the excess water out of her dress. 'Now you just sit there until she comes out. If you move I'll kill you.'

Georgie sits with her hands folded in her lap for about thirty seconds. She doesn't mind the wet hem of the dress, she can hold that out of the way, but her wet knickers are really bothering her. She peed in them, and Luke knows it. She doesn't want to sit in the evidence of her babyish behaviour for the rest of the day.

She waits until Luke's daddy's attention is elsewhere. Then she takes her knickers off.

Luke's attention has not been elsewhere. 'Georgie's got a bare bum, Georgie's got a bare bum,' he chants, again to the mystification of everyone but his father.

His teasing backfires by drawing his daddy's attention to him. 'You get out of there, mister, and dry up as well as off. Sit down and behave yourself, or I'll give you a fat ear.'

To Georgie, Luke's daddy says, 'What d'you think you're doing, young lady?'

'They're wet,' she explains, handing her knickers to him as she would to her mama. 'I peed in them.'

He refuses to accept them. 'I know that. Jesus Christ, I don't want your soggy knickers. You keep them and give them to Lia.'

'You take them,' she insists, pushing them at him as if he were her mama or her grandma or even Matty's mummy. 'I peed in them.'

He says several forbidden words under his breath, and then he throws her knickers into the fountain.

Georgie is horrified as well as humiliated. She begins to howl.

'Shut up,' says Luke's daddy in a terrible voice. 'Stop that bloody shrieking.'

Georgie doesn't stop. She wants her knickers. She wants her mama.

Luke's daddy leans over and smacks her on her bare legs and

bottom. His hand is so big that she feels the blow right across her entire back end.

She stops crying, out of shock and astonishment, for the measure of a breath. Then the sting hits her, and she lets out a real screech.

'I want Mama, I want Mama,' she weeps when she can speak.

Luke is absolutely bug-eyed at the revelation that his own backside is not the only assailable one. Knowing that his father's bad temper is inclined to be indiscriminate, he sits down firmly on the fountain's edge and remains as still as he can, watching Georgie throw a tantrum.

It's a very successful tantrum. Luke's daddy tries to ignore her, while all the non-English-speaking people in the piazza – everyone but him, that is – turn to stare at the ill-used *Inglese* baby. But eventually he is obliged to pick her up and comfort her, before her mama comes out of the church and finds her in hysterics.

Although he's the one who hurt and frightened her, when he picks her up she throws her arms around his neck and weeps against his shoulder. He cuddles her and says he's sorry he whacked her and will she please shut up.

She goes on wailing, though with less conviction. He walks away from the fountain with her and the drama disperses, along with the audience.

Georgie is still crying. Her bottom still hurts from the smack. Luke's daddy puts his hand under the damp hem of her dress and caresses her where he hit her. That comforts her, in spite of the echoes of the sting. She hiccups in the middle of a sob.

'Come on, sugar, cut it out. Here comes your mama.'

Georgie sees her mama coming down the steps of the church. She wriggles to be let down, so she can run to her mama, the best source of comfort. But Luke's daddy doesn't put her down.

'Hold on a tick, we'd better clean you up a bit.' He takes out his shirt-tail and dries her tearful face with it.

Georgie is so amazed by this that she gives up the crying altogether. 'You're making your shirt wet.'

'No, *you're* making my shirt wet.'

He puts her down as her mama comes up to them. Her mama wants to know why Georgie's dress is wet, and, a moment later, what's become of her knickers. Luke's daddy says it's a long story which he is not going to tell. Then her mama asks where Luke is, and his daddy says Over there by the fountain. They all look over there and see Luke splashing happily in the fountain, completely naked.

His daddy says *Christ* and heads for the fountain. Georgie's grandma has appeared, and goes to the fountain as well, to rescue Luke either from the fountain or from his daddy. By the time Luke has got his clothes back on again, Georgie's mama has forgotten about the damp dress and the missing knickers, and Georgie has forgotten about the smack.

At home Georgie's mama always gives her and Matty a bath and puts them to bed, and then her grandpa reads them a story. Here at the villa Luke's daddy gives him and Georgie a bath, and then her grandma reads them a story. All her mama has to do is come and say good-night at the end.

The bath here is bigger than the one at home. That one has feet with claws on them like an animal, and Georgie has a bad dream sometimes that the bath comes prowling and sniffing at her bedroom door, trying to track her down while everyone else is asleep. The villa bath, on the other hand, has no legs at all. It's a funny shape so as to fit into a corner of the bathroom. The bathroom is very large and has red tiles on the floor.

Bath time with Luke's daddy is more fun than with her mama, because he doesn't mind if Luke and Georgie get water on the floor, or even on him, since he's only wearing a pair of old shorts. He's not so good when it comes to scrubbing up. He calls it hosing them down. He tends to get soap in their eyes and is not very sympathetic about the consequences. Georgie has learned to keep her eyes tightly shut while he's washing her.

They climb out of the bath to let him dry them off. He does this with a cigarette between his lips, squinting as if he's concentrating but really because of the smoke.

There's a big mirror on the wall opposite the bath. Georgie looks at herself and Luke, both facing the mirror, and at Luke's daddy who is kneeling behind them, briskly towelling Luke's hair and ignoring his complaints.

'Why don't girls have a penis?'

She has asked this before of various people, when the occasion brings the question to her mind, but she's never had a satisfactory answer. Her mama says it's because girls can have babies when they grow up, but Georgie can't see any connection between the ability to have babies and the possession of such an entertaining organ. You can aim it when you pee. Luke peed on her the other day and got a smack from his daddy for it, but afterwards Georgie heard Luke's daddy telling her grandma about it and they were both laughing. Also you can make it stand up instead of hanging down. Matty did that in the bath once and Georgie was amazed, but her mama was not amused. Her mama told Matty it was rude to do that in front of other people. Georgie was therefore unsurprised when Luke did it in the wading pool here at the villa, because she has long since observed that if anything has been denounced as rude, Luke can be relied upon to do it.

Luke's daddy isn't paying any attention to her. He's telling Luke to go and get into his pyjamas and pick out the book he wants, and tell his mum – that's Georgie's grandma – that he's ready for bed. He opens the door to let Luke out and closes it again. 'What'd you say, sugar?'

Georgie repeats her question.

He sticks the cigarette back in his mouth and picks up a dry towel. He hunkers down in front of her, wraps her in the towel and starts to rub her all over. 'You've got a magic button instead.' He's talking out of the side of his mouth, on account of the cigarette.

'Where?'

'Down there.'

Georgie puts her hands on his shoulders to keep herself upright. He is a lot more vigorous than her mama when it comes to drying. 'How come I can't see it?'

'Because it's so small.'

This is the first that Georgie has ever heard of any mysterious magic button and she doesn't know if she believes him. But she also doesn't know if it's polite to say so. Her grandma said it was rude to call someone a liar, when Luke called Georgie a liar yesterday. She looks up into Luke's daddy's face to see if she can tell if he's teasing her. 'Is that true?'

'Sure.' He stops drying her and takes the cigarette out of his mouth. 'You've got lots of buttons.'

'Only one.' She looks down at her naval, as if to reassure herself it's still there.

'No, look.' He touches the tip of her nose with the tip of his finger, with the hand that isn't holding the cigarette. 'You've got a button nose, for starters. And two more buttons here.' He presses each of her nipples with his fingertip, like ringing a door bell. 'And here's another one.' He pokes her tummy button, which makes her giggle. 'And one more down here.' He touches her down at the very bottom of her tummy.

The touch makes her feel sort of itchy inside. She giggles again and pushes his hand away. She backs off from him, with the towel still draped over her shoulders like the Indian chief in one of her picture books. 'Mama says it's rude to touch yourself there in front of other people.'

'I guess she's right. But it's okay when you're in private.'

153

She comes closer again, curious. She ventures into the V-shaped space between his knees. 'Are we in private?'

He's smiling, as if she has said something funny. 'We sure are, sweetheart.'

She comes closer still. 'Why is it magic?'

'D'you want me to show you?'

She doesn't answer. She's sort of scared of him. She never knows what he's going to do. He does and says all sort of things that her grandpa never would. But all men are sort of scary. They're big and hairy, with deep voices. They get to do things that other people don't.

Luke's daddy puts his arm around her, outside the towel, the arm with the hand that has the cigarette. She likes that. She puts her arms around his neck and leans against him. His chest feels furry where it rubs against her skin, tickling her pleasantly. He puts his hand down to the bottom of her tummy again. That tickles, too, in a different way.

This time she doesn't push him away.

Her heart is thumping hard and fast. She's breathing as fast as her heartbeat, as if she was scared of something. Scared of what he's doing, maybe.

She sits down, falls down, into his lap. Her legs won't work. She thinks she must have peed herself. She's afraid and ashamed.

She starts to cry.

He has both his arms around her now. 'Hey, sugar, don't cry.'

'You made me pee,' she sobs.

'No, I didn't. You're all right, you didn't pee.'

He's right, she realizes. She hasn't peed herself. But she's still scared of whatever it was that happened.

He wraps her up in the towel again, and kisses her and cuddles her and talks to her to take away the scary feeling. She likes that. She likes it much better than what he did before. She's not scared of him now.

She wishes she had a daddy. She's never been able to understand how her grandpa can be Matty's daddy but not hers. Other children have daddies, even if they've gone away, or live somewhere else.

Maybe her grandpa just doesn't want to be her daddy.

He doesn't hug or kiss her. She can hug and kiss him when he's carrying her or she is sitting on his lap, but he never seems to do it to her. It's not on account of him not being her daddy, because he doesn't do it to Matty either. And although he reads to her and Matty, he never talks to her like Luke's daddy is doing now, talking like her mama does, not talking about anything really, just talking to make Georgie feel good.

154

Luke's daddy doesn't sound or smell or feel like her mama or her grandpa. He sounds smoky and husky. He smells all sunny and salty. His chest and arms and legs feel hard and furry, like a pony she once patted at the zoo.

She wishes she had a daddy.

She wishes Luke's daddy was her daddy.

16

My iniquities have taken hold upon me.

The memory was relived rather than recalled, yet it happened in an instant, a literal flashback. Like being dunked in a cup of yesterday.

When Georgie reached the flat, the rags and tatters of that experience were still hanging about her like shattered cobwebs, and she was shattered too. By the import and intensity of what she had remembered. By the violence and primitive physicality of the encounter with Nick on the stairs.

Primitive was not too strong a word, now that she thought of it. She hadn't realized that sex could even get that basic. As if she had lost her identity and individuality, even her humanity, and become merely a female penetrated by a male. A sort of living definition of the sex act.

Afterwards they had had to prop each other up: not lovers but survivors of some near-fatality.

Nick had cradled and caressed her and muttered breathless husky words into her hair, though half of what he said was only talking to himself. Jesus, he said, what a fucking stupid thing to do. I must be fucking crazy, he said. Christ, I'm sorry, sugar, he said. I shouldn't have done that to you, he said, I didn't mean to screw you. He said.

Georgie was still so stricken by the remembrance of things past that she thought at first he meant what he had done long ago. But he was right either way. He shouldn't have done it, then or now. She wanted to ask him why he had, but when she opened her mouth to speak, her voice dissolved in tears.

As in the pub, he didn't try to discourage her, he just held her and let her cry, literally on his shoulder. The least he could do was console her, she thought bitterly, since it was all his fault. She didn't try to get away from him, any more than she had at the age of three when he had spanked her and then soothed her. That comfort was too necessary to her.

'What do you mean, you didn't mean to screw me?' she demanded, still weeping. 'You did it in a fit of absent-mindedness?' She meant it sarcastically, but maybe it was true. Absence of mind was precisely what she had experienced while he was doing it.

'No, not that. Maybe just the opposite.'

What was the opposite of a fit of absent-mindedness? But she knew the answer to that. A spell of remembering.

'Matty, I need a drink.'

'You look like you've already had one. At least one.'

Georgie peered at her flushed face in the mirror by the door. 'Well, I have, but I need another one.'

She went into the kitchen and fixed herself a large vodka and tonic. Matthew followed her. 'What happened?'

'Nothing,' she said automatically.

'He wasn't there again today?'

'Who?'

'The little man who wasn't there. Your mysterious father. Isn't that who you went to see?'

'Oh, yeah.' The encounter with the man who was not her father seemed so long ago she could hardly remember it. She had lived through several harrowing years since then, it seemed. She sank down on to the sofa and swallowed half her drink at one go. 'No, he was there.'

'And?'

'And he's not my father.' She added hastily, 'I don't think you'd better tell your parents that. It won't do my mother's stock with your father any good.'

'Did he suggest any alternative suspects?'

'Nope. He didn't have a clue.'

'So the trail's gone cold. You don't sound terribly cut up about it.'

Georgie shrugged. 'I guess I'll just have to ask my mother.' She held up her glass, empty except for the unmelted ice. 'Matt, can you be a honey and fix me seconds?'

'What about this dinner you're supposed to be cooking?'

'I'll get around to that, but first I need stiffening. And don't you go all holy on me. You've gotten plastered just about every night while I've been here.'

'But only after dinner.'

He took the glass away to deal with her drink. She leaned her head against the back of the sofa and closed her eyes. God, she had really messed things up. She had let Luke's father screw her. Not just *let* him: she had really *wanted* him to do it. Had desperately

156

wanted her grandmother's husband, her mother's stepfather, her lover's father, to stick his prick into her. As he had said of himself afterwards, she must have been fucking crazy.

Well, at least there was no mystery about how he had managed to seduce her so easily. It was the second time around.

How could anyone seduce a three-year-old, for God's sake?

Of course, according to Freudian theory small children were simply seething with violent sexual passions, not to mention murderous inclinations, all of which eventually got firmly repressed, internally and externally, in the interests of civilization and its discontents. She had always thought that was so much hooey, but now . . . maybe not. Now she could recall very vividly having distinctly, specifically, intensely sexual feelings within a week of her third birthday. And after all, babies played with themselves, didn't they? Adults were constantly telling them to cut it out. So why else would they persistently do it, unless it made them feel good?

The funny thing was that, now she had had a little time to reflect, she didn't feel totally disgusted with Nick. She might have if it had been a tale told of someone else, some abstract infant innocence. Then she might have denounced him as a pervert and a paedophile. But all he had done was . . . well, just what she had innocently invited him to do. It wasn't a terribly wise or righteous or mature way to behave, but perhaps it wasn't, under the circumstances, totally wicked either. He hadn't frightened or hurt her, or forced her to do something she didn't want to do. On the contrary, he had cuddled her and made her feel good.

And anyway she knew from her anthropological studies that in plenty of cultures where parents didn't have the advantage of plastic pacifiers, they routinely addressed their attentions to the bottom end rather than the top end to get the baby to shut up and go to sleep. Nobody in those places called it child abuse, or indeed thought anything of it. Quite likely there were subcultures in the so-called civilized world where the same methods were employed. It would certainly go unremarked, for instance, in those benighted pockets of rural poverty where, when a woman died or disappeared, the eldest daughter was expected to take her mother's place, not omitting the father's bed.

But even as she recited these facts in her head, she could feel her body going rigid with shock and revulsion. She hadn't been brought up like that. She had always regarded her body as her own domain, to bestow or withhold as she chose. Though there were many women, maybe most of the women in the world, who never enjoyed that luxury.

She crossed her legs and wrapped her arms around herself. The recollection of her earliest sexual encounter roused a feeling of shame in her almost as intensely as the knowledge of what she had done just that afternoon. But at the time, at the age of three, she knew she had felt no shame at all.

And why should she? Whoever had done wrong, it wasn't the little girl who had been Georgie. Yet now, looking back, she found herself feeling ashamed. Of her own three-year-old feelings, rather than what Nick had done to her three-year-old self.

Someone, something, had afterwards attached a bad name and bad emotional responses to those events, and it was that later reaction she was feeling now. Nothing good or bad but thinking makes it so. And it seemed to her now that having at some point been made to feel ashamed for what had happened then was the worst thing of all, far more damaging than anything Nick had done.

Why had he done it? Did it mean that her grandmother's husband was a pervert?

He had shown her that very afternoon, in the most graphic and incontrovertible way, that little girls were not the biggest item on his sexual agenda.

At three she wouldn't have known about or noticed any signs of arousal in a grown man. She couldn't recall any now, thinking back. His whole attitude had been curiously matter-of-fact, as if what he was doing was perfectly normal.

Well, Matthew seemed to think that letting strangers go down on him was a perfectly normal way to behave. Some men regarded sex with prostitutes as an ordinary part of life. She knew from her own experience and observation that an astounding, absolutely astronomical number of men were prepared to go to bed with almost any willing female. And lots of them didn't care if she was willing or not. Others didn't even demand that the female in question be human; a ewe or a chicken would do, if nothing better offered. Not to mention the men who went into dark rooms, not caring who or what did what to whom.

All of these behaviours were equally bizarre as far as Georgie was concerned. It was even possible that most men were perverts in one way or another, at least from a woman's point of view. She couldn't make sense of any of them, and found it too disturbing even to try.

In spite of the ice, the second vodka warmed her up again. The only trouble now was that she couldn't seem to get up. When she did manage to stand up, she had to sit down again before she fell down.

'Oh, Matty, I think I'm drunk.'

'I warned you. What about dinner?'

158

'Come and help me get it ready.' She struggled to push herself up again. 'But first help me get up.'

He hauled her to her feet. She swayed and clutched his arm.

'I feel sick.'

'I'm not surprised. You're pissed.'

'I mean really sick. I need the bathroom.'

She staggered out of the room, bumping from one piece of furniture to the next. She made it to the bathroom, remembering to shut the door, and threw up in the toilet. She came out looking and feeling green.

'I can't make dinner. I can't face food.'

'Georgie, what the hell have you been doing all day? Drowning your sorrows when you discovered that you're fatherless again?'

'Something like that. I've got to lie down.'

She went into the bedroom and lay down on the bed. The room reeled around her. She saw Matthew's face looking down at her. It merged with her memory, once lost and now so clear, of his face at three years of age. He had been a beautiful child and was now a beautiful young man. Ditto Luke.

Luke. She had done something dreadful to Luke. She tried to recall what it was. When she remembered, she was overcome with shame. 'Oh, Matty, I've done the most unforget – no, unforgivable thing.'

'What have you done, you wicked woman?'

'I am wicked.' She rolled over and buried her face in the pillow. She had to wait until the room stopped rolling and she was quite sure she wasn't going to be sick again. Then she whispered into the pillow. 'Luke's daddy made love to me.'

'Jesus.' Matthew sat down quite heavily on the bed beside her. 'That's pretty unforgivable all right. On both sides and several counts.'

'Don't bounce the bed, I'm going to be sick.'

'Then you'd better get back into the loo.'

'I'll be all right if you don't bounce around.' She hugged the pillow and swallowed several times and felt the sweat break out all over her. 'Oh God, I feel so rotten.'

'You deserve to feel rotten. You are rotten.'

'Don't yell at me, you'll make me cry.' She was crying anyway. 'What am I going to do? I can't even look at Luke right now.'

The door bell rang. 'That's likely him,' Matthew said. 'I'll tell him you're sick and get him out of here. You close your eyes and play dead.'

'Oh Matt, you are good.'

159

'I know. Shut up and keep still.'

She could hear Luke's voice in the living-room. She wanted him to come in and comfort her. Comfort her for having sinned against him. She wanted to confess and be absolved, but she could never never tell him.

Yesterday she had been so happy, it seemed in retrospect. Yesterday she was going to meet her father, she was going to live with Luke. Now she had no father, and if Luke ever found out what she had done she would have no Luke either.

She heard their voices at the bedroom door. They must have been looking in on her.

'She'll be okay in the morning,' Matthew said. 'Let's go out and get something to eat.'

They went away. She slept, and woke and wept a while, and went to sleep again.

Georgie is in love with Luke's daddy.

When they all go out anywhere, she insists on holding his hand. If anyone is going to carry her, it has to be him. She sits on his lap whenever possible. Whenever he'll let her, that is. Sometimes he calls her a persistent little cat and sets her down again and tells her to go away.

She hears her mama say to her grandma, 'I think Georgie's got a crush on Nick,' in a pleased and amused sort of way. And her grandma says, also pleased and amused, 'Well, little girls do that, don't they? They always prefer the men.'

Georgie feels absurdly pleased with herself, and rather superior, the way people with secrets always do.

The secret is what Luke's daddy did. Tickling her button or whatever it was. He didn't say it was a secret or tell her not to tell anyone, but all the same she isn't going to tell. That makes it special, something secret between them. Only to be done in private, he said. And he can't have ever done it to Luke, because Luke doesn't have a magic button.

After their bath the next night, he dries her first instead of Luke and sends her off for pyjamas and a book. She is horribly disappointed that he didn't want her to stay so he could cuddle her.

When her mama comes into the bedroom to say good-night, after her grandma has read them a story, Georgie makes her promise to send Luke's daddy up to say good-night again.

When he comes up he has changed out of the old pair of shorts he had on to bathe them. He's wearing jeans and a shirt. He sits down on Georgie's bed and she holds her arms up to him. He bends down

160

so she can put her arms around his neck, and he puts his arms around her and she feels absolutely blissful.

She whispers in his ear. 'I love you.'

'I love you too, sugar.'

'Can you be my daddy?'

He unhooks her arms from his neck and sits up. She thinks she must have annoyed him by asking, but he is laughing. 'The problem isn't a shortage of daddies, it's too many fucking mummies,' he says, and he goes away, still laughing.

Luke has overheard the exchange. 'He can't be your daddy,' he hisses at Georgie. 'You haven't even got a daddy, and anyway you don't live with us.'

'I do now.'

'But you won't when we go home.' He adds the final clinching rejection: 'There's no room for you at our house.'

He falls asleep right away after that. But Georgie stays awake for a long while and cries.

17

Who can understand his errors?

After fourteen hours of troubled sleep, Georgie woke up feeling fine.

She was surprised to discover Luke asleep beside her, sprawled fully clothed on top of the comforter. He refused to wake when she shook him.

She went into the living-room and there was Matthew sleeping on the sofa with the same haphazard profundity. They must have come home too late and too drunk for Luke to do anything but crash for the night. Matthew had let him sleep on the bed because Georgie was in it. Gentlemen all.

She brewed coffee and eventually managed to rouse them. They seemed to be suffering from the hangover that she had somehow avoided.

'Did you people have a good time last night? You sure look like you did.'

Luke frowned, evidently trying to recall what a good time might be and whether or not he had had one. 'I guess so. We just went downstairs to the pub.'

'You spent the whole evening there?'

'Well, we got into an argument about something and it went on for a while. Till closing time, I think. And then we just staggered up here to continue the argument. You were still out for the count.'

'What was the big argument about?'

Luke glanced at Matthew for assistance. Matthew shrugged, rather painfully, to disclaim any recollection. 'Can't remember now,' Luke confessed.

Georgie cooked a proper breakfast, scrambled eggs on toast, and made her two semi-uncles eat it. Her father – her non-father, Tom Payne the doctor – maintained that a square meal was the best remedy for a hangover, and she had never come across any better nostrum herself. Her patients protested and complained of nausea and lack of appetite, but she was pleased to observe that they looked much less pale by the time they had obediently cleared their plates and started working on a final cup of coffee.

'You guys should get a job,' Georgie said severely. At the moment they looked pretty well unemployable: Luke's hair and clothing still rumpled the way he had slept, Matthew's eyes vaguely unfocused as if the alcohol had not completely worked its way through his system. 'It's not good for your soul, having nothing to do all day.'

'I have a job,' Luke protested. 'I'm an artist.'

'That's why you were up and whistling at your work by nine o'clock this morning, I suppose. My father says that people whose jobs don't oblige them to get out of bed in good time every day are more prone to depressive illness and substance abuse.'

The breakfast had not yet worked its way through Matthew's system either, apparently. 'Which father would this be?'

Georgie looked at him in pained surprise, as if her own dog had just bitten her. 'I mean my stepfather. My mother's husband. You know what I mean, Matty.'

Luke roused himself. 'That reminds me, what happened yesterday? You were going to confront your onlie begetter, as I recall, but Matt told me you came back pissed as a newt.'

'Drunk as a skunk,' Georgie amended, 'and anyway I wasn't. I just got sick, that's all.'

'Well, it sounds to me like you should get a job too. What happened with your father hunt?'

'He took me to the pub and we had a long chat.'

'You mean he got you drunk. Didn't Matt's mother say he'd done well for himself? Maybe you could try blackmailing him.'

'I can't. He denied everything.'

'Well, he would, wouldn't he?'

162

'Yes, but I believe him. He said my mother had told him he wasn't my father.'

Georgie reflected that the history of her life now appeared to be nothing but a succession of false fathers, asserted or adopted or assumed. Maybe she would never find the real one. And maybe it didn't matter after all. Right now the truth seemed to her less important than the lies.

Her mother's lies.

Luke was staring at her. 'So who is your father?'

Georgie shrugged. 'Who knows?'

'You don't sound much bothered about it. I thought you were all upset. Having an identity crisis or something.'

'I'll have to postpone all that until I see my mother. For now I seem to have hit a dead end.'

She kept her voice deliberately matter-of-fact. There was no point throwing wobblies now. There was no point even thinking about it, because there didn't seem to be anything more she could do. And to brood on it was only to throw herself down that well of emptiness from which she had been rescued yesterday by Nick.

If you could call it a rescue. A distraction, more like. Taking her mind off her original concerns by creating other problems for her. She had already been feeling guilty about what had happened with Matthew – even though she still didn't see how she could have done anything different, and even though that was before Luke had become her lover. But now she had stupidly entangled herself in another and far more dangerous situation. If Luke ever found out about Matthew he would be apoplectic. If he ever found out about Nick he would be – well, apocalyptic.

She could say she had been drunk.

But she hadn't been, not really, not then. She had enjoyed and remembered every minute of it. Enjoyed a pleasure that she hadn't yet had with Luke, or anyone else. She had thought she had come for the first time ever, and then discovered it wasn't the first time. That discovery was another black hole she didn't want to let herself fall into. Mentally she edged around those ancient memories, so fresh from having only just been unearthed. She wasn't going to think about that either.

She had to get things settled with Nick. Urgently. Just in case . . .

She refused to think about in case of what.

She went down to Chelsea with Luke. They did some browsing in boutiques. Georgie bought an enormous black straw hat. It looked quite stunning with her pale blonde hair, she thought, and Luke obligingly agreed with her. She had lots of money, because she had come over expecting to have to pay for accommodation and instead she was staying for free in her grandfather's flat.

Then they went to Luke's house and upstairs to Luke's room and made love on Luke's bed. She had been hoping she would come, if only to make herself feel less guilty and unfaithful, but it didn't happen. Maybe because she had been worrying about it.

They went downstairs and had a snack, went back upstairs and screwed again. It was very nice and exciting but nothing happened like what had happened with Nick. Maybe she should take Luke for a ride on the Circle Line and see if that did the trick.

Instead she took him grocery shopping. There was no proper food in the house, she knew from her previous stint as cook. The consequence, she supposed, of two men living womanless, at least for domestic purposes. It was all very well to say they should have been able to fend for themselves but it was clear that her grand-mother had arranged all that sort of thing for them, and neither of them had gotten around to making the appropriate adjustments. Anyway, they did fend for themselves, Luke pointed out: if he got hungry he went out and found somewhere to eat, and his father did the same thing. Man the hunter in an urban context.

'But it's not good for you to be eating out all the time,' said Georgie the doctor's daughter. Stepdaughter.

'Is that why we're going to move in together, so you can improve my diet?'

'Plenty of room for improvement there. Chip butties indeed.' She piled salad fixings into the trolley, lettuce, radishes, green onions, tomatoes, peppers, cucumber, celery. The stuff of life as she knew it. 'Do you think your father will get married again?'

'I'd be very surprised if he did. Why should he, when he has it thrown at him every time he turns around?'

'Don't be crude.' Georgie concentrated on selecting the smallest, freshest mushrooms, just in case she might be blushing. 'Marriage isn't only about sex. And you don't get married for that anyway, not nowadays. You don't need to. People marry because, well . . .'

She trailed off, thinking about babies. She dropped the mushrooms into the trolley Luke was steering, put her hands over his and looked up into his face. 'Do you want to marry me?'

'Since I know that's a legal impossibility, I can safely say yes.'

He was smiling when he said that. Fortunately. 'Why?'

He stopped smiling. He brought his face down to hers so that no one could overhear, although no one was near. She could feel his

164

breath on her lips when he spoke. 'Because you belong to me, and I'd like a piece of paper that says so.'

She felt an atavistic thrill. Modern independent educated career-minded woman seeks caveman to haul her home by the hair. And Luke was big enough and strong enough to do it. 'Well, then, see? There *are* other reasons.'

'Maybe so, but they don't apply to my old man. He hasn't got an emotional bone in his body. And if he wants a housekeeper or a cook or a social secretary he can buy one. Come to that, he can buy a woman for his bed.'

'But he married your mother, didn't he?'

He smiled again, sourly. 'He wasn't rich in those days.'

'Why are you so keen to make your father out to be an awful person?'

'Why are you so keen to make him out to be a nice one? I know him better than you do.'

Up to a point, thought Georgie. But she couldn't look at Luke when she thought it.

They were in the middle of making dinner – at least Georgie was making dinner, while Luke provided moral support and companionship (two more reasons for marrying, she thought) – when Nick came home.

Luke muttered something profane when he heard the front door. 'I hope you're not going to have to feed him.'

'I don't mind.'

'But I bloody well do.'

'Well, why don't I go and find out?'

Nick was just starting up the stairs when Georgie came into the hall. He stopped and smiled when he saw her. He was wearing the faded jeans and well-worn shirt that seemed to be his working uniform. The sight of that shirt unsettled her. She remembered how it felt – under her fingertips, against her bare breasts. Forbidden knowledge.

Nick gave no sign of being similarly disconcerted by the sight of her. 'Have you decided to take the job, then?'

'What job?'

'I offered you a job as my cook, remember? That smells great, whatever it is.'

She gripped one of the banister rails. 'Are you home for dinner?'

'No, I'm just going upstairs to have a shower and get changed to go out again. Unless you want to make me a better offer . . .?'

Luke was right, his father was a dreadful man. 'Cut that out,' she told him in a soft but steel-edged tone. 'Luke's in the kitchen.'

165

'I imagined he might be.' But he came down and leaned over the newel post to speak more quietly. 'How're you feeling, sugar?'

That was not an idle enquiry but a specific question about several things, she understood. About her father (or absence thereof), about her distress yesterday, about what had happened between them. How was she feeling about all of that? She didn't know because she had refused to think about it.

'I have to talk to you,' she whispered.

'I've got time for a drink before I go.' He straightened. 'I'll see you in a few minutes.'

She was not surprised to find Luke standing in the doorway behind her, morosely watching his father go upstairs. 'Does that mean he won't be taking advantage of your kind offer?'

He's already done that, she thought. Even when I didn't actually offer.

She poured a glass of wine for herself and Luke and took the glasses out into the garden. Nick emerged in a quarter of an hour, all tidied up and wearing rather a lot of money on his back. He looked amazingly good for a middle-aged man.

Well, she already knew how good he looked. Good enough to take to bed.

She wondered who he was going out with tonight, and felt a pang of jealousy, then a surge of self-disgust both for wondering and for the jealousy. And then she wondered if he would have stood her up, whoever she was, if Georgie had offered to go out with him instead.

She knew why she was doing that. She told herself why. Because long ago when she was a very little girl looking for a daddy he had captured her infant imagination, both emotional and erotic. That pathetically fatherless little girl was still alive inside her, wanting him to love her. And even at three she had understood, with the wisdom of proverbial babes and sucklings, that the only way he could love was through the body.

Was that why he had screwed her in the Morlock well? Had he just been fucking her, or was he maybe actually making love to her?

Well, what difference did it make? He really was a truly dreadful man, she decided. Just being around him was enough to corrupt her. She perched on the arm of Luke's chair and stayed there.

Nick finished his whisky and said he had to be going. As he turned to go inside the house, Luke asked in a sarcastic way, 'Will you be coming home tonight?'

Nick glanced back with a look to match his son's tone of voice. 'I don't know. How about you?' His eyes flicked towards Georgie. 'No, you're sleeping here tonight, aren't you?'

166

Georgie waited till he had gone in. 'I told you he knows.' He knew because she had told him, if for no other reason, but she couldn't say that.

'So what? He doesn't care. He just can't resist a chance to behave like a bastard.'

'I have to go and check on dinner. Give me your glass, I'll fill it up for you.'

'Better still, bring the bottle out.'

Nick had just opened the front door, on his way out, when Georgie caught up with him. Safest in the open, she decided. She slipped out in front of him, through the partly open door.

He followed her out and shut it. The evening sun flooded down the street, filling the air between the two rows of high houses with a golden-red light. Georgie felt as if she had stepped into the heart of a flame.

She turned to face him. 'You were right, we shouldn't have done that.'

'Done what?'

'Yesterday.'

'Why not?'

She could have shaken him, and not for the first time. He was only doing that to make her spell it out. 'Because of Luke.'

'Luke didn't stop you yesterday.'

'Well, I was drunk. And upset. You knew I was. You took advantage of me.' Just like he had done before. All those years before.

He looked at her with cool gravity. 'It's easy to do that on a rush hour train.'

'You know what I mean,' she said angrily.

'I know exactly what you mean, sugar. What I mean is that you're a liar.'

She didn't know how to respond to that. *I am not* didn't have much force or conviction. *I hate you* was not only irrelevant but might even convey the opposite meaning to him. 'If you're trying to tell me I'm not in love with Luke – '

He cut her off brusquely. 'I'm not trying to tell you anything about Luke. I don't know a fucking thing about your relationship with him. If you want to screw him, go ahead. Just don't tell me lies about yesterday.'

What was the truth about yesterday? When he went down the steps, she ran after him and caught his arm. He kept on walking.

'Nick.' She skipped alongside him, trying to sound matter-of-fact, to keep the pleading note out of her voice, but not quite succeeding. 'You won't say anything, will you?'

She saw with relief and some embarrassment that he was amused. 'I told you I don't give away other people's secrets.'

Which was just as well, since he seemed to hold a lot of them. 'But it's your secret too.' She tried without the slightest success to drag him to a halt. 'You said you shouldn't have done it. Why did you say that, if it wasn't because of Luke?'

He did stop then. He looked at her in a funny way, almost as if he was thinking of something else entirely. And what he said surprised her, especially coming from him. 'Your mother wouldn't like it much, would she?'

Did that mean he really was ashamed of what he had done? That was even more surprising. 'Then why did you do it?'

He was still looking at her, but not seeming to see her at all: fixing her with a wide blind blue-eyed stare. Because of the sun, maybe, shining in his eyes. Then he turned away, muttering something she didn't catch.

She grabbed his arm. 'What did you say?'

He shook her off, took himself out of her reach. 'You've got her face, haven't you?'

She stood in the flood of sunlight, watching him go, feeling like her own ghost. Her grandfather had said it too. Said she looked like Emma.

All that time she had been responding to him as if she were still a three-year-old looking for a daddy, and he had been seeing his dead wife in her face. *I didn't mean to screw you.* He hadn't really been screwing her at all. She was only a stand-in.

She went back up the steps, into the house. She met Luke coming down the stairs with a scowl. 'Where the hell have you been, Georgie? I called you and called you and you didn't answer.'

'I was just outside. Saying goodbye to your dad.'

He stopped on the bottom stair. The way he was looking at her made her feel very uncomfortable. 'Saying goodbye or kissing goodbye?'

'Nothing like that, for heaven's sake,' she protested, with the indignation of a bad conscience and the righteousness of the reformed sinner. 'Why are you talking like that? Who do you think I am? What do you think he is?'

'I don't have to think about it, I know exactly what you both are. You're female, and he's completely unscrupulous.'

'And you're paranoid.'

She began to walk away, to go back to the kitchen, but he caught her arm. When she had caught Nick's arm in the street, he had kept on walking and she had had to scramble after, in order to say what she wanted to say. When Luke caught her arm now, he held her

168

pinioned and immovable. But the look on his face would have transfixed her in any case. He looked quite murderous. Maybe he really did hate his father, as he had declared that summer long ago.

'Listen to me, Georgie. Just bloody well keep away from him. Six feet away at a minimum. He's poison.'

'Are you giving me orders?'

'I'm giving you a warning.' He had both her arms in a painful grip. Maybe he just didn't know his own strength. Or maybe he did. He dragged her up against him. 'And here's another one. Remember I told you about all those slags who used to follow me home in the hopes of meeting him? Well, if you turn out to be one of them I'll kill you.'

18

Thou knowest that I am not wicked.

'How did you get on with Charlie?'

Althea had decided to bring up the subject at the dinner table on Saturday evening, for reasons that Georgie couldn't guess at. Maybe she thought the whole business of Georgie's mysterious father was just an Interesting Experience, like having shared one's train compartment with a harmless lunatic, and therefore suitable for dinner-table diversions. Maybe she thought everybody there was agog to hear the news. Or maybe she was just curious about Charlie, an old acquaintance she hadn't seen for twenty years.

Georgie glanced at her grandfather's face. Largely impassive, but with a faint hint in the tilt of the eyebrows and the set of the mouth that he was heroically ignoring some minor unpleasantness. A dead mouse on the doormat, for instance, gift of the equally unwanted cat. She knew he didn't want to hear about Charlie. He had disapproved of Charlie as his daughter's boyfriend, and even more as the father of his daughter's child. But the one thing that he would disapprove of still more vehemently than that, was the news that Charlie was not the father of the said child. So Georgie wasn't going to give him that news.

She said cautiously, 'We had a long talk.'

'Tell us,' Althea encouraged. Demanded, more like.

This time it was Matthew that Georgie's eyes lighted on. He was looking both sympathetic and amused, and very slightly mischievous. She would have to try to say something true, without giving

169

the game away. 'Well, he recognized me as soon as he saw me. He said I look like my mother. He asked about her. He was very nice.'

She paused, thinking hard, keeping an eye out for Matthew's reaction. 'But that's all dead and buried, isn't it? He's got a family. There didn't seem any point in . . . well, at the end he just sort of shook hands and said good luck and goodbye.'

The faint cloud lifted from her grandfather's face. The mouse had been removed from the doormat. 'That sounds like the most sensible thing,' he said briskly. 'As you say, there's really no point in raking up the past.'

He could talk like that, thought Georgie, because the missing piece in his own past had been partly restored when she turned up on his doorstep. But her past was proving to be far more complex and threatening than she had ever imagined when she first set out from her cosy Canadian family nest, her own personal fool's paradise. Would it have been better not to have come looking? To have left her mother's secrets undisturbed, and never to have discovered that her mother had lied to her?

There wasn't any answer to that. You could never know about what hadn't happened. Or was there some inherent virtue in truth, that gave it priority above any other consideration?

The truth shall make you free, it was written somewhere. If freedom was what you wanted. It didn't say the truth would make you happy. But the truth had to be known to someone, her mother or father or grandmother or even Nick, and if they knew the truth and she did not, she would be for ever to them as a child to a grown-up: *She doesn't know, it's better for her not to know.* So the truth really did make you free. It made you equal and adult and left you to make what you would or could of the cold hard world. Truth was good but it wasn't nice. Scary was what it was.

After dinner she went for a walk with Matthew, to enjoy the evening. When the daylight faded it was normally not possible to walk in the countryside, because the night, to a city-dweller's surprise and consternation, was so very uncompromisingly *dark*. But here, if there was a moon – and there was, a first-quarter moon already going down in the west – you could walk along the lane, because the white chalk soil gleamed in the moonlight to show you the way, like a demonstration of divine providence.

'How do you go about getting a job in this country?'

'Don't ask me, I've never had one.'

'What, never?' This struck Georgie as somehow deeply immoral, that somebody could reach the age of twenty-one without ever having had to work for pay. 'It's high time you got one, then.'

170

'So you've already said. Or is this a sponsored message from my father?'

'If he thinks you should get a job, he's absolutely right. But I wasn't taking a dig at you, I was asking for information. What sort of papers do you need?'

'Just a National Insurance number, I think. You'd better get one of those anyway, you need it to go on the dole.'

'I'm not eligible for that, surely?'

'Yeah, you are. You just take your birth certificate to a DSS office and ask for a National Insurance number, and then you can sign on.'

'But don't I have to have worked here for a while, or at least lived here for a while?'

'Nope. As soon as you get off the plane you can go and demand your rights. You're eligible for cash benefits and they're supposed to find you a place to live.'

'That's crazy.'

'Well, they can't leave people to starve or freeze to death, can they? This is at least nominally a civilized country.'

'What about all the beggars? London is full of them. So is Brighton, for that matter.'

'They get the same money I do. Or more, maybe. Theoretically they're entitled to a place to live, and they could sleep in a hostel if they wanted, but a lot of them don't. Either they get thrown out because they're drunk or deranged, or else they can't stand the hostels because everyone in there is drunk or deranged. Anyway, if you want a permanent home you pretty well have to get pregnant.'

Georgie stopped walking. 'You mean if I was pregnant they'd find me a place to live right away?'

'Yeah, they probably would, but you wouldn't like it. It'd likely be on the tenth floor of some grotty high-rise slum.' Matthew had walked ahead when she stopped, and now turned to look back at her, whatever he could see of her in the darkness. 'Why, are you going to get yourself knocked up?'

'I was just wondering, that's all. Luke and I have to find somewhere to live. His father is moving out of London soon and Luke hasn't got anywhere to go. Anyway, this being in two places is starting to get me down.'

'Why don't you go and stay with him, at least until the house is sold? I thought you said his father knows about you.'

They had lowered their voices automatically, perhaps in case the drowsing sheep in the fields on either side might wake and hear and be scandalized. 'He does,' Georgie allowed, 'but Luke won't hear of it. In fact he doesn't want me to come to the house at all, in case his

171

father turns up while I'm there. He's pathologically jealous of him. Luke is jealous of his father, I mean.'

'I took your meaning the first time, and I don't blame him. You're a little tart.'

He said this in an amiable way and she didn't take particular offence. 'I am not. And you're no one to talk. And besides, he doesn't know about . . . about what happened with Nick. He's just jealous on general principles.'

'Then he's got a very specific surprise in store, hasn't he?'

'He does not, because he's never going to find out.'

'Maybe that's what your mother said about Charlie Cahill.'

'It's not the same thing.'

Or was it?

She was doing to Luke what her mother had done to her: not telling him something of great importance to him. But it wasn't really his business who her lovers had been, even if one of them, for only one hour, had been his father.

On the other hand, that had happened not in some distant past but at a time – now – when Luke thought he was her real, true, only lover. When he had thought and expected, and she had led him to expect, that she was being faithful to him. And she had betrayed him with the one person whose treachery he most feared.

Yet there wasn't any point in telling him. What was he supposed to do with the information, except go mad?

As she had gone mad, on finding out that her father wasn't her father. That she had no father.

Maybe her mother had done right to lie to her. No, no, she couldn't believe that. Her life was her own to shape. She had a right to the truth, to grow up, to make her own choices in the bleak landscape of reality, however unhappy it made her to have to do so.

So why didn't Luke have that right?

It wasn't really anything to do with him. Not like who her father was.

But it was *his* father who had done it. How could she say that wasn't anything to do with Luke, the fact that his father would do that to him, right after she had told him about herself and Luke? Well, he was already convinced his father was a two-timing bastard; he didn't need any extra evidence on that score.

And besides, he had said he would kill her if she did anything like that. Anything like what she had already done when he said it.

Just think, once upon a time she had imagined that sex was nothing much more than a pleasant sort of recreational activity, a two-handed version of volleyball, with consequences no more serious than might attach to a volleyball game.

Matthew interrupted her broodings. 'Why did you do it, anyway?'

'Do what?'

'Screw his father.'

'You know why. I was drunk.'

'Not so drunk you didn't know what you were doing. And how drunk was he?'

'He wasn't. Well, okay, I wasn't really drunk either, not all that drunk.' Georgie paused to recall events, and wondered how on earth she had ended up having sex with anyone, let alone Luke's father, under such extraordinary circumstances. She slowed to a standstill with the effort of recollection. The girl who couldn't think and walk at the same time. She considered and rejected the idea of blaming everything on Nick: he mesmerized me, she could say, not untruthfully. But Matthew wouldn't believe it anyway. 'I think . . . actually I think it was all a misunderstanding.'

Matthew stopped too. 'Do tell me more. In my experience misunderstandings are more likely to end in a fuck-up than a fuck.'

'Maybe misunderstanding isn't the right word. But I don't know how else to describe it. He was cuddling me, just to be kind, I think, and it felt really good, and then it started to feel good and sexy, and . . .' Georgie found she had somehow drifted into Matthew's arms. It was easier to talk about intimate things that way, close to. 'Listen, Matty, I was really freaked out when I found out this guy Charlie Cahill wasn't my father either. In a way it was worse than when I saw my birth certificate. It sort of deranged me. I really needed some kind of . . . well, some kind of consolation.'

Matthew should have understood that. He himself had been in no less desperate need of consoling, not too long ago. The same kind of consolation, as it happened.

But he wasn't inclined to let her off the hook so easily. 'Okay, so you're pleading temporary insanity. What about him?'

'I think in a funny way it was the same for him. I asked him afterwards why he'd done it, and he said You've got her face. Meaning my grandmother, I guess. Your dad said I looked like her.'

'How romantic. And you swallowed this excuse, of course.'

'Yeah, I did actually believe him. I could tell at the time he wasn't just getting it off with me.' She felt betrayed, remembering. 'He said something funny. He always calls me sugar, but right when he . . . you know . . . well, he called me kitten. Only I don't think he meant me.'

She was trembling now, glad of Matthew's embrace. He said drily, 'Much more tasteful than snookums or bunnikins, whoever he had in mind. Talk about darkling plains and ignorant armies, we should all be issued with ID tattoos and illuminated name tags. Listen, sugarpussy, do you want your Luke to come and live in the flat with us?'

That was precisely what she wanted, but hadn't dared to ask. 'Would you mind?'

'Mind? Me? Mind Luke? Of course not.'

'But what would your parents say?'

'They're not likely to find out. They never use the flat during the summer. Anyway, we could always say his father had chucked him out and gone abroad and he's looking for somewhere else to live, which is all true. I have the impression my father regards Luke's daddy as something that crawled out from under a rock. I mean, if a man's not even good enough to marry your ex-wife, he must be really appalling.'

'Oh, Matt, you are good. How can I ever thank you?'

His dark eyes gleamed, maybe only with the light of the westering moon. Or maybe not. 'What about a fuck?'

'Ha ha. You know I can't do that.'

'How come it's okay with Luke's old man but not with me?'

'It wasn't okay with him. It was totally wrong. And even he was sorry afterwards.'

'Well, okay, let's just say it's totally wrong and do it anyway. I can say sorry afterwards too.'

She pulled away from him. 'Don't be such a cynic. You're going to grow up to be just like him if you're not careful.'

'What a dire prospect. Rich and famous, and beautiful women throwing themselves at me.'

'But I don't think he's very happy, in spite of all that.'

'Well, I'd rather be rich and famous and good-looking and unhappy than poor and insignificant and ugly and unhappy.'

He seemed to have accepted her refusal in good spirit. She hoped it wasn't going to make him change his mind about letting Luke stay in the flat. Aside from everything else, Matthew wouldn't be making suggestions like that with Luke around the place.

Unless, of course, he started making them to Luke.

19

They are sottish children, and they have no understanding;
they are wise to do evil, but to do good they have no knowledge.

On Monday morning Georgie decided it was time to start getting on with the rest of her life.

She took her birth certificate (or certificate of bastardy, as she had begun to think of it) and inserted that proof of her existence into the machinery of state bureaucracy, in order to get the magic number she needed for a job. Then she signed on at a temp agency, where somewhat to her dismay she was given an address at which to turn up the next morning. She hadn't been expecting the rat race to begin quite so promptly.

After that she went on a shopping spree. The clothes she had brought over with her were suitable for a student's summer travel, not for an office worker. Besides, everybody seemed to dress more formally here than in Toronto. She spent the afternoon formalizing her wardrobe.

While she was reviving herself with a cold drink in a café, she wrote out a postcard to her parents – that was, her mother and spouse. *Having a wonderful time, never coming home.* They could make what they liked out of that.

After depositing her shopping at the flat, she went down to the supermarket to get ingredients for dinner. Luke was moving in tonight. She would have two men to cook for, and was rubbing her hands with pleasure at the prospect. It was so nice to be cosy and homelike, to have an ordered life and family of sorts. Her (step)father, being a doctor and the son of a doctor, had no real concept or hope of a serious domestic life. Her mother, for as long as she could remember, had either been studying or disappearing up North to track wolves. Their family life had to fit into the interstices of her parents' other activities. It wasn't her idea of proper domesticity.

Now, very soon, one way or another, she would be setting up her own domestic arrangements with Luke: a home of her own and her own true man. Soppy, romantic, Dark-Age stuff. But she couldn't even manage to feel ashamed of herself.

The arrangements in the flat would do for practice in the meantime.

Luke and Matthew were happy to be practised upon, even when she dragged them away from television to wash the dishes. Later on Matthew went out, leaving Georgie and Luke free to use the sofa for what they regarded as its primary purpose. Matthew was not quite so selfless as to give up the bedroom on their behalf, and the bed that the sofa made into was not quite a double bed, especially when shared with someone the size of Luke, but Georgie thought it was total bliss all the same.

'Aren't you glad I've got work? Now if you get a job, we can find somewhere to live on our own.'

'I've got my dole money and my mother's money. That'll do to be getting on with.'

'I said a job, J-O-B.'

'What is this obsession with nine to five employment? I've got a job, I'm an artist, A-R-T-I-S-T.'

'And where are you going to practise your artistry when your father's sold his house?'

'Well, if we find a two-bedroom flat I can have a room to myself.'

'It won't likely be very big,' she said doubtfully. And what if we have a baby, she didn't say.

'Are you going down to Sussex again this weekend?'

'I guess so. They're expecting me.'

'Can't you stay here and let Matt go down by himself?'

Georgie knew that that wouldn't happen; if she didn't go, Matthew wouldn't. But she didn't want to let Luke know that. He was inclined to be jealous of her relationship with Matthew, whatever he imagined it to be. 'I can't just live in their flat and never go down to visit them,' she pointed out.

'Paying the rent, is it?'

It was, a bit, but she didn't like him to say so quite so bluntly. 'Well, I like to see them. I have eighteen years to make up for.'

'And have I got to keep out of sight for the next eighteen years?'

'Just be patient for a little while. The right moment will arrive eventually.'

Matthew arrived eventually too, just about the time the pubs were closing. But that was only coincidence tonight, it seemed, since he appeared to be relatively sober. He produced what he claimed was top-quality dope and invited Luke and Georgie to smoke some with him.

Georgie agreed, to be polite. 'But I can't stay up all night,' she pointed out. 'I have to get up and go to work in the morning.'

'Why are you so set on this stupid job?' Matthew demanded. 'I thought you said you still had lots of money left.'

'I do, but I've got to get started earning some more, if I'm going to stay over here. I can't just float through life on the dole.'

'Why not? Everybody else does.'

'I'll bet it gets boring after a while. And I'll feel better with some money coming in.'

'I also thought you said you wanted to be an archaeologist.'

'There weren't any vacancies for archaeologists in the jobs column. Don't be silly, Matt, I'll get around to doing something about that in good time. Right now I just need any old job.'

Matthew handed her the joint to shut her up. 'Luke, are you sure you want to get involved with this madwoman?'

'Well, if I can't pull an heiress, the next best thing is a woman with a steady job.'

'It's only a temp job, and a deadly dull one at that. Mucking about with invoices, didn't you say, Georgie?'

She nodded, still stuffed with smoke. She opened her mouth to let it drift out, and watched Luke as he inhaled on the joint. She liked that look of intensity on his face, as if he were listening to some inner voice. Even though he didn't believe in still small voices.

She laid her head in his lap, to look up into his face. He bent down and blew smoke directly into her mouth, like the kiss of life.

At the other end of the sofa, Matthew had taken possession of her bare feet and begun to play piggies with her toes. She wiggled her feet to discourage him. 'Stop that, Matty, you're tickling.'

'I am not.'

But he was, definitely and deliberately. Even biting her little toe, which made her jump although it didn't hurt. 'You are too. Luke, make him stop.'

Luke turned on Matthew with an amiable growl. 'She wants you to stop.'

'How about massage? Ask her if I can massage her feet.'

'Tell him that's all right, but absolutely no tickling.'

Luke made sure to pass on the message. 'Did you catch that, mate? No tickling, she says.'

They sat like that for a while, smoking in companionable silence, Luke and Matthew propped up at either end of the sofa, with Georgie stretched out between them. Luke stroked her hair and Matthew stroked her feet, while she drifted in and out of sleep.

After a while they began to talk across her, in a desultory way with long pauses for reflection, like two taciturn old Yankees in rocking chairs on the veranda. Georgie couldn't make much sense of the conversation, either because she kept falling asleep or because she was stoned or because they were stoned, but it pleased her that

177

they should be talking like that, like good friends at ease with each other. Like the brothers they might have been, rather than nothing at all.

While sliding in and out of consciousness she thought about brothers, what they were and weren't. Luke and Matthew were brothers to the same person, her mother, but no relation to each other. Yet they were now closer to each other than to her mother, who was a stranger to them both. To say that Luke was her mother's brother in the same way that Alex was her own brother, was theoretically true but actually nonsense.

Alex *felt* like a brother to her. She had known him from birth, played and fought with him, called the same pair of people daddy and mama, and another pair grandma and grandpa, and so on. He would still feel like her brother even if somehow he turned out to be no blood relation at all. Whereas Luke and her mother were strangers to each other in that familial sense, however they might be related.

So what was family?

Was it only people you were related to genetically? If your biological father was unknown, you had no real father. Like missing an arm or a leg. No substitutions allowed. Paynes could not legitimately pose as Becketts or Hardys. And on the other hand you might be obliged to treat some stranger as your father or brother, if he had the papers or the DNA to prove it. Feelings and interpersonal history didn't come into it.

Or was it feelings that made a family? Was Tom Payne her father because she had always called him that, and loved him as a father? And loved his blood relations, thinking of them and calling them by kinship titles. Then it was these Englishmen, these Becketts and Hardy/Winters, who were the frauds and pretenders. They were certainly the strangers – or had been, weeks ago.

At school they had taken a deliberately amorphous view of what might make a family, so as not to make kids feel bad if they happened to be short of a parent or two, or had too many of one sex, or only had temporary ones. Georgie used to feel sorry for those kids, not knowing that she was one of them herself. Now she knew, and felt even sorrier for them.

Was a family just a household, everybody who lived together under one roof and sat down to dine at the same table? You could get a family by moving into a house, and lose your family by moving out.

Or did family include anyone who was related to the man in your mother's bed, whoever he happened to be? If he had children, they became your brothers and sisters. If he left and someone else took

178

his place, you acquired a whole new family, and lost the previous one. Like changing jobs or schools, and acquiring a whole new set of friends.

Or maybe not, if you didn't get on with them.

When you got old enough, you became the family-maker, with whoever was sleeping in your bed.

Nothing was for ever now, nothing was forbidden. Everybody could do what they liked, as long as they didn't hurt anyone: on this one commandment now hung all the law and the prophets. Everyone was free to pursue their own happiness in their own way.

So why not Luke and Georgie? They weren't hurting anyone.

Georgie's grandfather and Althea were going to France for two weeks. A fortnight, her grandfather called it, which sounded delightfully old-fashioned. He invited Georgie to go with them. 'You're welcome to come along too, Matthew, if you can spare the time,' he added sardonically. 'I know you're a seriously busy person.'

Matthew chose to ignore his father's gibe. 'It's Georgie who's seriously busy. She's got a job.'

Her grandfather and Althea both looked at her. She felt like blushing. 'It's just a temp job. Something to be getting on with.'

'Are you going to stay on, then?' Her grandfather looked quite pleased at the idea.

'I think I will, if I can find somewhere to live. Everything seems to be very expensive.'

'You'll probably have to share, if you want a decent neighbourhood,' Althea said briskly. 'Matty, do you know anyone who needs a flatmate?'

'Yeah, I do, but they also need a flat.'

'Well, I expect you can work something out. If Georgie can get a job in just a few weeks, why can't you find something to be getting on with?'

'That's my life you're talking about, Ma. It's not just something to be getting on with.'

'I told you before, if you'd make up your mind what you're interested in, I might be able to pull some strings to find you something suitable. But it's no use my doing anything unless you're prepared to take it seriously.'

'I'll let you know when I've made the big decision.'

He didn't trouble to disguise his sarcasm, so Georgie was not surprised to catch her grandfather glaring at him. 'When you've decided what you want to do when you grow up, you mean?'

Althea only looked mildly irritated, as if her son had refused to lift his feet to let her vacuum the carpet underneath. She returned her attention to Georgie. 'What's Lia going to say if you decide to stay?'

Georgie shrugged. That was part of the point of staying. To punish her mother for telling lies. 'Maybe she'll break down and come over herself.'

Althea looked at Georgie's grandfather, who was looking at Georgie. Georgie couldn't tell if the prospect pleased him or not. Nor could she tell how much irony was in his voice when he said, 'That would be nice.'

She had promised to ring Luke. After dinner she walked into the village, escorted by Matthew, to use the pay phone at the pub and avoid any awkward questions from her grandfather or Althea.

She didn't have anything to say, it was just electronically holding hands. She told Luke she missed him. He said he missed her too, and told her in exactly what respect he missed her most, with graphic anatomical details.

She was still pink and giggly when she came back to Matthew, who had bought himself a drink while he waited.

'An obscene phone call, was it?'

'How did you guess?'

'Your spirit shines through you, as Macbeth said to the murderers. Can you survive till tomorrow night?'

She sighed. Luke was addictive; the more she saw of him, the more she needed him. 'I'll have to, won't I?'

'Not necessarily. Consolation is available on request.'

'Listen, Matty, you're gorgeous and sexy and I love you dearly, but my heart belongs to Luke. I accept no substitutes.'

'Except his father. Almost the same thing, I suppose.'

'Don't go on about that,' she said fiercely. 'I'm sorry I told you.'

'But not sorry you did it.'

'What do you want me to do about it now? I told you how it happened. And if you don't tell him, he'll never find out, and no one will be hurt by it.'

She didn't speak to him all the way back. She didn't know why he was so concerned about what had happened with Nick. It was almost as if he was jealous, not of Luke but of Luke's father. Maybe it was because he was chummy with Luke. Maybe he was jealous on Luke's behalf, since Luke in his happy ignorance couldn't be jealous on his own behalf. Whatever, she wished he would cut it out. She was trying to forget the whole thing.

Not easy, when there was so much more to it than just a quick

180

poke. A sort of life history, in fact. But she hadn't told Matthew anything of that.

The forbidden cat was sitting on the wall by the unused front gate, just about where Georgie had first seen him. She only saw him now, a black cat in darkness, when he turned his bright round eyes on them. The eyes appeared so suddenly they startled her: a human caught in the animal's headlight beam.

It startled her out of her sulk. 'There's your cat.'

'We don't have a cat.'

'Yes, you do. He's right there by the gate.'

The cat must have blinked, or looked away. The eyes had vanished, the only visible part of him. 'There's no cat there.'

'Well, he was. It's extraordinary how nobody pays any attention to him, even though he's always around. You'd think he was a ghost. I'd like to know how he gets into the house, if he's not allowed.'

'Oh, *that* cat. He isn't ours, but he seems to think we're his. My mother thinks he's a ghost too, because he can walk through walls. Actually he just opens the door.'

'How?'

'Same way you would.' They arrived at the back door, allowing Matthew to demonstrate the cat's technique. 'He jumps up and pulls down on the tongue of the latch, like this, and then he pushes on the door.'

Georgie thought he must be making this up. 'How do you know that?'

'I've seen him do it.'

'So he's not a ghost.'

'Not at the moment, anyway. But he's the sort who might come back to haunt you, don't you think?'

When they got back to London on Sunday evening, Luke had collected half a dozen telephone messages for Matthew. 'And one heavy breather. I presume that was for Georgie.'

'More likely it *was* Georgie,' Matthew suggested.

Georgie ignored him. She hadn't quite forgiven him for his persistent needling the night before. She said to Luke, 'Did you really get a breather? They usually hang up when they get a man. Is there such a thing as a gay breather?'

'Well, he didn't actually breathe, he just hung up.'

Matthew said, 'If a man answers . . .'

Georgie glared at him, until she realized Luke had noticed the glare and was staring at her. She panicked and went and locked herself in the bathroom. As long as she was in there she decided to have a bath, which would give Luke plenty of time to forget about Matthew's dirty rotten remark.

It seemed to work.

The next night the phone rang while Georgie was making dinner. Since the phone was in the kitchen, she answered it, rearranging the sauté onions in the frying pan with her other hand.

'Hi, Georgie.'

She nearly dropped the spatula. The voice on the line was all husky from forty years of cigarette smoke being dragged across the vocal chords. At least she supposed that was why he sounded like that. The alternative, not much less likely, explanation was that he was about to murmur intimate obscenities into her ear. She tried to sound brisk when she replied, but in her discombobulation it came out unfortunately breathy. 'Who is it?'

'You know fucking well who it is. Has Luke moved into your bed, or has he jumped off Tower Bridge?'

Obscenities it was, then. She managed to sound a little less potentially passionate this time. 'Did you want to speak to him?'

'No, I just wanted to make sure he's still alive, since I haven't seen or heard from him for a week. You're the one I want to speak to.'

'Well, now's your big chance.'

'Right. I'm off to New York on Wednesday and Christ knows when I'll be back in London. D'you fancy dinner tomorrow night?'

'What about Luke?'

'He can forage for himself.'

'No, I mean – what's going to happen to him if you're leaving London?'

'The lucky bugger's living with you, isn't he?'

'But he – aren't you going to tell him where you're going?'

'You tell him for me, sugar. He'll know where to find me if he needs me. What about tomorrow night?'

She couldn't say no, he was her grandmother's husband. On the other hand she couldn't say yes, because of Luke. 'What about lunch?' That was safer. She would have to get back to work on time.

'That's okay, but I won't be free till two-ish.'

'Oh, that's no good. It's my job, you see,' she explained, gabbling somewhat. 'I've got this temping job, and the place I'm at, you can only go to lunch at twelve or one.'

'Why don't you just take the afternoon off?'

'No, I can't do that, they wouldn't like that at all.'

'What've you done, signed up with the fucking army? Listen, I'll buy you a drink after work. It sounds like you'll need one.'

'Yeah, okay.' She poked at the onions. She had forgotten them and they were starting to blacken.

'Where are you working?'

'Finsbury Circus. It's very handy, about five minutes from the flat.'

'Then I'll meet you there. Five thirty, all right?'

'Okay.'

She hung up. Luke was leaning on the counter opposite, looking grim. 'Who's your friend?'

'No friend. It was your dearly beloved daddy.'

'I thought it might have been. Just rang up to have a chat, did he?'

She busied herself with mincing the garlic impossibly fine and tossing it in with the frazzled onions. 'No, he wanted me to tell you that he's going to New York on Wednesday and won't be back. He said you'd know where to look if you wanted him.'

'No bloody chance of that. What's this about lunch?'

'Nothing about lunch. Since you were eavesdropping so intently, you should have gathered that lunch was not happening.'

'Why'd you make excuses? Why didn't you just tell him to fuck off?'

'Maybe because I'm more polite than you.' It was the broccoli's turn for attention. She reduced it rapidly to fork-sized florets. 'Anyway, he's your father, you can be as unpleasant to him as you like and it won't make any difference to anything between you. I don't have the same privileges with my mother's stepfather.'

He stood very close to her, watching the broccoli join the onions and garlic. He said in her ear, 'Where?'

'Where what?'

'Where are you meeting him?'

There was no point trying to explain. This was clearly a monomaniacal subject with him. She tried evasive tactics instead. 'What makes you imagine I'm meeting him anywhere?'

'Because you told him where you're working.'

'Because he asked. Is that classified information? Now go away, you'll make me burn the dinner and you'll be the first to complain.'

He moved away moodily, then returned to poke a finger in her ribs and make her jump. 'Remember, I said six feet minimum.'

When Georgie wakes up from her nap, the villa is all quiet. Luke is still asleep on the other bed. Maybe everyone else is asleep too. She knows her mama and grandma usually have a nap. Only they call it a siesta.

183

She goes into her mama's room. Her mama isn't there.

She goes into her grandma's room. It's empty.

She goes downstairs. There's no one in the living-room or kitchen. There's no sound or voice at all. Maybe they've all gone out, and left her and Luke alone.

The idea scares her. They're not at home, they're in a strange country. She can't even do what her mama always told her to do if she got lost, namely, find a policeman and tell him.

She goes outside, on to the terrace by the swimming pool. And there, to her vast relief, is Luke's daddy. He is stretched out on the li-lo with a floppy greeny-browny hat pulled down over his eyes. Having a siesta, she supposes.

She stands beside the li-lo and works up her courage to wake him. He might be cross.

While she hesitates she studies him. He is wearing the tatty faded shorts and nothing else. His body is golden brown from the sun. His chest and legs and arms are covered with short fair curly hair. With his face half hidden under the hat, he looks more like a tawny animal than a person.

She decides to play safe by making it as hard as possible for him to reach her, in case he is cross at being wakened. She stands at the foot of the li-lo and wiggles his big toe.

He grunts. That's all.

She tries the little toe. Much more sensitive, in her personal experience.

He raises himself up on his elbows to glare at her. The hat falls on to the paving stones. 'Georgie, what the hell are you doing?'

'Where's Mama?'

'Gone shopping with Em.' Em is his name for her grandma. 'Where's Luke?'

'He's still sleeping.'

'Good for him. Why don't you do the same thing?'

Seeing he isn't going to smack her, she comes round to the side of the li-lo and picks up the floppy hat and gives it back to him. Then she climbs up on to the li-lo and perches herself astride his middle.

He replaces the hat and lies back again with his arm behind his head. 'Why don't you go back to sleep for a while, sugar?'

'I'm not sleepy.'

'Then lie still and sunbathe.'

With his free hand he pulls her down till she's lying flat on top of him with her head on his chest, just under his chin. Her mama put her down for her nap with only her knickers on, so she can feel the warmth of his skin and the pleasantly furry sensation of the hair on his body, all up and down her own body, like lying on top of a tiger. He puts his hand in her hair, stroking her short blonde curls.

After a while the stroking stops. She raises her head to see if he's gone to sleep again. Under the brim of the hat his eyes are closed. His breathing lifts and lowers her in a drowsy rhythm.

She lays her head back down on his chest, sticks her finger into her mouth and sucks it for a while. Getting bored with that, she locates his nipple amongst the hair on his chest, and starts pressing it with her forefinger.

That wakes him up again. 'Georgie, for Christ's sake. What're you doing?'

'I'm pressing your button.'

He laughs. That makes his chest move up and down more quickly. She moves up and down with his laughter. 'Is that a hint?'

She doesn't know what he means. She sits up as if she were riding him. She wiggles against him, enjoying the ticklish sensation of his furry chest under her own soft skin.

He grunts, but not with displeasure. He's smiling, in a lazy sleepy way. 'Come on, lie down and go to sleep. Stop bouncing on me.'

'I'm too hot.'

'You can wear my hat, all right? That'll keep you cool.'

He puts the hat on her head. It's too big for her. She pulls the brim down over her ears and giggles. He flops his arm across his face to shade it from the sun, and pulls her down flat again with his other hand till she is splayed across his chest like a little frog.

It's cooler under the hat. She squirms to get herself comfortable; his body is a lot harder than her mama's. He strokes her: not her hair this time but her bottom, because her hair is under the hat.

She stops wriggling as he pats her back and bottom. The strokes get more irregular as he starts to doze off.

She falls asleep again, just about the same moment as he does.

20

How shall I pardon thee for this?

Georgie was early for her rendezvous, a bad habit of hers. It meant she had to hang around the steps that went up to the wine bar. The bar was jam-packed inside, though why anyone would squeeze themselves inside a smoky pub when they could be drinking outside in the summer sunshine was beyond her.

While she waited, she unfastened the top button on her blouse to make herself look less like a refugee from office life. She was half hoping that Nick wouldn't come, so she could go home with a clear conscience.

On the other hand, Luke had no right to carry on like that. Well, maybe he did, if he only knew, but he didn't know, so his obsession was quite unjustified. Anyway, it wasn't as if she'd been having an affair with his father. It had only happened once, and almost by accident.

No, not accident. Exactly the opposite. The opposite of accidental was not deliberate but fated. There was an old Scottish expression about dreeing one's weird (doubtless some relation to the three weird sisters in *Macbeth*) and it seemed to Georgie now that something like that must have entangled her with Nick. That she had had to wait eighteen years to get him out of her system. Maybe what had happened on the stairway to the bottom of the world had been an exorcism, a consummation that had haunted and taunted her like a malicious ghost, without her conscious knowledge. Committing the dreaded and desired and – to her three-year-old self – unknown sin, getting it over with and out of the way. Literally laying the ghost. Her feelings for Nick, she understood now, had been brought with her from the distant past, her own forgotten past, archaeology rather than history.

Now he was leaving London. It might well be another eighteen years before she saw him again, and she hadn't even had a chance to talk with him, in the way she had talked with her grandfather Beckett. He hadn't told her anything about her grandmother, or even about himself. She knew nothing about him, nothing of importance to either her or him. And yet he was a vital piece of her past.

Her only close encounter with him had been a sort of carnal collision, which had left her bruised and confused. And him too, maybe, to guess from his reaction. Guessing was all she could do, where Nick was concerned.

The subject of her thoughts came up and touched her shoulder, startling her because she had been looking in the opposite direction. 'I'll be right back,' he said in her ear, and disappeared inside before she had a chance to be meaningfully cool as she had intended.

He came back down the steps almost immediately, with a bottle of wine and two glasses. There must have been a million people in there trying to buy a drink, but he was obviously the sort who acts as a magnet to the bartender's eye. Come to think of it, she could have guessed that much about him even without this evidence.

He was looking very respectable. Dressed up for a dinner date, maybe? She squashed the little niggle of jealousy that reared its head at that thought; it could have been her if she had said yes to his invitation. In the sea of conservative pinstripes surrounding them, his cool grey-green stylishly-cut suit stood out like a peacock's feathers. Not that he would care, she thought as she followed his broad back through the crowd, searching for an untenanted bench or even a vacant patch of grass. It was in the set of his shoulders, the casually confident stride, the air of a man who knows that whatever he does is the done thing. And why not? Defining fashion was how he made his living.

They found a place on the lawn. He handed her the spoils from the bar, peeled off his jacket and discarded it on the grass. She kicked off her sandals, sat down cross-legged beside him and poured wine into the glasses. He hauled the knot on his tie down to half-mast and undid the collar button on his shirt. So much for the image of respectability. It was only an illusion anyway, as she had good reason to know.

It was time to say something, before he said something she didn't want to hear. 'Are you going to live in New York?'

'I've had a flat there for years, just to make my life easier. I hate hotels. But no, I wouldn't want to live in New York. Christ, what an appalling idea. Have you ever been?'

'Once. Just for a weekend.'

'That's about long enough. I think it's a fucking lunatic asylum. But I guess that's okay if you're crazy.'

'So where will you go?'

He grinned. 'Why, are you going to write to me? Or better still, come and visit me?'

She sipped at her wine to avoid his eyes. 'That depends where you go. Somewhere nice and warm, with a private beach and a yacht . . .'

'Okay, you've convinced me. You pick it out and I'll buy it.'

She had been half joking, half fantasizing. But why couldn't it be true? Luke had said his father was rich. If Nick went to live in the Caribbean or the Mediterranean – if she could cure Luke of his absurd obsession about his father . . .

But she had more prosaic property concerns. 'If I pick out a flat in London, will you buy it?'

'Are you really going to stay over here?'

'Yeah, I think I will.'

'Because of Luke?'

'Mostly.' She glanced sideways at him. 'Is that a problem for you?'

He shrugged. 'Hell, no. He wants looking after, and if you're keen to do it, you're welcome.'

Georgie drained her glass, out of nervousness. This was her big

187

chance, her one chance. He would be leaving town tomorrow. And Luke refused to realize how lucky it was that his father didn't seem to care about the fact that the girl his son was living with was also his son's niece. On second thoughts, she didn't know if that was lucky or not. It was just what she would have expected of Nick. Besides, she was only a semi-niece, and a purely notional one at that.

She plucked grass to occupy her hands while she made her sales pitch. 'Listen, Nick, it's not that simple. I'm staying in a flat that belongs to my grandfather. It's only got one bedroom, so it's pretty crowded even with just Matt and me. But I don't really have the right to invite Luke to live in a place that isn't mine, especially when it means putting Matty out so much. I've got this temp job, but it doesn't earn much money.'

She leaned towards him confidingly and looked up directly into his eyes. That usually went down well with men, the wide-eyed blue gaze. 'I don't know what to do.'

Nick returned the look, with evident amusement. 'Sure you do, sweetheart. You're doing it right now.'

He was deliberatey looking down the front of her blouse. She felt like doing up the buttons again. Except – well, she had invited that, hadn't she? Flirting was how she often got her own way. Success had made it second nature to her, so that she did it without even noticing. But he had noticed, and was letting her know. Well, if he was going to talk turkey she could do it too.

'Why don't you do what my grandfather did – buy a flat for when you need it and let Luke live in it the rest of the time? You're going to have to come to London anyway from time to time, aren't you? You could use it just like your flat in New York.'

He didn't answer right away. Maybe she had gone too far, been too blunt. She picked up the wine bottle and he held out his glass for refilling. She filled up her own glass and waited. She had spoken her piece, it was his turn now. Even if the answer was no.

'Well, I might do that. But not for free.'

'We could pay rent. Not the market rate, but something.'

'That's nice of you to offer,' he said drily. 'But it wasn't what I had in mind.'

She waited uneasily, frowning at her toes, for him to elaborate. After a minute of silence she glanced at him, and went quite red as an awful thought crossed her mind. 'You don't mean . . .'

He smiled. A broad but not totally comforting smile. 'Get your mind out of the gutter, sugar. I just meant that I'm going to want a favour from you in return, some day.'

'What kind of favour?'

188

'I'll tell you what it is when I want it.'

She looked at him through her lashes. 'That sounds like a folk-tale sort of bargain. The kind that leads to trouble.'

'Well, that's the deal, take it or leave it. What d'you say?'

She stared at her hands in her lap. She laid the right hand down on the grass between them, palm upwards.

He took it and ran his thumb across her palm, as he had done the first night she met him. It had caught her attention then, and it felt pretty good right now. She curled her fingers over his thumb. His hand closed around hers. She remembered that hand. Remembered how much bigger than hers it had seemed, long ago. And still was. He was full of ghosts, this man, and he raised them in her.

'You shouldn't do it for me, you should do it for Luke.'

'I don't reckon to need any favours from Luke,' he said drily.

'I mean because he's your son. You're supposed to want to do your best for him. Fathers do, don't they?'

'I couldn't say what fathers do. Does yours feel like that about you?'

It was a pointed question, not an idle one. Not a question at all, but a deliberate gibe.

She tugged her hand free of his. 'Luke was right, you are a rotten bastard.' She stood up, searching blindly with her toes for her sandals. 'Forget the flat. Forget the whole conversation. I don't need any favours from you and neither does Luke.'

She was horrified to find herself on the verge of tears, as if she were a little kid again, being taunted about having no daddy. She bent down to pull on her sandal and nearly lost her balance.

He caught her other hand to steady her. This time she didn't yank it away. There wasn't much point. What a pathetic person she was, sucking up to such a terrible man. Crying because he had said something nasty to her.

Wanting him to hold her.

She would have walked away, but he still had hold of her hand and wasn't going to let go. She had to wait till he had picked up his jacket and slung it over his shoulder. So they walked out of the park hand in hand, heading towards Moorgate and the Barbican.

She refused to look at him. 'You should be good to Luke for my grandmother's sake, even if you don't get on with him yourself. Anyway, it's partly your fault if he doesn't like you. Because you . . .'

'Yeah? What did I do?'

She realized she couldn't say it: Because you seduced his girl-friends. She couldn't say it because she was one of them. A truly pathetic person.

'You haven't treated him very well.'

'Maybe he hasn't always been Mr Nice Guy himself.'

She shook his hand impatiently. 'But he was the kid, you were the adult. Parents ought to love their children no matter what. People have to grow up with that reassurance that somebody loves them absolutely. Otherwise they haven't the nerve to love somebody themselves.'

'Love takes nerve, does it?'

'Sure it does. It's scary. You're making yourself vulnerable, giving someone else power over you. It's like signing a blank emotional cheque. You can't will yourself to stop loving someone just because it starts to hurt.'

Maybe he didn't understand that. She recalled what Luke had said about his father's unknown family.

She also recalled a much more vivid and painful memory, of Nick holding her small self, telling her he loved her. The first man ever to tell her that.

They had reached the kerb at Moorgate and had to wait to cross. Moved by the memory, Georgie turned to face him.

'I've remembered why you call me sugar.'

He must have known what she meant, what else she had remembered, but he didn't show any sign of being bothered, or of any emotion other than slight amusement. 'Did you? I told you you would.'

'I mean I've remembered everything,' she persisted. She hesitated over how to phrase it. Well, she just had to say it. She hadn't been the least bit ashamed of herself at the time, why should she be embarrassed now? It was he who ought to feel embarrassment. At the very least. 'I know what you . . . what you did to me.'

He looked at her then, turning to confront her. She saw that he was serious at last. Or at least not completely unamused. 'Hellishly traumatic, was it? Scarred you for life? Drove you into therapy for years?'

'Don't be silly,' she said automatically. Too late, she bit her tongue. 'No thanks to you, though, was it? Be serious for once.' She said it furiously, wrenching at his hand. 'It's not funny, messing around with a little kid like that.'

'I thought it was the other way round. You were pretty keen at the time.'

'Not like that! I didn't understand . . .' Georgie found that she couldn't explain what it was she hadn't understood; it was too humiliating. By way of explanation she burst into tears, which was even more humiliating.

Nick was the best – or possibly the worst, in view of what had happened the last time he consoled her – man in the world to cry in front of. He didn't back off or get embarrassed, he just put his arm around her and held her while she cried. Even though, she reckoned, nine times out of ten he was probably responsible for the tears in the first place.

She spoke in sobs. She couldn't help it. 'I didn't understand what you were doing.'

'You mean you didn't have a word for it.'

'I do now.' She spat out her accusation. 'Child abuse.'

'You felt abused, did you?' His voice had gone cold, but he didn't take his arm away. 'Physically damaged, betrayed, treated like shit for someone's enjoyment, because you were the nearest thing when he fancied a fuck? Knowing he doesn't bloody care if he hurts you, and there's not a bloody thing you can do about it anyway?' He took a breath as if he badly needed one. 'Like that, was it?'

He had surprised her again. In spite of his sardonic tone, the underlying intensity of the words implied some unexpected personal understanding of . . . well, of a different sort of experience. Not hers. 'Well, no, of course it wasn't like that. But . . .' She stopped, not knowing quite but what.

He said drily, 'But now that you're all grown up and educated, you know how you should have felt.'

'I didn't mean that. You know I didn't mean that.'

'Then what do you mean?'

Still he hadn't let her go. Still she found herself clinging to him, between the roar of traffic on her right-hand side and the rush of pedestrians on her left, while she considered what it was she meant. She couldn't face him, she had to speak into his shoulder. 'Well, first of all I think you were taking advantage of me, because I wanted, you know, wanted to have a father.'

He took so long to respond that she nerved herself to look up at him. But she couldn't work out the expression on his face.

'No, sugar, believe me, I wasn't doing that.'

'I don't believe you.'

'If you don't believe me, what's the use of asking?'

It was an unanswerable argument. She looked away. 'Okay, okay, I believe you.' But she didn't know if she did.

'All right, here's something else to believe. I didn't do it for my own wicked pleasure. Little girls don't turn me on. I was just showing you something. Like kids' games. And I thought you liked it.' He took her face in his hands, made her look at him. 'Didn't you like it?'

'I don't know. It scared me.' She lowered her gaze, used her eyelashes to protect herself from that demanding stare. 'But Nick, the thing is . . .'

'But again. But what this time?'

191

'Well, it's . . . well, it's not like playing tag, is it? I mean, if you . . .' She was mumbling, stumbling, trying to articulate a point of view that until this summer she herself would have dismissed as superstition. 'It's not like kids' games, because you weren't a kid. You were an adult, an important person to me. So if it was a game it was an important game, at least to me. And I don't think – now – ' she added with humble honesty, 'that sex can ever be just a game. It's too close to your self. It touches you, whether you know it or not, and you can't tell how it's going to affect you, or the other person for that matter. The younger you are, the more impression-able you are, the more powerfully it affect you. That's how people get hooked on perversions. Everything that happens when you're very young becomes part of your own private myth, just the way cultural myths are created when the culture is young and unformed. What you were doing was messing with my head.'

Georgie spoke slowly, feeling her way. Nick had bent his head to hear her properly against the noise of the rush-hour traffic. Now he kept his head bowed a moment longer, brooding, it seemed to her, in a most uncharacteristic way. He usually had an answer, and a sarcastic one at that, ready on the instant.

'So what are you trying to tell me?' he said at last. 'That I put my big fucking feet in your personal mythology and messed it up, and on account of that you're doomed to fancy the likes of Luke?'

That made her laugh, against her inclination. 'Something like that.'

'Well, okay, sugar, you have my apologies. I'll admit that sounds like a pretty bloody insensitive thing to do.' Before she could decide if he was in any way serious, he exclaimed, 'Hey, let's go, there's a taxi pulling up over there.'

A magnet for cab drivers as well as barmen, it seemed. He dragged her through the traffic to the far side of the street and engaged the taxi while the previous passenger was still settling the fare.

He shrugged into his jacket beside the open cab door. 'D'you want to change your mind about dinner?'

'I can't,' she said candidly. 'Luke wouldn't like it.'

'He makes the rules, does he?'

'No, but – well, I don't want to make him unhappy.'

'So you're going to make me unhappy instead.'

He smiled when he said that, so she smiled back. 'That's not in my power, is it? To make you happy or unhappy.'

And when she had said it, she wished it were. She wished to be closer and dearer to him, just as intensely as she had wished it eighteen years ago, though not – she thought – in a sexual way. Assuming that it was possible, where Nick was concerned, to separate the sexual element from all the rest. Or was it ever possible, for any man? Could they respond to any female, of any age or condition or relation, entirely above the belt? Maybe he was simply more open about it. At any rate she had to take him as he came, whatever the consequences. You couldn't change your wishes just because you wanted to.

The weight of her longing, a lifetime's worth, made a vacuum within her, a hollow hurt that threatened to drag her innards into emptiness. She put her arms around his neck to relieve that inward ache. She felt him pull her against him. She held to him as tightly as she could, as if she were a little girl again.

The lost little girl inside her whispered to Luke's daddy. 'I love you.'

Luke's daddy said what he had said long ago. 'I love you too, sugar.' He put his hand on her head, held her against his shoulder and stroked her fluffy fair hair. 'Sure you're not going to come with me?'

To dinner, she wondered dizzily, or to New York? 'You know I can't.'

He let her go, and got into the taxi. She watched it, and him, disappear into the traffic. Did she believe him about loving her? What sort of love did he mean? She found herself in turmoil at the thought, at the words.

She took a deep breath and turned to go down the little side-street, towards the escalator up to the Barbican. She bumped into someone standing right behind her.

Luke.

The look on his face reminded her of something. It reminded her of the drawings of American soldiers in some old war comics she and her brother Alex had found in her grandparents' attic, and treasured as a secret hoard. Luke looked like one of the GIs in those comics: maybe one who had just made his way through a swamp and fought off a boa constrictor and lobbed a grenade or two into a machine-gun nest and chucked his useless rifle aside because it was out of ammo, and was now confronting an enemy tank as it advanced down a sand dune on him, preparing to take it apart with his bare hands. And teeth. Luke was baring his teeth.

He grabbed her wrists. Not being a tank, she had neither the nerve nor the means to get free of him. He brought his face with those gritted GI teeth down close to hers.

'Well, that was nice, wasn't it,' he said in a terrible conversational tone. 'I'm really chuffed that you get on so well with my dad. There can't be many old bastards who'd get a hug and a kiss like that from their son's girl. I'll bet he really enjoyed that.'

She would have let him wear himself out with raving in that vein, only he was virtually crushing her wrists and her hands were about to fall off. 'Luke – '

He jerked her up against him. 'Where've you been, you little scrubber? You had lunch with him, didn't you? You've been with him all afternoon.'

'I haven't, I've been at work. I just met him – '

He thrust her away from him, not letting go of the wrists. She stumbled and he dragged her upright again. 'What makes you imagine I'm meeting him, you said.'

'But I didn't say I wasn't. Anyway, we were only over in Finsbury Circus, having a drink.'

'It doesn't count if it's close to home, hey?' He gave her a little push backwards, into the stream of pedestrians in Moorgate. The passers-by parted to go around either side of them without apparent interest or attention, just like water flowing around a boulder in mid-stream.

'Luke, nothing happened. Really. And you're hurting me.'

'What does *nothing* mean in your mouth? You answer the questions I ask you, and if you lie to me you're dead. Got that?' He punctuated each sentence with a shove. 'Did he fuck you?'

She tried to make herself say it. *No.* She couldn't say it just like that, a plain flat big bald lie. Maybe he meant just now. But he hadn't said that, and if she were to say *Not today* it would be the same as saying yes.

She stared at him, speechless, unable to defend herself. And he took her silence for answer.

He lifted his arms, still holding her wrists, like Samson in chains about to bring the temple down. He called her half a dozen names of the sort that Samson might have used upon Delilah. And with the heedless strength of Samson he threw her away from him.

Her feet must have actually left the ground, because she couldn't do anything, anything at all, to control the movement of her body. It was like a nightmare, with time slowed down to increase the terror. She saw the faces of strangers, gaping in astonishment. She saw Luke's face like a stranger's, coldly impassive now, as if he had flung off the GI berserker's fury along with her.

Then a sound like the crack of doom reverberating in her head. Not so very loud, yet loud enough to obliterate all the other sound in the world.

SECOND HALF

21

As for me, behold, I am in your hand:
do with me as seems good and meet to you.

'What exactly did he say?'

It was the fiftieth time Olivia had asked the question, though she knew very well there wasn't any point repeating it after the first time, since Tom only had the one conversation to report. She kept asking because she felt she ought to be doing something. Asking fruitless questions was all there was to do, until they had arrived.

They had arrived, as a matter of fact, but only at the hotel. An extraordinary thing, to come home and have to book into a hotel. She hadn't had time to make arrangements, even if she could have.

And she couldn't have. She didn't even know where her parents lived any more.

She didn't have time to think about that now. She hadn't come back to see her family, though that would have to happen. Georgie had sent a postcard announcing that she had 'found Grandpa Beckett', like Schliemann cabling home about the discovery of Troy. The only other word they had had from her all summer, according to Tom, was a card last week saying she was never coming home.

Which might turn out to be more terribly true than she could have meant.

Since they had to stop at the hotel to book in and leave their luggage, Tom was taking the opportunity to shave. He said to his own soapy face in the mirror, 'I could tell you exactly what he said, but since you're not a doctor you'd be none the wiser. The important thing is that she's had a bad concussion and she's in a coma.'

That was more or less how he had answered her every time. And every time Olivia wanted to ask the next question: Is it possible, might she die?

She didn't need to ask that question either. She already knew the answer. If he had been any other doctor she might have asked it anyway, hoping for reassurance: Will my daughter die? But she couldn't ask Tom because she would have been asking a different question. *Will your daughter die?*

She wrapped a towel around her wet hair and dried herself off with another towel. The shower had roused her from the fretful stupor into which she had fallen. She hadn't slept since – well, since about twice as long ago as Tom's last shave. When she was up North she had to learn to keep the same hours as the wolves, all hours that was, which was why it was easier to be on her own. So she had been out of doors, not asleep in bed, the night before last. When she came back to the cabin to go to bed at sunrise, there was a Mountie waiting for her.

They didn't bang on your door at dawn to ask to see your driver's licence. In this case the Mountie wanted to tell her that she had to go home.

After eighteen years, she had to go home.

It had taken her the rest of the day to get back to Toronto, even with the help of the Mounties. Then she had to pack, before dashing to the airport with Tom to catch the first standby seats available. There was no hope of tracking down Alex, who was camping and canoeing somewhere in the Yukon with a party of like-minded young masochists. She had to leave him to be dealt with by her parents-in-law. Another job for the Mounties, she supposed.

If she could just see Georgie, it would be okay.

If she could just see Georgie alive and breathing, it would be okay.

If she could just . . .

'I wish she hadn't come back here,' she said for the fiftieth time.

Tom didn't say anything.

Olivia brushed out her long hair. It was still damp but it would have to do. She knotted it up at the back of her head and fastened it with a sort of primitive giant hair grip: an oblong of leather with a hole in either end, and a pointed wooden rod about the size of a pencil that went through both holes, playing the part of the metal clip. Alex had made it for her Christmas present when he was twelve. It was one of her favourite things, for its simplicity and because Alex had made it.

She put on a sleeveless cotton dress because it was so warm outside. She looked at herself in the long mirror on the back of the bathroom door. She was nearly twice as old as when she had last been in London. By this time next year, she would have spent half her life in a foreign country. When she had left England she had still been a teenage girl. Now, at thirty-seven, with a grown-up daughter, she could scarcely claim to be a young woman any more.

She wondered if her father would recognize her, supposing she met him in the street.

She was brown all over from being out of doors all day. Her light brown hair had been bleached almost blonde by the sun. She kept it long, and fastened it up for minimum interference and bother. It wasn't very glamorous but the wolves didn't mind. Neither did Tom. Assuming he even noticed what she looked like any more.

Right now he just glanced at her to make sure she was dressed. 'Ready? Let's go.'

Georgie had been turned into a stranger.

People said things like that, *Your own mother wouldn't know you*, and Olivia was her mother and she didn't. Which was not surprising, because Georgie didn't look like anybody's child. She had tubes stuck into every visible orifice and into the veins of her arms. She was wired up to electronic boxes with screens like the control room of a spaceship. The left side of her face was bruised and swollen. Her head was swathed in bandages. And her eyes were closed, of course.

When Olivia saw her she had to sit down, the shock was so great. She looked away from Georgie in order to recover. Even Tom had gone pale, she noticed, and he must be used to such sights. But of course it was different this time. It was Georgie.

The consultant was nowhere around, naturally. He would only appear at his appointed time. But one of the junior doctors on duty – very junior by the look of him, which was about eighteen – came up to talk to them. As soon as he had established that Tom was a doctor too he addressed himself entirely to Tom.

That was just as well, because Olivia couldn't have taken in a word he was saying. Having got over the first shock of seeing Georgie, now she couldn't stop staring at her. It felt silly, at least with Tom and the doctor around, to try to talk to a person who plainly couldn't hear you, so she gripped the unresponsive hand and held on to that by way of letting Georgie know, if she was capable of knowing anything, that her mother had come at last.

The baby-faced doctor was saying something to Tom about operating to relieve the pressure. That had been done just this morning, she gathered. They had been doing things to her daughter's head without her knowledge or consent.

He was going on about reflex tests. 'If her condition stays stable overnight we'll try taking her off the ventilator tomorrow morning.'

Olivia caught that and broke into the medical *tête-à-tête*. 'What does that mean?'

Tom and the doctor looked at her as if she had been eavesdropping on a private conversation. Tom said, with the patience he reserved for his patients' parents, 'It's to see if she can breathe on her own.'

Olivia said it before she could stop herself. 'What if she can't?'

Tom and the doctor looked at each other. 'Then they'll have to try again later,' said Tom, not entirely convincingly. The baby-faced doctor simply shrugged.

199

They moved to the other end of the ward to continue their talk. Olivia didn't mind. It meant she could talk to Georgie without feeling foolish. Georgie, wake up. Georgie, it's me. Georgie, don't die, don't die, I love you, Georgie.

Georgie didn't answer. Or move, or open her eyes. Or even breathe her own breath.

Tom came back. 'Do you want to go back to the hotel and get some sleep? I'll stay here with her.'

'I'm not sleepy.' Olivia didn't take her eyes off Georgie's face. 'Did you ask him what happened?'

'He didn't know, exactly. He said it looked as if she hit something, rather than the other way round.'

'Hit what? A car?'

'He didn't know. He wasn't on duty when she came in, so he didn't talk to the police.'

'The police?'

'How do you think she got here?' Tom said wearily, not in his patient patients' voice. 'I've got the name and phone number of the guy who has all the gory details.'

'A policeman, you mean?' Olivia sounded stupid even to her own ears. Her brain didn't seem to be working much better than Georgie's right now.

'I presume so. Inspector John Sargent. He must have been extra pleased when he got his last promotion. Do you want to talk to him right now?'

'If he can come here.' She kept her eyes on Georgie. She wasn't going anywhere right now.

Tom went away and came back to tell her that Inspector Sargent was keen to talk to them and would be around in an hour or so. 'Do you want some coffee?'

'Tea, please.' Eighteen years abroad hadn't cured her of that preference.

'I thought coffee might help to keep you awake for a while.'

'I told you, I'm not sleepy. Are you?'

'Well, I am going to be wanting forty winks sometime this afternoon.'

'You can go back when you want. I'll stay here with her.'

'She's not actually critical right now, you know, Lia. Condition poor but stable is the technical term.'

'Go away, Tom, and get me my tea.'

She had another cup of tea an hour later when the inspector arrived, because Tom said it would be better to talk to him in the cafeteria.

Tom knew about the etiquette of hospitals, so if he said the cafeteria was the place to talk to a policeman, that was what happened.

The inspector looked to be about forty. About her own age, Olivia realized with a sense of dull surprise that was rapidly becoming familiar. Once you got past thirty-five, it seemed like the world was being entirely run by people your own age. Terrifying, really, because how much could they possibly know about whatever they were supposed to be in charge of? And then it meant that whatever you hadn't done that you'd always meant to do, you had no more excuses.

In the case of the inspector, she was irrationally reassured by the remains of a Scottish accent. His first concern was quite properly for Georgie. 'How's your girl? Holding steady?'

'So far,' Tom agreed. He explained about the operation that morning, and about tomorrow and the ventilator. Olivia shut her ears to that bit.

'Well, we'll all keep our fingers crossed and say our prayers,' the policeman said with a brutal sort of sympathy. 'So will the lad that did it, I imagine. Otherwise he could be up for manslaughter, if not murder.'

Tom and Olivia stared at him, uncomprehending. The mention of murder had bewildered them. It had never crossed Olivia's mind that anyone might have done that to Georgie on purpose.

The inspector misread their amazement. 'Oh yes, we've got him. Turned himself in, as a matter of fact, yesterday morning,' he added with satisfaction, as if that circumstance redounded to the credit of the police. Perhaps it suggested they enjoyed such a terrifying reputation for efficiency that the villains gave themselves up rather than waste police time and public money by trying to postpone the inevitable outcome.

'We don't know anything about it,' Tom told him. 'What happened?'

'Well, it seems she was having an argument with this boy out in the street, and he gave her a real shove and she cracked her head on a sign post. Right in the street,' he repeated, though the involvement of the sign post had already made that perfectly clear.

Tom began to ask questions, unjustly aiming his indignation at the policeman. 'Where did this happen? When?'

'Moorgate, six o'clock or thereabouts on Tuesday evening. Plenty of witnesses.'

'And he just walked off? Didn't anyone try to stop him?'

'Well, they were a touch surprised, to say the least. No one had taken much notice up to then. They all said they thought it was just an argument with the boyfriend, and naturally they didn't want to get involved.'

'Naturally,' Tom echoed acidly.

'Well, he's a big strapping lad, Dr Payne, well over six foot. And she wasn't asking for help.'

'Who is he? Was it really someone she knew?'

'So he says. He says just what the witnesses all say, that they were having an argument. And he didn't mean to do it, of course. That goes without saying.'

'Of course. What was the argument about?'

'Now that he won't say. He seems a well-spoken young man,' the inspector added, rather mysteriously, Olivia thought. Possibly he meant to imply that a well-spoken person had less excuse for resorting to violence in order to win an argument. 'He asked if he could see her, but I said that was up to you. In any case he can't go anywhere until he gets himself bailed.'

'You mean he's still sitting in a cell? I thought they let everyone out these days – mass murderers, serial rapists, the whole lot.'

'So it seems they do, Dr Payne. And he'd be out by now too, only when his father tried to arrange bail he refused to take it.'

Olivia understood now. Georgie was the sweetest child in the world, but she had absolutely no sense of self-preservation. She was forever being put upon by dubious characters; she attracted lunatics like flies. Obviously she had got embroiled with some nutter and not known how to extricate herself. 'What's his name?'

'Luke Winter.'

If Olivia hadn't been sitting down she would have fallen down. As it was, she could only stare at the inspector, who now proved to be not as slow as he had let on. 'You know him, do you, Mrs Payne?'

'He's my brother,' she said faintly.

'Ah, well.' The inspector nodded with obscure satisfaction, as if this information had cleared up the whole case as far as he was concerned. 'He didn't tell us that. Maybe you'd like to come down and have a word with him, then, since he won't talk to your father.'

'He's not my father, he's my stepfather. And I can't go now. I'm going back to my daughter right now.'

She stood up and swayed, and grabbed the edge of the table. Tom jumped up to support her, and the policeman put his hand on her arm. 'All right, are you, Mrs Payne?'

'Lia, you must be dead tired. I'm taking you back to the hotel.' By the tone of Tom's voice, she was not now the patient's mother but the patient herself.

'Later. Let me go back and see Georgie first. One of us should stay with her the whole time. Just in case . . .'

In case she woke up. Or in case – in case of the opposite . . .

As they were coming down the corridor to the intensive care ward where Georgie was lying dead to the world, a nurse came up to meet them.

'Dr Payne?' It was clear that Tom's status as a doctor had also transformed him into the undisputed Next of Kin. Olivia as a mere non-medical mother possessed no authority at all. 'Dr Payne, there's someone here to see your daughter. He says he's Georgie's brother, but you hadn't mentioned . . .'

Tom looked at Olivia. 'Another member of your extended family?'

Olivia was looking over the nurse's shoulder at the young man standing by the nursing station. He was about her own height, slim and dark. Her father's nose. Althea's mouth.

'Matty,' she said.

He couldn't have heard her, over that distance. But he turned his head and saw her, and she saw that he knew her. He had been not quite four years old when she last set eyes on him.

'It's okay,' she said to the nurse. 'He's my brother, not Georgie's. But it's okay, he can go in.' She went right up to Matthew, who was waiting politely at the desk. She thought maybe she should hug him, he being her brother and all, but on the other hand, after eighteen years of silence that might seem a bit presumptuous. Even though once upon a time she had loved him like her own child. 'You're Matty, aren't you? I'm Lia.'

He didn't show any sign of being inclined to embrace her. He was smiling, her father's small cool smile. 'I know.'

'Surely you didn't remember me after all this time.'

'You look like Georgie.'

Of course he knew Georgie. She would have met them all by now. Would have been wondering why on earth her mother had chosen to disown such a swell bunch of people.

Would have been . . . if she hadn't had all the thoughts knocked out of her head by one of the swell bunch.

She put her hand on Tom's arm, bringing him forward. 'This is my husband Tom. Georgie's father.'

Tom extended his hand automatically. Matthew looked him up and down distantly before consenting to shake it. 'How interesting to meet you, Georgie's father.'

Olivia could see that the little boy she had left behind had grown up a lot since she last saw him, but not entirely in a helpful direction. She must have become a hissing and a byword in her father's household for having left them like that. And serve her right too.

She asked Matthew, 'Where's Daddy? Does he know what's happened to Georgie?'

Matthew gave her a dose of the almost insolent survey he had given Tom. 'He's on his way back from France with my mother. They should be here sometime this afternoon. It took a while for the gendarmerie to track him down.' He paused. 'Can I go in and see Georgie now?'

They all went in and stood by the bed. Georgie looked just as she had half an hour ago, totally unrecognizable.

Matthew gazed down at her impassively. Olivia glanced at his face, then at Georgie. She wondered in an abstracted way what sort of relationship her brother and her daughter might have developed over the summer. Long ago they had lived together in her father's house like brother and sister.

'You look jet-lagged,' Matthew said to Olivia.

'I guess I am,' she admitted, finally allowing herself to feel her exhaustion. 'I haven't slept for two days.'

'Do you want me to sit with Georgie while you get some sleep?'

Olivia glanced at him in surprise. He might have inherited her father's nose, but not, evidently, her father's limited awareness of what went on inside other people's heads. 'Could you? That would be wonderful. Tom and I are both feeling rather whacked. We won't be gone more than a couple of hours.'

'Take your time. I've got nothing else to do. And our mutual daddy should be showing up sometime soon, to do his bit at the bedside.'

'I think that kid's inclined to be a smart-ass,' Tom observed as they were on their way out.

'Self-preservation, I expect.' Olivia's eyes were so tired that when she blinked in the sunlight she had to struggle to get the lids apart again. 'He's my father's son, after all.'

22

None of them can by any means redeem his brother,
nor give to God a ransom for him.

Tom hadn't wanted her to go. Had objected strongly, argued with her. Given orders, for what that was worth. 'You keep out of it, Lia. Let him rot, for God's sake. Look what he did to Georgie. You're Georgie's mother, not that punk's.'

Olivia didn't need any reminding about whose mother she was. 'But he wouldn't let Nick bail him. And I don't know how to get hold of my mother.'

'That's her problem. His problem. He sounds like a nutcase anyway.' Tom was fond of using clinical terminology.

As reported, he did sound like a nutcase. But Olivia had in her head a picture of a small blond boy, Georgie's playmate. She couldn't leave her little brother to rot, no matter what he had done. And she wanted to know just what he had done, and why.

She had imagined herself sitting on one side of a vertical grille, like in cartoons about a prisoner being visited by his wife or attorney. But Inspector Sargent showed her into an ordinary room and sat her down on one side of a table. Maybe the grille devices didn't come into play until you had actually been convicted.

Another policeman brought her brother in.

Not a small boy but a big shock. Not her little brother but Nick's son. The sight of him rocked her like a physical blow. If she had caught a glimpse of him in the street, she might even have thought . . .

But he was bigger, younger, more vulnerable than Nick, even though just now he was deliberately looking sullen and yobbish. Nick's son, unmistakably.

He was leaning on the back of a chair, staring down at her. The policeman stood behind him, between him and the door. As if he would have done anything as mad as trying to make a break for it when he had already refused to be bailed by his father.

He was staring at her with Nick's light blue eyes, devastating her. If Georgie died, this man would be her killer.

She cleared her throat and managed to speak. 'Luke?'

'You're Lia.' He spoke grudgingly, as if even that much was a concession to authority.

The sound of his voice released her anger. She stood up to confront him, defending her daughter after the fact. 'What have you done to Georgie? What right did you have to hit her? Did they tell you she might die?'

Luke sat down in the chair next to the one he had been leaning on. He was a big lad, as the inspector had observed, and his movements were unavoidably vigorous, with the overflowing energy of an athletic young man. When he dropped into a chair, the table trembled. He leaned on his hand, half covering his face with it. 'Oh Christ, I know. I'm sorry.'

Easy to say sorry now, Olivia thought, unmoved. Sorry when it was too late.

'Christ,' he said again, slowly, thickly, making a groan of it. He didn't look up at her. 'Jesus. Jesus.'

The set of his wide shoulders, defeated, defenceless, moved her against her will. 'Why didn't you let Nick bail you out?'

He glanced sidelong at her. She could see his face go stubbornly blank again. 'I don't need any favours from him.'

Olivia felt a small twinge of sympathy for him. She knew what it was like, not to want to take favours from Nick. But she was more concerned on her mother's behalf than for this graceless manchild. 'What about your mother? She can't want you to be locked up in here.'

He took his hand away from his head and gave her a very odd look. His mouth twisted. 'Did you really not know? She's dead.'

For a merciful moment she didn't believe him. In that instant of disbelief her mind and body braced themselves for impact. 'What do you mean?'

'Dead only means one thing, doesn't it?'

'When?' Not that it mattered; she only asked to keep from feeling. 'How?'

He spread his big hands out on the table and looked at them with a detached air, as if they might have belonged to someone else. 'After Christmas. Brain haemorrhage. They wired her up to a life-support machine. And then they turned her off.'

He glanced up, into her face. She didn't know what expression he saw there, other than stunned horror, but whatever it was, it moved him to add with cool brutality, 'What do you care? She could have been dead for eighteen years as far as you were concerned.'

This boy had Nick's own tongue in his head. The notion of civility did not exist for him. But he had done her a favour with his deliberate cruelty, maybe, like slapping someone in the throes of hysteria. And she deserved the rebuke. From his point of view, her mother's point of view, Olivia had deserted them.

Guilt gave her patience – a little – and held the edge of her anger. Why should she be angry with him because her mother was dead? Angry with him over Georgie, certainly, though he genuinely seemed to be at least as sorry himself. But his mother too had died last Christmas.

She said it, the words that Tom had told her not to say. 'Actually, I came to bail you.'

'If you're fool enough to want to do it, go ahead.'

She forgave him for that gratuitous bit of bravado, because he was Nick's son. Even as a small boy, she recalled, he had always taken things further than was wise. She spoke briskly, before she could change her mind. 'I'll have to find someone to arrange it. Who is your father's solicitor, do you know?'

'Not a bloody clue.'

'Then give me Nick's phone number. I'll find out from him.'

'He's not here any more.'

'What do you mean, not here?'

'He's gone away. Left home. No longer living in London.'

'Where is he, then?'

Luke didn't answer.

The inspector interrupted, addressing him with brisk acerbity. 'Come on, lad, we don't want you taking up space in our cells one minute longer than necessary. We've plenty of others to put in your place. Tell the lady what she needs to know.'

'He's gone to New York,' Luke said sulkily. 'He has a flat there. The house over here is being sold.'

Olivia repeated what she understood him to mean. 'He went to New York and left you here in jail?'

'Nothing to do with him any more, was it? He did his bit and I turned him down.'

She was not much given to bad language but she really felt the need of it right now. Her brother and his father were a prize pair of pig-headed pea-brained stupidly self-absorbed irrational idiots. She said as much to herself. Aloud she only said to the inspector, 'Never mind, I'll sort it out myself.'

The silent policeman took Luke away. The helpful inspector explained to Olivia what she needed to do. Olivia thanked him and said she would get right back to him.

Then she went to find a phone booth and rang the number of her father's flat, which Matthew had given her. She still hadn't seen her father but she would see him tonight. She and Tom were going to dinner at the flat, which was in the Barbican and therefore only a few minutes from the hospital. Tom was on duty with Georgie at the moment.

Matthew answered the phone. Olivia recognized his voice. 'Matty, it's Lia. I need a solicitor. Can you ask Althea to recommend me one?'

'I already have.'

'Have what?'

'I've already got the name of a lawyer for you,' he said patiently. 'It's for Luke, yeah?'

'Yes, but why did you –'

'Well, somebody had to, didn't they? Especially after Dumbo told his old man to get stuffed. I sympathize with the sentiments, but really he's not very bright, that boy. Okay, are you ready to write this down?'

It took Olivia ages to get back to the hospital. She had contacted the solicitor and explained matters and arranged to meet him at the police station. She waited outside in the street for him because she wanted to explain a few more things in person.

This time she suppressed her sense of surprise when he turned out to be a man of her own age. Perhaps it was coming back to London that had done it. In a place where she had only been young, been the child instead of the parent, she still expected all the authority figures to be her parents' age. And so they were, the age that her parents had been when she left home.

'Listen, Mr Sawyer, this boy you're going to be acting for – '

'Your brother, didn't you say?'

'Yes. He doesn't have any money, but his father does.'

'Has your father agreed to pay on his behalf, Mrs Payne?'

'He's not my father. Luke's only my half-brother. And my mother is dead,' she remembered and added in surprise.

'I see,' the solicitor said impatiently, obviously neither seeing nor caring but going straight to the nub of the affair. 'So where shall I send the bill?'

The man was only trying to make a living. He had a right to make sure he was going to get paid for his work. But Olivia was damned if she was going to pick up the tab for some lawyer to defend Nick's psychopathic son from the consequences of trying to murder Georgie. On the other hand, she didn't know Nick's address, neither here nor in New York. 'Well, all right, send it to me at Luke's address. He's an idiot but I presume he knows where he lives.'

The solicitor seemed satisfied with that. It sounded iffy to Olivia, but after all he knew Althea and knew that she was Althea's stepdaughter, so he always had another way of coming at her if the bills came back marked *Not at this address*.

After all the tribulations of the morning it was almost a relief to get back to the hospital. There was no change in Georgie's condition, but some deterioration in Tom's. He had been trying to do the crossword in *The Times*, with a complete lack of success.

'I haven't understood a single clue, not one,' he complained, as if that were the fault of the crossword compilers.

'They're cryptic clues,' Olivia explained. 'They don't work like the ones in the *Globe and Mail*. My father can explain them to you.'

Tom threw the paper on the floor and deliberately stomped on it to express his contempt for cryptic crosswords. 'Did you actually go to see that thug?'

'Yes, I did.' She took a deep breath. 'And I got him bailed.'

'I told you not to do that, Lia.' He glared at her, furious with the world in general and with her in particular. Blaming her for her brother's assault on his daughter. 'I told you, let him rot. At least as long as Georgie is . . .' He gestured at the bed.

208

Maybe for ever, then.

'Tom.' She remembered again. Funny how it kept slipping out of her mind. As if she was determined not to know. If she hadn't come back, she might never have known. 'Tom, my mother's dead.'

'What? When?'

'Last Christmas. Luke told me. I . . .' She looked down at Georgie and thought of Luke's description of her mother. Turned off. 'Tom, I . . .'

She crumpled. Her legs, her composure, the buttress of busyness that had kept her going for three days. She collapsed on to the corner of the bed and cried, wringing her helpless hands in her lap, too shattered even to cover her face.

'Hey, come on. You can't cry here, you'll scare the other patients.'

That was the sort of thing he would have said to his paediatric patients, to distract them and jolly them over their pain. Now he said it to her because the sight of her tears alarmed him. What was wrong with tears? They were distracting in themselves. But she wanted consoling, not distracting, and there was no consolation to be had.

He could have said more or less what Luke had said: Look, you haven't seen your mother for eighteen years, you deliberately took yourself right out of her life. What serious difference could it possibly make to you that she's dead? But that only made it worse, what she had done to her mother. She should have come home of her own accord, now that Georgie was grown up. Not waited for Georgie's genealogical curiosity to break the ice.

Only, how could she ever have explained her long absence? Over eighteen years she had never been able to think of any acceptable rationalization. What did you say, when the truth wouldn't do? So she had dithered and delayed, thinking always in the back of her mind that one day she would go back home, make it up with her parents somehow and regain the half of her life that had been lost to her. Now half of that half was gone for good.

Tonight she would meet her father for the first time in eighteen years. She still hadn't worked out what to say to him.

Her tears ran out eventually. Even with all the cause she had, she couldn't cry for ever.

Tom was still hovering, still looking discomfited. A crying woman is an embarrassment to any man in the vicinity. 'Listen, Lia, have you had any lunch? Your blood sugar must be at rock bottom. Let's go get something to eat, eh?'

There was no disorder known to man, physical, mental, or emotional, that Tom Payne MD didn't imagine could be improved, if not cured entirely, by a square meal. 'I'm not hungry. I want to sit with Georgie.' What if they turned Georgie off?

'Then I'll get you a sandwich. I'll be right back.'

It was perversely soothing to sit and watch the beat of her daughter's heart, the rhythm of her daughter's brain, electronically amplified and displayed. Her own heartbeat and brainwaves would have been bouncing all over the screen. Georgie's biorhythms washed across in perfect peace, undisturbed by knowledge or grief.

A nurse came over, one she hadn't seen before. 'There's a young man outside. He says he's Georgie's brother.'

The one person who was guaranteed not to be turning up was Georgie's brother. Tom had phoned his father last night but they had had no word from the Yukon. Alex was still incommunicado. 'No, he's my brother,' Olivia explained. 'Let him come in.'

She didn't take her eyes off the screens. When she felt a presence behind her, she turned her head briefly to say hello to Matthew. Only it was Luke.

He was staring at Georgie. He had gone pale with shock, as if a stranger had done this terrible thing to her and he had only now found out.

Olivia didn't feel at all sorry for him. But seeing he was a big man and looked as if he might faint, she got up from her chair. She didn't want him falling on top of Georgie. 'Here, sit down.'

He sat down heavily, hardly aware of her. He put his hand out to touch Georgie's hand, but withdrew it without making contact. Maybe he had recalled Olivia's presence. 'Sorry.'

'For what, exactly?' She meant why, not what. Why had he done what he had done?

'I have no right . . .' He rubbed his hand across his face. 'I'm sorry I was such a shit back there.'

'You were.' I'll forgive you for that, she thought, but not for this.

He was still staring at Georgie and talking to Olivia. 'I know it sounds stupid, but I didn't really mean . . .' He indicated Georgie.

Olivia said icily, 'Then what exactly *did* you have in mind?'

He flushed. It showed up distinctly in his fair-skinned face. That was something that Nick could never have done; he never would have had the grace to blush. She began to feel just a little bit warmer towards Luke.

'Well, actually,' he said in his slightly husky voice, which sounded like the beginnings of his father's voice, without the cigarettes to roughen it, 'actually I felt like I wanted to kill her. But I didn't really. You know what I mean. This was an accident.'

The accidental result of being six foot three and fourteen stone, she supposed. Men and women hit each other all the time, according to statistics, but only the men succeeded in doing much damage. 'What was the argument about?'

'Something stupid. It doesn't matter now.' He stood up. 'Here, have your chair back. Sorry. Thank you for what you did for me. Do you want me to go away now?'

'Not before you've written down your address and telephone number, and your father's address and phone number in New York.'

He produced a pocket diary, that indispensable aid to English social and business life, and sat down again to carry out her instructions.

While he was copying everything out for her, Tom came back with her sandwich and a cup of tea. He stared at Luke, who carried on writing, not looking up.

'This is Luke,' Olivia explained.

Tom went as white as Luke had done, but with anger rather than shock. 'Get him out of here.'

Olivia felt obliged to put a restraining hand on her husband's chest. Aside from the embarrassment of a possible scene, she didn't want him tangling with what might yet prove to be a homicidal maniac. Or even a young man who dealt death by accident. 'He's just going now.'

So he was. He handed her the promised information and left, without taking any notice of Tom. Perhaps it had seemed to him the most politic course of action, under the circumstances.

Tom stared after him, obviously contemplating a serious assault on his own account. 'What'd they let him in for?'

'I said he could come in. They said my brother and I thought they meant Matty.'

'Well, he's not getting in again. I'll tell them at the desk. You shouldn't have bailed the bastard.'

'Don't be silly, Tom, I had to. He's my brother.' She meant, my mother is dead.

Tom gave her the sandwich and tea and a black look. 'Yeah, I know. Jesus, Lia, what a family you've got. A bunch of psychopaths. Murderers and perverts.'

'Perverts?'

He had started for the door of the ward, presumably to warn the nurses about Luke. He stopped and looked back at her, a long cool significant look. 'You heard me.'

211

23

The heart knows its own bitterness;
and a stranger does not intermeddle with its joy.

It didn't seem right to be going out to dinner with Georgie lying there. But they weren't going very far away, and the hospital had promised to ring them at once if there was any change, and Tom said anyway it wasn't good for Olivia to be sitting fretting at the bedside all day and all night.

And besides, of course, what she was really doing was going to meet her father.

She had spoken to him yesterday, a brief and businesslike chat to establish who was going to be with Georgie when, because the hospital disapproved of family parties in the intensive care ward. Then Althea had invited her and Tom over to dinner tonight. They wanted to hear about Georgie, Althea said.

It was guilt, Olivia admitted frankly to herself, that made her so reluctant to see her father. In this matter at least he was the innocent injured party. Almost.

He had virtually thrown her out of the house when she had told him she was going to Canada and not to university. She had sent him a postcard when she got to Montreal, just to say she was okay, but never got a reply. So she had left it there, not wanting to take the risk of trying to re-establish contact, even with her father, when he had pretty much said he didn't want anything to do with her any more. He had already forgiven her for Georgie and then she had done it again, destroyed his hopes for her future, and for no cause that she could tell him.

She held on to Tom's hand, going up the stairs to the flat. She told herself she had Tom for her ally, but it wasn't really true. None of the others counted: Tom, Althea, Matthew. She had to deal with her father on her own. Like crossing the River Jordan.

Matthew opened the door, which was a relief. Matthew was neutral territory; he harboured no grudges as far as Olivia could tell. She kissed him, sister to brother, and he gave her a little pat on the shoulder. Maybe he was okay.

Althea came up and kissed her as well. It was definitely a cold greeting, only a brush against each of Olivia's cheeks with her own exquisitely made-up and scented cheeks. More of a non-kiss really. She greeted Tom with slightly more warmth.

She was as beautiful as ever, Olivia decided. Only now her appearance was rather more studied and deliberate, as if she spent a lot of time on it, instead of just waking up every morning looking like that.

After greeting them, Althea glanced at the door leading out of the sitting-room. 'Ross will be out in a minute. He's wrestling with his tie.'

Olivia decided to take the situation by the horns. She went over to the door that Althea's glance had indicated, and found herself in a small square inner hall. 'Daddy?'

He came out of the bedroom, shutting the door behind him. 'Lia?'

Olivia stared at him. Her father stared at her.

His hair had gone grey. His shoulders were slightly but unmistakably stooped. He was thinner, almost brittle. His cheeks were rather hollow, his face rather haggard, his mouth indisputably grim. He was handsome still, in an austerely abstract way, like a drawing someone might have done entitled *Head of a handsome old man*.

Her father was an old man.

She had left him in his prime and come home to find him old. It was like the legends about a person who spends a night in fairyland and comes back to find everyone aged by twenty years.

Or, in her mother's case, dead.

She put up her hand to her mouth. She was afraid she was going to cry, and for the wrong reason. Not because she loved him and had missed him. She did, and had, but she had also missed him in the literal sense, missed eighteen years of him, and now she saw him so changed and somehow diminished, and she was going to weep for pity and terror.

She forbade herself, quite uselessly, to cry. He was looking at her and she had to hide her face from him. The only way she could do that was by going up and hugging him.

He stiffened when she put her arms around his neck. He had never known how to cope with her affection, had always felt it not as a gift but as a demand. He put his arms around her anyway, out of duty perhaps. She felt his bony rigid body against hers. She began to cry.

He was worse than Tom when it came to weeping women. Not being a doctor, he didn't have a bedside manner to bully them out of it. And being married to Althea, who thought tears were a sin, he hadn't had much practice lately.

He did hug her for a moment, really hug her, before starting to disengage himself. 'Lia, don't cry. She'll be all right.'

Well, if he wanted to think she was crying over Georgie, that was okay. It gave her an excuse for her tears. 'Sorry, Daddy.'

Sorry for everything. Sorry for eighteen years.

She slackened the intensity of her embrace enough to dry her eyes and blow her nose. 'Did you know that Mummy died last winter?'

'I didn't know until Georgie told me.'

'You were married to her for fifteen years,' Olivia said indignantly. 'How could you not know she was dead?'

'Contrary to popular romantic belief, domestic intimacy doesn't necessarily create eternal psychic bonds. If her obituary wasn't in *The Times*, I had no other way of knowing.' They pulled apart and he added in a dry cold tone, 'She was your mother all your life and you didn't know either.'

'Oh, Daddy.' She started to cry again. He had said that to hurt her, not on her mother's account but on his own. And she had deserved it. She had no defence but the one she could never employ.

She made a cowardly escape. 'I've got to go to the loo.'

The loo turned out to be the third door in the little hall, not the bedroom on the right, not the broom closet in front of her, but the left-hand door that shared a wall with the kitchen. She ducked inside and locked the door and wept. It was unspeakably awful. She had ruined everybody's life. Everybody but the one who was the cause of it all. And she hadn't even had a chance to say sorry to her mother.

By the time she came out, red-eyed but relatively composed, her father had been introduced to Tom and they were all chatting politely.

How did you chat politely to your son-in-law who was a total stranger, who had come over on account of your granddaughter who was lying near to death in a hospital bed? Well, if you were Althea, you asked about the weather in Toronto and the flight over to England.

Matthew had different ideas about politeness. When Olivia appeared he said to her abruptly. 'How's Georgie?'

'No change,' Olivia told him. 'She just lies there and . . . and breathes.'

'How long does this go on for?' Now he was challenging Tom, the medical doctor. 'Isn't she in, what do they call it, a vegetative state?'

'Strictly speaking, yes.' Tom looked faintly alarmed at having to contend with a layman who had apparently armed himself with some knowledge of the jargon of medical mysteries. 'But you're thinking of something much more serious, PVS or persistent vegetative state.'

'How many days before it's persistent?'

214

You're already persistent, Tom's look said. 'Well, there isn't any official demarcation. People have been known to recover without ill effects after weeks or even months. But obviously, the longer it goes on the worse the prognosis.'

'So it really matters, how soon she comes to?'

'Well, it might. It's not desperate yet, three days is hardly indicative. When someone sustains a concussion, what actually happens is that the brain gets bruised by being knocked against the skull, like a passenger in a car being thrown on to the dashboard when the car hits something. The danger there is that it takes a day or two for the swelling to come up, and the resulting pressure can kill or cause permanent damage. They've taken action to relieve the pressure, and the swelling should start to go down now, so we can live in hope. And she's off the ventilator, that's a good sign. But as I said, the sooner she comes to, the better.'

'What do you do to make her wake up?'

'Nothing very scientific, I'm afraid. Talk to her, stroke her, play music – anything to get her attention.'

Olivia held her breath, not daring to interrupt. Matthew was asking all the blunt questions that she herself couldn't. She couldn't ask them of the consultant, because the consultant would only speak seriously to Tom; Olivia just got a pat on her pretty little head. And she couldn't ask them of Tom, because . . . because it was Georgie.

'That doesn't sound scientific at all,' said Olivia's father. 'Do you mean to imply that even when she's unconscious her awareness is still around somewhere? How can that be? If awareness is a higher function of the brain, and the brain isn't functioning on any level beyond the most basic autonomic activities . . .'

'God knows,' Tom said bluntly. 'I certainly don't. All I can tell you is that coma patients sometimes regain consciousness when they hear familiar voices. They really can be . . . called back from the dead.'

He said that last bit in a rush, out of embarrassment, Olivia knew, because as her father had just pointed out it wasn't remotely scientific. Come to think of it, though, there was nothing remotely scientific about the whole idea of life and death. Some things were alive and some were dead, and some were first the one and then the other, and nobody had the faintest idea what really made the difference.

Matthew changed the subject. Apparently. He said to Olivia, 'How did you do with Luke?'

'Well, he's out of jail.' She glanced at Tom. 'First thing he did, he came to see Georgie.'

'What a cheek,' Althea said indignantly. 'Matty, I wish you'd

215

asked us beforehand about letting him stay here. This isn't a dosshouse, you know. And his father could afford to put him up at the Dorchester if he wanted.'

'Well, I don't think his father wanted,' Matthew said drily. 'And he is a relative, in a roundabout way. At least he's related to Lia and Georgie, and they're related to us.'

'Well, he's nothing to do with Ross or me, thank God, or you for that matter. I'm sorry his mother is dead and his father is a rotter, but he's well grown up in anybody's books and he'll have to look after himself.'

'Ma,' said Matthew, surprisingly gently – maybe he really did love his unlovable mother, Olivia thought in wonder – if they gave you the sack tomorrow, and the old man threw you out the next day, where would you go?'

'To see my solicitor,' Althea said with spirit. 'And maybe I would go home to Mummy and Daddy for a little while, Matty, which is what I suppose you're getting at, but in the end I'd have to look after myself.'

'So will Luke, in the end,' Matthew agreed, laughing without malice at his mother. 'All I wanted to say, believe it or not, is that Georgie knows Luke's voice as well as anyone's, and he's got nothing else to do with his time but talk to her.'

'He's not getting within a mile of her,' said Tom. They seemed to be taking it in turns to express righteous indignation, and this was Tom's go. Olivia was surprised, and amused in spite of herself, to see her father's face show approval of her husband's statement. 'If I'd been beaten up, the last person I'd want at my bedside is the son of a bitch who did it.'

Althea said, to Olivia's relief, 'I think the dinner's ready to be served.'

While Tom was in the hotel bathroom, brushing his teeth or whatever he did before bed – in all the years of their marriage Olivia had never discovered what took him so long, because he always locked the door – she decided to try the New York number Luke had given her. New York was the same time zone as Toronto, wasn't it? Which made it early evening there.

She rang without getting any answer. She let it ring until the automatic cut-off disconnected her. Then she redialled and did the same thing again, in case she had got a wrong number the first time.

Tom came out of the bathroom just as she was disconnected for the second time. He was wearing his dressing-gown, brought along in case of a fire in the middle of the night. Olivia was wearing a

216

night-gown in deference to the same hypothetical emergency. At home they never wore anything to bed. When they first started living together they used to get ready for bed every night by putting on pyjamas; then they would get into bed and promptly take them off again. After about two weeks of this Olivia had suggested they save themselves the trouble. The reason for the nudity had died down as she became seriously pregnant with Alex, and never revived to anything like the same intensity, but by then they had acquired the habit of no habit.

'Who are you calling this time of night? I've already spoken to my mother.'

'I'm ringing Luke's father. But he doesn't seem to be there.'

'What do you want him for?'

'Because he's gone away and left Luke locked up, as far as he knows.'

'Just what I'd've done, if my kid had tried to kill somebody.'

'You would not,' Olivia said severely. Though of course Alex would never have done such a thing. 'Anyway, he's going to have to pick up the tab for the lawyer, whether he likes it or not.'

'Why don't you just let Luke worry about that? He's all grown up, officially.'

'He's grown up like Georgie's grown up. Hardly at all.' She wished she hadn't said that. Would Georgie live to grow up?

'So what? I can't see that he's your responsibility. When you were twenty-one you were married with two children. And you'd left home for good.' He took off the dressing-gown, tossed it at a chair, missing the chair, and rolled himself into bed. 'Let's go to bed, eh?'

Olivia sat down on her side of the bed and inched herself under the covers, trying to keep her night-gown from bunching up. She knew what was going to happen next, and dreaded it. But it happened anyway.

'Are you over your jet lag?'

That had been her excuse yesterday. Tonight she wasn't allowed to have any excuse. 'I guess so.'

He slid towards her, pushed back the bedclothes and pulled up the night-gown she had so carefully kept down over her legs. 'Christ, it's been two whole months. I hate those goddamn wolves.'

She put her arm around his neck to show willing. 'It would have been another two weeks if all this hadn't happened. And abstinence is supposed to be good for the soul.'

'Don't give me that crap. It's a wife's duty to keep her husband happy. Especially a wife who's only there three-quarters of the time.'

He kissed her mouth and stroked her crotch. After about thirty seconds she edged herself to the right and him to the left so that he was over her, and with her hand she invited him to enter her. There was no point waiting. As far as she was concerned, it was just a matter of getting things over with as quickly as possible. He didn't seem to mind, or even to notice.

It was an unspoken bargain between them that if she was going to be up North three or four months of the year, she had no right to say no for the rest of the time. That was the price of his going along with the inconvenient career she had chosen. Men could be sailors, soldiers, travelling salesmen, doctors working all hours, and their wives just had to put up with their absences. But husbands were not brought up to be so obliging. Tom wasn't terribly demanding: twice a week was enough to keep him happy, with co-operation rather than a professional performance on her part. And it was comforting, sometimes, to be close to another body.

Other times, like tonight, it only increased her loneliness.

He was a good man, and she loved him as much as she could. He seemed to love her and he certainly loved Georgie. And Alex, of course, but Alex was his anyway. He had saved her and Georgie when they most needed rescue. He had married her and given her his family for her own. The fact that for all their married life her body might as well have been asleep whenever he made love to her, was hardly relevant in the face of all that.

When he had brought himself to climax with the use of her body, he rolled over and went to sleep right away. She always knew when he was asleep, by the sound of his breathing. After nearly eighteen years the rhythm of his lungs in the darkness was as familiar as her own.

She wasn't lying awake in sexual frustration. She didn't even get as far as that. She had learned how to avoid it by turning herself right off. At the beginning she had tried masturbation, but that meant invoking fantasies, or memories, that made everything worse rather than better. If the price of physical satisfaction was an unappeasable ache in her soul, she would rather go without it.

When she had started university as a 'mature' undergraduate in Toronto, she had had no time to waste in student socializing, and besides, her classmates were nearly all babies as far as she was concerned. But when she got to graduate school, everybody was older and the process of education more informal. What with raising two children, and working at her studies, and Tom simply taking her for granted, it was a long time since she had been aware of herself as a desirable woman, attractive to men. It came as a shock when one of her fellow students made advances to her.

She had turned him down – it wasn't a real temptation, she didn't like him much – but the episode opened her eyes to a world she had never noticed, a demi-monde of infidelity. All you needed to gain entrée was your own internal consciousness of a restless desire. It seemed to give you a kind of badge, a Masonic handshake, a mark of Cain, so that other denizens of that world would recognize and approach you. It was true what her grandmother used to say, that trouble came and found you if you were looking for it.

She decided she didn't want it. She tried it once, with a man she quite liked. It was exciting at the time but she felt quite ill afterwards. Perhaps she was allergic to adultery.

She stopped wearing make-up, or dressing up at all, except when she was out with Tom. She derailed her train of thought whenever she found herself day-dreaming or speculating along forbidden lines.

It seemed to work. At any rate the mark of Cain must have disappeared from her forehead. She was no longer constantly aware of moving in a sexual context, no longer knew who was sleeping with whom. She seemed to have become invisible again to men looking for adventure.

That was the end of any fantasizing. She couldn't have an affair, because it would be wronging Tom, and it wouldn't have the desired result anyway. She couldn't have an alternative sex life of one-night stands with strangers, because it was dangerous and because the strangers weren't strangers to themselves. Nobody on earth went around with a name tag labelled Stranger. So the consequences were incalculable.

Anyway, she told herself as she lay in the darkened hotel room listening to her husband breathe, she should be grateful for what she had. She would gladly have forsworn all sexual activity for the rest of her life, if that were the price of having Georgie well again. And what would she have given for the chance to see her mother once more? Just to hug her and cry in her arms as she had with her father. Just to say, Sorry, sorry, it wasn't because of you.

24

We ought always to pray, and not to faint.

She dreams of Noah.

Dead Noah, that is. She might well have dreamt of Noah as he had been: a playful cub, an energetic hunter, an amiable friend, a responsible father. A lovely creature, to her non-wolf eyes. But that is not the Noah that comes to her now in dreams.

Blood stains his muzzle, and the leaves under it. He must have dragged himself a long way, looking for help. What help could there be for him anywhere, a wolf in the wilderness? She might have helped him but he couldn't know that. Maybe he was only looking for a decent place to die.

Booboo finds him. She never takes Boo near the wolf dens, in case they attack him, but after seven years she knows where the wolves seldom go, which is mostly where the deer trails don't go. She has a rifle in the cabin but she never takes it out with her. It's there to defend her from human depravity, not from wolves. Where the wolves are concerned, her own presence is enough to protect Booboo, though naturally Boo thinks things are the other way round.

Led by Booboo's nose and curiosity, she finds Noah, lying under an outcrop of rock. She knows him by his markings: a beautiful black wolf with a silver ruff.

The great glaciers of prehistory robbed Peter to pay Paul, stripping the Shield of its precious skin of soil in order to create the deep black tall-grass prairie to the west and south. The podsol left here is thin and acidic from conifer needles. The bedrock bursts through it everywhere, the bones of the earth revealed without the fat of the land. Before white men came, the only living to be had here was by hunting and fishing. Now there are a few other occupations, mining or logging.

But someone has gone hunting Noah.

More likely they shot him from fear, or for fun. It's a criminal offence, wolves are a protected species, but here in the wilderness who is to know? She knows of the crime now, but not the criminal.

Booboo sniffs irreverently at the corpse. The scavenging foxes and ravens haven't found him yet. He can only have been dead a few hours. If she had come sooner . . .

No, he wasn't a pet. He would never have let an alien, even a known alien, come near enough to touch him as long as he had breath in his body. And she isn't a vet. She knows all about dead animals, but not very much about how to keep them alive.

She can see the small hole in his coat, in his shoulder, where the bullet has gone in. Death in delayed guise, leaving his life to bleed away internally.

You don't come across a dead wolf very often. As a biologist maybe she should take the opportunity to dissect him. To assess his age and state of health – before being shot, that is – and other items of interest to a scientist. But she knows all that already. She knows his whole life story. He was four years old, and his father was Esau, presumed dead, and his mother is Rachel, retired matriarch of the pack, too old to hunt but a useful baby-sitter for the cubs. This spring for the first time Noah fathered cubs himself: Shem, Ham, and Japheth.

She has taken to naming her wolves from the lists of begattings in the Bible. Someday maybe she will get as far as Joseph the carpenter and his son. What would a wolves' messiah be like, how would he set about saving his people? Like mankind they are in sore need of salvation, but biologically rather than spiritually. Well, maybe both; what does she know about the souls of wolves?

She doesn't bury Noah. The soil is too shallow to put him out of reach of scavengers. Anyway, he had to die sometime. Four years, eight years, a bullet or pneumonia, what difference does it make in the end? His natural destiny was food for the foxes. Nothing to cry over.

She woke up and remembered her mother. Fifty-six or eighty, what difference did it make in the end? Nothing to cry over, right?

She went into the bathroom to weep, so as not to wake Tom.

Next morning, while Tom was having a bath, Olivia tried New York again.

It was three o'clock in the morning there. He had to be at home now – assuming he was sleeping in his own bed. She wouldn't be surprised if that was not the case. It rang so long she thought the line was going to disconnect itself. Then the ring was abruptly interrupted by a voice that sounded like a bear roused untimely from his hibernation. 'Yeah?'

'Nick?'

'Who the fuck is that?'

'It's Lia.'

He didn't say anything for a long minute. She knew he was still there because she could hear him breathing. The post-hibernatory bear filling his lungs, to start his brain working again. Maybe he was trying to remember who she was. 'What d'you think you're doing, for Christ's sake? It's three o'clock in the fucking morning.'

'It's eight o'clock here. And you weren't in last night.'

Another silence. This time perhaps he was working out where she must be if it was eight o'clock where she was. 'Are you in London? How's Georgie?'

'Still unconscious.'

'Oh, Christ.' A long pause. 'I'm sorry, kitten.'

She was outraged. How dare he call her by that name after all this time, after what he had done? 'That hardly matters,' she said coldly. 'What does matter is that you ought to be here instead of there.'

'What for? I'm not a doctor.'

She could hear Tom splashing about in the bath. She cupped her hand around her mouth and the telephone receiver to make sure her voice went to New York and not into the bathroom. 'You know very well why. You had no business going off like that in the first place. I've hired a lawyer for Luke and you're going to pay for him.'

'It was business that brought me over here, sweetheart. And Luke and his lawyer don't need me around as long as they know where to send the bill.'

'I didn't even know that much,' she hissed down the line. 'I had to get Luke out of jail in order to find out where you'd got to and how to get hold of you.'

More silence. When his voice came again it was colder even than hers. 'Well, that's an option Em didn't have, isn't it? You didn't even leave a forwarding address.'

'And you know why.' She had to close her eyes and pause for a moment, to get her breath back after the wave of primeval emotion – rage, revulsion, grief – that had swept her beyond speech. If he had been there in front of her, she would have . . . she would have tried to do to him what Luke had done to Georgie. 'For God's sake get back here, and for once in your life stop walking away from your responsibilities. It's *your* child we're talking about.'

'Lia, if you really want me to come back, why don't you just ask me nicely?'

She hung up.

Tom was standing in the doorway to the bathroom, still dampish from the tub, a towel tucked around his middle. 'Who was that you were exchanging pleasantries with?'

Olivia sat down on the bed, feeling drained. After eighteen years' absence, her stepfather was still a past master at reducing her to impotent hysteria in the most efficient manner imaginable. Not only did he not mind hitting below the belt, he didn't even acknowledge where the belt line was.

'It was Nick.'

'Is he coming back?'

'God knows.'

She got up and found herself a clean pair of knickers and put them on. Then she pulled her night-gown off over her head. Tom came over to her and began to stroke her bare breasts. With his other hand he pulled the knickers down and stroked her between her legs.

222

She made an effort to discourage him. 'Tom, we've got to get going. We haven't even had breakfast yet.'

'Five minutes. Come on. We've got ten goddamn weeks to make up for.'

She knew the rules. She wasn't allowed to say no.

Now that she knew, from what Tom had said last night, that time was an enemy where Georgie was concerned, Olivia was even more reluctant to leave her bedside. She stroked her daughter's hand, her arm, her face, her eyelids and mouth. She whispered in her unresponsive ear. She kissed her and called her, feeling more and more like an amateur and unsuccessful Witch of Endor.

Or someone at a ouija board. The consultant had suggested asking Georgie to squeeze Olivia's hand if she could hear her. Sometimes Olivia thought she was getting a faint response and other times she decided it was only wishful thinking. Tom had tried it too and wasn't sure either.

She wished her old friend Megan were here. Meg would know how to go about it. Megan had a firm and unswerving belief in the existence of the soul and its priority over the body. Megan was the one person in her past life that she hadn't given up when she left England. She had told Meg where she was going, though not the real reason why, and in return for swearing secrecy had kept in contact with her. Megan was godmother to Georgie and Alex. She, and her husband and children, lived the nomadic life of medical charity workers in all the most appalling pieces of the Third World. At irregular intervals she landed in Toronto on her way from somewhere to somewhere else, and took an hour or a day to see Olivia.

Olivia was writing a letter to Megan, describing the catastrophe that had befallen Georgie. She had got Tom to write a note on her behalf, explaining the technicalities of the injury. Despite being a nurse, Megan believed in all sorts of weird things, long-distance healing and energy auras and whatnot, and Olivia was hoping her friend would try them all on Georgie from wherever she might be on the far side of the earth. She glanced at the return address on Meg's last letter. Malagasy, wherever that was.

Tom was off getting tea for her and coffee for himself when Matthew turned up. 'My shift now,' he told her. 'You can go outside and play for a while.'

'I don't want to. I can't think about anything else. It just makes it worse, not being here, because I worry more.'

'I've got a message from my father for you. He'll be coming round himself later on to see Georgie, but just in case he misses you, I've been asked to pass it on.'

She looked at him expectantly, thinking what an odd boy he was. Thinking how long ago she had lived in her father's house and looked after Matty along with Georgie. And loved him. 'Well? What is it?'

'Close your eyes and hold out your hand.'

She did that childish thing. He dropped something metallic into her palm. Keys. She opened her eyes again. 'What are they?'

'The keys to the flat. My parents are going back down to Sussex today, so you and Tom can stay at the Barbican.'

'What about you?'

'Your idiot brother has offered to repay my hospitality by inviting me to stay at his house. I thought I ought to take him up on it so as to keep an eye on him, since he obviously shouldn't be allowed out on his own. But that's only until his father has actually sold the house out from under him. He doesn't know exactly when that will be.'

'His father might be coming back,' Olivia warned him. 'At least I told him to.'

'Well, then. I'd better warn Luke. Since I've never to my knowledge met the gentleman, I have that pleasure to look forward to.'

'I wouldn't have phrased it quite like that myself. How is Luke?'

'He's lurking outside here this very moment, like a dog forbidden the company of his mistress and pining away for want of it. Can't you persuade Tom that he's not actually plotting to finish her off?'

'I'll think about it,' she agreed dubiously. It was no use her saying off her own bat that Luke could come in. The nurses took their orders from Tom, because of him being a doctor.

They moved their luggage out of the hotel and into the flat before dinner. Tom made a fuss about having to pay for a whole extra night at the hotel when they weren't going to be sleeping there. He grumbled to Olivia all the way down in the lift, and complained at the check-out desk. 'We haven't touched your damn bed-linen,' he pointed out to the clerk. 'You can rent the room out to the next person who walks in here.'

'Those are the rules, sir,' the clerk explained patiently. 'Check-out time is 11 a.m., and it's now half-past four in the afternoon.'

Tom's irritation was not appeased by this argument. 'I've got a good mind to go back upstairs and mess things around a little, just to get my money's worth,' he told Olivia as she dragged him away. 'Or keep the key till eleven tomorrow, and rent the room out to someone myself. For the price we're paying for that dinky room we could have rented a whole goddamn motel back in Canada.'

Not wanting to fuel his indignation, she forbore to point out the reason for this, namely that more people wanted to come to London than wanted to go to Canada.

That wasn't true of Tom, anyway. He spent all his holidays (when he could be persuaded to take them) at his parents' place on the St Lawrence River, or his brother's cottage on Lake Huron, where he could go sailing and fishing. Two years' study in London had exhausted his interest in foreign travel.

Olivia hated hotels, and the flat was closer to the hospital. Besides, it meant she could cook dinner for herself and Tom. On a holiday she would have been glad to get away from kitchen duty, but in this crisis her psychological ability to cope had been seriously undermined by the absence of domestic routine to occupy her nervous energy and make her feel she was doing something useful.

In the morning, Sunday morning, she got up early while Tom was still asleep. She hadn't slept properly for nearly a week. There was no point lying in bed awake while the sun was shining. She left a note for Tom, saying that she was going round to the hospital and would be back in time for breakfast.

She checked on Georgie – no change, though Olivia wished her good morning – and went out again to walk down to St Paul's. She walked all the way around the churchyard, then went inside to do what she hadn't done for twenty years, not since she had last gone to church with her grandparents. She went in to pray.

She had some trouble doing it. Not because, like King Claudius, her knees refused to make the unaccustomed bend, but because the interior of the cathedral had been roped off. The nave and aisles beyond the rope were full of chattering tourists and booths selling souvenirs. A brisk and unecclesiastical-looking woman manned the only gap in the barricades.

'That'll be two pounds, please. Would you like a guidebook?'

Olivia took some time to catch her meaning. 'But I only want to pray,' she protested, conscious of how cheap and feeble an excuse that seemed.

The woman sternly directed her to a chapel in the corner by the door. 'That's for prayers.'

The chapel itself was occupied by a couple of Germans who had decided to rest their feet and have a good natter while they were at it. Olivia slunk to the back and slipped into a pew of sorts, where she could huddle unnoticed and get her thoughts together.

Her thoughts wouldn't compose themselves. They just came blurting out, inarticulate whispered appeals to someone somewhere.

Please God don't let Georgie die. Please God bring her back to us. Please God tell Mummy I'm sorry I didn't get to see her again. Sorry she didn't get to see Georgie again. Sorry for everything, please God . . .

She had started to cry by that time. She went out of the chapel, past the ticket-taker and the throngs of sightseers and souvenir salesmen, to the steps outside, where she could blow her nose and sniffle. It didn't seem respectful to do it in church.

Then she went back to the hospital to see if it had done any good.

She had only just settled herself at the bedside – still no change – when the nurse came up. There was a gentleman wanting to see Georgie, her stepfather, he said he was, but Dr Payne hadn't mentioned him, and she didn't know . . .

The gentleman hadn't waited at the desk as he had doubtless been instructed. He had followed the nurse right on to the ward and was standing behind her, looking at Olivia with cool blue eyes.

'No,' said Olivia, calmly in spite of the shock, 'it's *my* stepfather. And it's all right.'

When the nurse turned to go and fetch him, he walked past her. The nurse exclaimed in surprise or annoyance, but since there was nothing to be done about it, she went away.

Yesterday morning Olivia had been ready to kill Nick. Today she fell into his arms and sobbed unashamedly.

Unlike every other man in the world, he didn't mind. Nothing ever embarrassed him, she recalled. He held her tightly, let her cry to her heart's content, and called her kitten, as if she were a young girl again.

'Glad to see me after all, are you?'

'I suppose I must be.' She recovered herself and put a little space between her body and his. What she had just done was quite the opposite of what she had intended to do when she saw him. 'How did you get here so soon?'

'It only takes seven hours.'

'But the flights are all full this time of year. Tom and I had to go down and wait on standby, and we only caught the very last flight out.'

'There's always room in first class, baby. Tell your cheapskate husband that next time.' He looked over her shoulder at Georgie. At her bandaged head and bruised face, the tubes and needles and wires. 'Jesus fucking Christ.'

Olivia turned to look at Georgie too. 'Didn't you see her before you left?'

'I didn't even know she was in here. Whatsisname – Ross's kid – rang me up and said Luke was in jug for doing her over and could I please bail him out. I thought he'd just knocked her about a bit. I would have left the stupid kid to suffer for a while but I had a flight to catch, so I got on to him right away. And might as well not have bothered. He said he wasn't taking any tainted money. I thought you might like that line.'

He still had his arm around her. He is still such a bastard, she thought, but she didn't try to move away from him. Just as she hadn't refused, once upon a time, to take his tainted money. 'What does Luke have against you?'

He shrugged. 'The usual adolescent grudges, I guess. And he thinks I behaved like a shit to Em.'

'And did you?'

'Sometimes, maybe. And sometimes not. For someone who calls himself an artist, that kid's got no sense of shading or perspective. Everything's black and white all the time.'

He set Olivia aside quite gently and sat down on the edge of the bed, looking at Georgie. 'What happens now with her?'

Olivia took the chair by Georgie's head, looking from her daughter to her stepfather. Unlike her father, Nick was obviously not an old man. He was nine years younger than her father anyway – nine years older than Tom, for that matter – and he looked to have flourished as the wicked proverbially do. But eighteen years had not left him untouched. His fair hair was flecked with ashy grey. The skin of his face didn't fit him as well as it used to. He was thicker around the middle than he had been. She knew precisely how much thicker, having just embraced him.

She explained about Georgie. 'They can keep her alive, for what that's worth, but they can't really do anything to bring her out of the coma. We have to try to get some response out of her, to wake her up.'

'What d'you mean, wake her up?'

'Well, from what Tom says, it sounds like she needs a witch doctor at this point. Someone to grab her attention, wherever that's got to, and persuade her to come back and open her eyes. I've been talking to her and calling her until I'm almost hoarse.'

She slumped back in the chair, despairing all over again. She said wearily, 'Why don't you try? You're a different voice, she might pay more attention to you.'

He certainly was a different voice. An arresting and unmistakable one to Olivia, who hadn't heard it for eighteen years but still would have known it anywhere – even, she thought, in a deep sleep like Georgie's. He took hold of Georgie's hand and ran his thumb across the palm in a slow caress, and spoke to her in a husky half-whisper. 'Hey, sugar, wake up. You owe me a favour, remember? Well, this is it. Wake up, your mama's waiting for you.'

Olivia closed her own eyes. He was talking now to Georgie as if she were the little girl of eighteen years ago, when he had last known her. Olivia tried to picture that three-year-old Georgie: her sweet sunny face and silver-blonde hair, her great round earnest blue eyes, her mouth caught in a smile of surprise. She tried to imagine, as maybe her friend Megan would have done, herself taking that small Georgie by the hand and leading her up to . . . where? To the grown-up Georgie on the hospital bed? Yes, why not?

She opened her eyes. Nick was still watching Georgie. Still stroking her hand and talking to her. 'Come on, sugar, wake up. You don't want to make your mama cry.'

Olivia leaned over to touch her daughter's face. For some reason she was hardly even surprised when Georgie opened her eyes and looked at her.

'Mama?'

'I'm here, Georgie.'

Georgie went on looking at her without speaking for a minute, maybe trying to recall how to go about conveying her thoughts in the clumsy physical world, after having spent so many days in some realm of the spirit. And her voice when she spoke again was shy and squeaky, as if from disuse. 'Where's Daddy?'

'He's here too.'

'Good,' said Georgie, and closed her eyes again.

25

And her spirit came again, and she arose straightway.

Olivia ran to tell the nurse, who went to fetch the doctor. They were almost as excited as Olivia. The doctors wanted to do checks and tests – making sure she hadn't just made it up? she wondered – and she found herself elbowed away from Georgie's bedside. She retreated into the corridor, where she encountered Nick, who had also been displaced.

'Come on, kitten, let's go and find some coffee.'

'Tea,' she said automatically, and then, 'No, I can't, I've got to go back and tell T – tell my husband,' she amended carefully.

'Yeah, okay, you go and tell him. Where are you staying?'

'At my father's flat in the Barbican.'

'Of course. How handy. That's where Georgie was living.' He stretched and yawned. After all, she thought, recalling his voice on

228

the telephone, he had only been roused from hibernation yesterday. 'I think I'll just go home and get some sleep.'

'Is Luke there?'

'Haven't a clue. I came here straight from Heathrow, just dropped my bag inside the front door on the way past. He never gets up till noon anyway.'

'Well, if he is there, don't forget to tell him about Georgie.'

'Now how could I forget a thing like that?'

He was looking at her, smiling faintly. She wondered how different she seemed to him, after all this time. She wondered if he was disappointed at all. If he still . . .

'I've got to go,' she said, and ran away.

She went back to the Barbican, where Tom was still asleep. She woke him up to tell him that Georgie was going to be okay. Then she phoned her father in Sussex to tell him. Because of the time difference, she had to wait till lunch time to phone Tom's parents in Toronto, but when she did call they had some news of their own. Alex had phoned the night before from Vancouver. He had travelled all the way back down the coast without encountering the Mounties who were looking for him, and he was flying home that morning. So everything was all right again all of a sudden.

At the hospital Tom had a long technical conversation with one of the doctors. He seemed pleased with whatever the doctor had told him. Olivia didn't need any doctor, not even Tom, to tell her that her daughter was going to be okay.

Georgie woke up again while Tom was there. 'Daddy, where's Luke?'

Whatever she remembered or didn't remember, she had obviously forgotten that Tom had never met Luke, as far as she knew. 'I don't know, honey. Why do you want to know?'

'I want to talk to him.'

'You want to take it easy right now. Did you know you nearly died?'

'Is that what it's like?' And she fell asleep again.

Later in the afternoon Olivia left Tom on guard and went back to the flat to get some sleep. The terrible tension within her had eased for the first time since the news of Georgie's accident, allowing her to feel the accumulated weariness of all the sleepless nights in between.

She opened the doors to the narrow balcony above the lake, to invite whatever breeze was available into the stuffy flat. She undressed and lay down on top of the duvet, and was instantly asleep.

Something woke her, just as suddenly. She wondered in a fuddled reluctant way if it was time to get up, but she couldn't be bothered to remember where the clock was. When she heard it a third time, she recognized it as the entry-phone buzzer. Tom must have come back from the hospital and of course she was the one with the keys.

She struggled up off the bed, draping his dressing-gown over her shoulders, and went into the sitting-room. A lovely light breeze was rising from the fountains on the lake. She pressed the entry button to let Tom in, and took the door off the latch so he wouldn't have to knock again when he got up the stairs. Then she slid her arms into the sleeves of the dressing-gown, wrapped it around her and tied it firmly at the waist.

She wandered into the kitchen and filled the kettle for tea. She really must have been down for the count; she was hardly awake even yet. Not surprising, since she had been living on her nerves for almost a week. She had never till now understood how true that phrase was.

She heard the front door of the flat closing. She poked her head around the corner of the kitchen cupboards to say hello to Tom, but it wasn't Tom. It was Nick.

'Oh, Christ,' she said before she could think. 'I thought you were Tom. What are you doing here?'

'What d'you think? I came to see you.'

'Tom will be back any minute.' She couldn't seem to stop saying entirely the wrong thing. Maybe she should just shut up and let him do the talking.

'I didn't come to see him, did I? Anyway, I've just been round to the hospital and he told me you were here.'

'Did you tell him you were coming here?'

'Any reason why I should?'

He took out a packet of cigarettes and lit one. He wouldn't think to ask if she minded, of course. Her father didn't approve of anyone smoking in his house. He hadn't approved, that was, eighteen years ago. The subject hadn't come up this time.

She went back into the kitchen to find an old saucer for Nick to use as an ashtray, before he could do something really unforgivable like dropping ashes on Althea's tasteful pastel carpet. 'Do you want a drink? I'm just making tea.'

'Have you got anything cool?'

She knew what he liked. In eighteen years she hadn't forgotten that. Tom had put some cans of lager in the fridge last night and her father had left half a bottle of whisky behind when he went back to Sussex. 'Cold lager or Scotch on the rocks?'

'I'll have the beer.'

He was standing by the open balcony door, eyes narrowed against the light, sun in his salty blond hair. He was wearing faded jeans and a faded blue shirt. They might have been the same ones he had been wearing when she saw him last, half her lifetime ago. She had lost eighteen years of him, just as she had with her father, only with him it didn't seem to make any difference, not like with her father. The time mattered where it shouldn't have, and didn't where it should. Where she had prayed that it would.

She poured the lager into a glass and brought it over to him. He took it and smiled at her. 'Em's views on civilization are still with us, I see.'

Her mother had always poured his beer into a glass before giving it to him, a needless refinement, as he used to point out. She remembered him sitting at her mother's kitchen table the first day he came to live in her mother's house, drinking beer that her mother had poured for him, sitting there looking at her when she came in the back door. Twenty-two years ago, almighty God.

He was looking at her now, in just the same way. She pulled the lapels of Tom's dressing-gown close across her throat and held it there, moving away from him. She wanted to go back to the bedroom and get safely dressed, but she didn't want to do or say anything that might make him think . . .

'Your kettle's just boiled.'

She scurried into the kitchen quite gratefully. She took as long as she could over making the tea, rinsing and warming the pot, waiting for it to brew properly before she poured it.

He followed her, lurking about the entrance to the kitchen area, watching her and smoking. She slid the saucer-cum-ashtray along the counter towards him. 'Watch your ashes, will you? It's not my carpet. My mother never succeeded in house-training you, did she?'

'I think she gave up after a while.'

Olivia concentrated on pouring the tea. 'Do you miss her at all?'

He was more amused than insulted. 'How am I supposed to answer that? Why not ask if I'd stopped beating her?'

'Did you?' He hadn't used to beat her eighteen years ago, but you never knew. Presumably Luke didn't hate his father for purely imaginary crimes against his mother. Her mother. And Olivia herself had every reason to know that he was capable of violence.

She swept past him and sat down at the table with her mug of tea. The table was safe, domestic, a barrier between them.

Nick sat down around the corner from her, bringing the ashtray saucer, she noticed, as well as the beer. He ignored her spiteful question. He wouldn't have bothered to defend himself, whether guilty or not. 'Do you want me to be missing her?'

'Yes, of course.' She was honestly shocked by the implication. 'You were married to her for twenty-one years. That's got to count for something in your life.'

'Would you miss your doctor if he died?'

She wanted to throw her tea in his face, only that would be letting him know he had got to her. She said as calmly as she could, 'I'd miss him enormously. He's a wonderful man and a wonderful father to Georgie and Alex, and I love him very much.'

'Well, that's all right then.' She knew he was mocking her, telling her he didn't believe her; but it was true, as true as she could make it. He lit himself another cigarette. 'If you really want to know, my life's been a shambles since Em died.'

That surprised her. Not that his life was a shambles, but that he would admit it. She said sarcastically, 'Because she's not around to do the washing up, I suppose.'

'I can pay someone to wash the fucking dishes. But mostly I just eat out. Remember how I told you, I don't want to be living like a kid when I'm fifty? Well, I'm fifty-fucking-four and I'm leading the same sort of life as Luke. Only difference is that I've got money, because people pay me for what I do, and he's broke because he does bugger all.'

'My heart bleeds for you. I thought it was every man's dream to be rich and fancy free.'

'Is that how your doctor would like to be?'

'Stop calling him my doctor. He's my husband.'

'How do you tell the difference, since they both get to stick things up your cunt?' Without giving her the chance to make any expression of shock or indignation, he pushed back his chair and picked up his empty glass. 'Any more of that beer?'

She grabbed the glass from him and stalked into the kitchen, seething. No, that was exactly what he wanted her to do. How was it possible after twenty-two years? Even allowing for eighteen missing ones, she should be inured by now to his deliberately outrageous habits of speech. She wasn't a kid any more. But he was, that was the trouble, still delighting to *épater les bourgeois*. Her mother had always been a sitting duck for that stupid game. And so, goddammit, was she.

She took another can of beer out of the fridge and pulled the tab on it. Immediately the lager bubbled over the top, because in her fury she had accidentally shaken it. She licked the bitter froth from her fingers as she carried the can back to the table. She tipped the glass and poured down the side of it to keep the beer from foaming over again. He sat and watched her do it, his amusement increasing her irritation.

232

'Now you're mad at me, aren't you?'

'How did you guess?'

'Doesn't your doctor use words like cunt? No, I guess no self-respecting quack would use a simple four-letter word when he's got the whole alphabet at his command. What's a handy fifteen-letter word for cunt?'

Olivia put the full glass and the empty can down on the table in front of him. 'Stop that, Nick. Don't be so juvenile.'

'Now that's the one thing I'm not being, baby. Fucking is for grown-ups.'

She looked at him, remembering . . . too many things. Things that made her shake inside. Her mouth went dry. Her voice shrank to a whisper. 'You didn't always think so.'

Her ears must have been affected by the memories too, because his answer sounded softer, more serious, without the jeering edge. 'Maybe I've grown up since then.'

He stood up suddenly, stepping to the left to stand right in front of her. He put his hands to her waist and picked her up, and she found herself sitting on the edge of the table. Before she could slide off again he pushed forward to stand at the table's edge, parting her thighs with his own.

The front of the dressing-gown fell open below the waist, so that her bare legs were pressed against the fabric of his jeans. The feel of the coarse denim and the unyielding muscle of his thighs beneath moved her like magic. Or rather it revealed to her what she would have known all along, if she hadn't been trying so hard not to notice.

She was still shaking inside, but from a different cause. From a longing she hadn't dared to feel for eighteen dreamless years.

He cupped his hands around her bottom. She put her arms around his neck. It felt so good, so good . . . his broad hands on her body, his heavy shoulders within her arms. Something lost and now restored to her.

An absurd, incomprehensible sense of pleasure and relief warmed her from the inside out, like the old heat of creation burning at the core of the earth. All of that in spite of danger. In spite of what she knew about him.

He was smiling, perhaps with that same sense of pleasure and relief. He leaned down to kiss the side of her neck, pushed the dressing-gown aside to run his mouth along the ridge of her collar bone and shoulder blade. She rubbed her legs against the denim, ran her hands into his hair.

'You've got a nerve,' she whispered. 'How did you know I'd have you?'

233

'Jesus, Lia, what did you think I came for? If I'd wanted a pint I'd've gone to the pub.'

He pulled out the wooden pin from Alex's home-made hair grip. Her hair came tumbling down into his hands, spilling around her shoulders, falling as far as her waist. He untied the knot in the belt of Tom's dressing-gown and opened the robe. He stroked her breasts with possessive eagerness. In his hands, her own familiar breasts felt voluptuous and sensual, the desirable object of his desire. He was the only man who had ever made her feel like that about her body.

'You've still got the most fabulous tits. I reckon they're bigger than they used to be.'

'You're right, they are. Because I'm fatter.'

'Who isn't? And so bloody what? You look fantastic.'

She didn't argue with him. She wanted to hear him say it, even if she knew it wasn't true; when he said it, she believed him. She had developed a definite tummy, and her breasts didn't hold themselves up the way they had at nineteen, and her thighs were by no means as firm as when he had last seen her. To say nothing of the presence of cellulite at the bottom of her bottom. Well, what the hell, his body was eighteen years older too. She unbuttoned his shirt to admire it.

Olivia had to admit, to be strictly honest, that his waistline did tend to crowd his belt just a trifle, but then so did Tom's and he was nine years younger, and her father's didn't but he was too thin. And anyway, as he had said, so bloody what? The fact was that Nick looked wonderful. She couldn't imagine how he might have changed in order to appear other than beautiful to her. Maybe – was it possible? – maybe it was the same for him, when he looked at her.

She unbuckled his belt, unzipped his jeans and pushed them down. He was still beautiful down there too. She stroked him just to make sure, holding his cock in both her hands, letting its broad head butt against her belly.

He must have caught the scent of it, her excitement for him. He lifted up her legs and laid her on her back, heels to arse at the table's edge, pushing her knees apart. He leaned over her, thrust into her with the blind urgency of eighteen lost years.

She felt him all the way up inside her, coming and going, the strength and heat of his desire coursing through her body, feeding and inflaming her. She felt those imperative reactions she had all but forgotten, making her move in compulsively consciousless ways and reach for him with the greed of starvation. She felt the convulsive rush and shudder, starting way down at the base of her belly and engulfing her whole body, up and down, inside and out, as he carried her with him to climax.

234

Oh Christ, she thought afterwards. When she was capable of thought again. Oh Christ, what have I done?

She didn't care. She had him again. She had her own desire again. He had given the life of her body back to her.

'Jesus, Lia.' Nick was sprawled across the table, slumped over her, propped on his forearms, breathing in great gusts as he looked down at her. 'Doesn't that goddamned quack ever fuck you?'

She could have said truthfully, not like that. But she didn't, because it would have been disloyal to Tom in a worse way than what she had just done. 'What about you? Anyone would think you hadn't been laid since my mother died.'

'Maybe just once or twice, to keep my hand in.' He pulled her against him with one arm, his hand and face buried in her unbound hair. She had forgotten the smell of him, smoke and sweat, the smell of remembered desire. 'If I'd known you were coming back, I'd have saved myself for the real thing.'

He was mocking her, she thought. Mocking her pathetic naked desperation for him, which she couldn't have disguised even to spare Tom's honour. She pushed him away. Only about six inches, but it might as well have been four thousand miles.

She struggled to sit up. Her hand coming down on the table met something cold and wet. So was the dressing-gown on that side, she realized now, cold and wet.

'Oh, God, look what you've done! There's beer all over the table and carpet. Althea will be rabid.'

Nick surveyed the wreckage with an indifferent eye, while hauling up his jeans and refastening them. 'Mop up and who's to know? I won't tell her if you don't.'

She shrugged out of the damp dressing-gown and tried to use it to dam up the liquid on the table, to prevent further spillage on to the carpet. She could feel her irritation returning at this characteristically cavalier response. 'But it might damage the finish on the table. And the carpet will take ages to dry out. Damn you, Nick, why couldn't you just drink your bloody beer and go home? Tom will be back here any minute now and there's no way he's not going to notice a stain in the middle of the carpet. Or the fact that his dressing-gown is sodden with drink.'

'That's not all it's got on it now,' Nick pointed out coarsely but correctly.

He tucked his shirt back into his jeans and stared at her, by no means in a loving fashion. Olivia felt uncomfortably exposed and faintly ridiculous, bending naked over the table, trying to rescue the disaster with a dressing-gown of some useless fabric that had never been meant to make a mop.

'Sod your old man's furniture,' he said suddenly, fiercely. 'I hope it rots. Sod your doctor's fucking dressing-gown. And sod you, sweetheart.' He grabbed her by the arm to shake her, briefly but savagely. In her surprise she dropped the dressing-gown. The beer promptly cascaded over the edge of the table, splashing her legs. Nick didn't even notice. 'Eighteen years!' He shook her again and pushed her back flat on to the table, right into the puddle of lager. 'You unbelievable little bitch!'

She levered herself upright, as wet and sticky as the dressing-gown but infinitely more indignant about it. 'And it was all your fault, you – you pervert!'

She had never said it before, not even to herself. And now she was saying it to no one, because he had already slammed the door behind him.

26

O Lord, thou hast seen my wrong; judge thou my cause.

She lies naked on the bed in the darkened room, aware of the intensity of heat and light beyond the shuttered window.

Her mother says that if you close the shutters in the morning and open them again in the evening – doing things backwards to an English maid – the villa will be relatively cool all the time. That isn't strictly true, she has discovered. At the hottest time of the day, mid-afternoon, her bedroom is hot too, but compared to the out-of-doors at that time it's at least bearable.

Georgie and Luke are having their nap in the room next door. Luke insists he's too big to be napping, but they went somewhere sightseeing in the morning and afterwards had a big Italian lunch, and when Olivia told him to go to his room, even if he didn't want to have a nap, because it was cooler there, he was asleep no more than a minute after Georgie.

Her mother is asleep in the room across the hall. Her mother has to have a nap, because she's pregnant and not very well. That's how Olivia and Georgie got to come along on her mother's holiday. Olivia is there to look after Luke (and Georgie, of course), so that her mother can lie about with her feet up, as the doctor ordered.

Not that Olivia minds. She doesn't live with her mother at home; she lives with her father and Althea. Since she has to deal with Georgie and Matthew at home, having Luke substituted for Matthew

236

doesn't make all that much difference. Except that Luke is much more inclined to do things he's been expressly warned not to. When a scandalized Georgie comes to report his misdeeds, he calls her a squealer and clobbers her. Then if Nick is around he smacks Luke for hitting Georgie, and Olivia's mother looks up from her book and pushes her sun-glasses down her nose to see what's going on, and starts to plead with everybody to play nicely now. It takes Olivia ages to calm everything down.

She is not asleep. It's too hot to do anything, even sleep. She's gone to her room because it's cooler there than downstairs. She's lain down to rest because there isn't much else you can do in a dark room. And she's taken off her clothes because even the coolest room in the house is still very warm.

The door of her room opens. She turns her head to see who it is, but the door has already closed again and it's too dark in the room to see that far. She knows who it has to be. She can hear him coming to the bed, standing over her, looking down at her. She can see him now in the faint echo of light that leaks in around the shutters, see his tall sun-tanned body, wearing only a pair of faded khaki shorts.

Her mother's husband.

He takes off the shorts and lies down naked on the bed, on top of her naked body, and makes love to her without a word.

It's unbearably exciting, his coming in and taking her like that, wordlessly, facelessly, unannounced, as if she and he were strangers who would never meet except in that anonymous coupling.

The next afternoon, when she hears him come in, she rolls over to face the wall so she can't see him at all, and lets him take her from behind.

The third afternoon she loves him so much she has to kiss his mouth and whisper to him. I wish you could sleep with me at night, she says, that's when I miss you most.

She wonders if he makes love to her mother at night, in spite of her mother being pregnant and ill and having to rest. He never says anything about whatever goes on between her mother and him. Which is only fair, she supposes, because her mother certainly doesn't know anything about what goes on between him and Olivia. But in any case she knows he can't be with her at night because he sleeps with her mother. Those are the rules and they aren't going to change.

In the evening she gives Luke and Georgie their supper and sends them upstairs with Nick to have their bath. At home her father is responsible for reading the bedtime story, but in her mother's household the paternal contribution to family life is the bath. While the children are temporarily occupied upstairs, Olivia has a chance to get started on preparing the grown-ups' dinner. Next, her mother goes up and reads them a story, while Olivia cleans up the remarkable mess that two small children and one man can make of a bathroom in less than half an hour. After that she goes to say goodnight to Georgie and Luke.

They look like twins, the same rosy round faces, the same huge blue eyes with silver brows and lashes, the same halo of fluffy fair hair, except that Luke is distinctly bigger than Georgie. He's bigger even than Matthew, who is five months older than him. He's also rougher than Matthew in his play, which Georgie has taken a while to get used to. She normally only has to deal with him on Sunday afternoons. Olivia's mother can't really cope with Luke at all, and she mostly doesn't try to; she sits on the sidelines and adores him. He is indisputably a beautiful little boy.

When Olivia has dispensed all the necessary good-night hugs and kisses and settled them in bed, she goes back downstairs to do whatever wants doing in the kitchen. The adults never sit down to dinner until there have been no complaints or calls for assistance from upstairs for at least half an hour. Olivia thinks this is almost the nicest time of the day, sitting on the terrace with her mother and Nick and a bottle of Chianti, watching the sunset beyond the hills, popping into the kitchen from time to time to tend to the dinner and enjoy the aromatic Italian cooking smells.

Her mother goes to bed first. Even though it's Olivia who has to get up earliest, which is whenever the children decide to. Olivia sits up playing rummy for pennies with Nick. They are not really pennies but tiny Italian coins worth even less than a penny. After he has won her entire fortune, he says if the kids are all right it would be nice to sit out on the terrace for a while before going to bed. Olivia says she will go up and check on them.

He doesn't mean the children, he means her mother. She puts her head into the children's room and hears their feathery baby's breath disturbing the darkness in two separate but equally even rhythms. She opens the door of her mother's room a little, just enough to catch the same regular rhythm of dreamless sleep. She goes into her own room and takes off her bra and knickers and puts her dress back on with nothing underneath.

Nick has already gone outside when she comes back down. She can smell his cigarette when she steps out into the darkness. She goes up to him and puts her arms around his neck. After a lot of kissing he unfastens her dress. When he discovers she is wearing nothing else he tells her she is a delicious little tart, a remark which she takes in the complimentary spirit he intended.

They make love on a li-lo by the swimming pool. He lies down on

238

it and she kneels over him. He likes that because he can enjoy her breasts more readily. She used to think they were too big, but he finally persuaded her otherwise. He holds her by the hips and pushes up against her, holding her so that she can only move her pelvis in a particular way, making a short steady insistent rhythm that quickly builds up an unbearable tension inside her. Their breath comes sharply in little groans, not like the effortless labour of innocent lungs upstairs. They know each other's body so intuitively and intensely that when some slight change in the pressure of her embrace warns him of her imminent release, he can let himself go and catch up and come with her.

Then she lies in his arms, still straddling and embracing him while he holds her and strokes her, an aftermath of affection that she likes as much as what has gone before. She says, I wish we could go to sleep like this, and he says, If you were Georgie's size I wouldn't mind either. Are you telling me I'm too fat, she says, and he says, You fat, don't make me laugh, you've got the greatest body I've ever seen but I'm not cut out to be a mattress.

After that they go inside and upstairs, she to her own room, he to sleep with her mother.

The holiday comes to an early end when her mother gets up one morning and starts to bleed.

Her mother is only seven months along and doesn't seem to take it too seriously. Of course she has already had two successful pregnancies, there's no reason to think this one will end any differently, though thirty-nine is rather old to be having a baby, Olivia thinks with youthful chauvinism. The doctor has told her mother to keep her feet up and her blood pressure down but there's been no suggestion of serious complications.

But there she is, bleeding when she isn't supposed to be. Nick takes her to hospital in Florence, leaving Olivia to mind the children meantime.

Olivia finds herself entertaining fantasies about her mother having to stay in hospital for a couple of days, just long enough to let her spend a night in bed with Nick. But maybe that would make things worse rather than better. Maybe it would only make her miss him more than ever at night, just like the more he screws her the more she wants him to.

He comes back in mid-afternoon, looking alarmingly grim, and tells Olivia that she's going to have to take the children back to England by herself. He has already booked a flight for them that evening. She asks what about her mother and the baby and he says he doesn't know, does he, they'll have to wait and see. He looks so forbidding she doesn't dare to ask why they can't just stay at the villa, at least till the next morning. Just for one night.

She does get to see her mother in hospital before flying home. When she sees her, Olivia feels horribly guilty about the sinful wishes she has been harbouring. Her mother is all doped up and has tubes fastened to her arm. Nick says they're trying to keep her from going into labour, but he can't tell more than that because neither his Italian nor the hospital doctors' English runs to much in the way of medical terminology.

Her mother comes back to London at the end of the week. The baby was born and then died, twelve hours old.

Olivia rings her father from Florence so he can come to meet her at Heathrow. She isn't going to try to take the tube home, with two large suitcases and two small children. Especially two excited and distressed children. Luke keeps saying he wants his mummy and Georgie keeps asking for Nick. She seems to have fallen in love with Nick at some point in the holiday.

There is more excitement in store for them when they get home. For Luke it isn't home at all, of course. He is going to have to sleep in Georgie's bed, in the room she shares with Matthew, while Georgie sleeps in Olivia's room. Georgie is adamant that she wants her own bed and Luke can't have it. She is only reconciled to her involuntary act of charity by the thought of sleeping with her mother all night. Matthew is ready for bed when they arrive, but he insists on staying up till the others go to bed too.

Olivia puts Georgie and Luke into the bath, in an effort to reintro-duce some routine and calm them down. She begins to understand how the bathroom at the villa got into such a state every night. Luke seems to have an intuitive understanding of the hydraulic principles involved in transferring water from one level to another, or to be precise from inside to outside the tub. When she tells him to stop it, he says he's making waves because they're having a storm. He also says his daddy always lets him do that. Olivia doesn't know what to say to that, because she's quite sure it's true.

She scrubs up Luke first and puts him out to dry while there is still some water left in the bath. Then she soaps up Georgie.

'Ouch, that hurts.'

Olivia pauses in her attack on Georgie's body with the flannel. 'Your bottom's sore?'

Luke perks up his ears. 'My daddy smacked her,' he asserts with more than a touch of *schadenfreude*.

240

Georgie is outraged by this slander. 'He did not! He was only tickling.'

Olivia looks at Georgie, who is glaring at Luke. 'Where did he tickle you?'

Georgie looks at her mother. She opens her mouth, then closes it as if she has just remembered something. She squats down in the tub without answering.

Olivia tries again. 'Can you show me where it's sore?'

'No,' says Georgie.

At some point, perhaps between the first and the second question, a thought has entered Olivia's head. Not really a thought, because it's so awful in its implications that she can't even form it in her mind. The suspicion of a thought, then, a suspicion of suspicion.

Georgie isn't going to co-operate with any more scrubbing. Olivia rinses her off and lifts her out of the tub and begins to towel her dry. When she comes to the suspect spot she say, 'Is it sore there?'

'No,' says Georgie loudly, and bursts into tears.

Olivia makes one more attempt, when Luke and Matthew have been settled in the nursery and she is putting Georgie down to sleep in her own bed. 'Is your bottom still sore?'

'No.' Georgie sticks the tip of her forefinger into her mouth, a habit of hers when dozing off.

'Aren't you going to tell me where Nick tickled you?'

Georgie mumbles something around her finger.

'Is it a secret? Did he tell you not to tell?'

Georgie takes her finger out of her mouth far enough to say No. But Olivia can't tell if that's an answer to the question or a general response to further interrogation.

What with worry about her mother and worry about Georgie, not to mention Georgie's small restless presence in her bed, Olivia doesn't get a lot of sleep that night. She wishes it were Nick in the Florentine hospital bed with needles stuck into his veins, so that she could hope for him to die.

He couldn't have . . . could he?

First thing in the morning she phones her friend Megan. Meg is in training as a nurse at the children's hospital in Great Ormond Street. That morning she has just come off duty. She invites Olivia to come down and have breakfast with her.

Olivia has no appetite, but she equips herself with a slice of toast and a cup of tea, and watches Megan tuck into scrambled eggs with sausages and mushrooms. Well, for Megan it's really dinner, because she'll be going to bed soon.

'How was the holiday?' Megan asks between mouthfuls. 'I thought you weren't due back till this weekend.'

'We weren't, but my mother started to haemorrhage. She's in hospital in Florence. Nick's down there with her, but he sent me back with the kids.'

'Best thing, I'd imagine. Less for him to worry about.'

Olivia wonders if Nick ever worries about anything at all. She already knows he is incapable of regret or repentance. She takes a deep breath and says what she has to say. Sort of. 'It's me who's got something to worry about, Meg. I really need your advice.'

Megan drinks tea and looks at her and waits. 'Well?'

The careful phrases that Olivia has formulated go clean out of her head. All that's left is the blunt reality: I think my stepfather has been doing things to my daughter.

Olivia couldn't have said that even if she wanted to. Her mouth just wouldn't make the words. 'I think maybe – something Georgie said . . .' She stammers on the 's's, leans towards Megan's ear, inarticulates her pathetic story. 'Somebody did something to her and told her not to tell.'

Instead of being shocked, Megan goes all professional. That makes it easier for Olivia. 'Was she traumatized?'

Olivia does her best to be honest and fair. 'No, not really. Sort of spooked, maybe.' It's Olivia who is traumatized.

'Are there any indications of physical injury?'

'She said she was sore. But she wouldn't let me look.'

'Well, you'd better take her to your GP, Lia.'

That's the second thing Olivia has been having nightmares about. 'Meg, I can't. He'll tell Daddy and Daddy will go berserk. And won't the doctor have to notify the police and social workers and so forth? And then Daddy – well, what's a word that means berserk to the power of ten?'

'I see your problem,' Megan allows.

'I thought maybe if you looked at her . . .'

'I don't know anything about child abuse, Lia. You really do need a doctor. Even just to make sure she's okay.' Megan ponders while she finishes her tea, frowning in concentration like an earnest angel. 'Maybe you could talk to Tom Payne.'

'Who's Tom Payne?'

'Oh, Lia, he'd be devastated to hear you say that. You met him when you had lunch here last time. Every time I see him now, he asks me when you're coming in for lunch again.'

Olivia tries to recall. Two young doctors shared a table with her and Megan, both of them tall and slim and dark-haired. 'Was he the Canadian or the South African?'

'He's the one from Toronto. The important thing is, he doesn't know your father and you could probably twist his arm to stop him saying anything to anyone else. Do you want me to have a word with him?'

'Could you? Today?'

'Why not, if he's on duty? You go back home to Georgie and I'll give you a ring when I've fixed something up.'

'Oh, Meg, you are good,' Olivia says with feeling.

'Yeah, I know,' says Megan placidly.

Olivia remembers Tom Payne when she sees him. He was the better-looking of the two doctors at lunch: tall and rangy, with blue eyes and a wide, engaging, slightly conspiratorial smile. At least it's conspiratorial when he smiles at Olivia. He seems very pleased to see her again.

'Did Meg explain what the problem is?' she asks, before he can get any potentially awkward questions in.

'I guess she did, in a roundabout way.' He sounds more curious than shocked by whatever Megan has told him. He glances at Georgie, in her mother's arms, with the same curiosity. 'This is your little girl, I take it.'

'This is Georgie,' Olivia agrees. To Georgie, who is clinging to her like a koala under threat of extinction, she explains, 'This is Tom. He's Megan's friend. He's from Canada.'

Tom speaks directly to Georgie, which pleases Olivia. People don't always, even when Georgie is the subject of discussion. 'Have you ever been to Canada, Georgie?'

Georgie looks at her mother, then shakes her head. 'Italy.'

'She means she's been to Italy,' Olivia translates. 'We went with my family and we've only just come back.'

Tom says to Georgie, 'What's Italy like?'

'Hot.'

'What else?'

'Lots of churches.'

'Did your mother take you to church?'

'Just to look,' Georgie says, with a remarkably sophisticated understanding, Olivia thinks proudly. 'I lit candles.'

'What else did you do in Italy?'

Olivia lets Georgie ramble on for a while about Luke and the swimming pool. Then, not wanting to waste the doctor's time, she says, 'And didn't you get smacked?'

'No!' Georgie pushes at her mother. 'He tickled me.'

'But you said your bottom was sore.'

Georgie sticks her finger in her mouth.

Tom cuts in again. 'Are you ticklish, Georgie? Do you like being tickled?'

Georgie hides her face against her mother's shoulder.

'Are you ticklish there?' Olivia tickles her under her arm. Georgie wiggles and giggles. 'Where else are you ticklish?'

'No,' says Georgie.

'Tom wants to have a look at you. Can you sit on his lap for a minute? I'm not going anywhere,' Olivia adds hastily when Georgie looks dubious. 'I'll stay right here.'

'No tickling,' says Georgie.

'No tickling,' Tom agrees, taking her into his arms and settling himself on a stool. 'Now you'll have to tell me, where don't you like being tickled?'

'No,' says Georgie, repeating her mantra. And then she adds, 'Button.'

'Have you got a button?'

No answer.

'Have I got a button?'

Georgie considers him for a moment as if he were half-witted. She prods his nose with her finger. 'One.' She pokes the right and left sides of his chest. 'Two and three. Four.' More tentatively she touches his midriff, pauses and puts her finger in her mouth. 'You haven't got any more.'

'Have you?'

She nods without removing her finger from her mouth.

'She didn't get any of that from me,' Olivia hisses at him over Georgie's head.

Georgie is not helpful when it comes to being examined. She refuses to let her mother take her knickers off. 'It's rude.'

'It's all right, he's a doctor,' Olivia explains. 'Even I have to take my knickers off for the doctor sometimes.' She reddens when she catches Tom looking at her.

Georgie has her own standards of modesty. 'Are we in private?'

'We certainly are. There's nobody here but you and me and Tom.'

So that's all right, it seems. She shows a stoic indifference to the examination itself. When she is dressed and in her mother's arms again, Tom says, 'There's no evidence of penetration, either vaginal or anal.'

'Thank God.' Olivia holds Georgie closer to her. 'But something must have happened or she wouldn't be talking like that.'

'She doesn't appear to be traumatized by the incident, whatever it was. Very young children often aren't, if it doesn't involve violence or fear or pain. They're too young to understand.'

'What they don't know can't hurt them, you mean?'

She was sarcastic, but he is serious. 'Well, not quite. But you could say they're protected by their innocence. Sometimes the reaction of adults can be a greater trauma than the original abuse.' His gaze moves from Georgie to Olivia. 'Forgive me for asking, but are you – er – married?'

'No, I'm not.'

'Are you living with Georgie's father?'

'I'm living with *my* father.'

'I see.' But whatever it is he sees, he doesn't say. Instead he looks at his watch. Then he looks at her, with the same inviting smile he had given her across the canteen table. 'I'm due off for lunch in half an hour, but I wouldn't suggest subjecting Georgie to hospital food. Maybe we could get some sandwiches and have a picnic in the square.'

Olivia smiles back at him, letting him read whatever invitation he cares to in her response. 'Okay, we'll get sandwiches and see you in the square.'

They sit on the grass in the sun and talk, while Georgie feeds her crusts to the pigeons, or tries to. She is unintentionally doing better service as a pigeon-scarer than a bird-feeder.

Tom says he will be going back to Canada for good in November.

Olivia says she will be starting university in three weeks.

He says his father is a doctor in Toronto.

Her father is a historian, she says, a senior university lecturer.

Georgie comes back for something more to offer to the pigeons. Olivia hands over her own sandwich. Tom says, 'You haven't eaten a thing.'

'I'm not hungry.'

They both watch Georgie trotting over to the pigeons, all of which promptly scatter. Tom says, 'You can't just do nothing, you know.'

'I know.' Olivia shuts her eyes and adds in a rush, 'I'm so scared, I don't know what to do. I have no money and nowhere to go.'

'What would you do if you could?'

'I'd go away. Somewhere really far.' She hugs herself, then looks at him with a faint smile. 'Canada, for instance.'

He opens his mouth to say something. Instead an electronic squawk comes from his breast pocket.

'Dammit, there goes my bleeper. I've got to get back.' He stands up and turns off the bleeper and looks down at her, irresolute. 'Lia, what's your last name? Where do you live?'

Olivia stands up too. She takes the pen out of his breast pocket and writes her father's phone number on the back of Tom's wrist.

She has to wait to confront Nick. He had brought her mother back to London, unpregnant and babyless, and the next day taken her and Luke down to stay with Olivia's grandmother in Devon. It's nearly a week before Olivia sees him again.

She wants to meet him somewhere neutral, somewhere safe. She doesn't trust him at all. Has she ever trusted him? What had he done to earn it? She must have been mad.

She arranges to meet him at a pub near his studio. It has a garden out the back, alongside the Thames. They sit in a corner by the wall, under an enormous weeping willow tree. Italy seems a thousand years ago.

She opens neutrally, with a question she really wants an answer to. 'How is Mummy?'

'She'll be okay in a while. She's depressed right now. All those hormones switching on and off, I guess.'

'Of course she's depressed. She thought she was going to have another child and now she's got nothing. You should be depressed too.'

He shrugs, as if the possibility of grief has never crossed his mind, as if it were a peculiarly feminine failing. 'No hormones, I guess.' He lights a cigarette, concentrating, then smiles at her. 'Thanks for looking after Luke.'

'My pleasure. He's lovely.'

She looks down at her wine, then up at him. At the blue-eyed English face of her faceless Italian lover, the fantasy man who came to her room in the Tuscan afternoons. No doubt it is a failure of imagination on her part, but she simply cannot see him as a paedophile.

Yet she has to ask. Something happened that was not a fantasy, and Georgie left no doubt that it had to be him. What if he denies it, what would she believe? Georgie is only a baby after all, and Nick has never to her knowledge told her a lie. A funny sense of honour he has. Or maybe he just can't be bothered to lie.

She decides if he denies it she will believe him.

'What are you looking so down about, kitten?'

There is no point beating about the bush, she'll just have to say it. 'Georgie said you were tickling her.'

He doesn't seem much interested. 'So?'

'She called it tickling. That isn't what I'd call it.'

246

He still doesn't show any sign of concern. Amusement, rather. 'What d'you want to call it?'

What does she want to call it, to give it a name? 'How about child abuse?'

'Oh, for Christ's sake, Lia.' He flicks the tip of his cigarette in the general direction of the ashtray. 'I abuse Luke too, you know, I wallop his arse from time to time. Are you going to turn me in for it?'

'I'm not talking about Luke, I'm talking about Georgie. And I'm serious.'

'I can see that, but I can't believe it. How can you possibly get so worked up about the idea of tickling a baby's fanny?'

She stares at him, rigid with horror. 'So you admit you did it.'

'Yeah, I confess,' he agrees, heavily sarcastic. 'And so fucking what?'

Olivia hears her own voice, surprisingly level, as if she were listening to someone else speak. 'But, Nick, that's sexual abuse. Don't you understand? It's a serious crime.'

'Touching my own kid is a crime, is it?'

'You didn't just touch her.'

His pale eyes flicker and freeze her. Something in that glance penetrates through the daze of shock and scandal, something hits her in the heart and stops it, just for the spell of one cardiac contraction.

'You know all about it, do you?' His tone matches the glance, a quick tight thrust with a blade of ice, thawing a moment later into grim amusement. 'Whatever I did to Georgie, it was hardly even sex, let alone abuse.'

Olivia's pulse recovers its rhythm. The terrifying look has vanished from Nick's face. She tries to work out what sort of look it was, what it might have meant. To call it a bleak expression is like saying Antarctica is cold. Another time she might have asked him. Right now she only wraps herself in her anger and keeps her thoughts on Georgie. 'Whatever you did, you told her not to tell me, didn't you?'

This time the stare holds only astonished contempt. 'Now why would I do that? Would anybody in his right mind expect a three-year-old to keep a secret? And it's no bloody secret anyway. We're all born with the right kit, aren't we, for Christ's sake. Though in your case I guess it's theoretically possible you didn't develop a pussy till the age of fourteen.'

She goes quite numb, so choked up with violent emotions that she feels nothing at all. She can't even speak above a whisper. 'You're a monster.'

For the first time he appears to take her outrage as something more than a joke. 'Look, Lia, this really is not a big deal and you're turning it into one. A serious crime, Jesus Christ. But if it makes you feel better, you write up a list of rules – no hands below the waist, whatever the hell pleases your puritanical little mind – and I'll go along with it. She's your kid, you make the rules.'

'She's *your* kid!' Olivia spits at him. 'How could you do that to your own child?'

'Why not?' He is looking at her in a convincing approximation of real puzzlement. 'What's the matter with you, Lia? I'm not bloody likely to be fooling about with someone else's kid, am I? You'd have to be a pervert to do that. You know, one of those buggers who hang around schools. And anyway, I'm not particularly crazy about kids. If Luke and Georgie weren't my own, I'd never have taken any notice of them. I mean, why would I? I think they're terrific, but that's because they're mine. Other people's brats are just a fucking nuisance.'

Olivia can't make any sense of this, and sees no reason to try. 'Well, you won't have to bother with Georgie from now on. I'm making the rules, just like you said, and the only rule I'm making is that you're never going to see her again.'

'Lia, for God's sake – '

She's not going to argue any more. She gets up and walks away, through the garden, through the pub.

He doesn't come after her.

Why should he? It's a stupid, toothless threat. When her mother rings up in a fortnight's time to invite her and Georgie over on Sunday, is she going to be able to say, Not unless your husband isn't there?

Is she hell. Nor can she tell her mother she isn't coming over at all. And since she lives with her father she can't invite her mother and Luke to visit her, *sans* Nick. There is no possible way she's going to be able to explain to her mother why she doesn't want Georgie and Nick in the same place at the same time. Neither can she follow Georgie around the whole time she's visiting her mother, making sure her daughter is never alone with her stepfather. And what about when Georgie gets big enough to visit her grandma on her own? She can't prevent that happening. And it's going to go on like that for ever. Maybe getting more dangerous the older Georgie gets.

She has no way of warning Georgie to keep away from Nick. As he himself has pointed out, you can't stop a three-year-old from saying the wrong thing at the wrong time, from telling her grandma that her mama has said that she's not allowed to sit on Nick's lap or whatever.

If Georgie had been traumatized by her experience, she might keep away from him of her own accord. But instead she seems to be quite dotty about him. She is still asking for him every night at bath time.

In a week of obsessively dwelling on the problem, Olivia hasn't thought to connect the two ideas. Now that she has, she is appalled. Surely Georgie can't have liked him doing that to her . . . could she?

Well, why not? She likes it well enough when she accidentally does it to herself, as Olivia has had plenty of occasion to observe. Because she's so small, she readily seems to forget which particular confluence of physical contact and body movements produced the sensations that made her want more of them. Which is just as well, because in a child too young to have developed a sense of decorum it tends to produce embarrassing situations.

So what's the difference between Georgie doing something to herself, and Nick doing it to her, supposing she doesn't object?

It's totally disgusting, that's the difference. It's outrageous and immoral and exploitative and the thought of it makes her want to go round to her stepfather's house and kill him. And just because he hasn't done anything worse doesn't mean he won't do something worse later on. If she doesn't take Georgie away from him.

And the worst, worst, worst thing of all is her sense of betrayal. How could he do such a thing to his own daughter? How could he do such a thing to *her* daughter? She believed that he loved Georgie. She thought he loved *her*. He wouldn't say it, of course, not him, but how else could he have carried on a passionate affair with her for all that time? And now it's like she has fatally misunderstood everything that ever happened between them. Like he never loved her and Georgie at all. The two of them were only a source of entertainment for him, bodies in a harem when he wanted one. Some sort of carnal cannon fodder. She can't bear the thought of touching him now, of even having to look at him.

But she has no money and nowhere to go.

'If you really want to go to Canada,' says Tom Payne, 'I've found a job for you.'

He has taken advantage of the racket in the pub to sit close to her and bring his head down to hers. Now he puts his arm across her shoulder.

It's only the second time she has been out with him. The first time, he kissed her good-night in quite a gentlemanly fashion, at the top of the street where she lives. Olivia hasn't really gone out with any boys since Georgie's birth. School and the baby have left her little time for a social life, and her sex life was already spoken for. But Tom is a man, not a boy.

She looks at him in surprise and vague dismay. 'Doing what?'

'Don't look like that, you don't have to do it if you don't want to. A friend of mine in Montreal is desperate for a nanny.'

Now she is even more surprised. 'A nanny?'

'Is that too ghastly to contemplate? English nannies have real cachet over there.'

'But what about Georgie?'

'She's your relevant experience, isn't she? Anyway, there's a job for her too. Their little girl is two and a half, and a nanny who comes with a playmate attached would be a bonus.'

'What about – '

'Private accommodation provided for you both,' he goes on remorselessly. 'Air fares paid. Free food. And they even pay you a salary.'

'Are they nice?' she asks timidly. Not that it makes any difference.

'Of course they're nice. What kind of friends do you think I have? Besides, they'll know you can complain to me if they don't treat you right. I'll be going home in a couple of months, remember? And Montreal's only a few hours' drive from Toronto.' He smiles, as wide as ever, but a little crookedly. It dawns on her that he is nervous. 'If that's a good thing.'

Tom being there will make it better, less of a leap in the dark. Give her the courage to do it, even. 'That's good.'

His arm draws her against him and that's good too. Warm, comforting, safe. He's a safe sort of man.

Not like Nick.

It's a terrible, terrifying thing she is planning to do. There is no point going half-way round the world to escape a dilemma if the dilemma is going to follow her. She can't be bringing Georgie back for visits or having her mother decide to visit her. And she can't do that to her mother without doing it to her father too. She is going to have to leave them all behind.

Tom is already making his own plans. 'You can come and spend Christmas with us. My parents have an island in the river near Kingston and we always do Christmas there. So you won't be homesick.'

That sounds even more scary than the nannying, but at least it means he understands what she is doing. She doesn't know what

250

his parents will think when she and Georgie land on their doorstep, two waifs from overseas.

She also doesn't know, and will only find out at Christmas, that Tom has a girl in Toronto whom his family is confidently expecting him to marry when he gets back. Or that by the time she sets foot on his father's island she herself will already be pregnant with Alex, and wondering, when she learns about the other girl, if Tom intended her pregnancy to be the unanswerable argument against his family's disapproval.

But all of that, the first part of the rest of her life, the first meeting with her new family, all that is still in the unknown future when Tom kisses her in the pub in Lamb's Conduit Street.

She tells no one but Megan at first. She doesn't say why she's doing it, and Megan, surprisingly, doesn't ask. Maybe she's guessed.

Olivia has to work out how to break the news to everyone else. Her father will go mad, because it means giving up her place at university.

Megan has more practical concerns. 'What if it doesn't work out? What if they don't like you, or you don't like them? What if the arrangements aren't the way Tom says they are?'

Olivia is shocked. 'Why, do you think he's making it all up?'

'No, no, of course not. But you can't afford to take chances, can you? I mean with Georgie and all you can't just go out and get another job. In fact I don't think they'd let you. If you go over as a nanny, you can only stay as a nanny. I think they're quite strict about that.'

Olivia considers the prospect of being stranded penniless in Montreal, with Georgie dependent on her. If it were just herself she would chance it, but she can't take risks with Georgie. 'I need some serious money, don't I? How am I going to find money in a hurry, Meg? Without going on the streets, I mean.'

'What about Nick?'

Olivia stares at her. Megan gazes back, unruffled. 'What do you mean, what about Nick?'

'Well, he's Georgie's father, isn't he? If you'd made a fuss about it, he'd have been forking over every month for the past three years. It seems to me he owes you something. Or at least he owes Georgie something.'

Olivia is certain now that Megan has guessed what the problem is. But she also knows that neither of them is going to say anything about it. It really won't bear the light of day, or discussion. 'But Meg, I don't want anyone to know about him.'

'They don't need to. Just go and ask him for money.'

'He won't give it to me.'

'He has to,' Megan says flatly. 'Georgie's his kid, he owes you for her. Listen, Lia, if it makes you nervous I'll go with you to talk to him.'

She would too. Olivia can easily picture Megan alongside her, a sort of solicitor and bodyguard and avenging angel all rolled into one. But she isn't sure that even Megan could get blood out of Nick. 'That's okay,' she says hastily. 'He doesn't know you know about him, see, and – well, I'd rather keep it private.'

Megan is still pursuing her line of thought. 'Better still, why not take Tom along? That would be rather fun, don't you think?'

'That would be absolutely appalling and mortifying,' Olivia says firmly, closing her mind to the apocalyptic visions raised by Megan's suggestion. 'Funny idea of fun you have, Meg. The last thing I want is for Tom to know about Nick.'

'Well, okay, do it yourself then. Just don't go losing your nerve.'

Megan sounds just a little disappointed. Olivia reflects on her future life in Canada, a life without Megan to hand. 'Meg, you'll come and visit me, won't you? I couldn't bear to lose track of you.'

'Sure. On one condition.'

'What condition?'

'I want to be the bridesmaid at your wedding.'

'What wedding?'

'When you marry Tom.'

Olivia doesn't make any advance arrangements to meet Nick this time. She just goes to his studio at the end of the day and waits outside, by his car. She doesn't trust him enough to go upstairs. She doesn't trust him anywhere without a witness. And he has to come down sometime.

When he comes down he doesn't seem surprised to see her. At least, if he is he doesn't show it. He walks over to the car as if she has often turned up like this before. 'Did you want something?'

'Yes. I want a thousand pounds.'

'Don't we all? Good luck in getting it.'

He reaches for the handle of the car door. She grabs his arm. 'Don't be funny. I want it from you.'

He looks at her, still without surprise. Looks at her hand on his arm. 'Is this begging or blackmail?'

'Neither. It's overdue child support. I've got a job in Canada starting October the first and Georgie's going with me and I want some money for her.'

She has half been hoping he might ask her not to go. Might even say he's sorry, he knows he's done a dreadful thing and he'll never ever do anything like it again if only she will stay. Say he loves her unendurably and can't live without her.

Fat chance. All he says is, 'What the fuck are you going to do in Canada?'

She realizes she is still clutching his arm. She takes her hand away. 'I'm going to be a nanny.'

'Well, like I said, good luck.'

He opens the door of the car. She pushes herself into the space between the door and the car, to prevent him getting in and driving away. 'What about the money? I mean it.'

He looks at her as if she's a dosser who has come up to him in the street. 'D'you really think I'm going to give you money so you can take Georgie away from me?'

'Don't you dare talk like that,' she says hotly. 'You don't care about her.'

'How d'you know what I care about?'

Olivia has no answer to that. She realizes, not for the first time, that she has absolutely no idea what goes on inside his head. Her understanding of him is like one of those pictures she used to make in school, where you cover a sheet of paper with every different colour of crayon, and then you cover the colours with black crayon, and after that you scratch a design on the paper to reveal the underlying colours in a mysterious pattern. In the course of her relationship with him, she has scratched the surface of Nick here and there to catch a glimpse of the colours inside him, but only random glimpses that tell her nothing of the hidden patterns that make him whatever he is.

'If you did care about her, you'd never have . . .'

She doesn't need to finish that. He grabs her arm. It hurts. 'Don't you fucking try to tell me how I should feel about Georgie. She's my kid just as much as yours. You've got no divine right to be making all the rules. My goddamn feelings are as good as yours, you prissy little bitch.'

She doesn't want to know about his feelings, and he isn't going to tell her anyway. Nick's emotional life is the best-kept secret in the world. 'I want that money,' she repeats stubbornly. 'You owe it to me. She's your daughter and you've never paid a penny for her.'

He lets go of her arm, his anger gone cold as quickly as it flared up. He shrugs. 'So sue me.'

'Don't be silly, that's no answer.'

'Sure it is. You want maintenance money, you take me to court. Tell the world whose kid she is.'

Olivia runs her tongue across her lower lip. 'You don't mean that.'
'Try me.'

He's probably bluffing, but she can't be sure and she doesn't have time to find out. She certainly doesn't have time to take him to court.

And she can't do that anyway. She can't tell her parents that her mother's husband is the father of her child. She can't tell her friends and neighbours, she can't tell anyone. It's simply too shameful and scandalous. And she can't tell Georgie, when Georgie is old enough to understand.

There are lots of other reasons. Why ruin her mother's life as well as her own? And the last thing she wants to do now, knowing what she does, is anything that would create an official bond between Nick and Georgie. Anything that could give him a legal claim on her.

She puts her hand on his arm again. He was right to look at her as if she were a beggar. She is a beggar. 'Please, Nick, just give me the money. It's the least you can do, after . . . everything you've done.'

She's forgotten how cold his eyes can be. What an absolute, unmitigated bastard he can be, without really even trying. 'Fuck that. If you want the money you'll have to work for it.'

'What do you mean, work for it?'

He's looking around, looking for something, with those icy blue eyes that even the hot Italian sun would never have warmed in a million years. 'That passage over there will do. It goes down to the river.'

She doesn't ask again what he means. She just follows him down the steps of the passage between high walls, down to the river, and lets him screw her standing up against the wall like a streetwalker, which is just what she is in this instance and he wants her to know it.

Afterwards he writes her a cheque for the money. 'A thousand pounds for the worst fuck I've ever had from you. D'you want a lift home?'

Well, why not? She gets into his car and he drives her to her father's house without another word. She is one thousand and two pounds and twenty pence in pocket when she gets out. A thousand pounds for the fuck and two pounds twenty saved on tube fare.

27

Who can bring a clean thing out of an unclean? Not one.

Tom came home in high spirits. The spring of his foot in the corridor gave him away to Olivia. He almost literally bounced in the door, when she opened it. Not only was Georgie going to live, but as a doctor he always liked to see his patients getting better.

'Everything okay?'

'Fuckin' ace, as we say back home.' He sniffed elaborately in the direction of the kitchen. 'Hey, that smells fantastic, whatever it is.'

'It's supposed to taste fantastic too. A celebration.'

An expiation, more like. The graduate student had never really represented a threat or a betrayal. What she had done that afternoon was both.

Before getting to grips with dinner, she had had a shower and washed her hair. Then she had rinsed the beer out of the dressing-gown and hung it over the balcony rail to dry, which was almost certainly against the rules of the Barbican. She had also tried to dry out the carpet with Althea's hair drier, but gave up after a quarter of an hour and moved the table a foot to the right instead. Now she handed Tom a glass of lager before he could open the fridge and find out that someone had already consumed half his supply.

He took his beer over to the open door to the balcony and stepped out to view the setting sun. 'What's my dressing-gown doing out here?'

'I spilled something on it. Sorry.' Olivia followed him out with a glass of chilled white wine. 'Was Georgie fully conscious when you left?'

'She was sleeping. Completely natural sleep, as far as we could tell. Her brain functions seem to be all okay. She should recover quite rapidly now.' He swallowed beer and added, 'She had no recollection of what happened to her.'

'Did you tell her?'

'I just said she'd hit her head.'

'You didn't mention Luke?'

'No, and don't you do it either. If she ever does remember well enough to give evidence, we don't want him claiming she only remembers what we told her.'

Olivia looked at him in surprise. 'Did Mr Sargent tell you that?'

255

'It had already occurred to me,' he assured her. 'But I discussed it with him, when I phoned him to let him know she'd regained consciousness.'

She hadn't thought about the police. 'How likely is it to come to court, especially if she doesn't remember anything about it?'

Tom shrugged. 'Plenty of witnesses, he said. And why should that bastard get away with assaulting her, even if he is your brother?'

'That's right, blame me for it.' She was only half joking. She took the empty glass out of his hand and went to refill it in the kitchen.

When she came back to the balcony he said, 'Speaking of your appalling family, your stepfather turned up at the hospital this afternoon. A bit of a rough diamond, is he?'

'Rough, yes, but I don't know about the diamond,' Olivia heard herself saying. That must have been some interior automatic pilot. The rest of her had gone into a tailspin at the mention of Nick, and not only because of events on the table.

She hadn't dared to tell Tom the whole true story of what had happened at the hospital that morning. She had only said what was perfectly true as far as it went, that Georgie had opened her eyes and spoken to her mama. She had made no mention of Nick, neither his presence nor the part he had played in the resurrection of Georgie. It wasn't just that Tom would inevitably, irrationally, be jealous that another man had brought his daughter back to life where he had failed – and him a doctor. There was also the implication, in the sequence of events, that Nick had come back for Georgie's sake rather than Luke's.

It's your child. What would Tom have made of that, if he had overheard her? She had never told him the truth about Georgie's father. She hadn't told any lies either. From the beginning it had been forbidden territory for him, and he had respected that. She assumed that he assumed someone like Charlie.

How right she had been to leave home, how disastrous coming back was proving. The lies she had left behind still lurked at hand, threatening to corrupt the life she had made for herself half a world away.

Tom was talking. She made herself listen. 'He kind of reminded me of your father.'

Olivia was incredulous. 'Nick reminded you of my father?'

'Yeah. They both struck me as pretty cussed types.'

She thought about that and started to laugh. 'My mother's taste, I guess. She must have liked bolshie bastards.'

The phone rang twice during dinner. Both times Olivia ran to snatch it up in alarm, thinking it might be the hospital phoning to say Georgie had taken a bad turn. The first caller was a girl wanting

Matthew, and wanting to know where to get hold of him when told he wasn't there.

She came back to the table after the second, longer call. 'That was Althea, inviting us to bring Georgie down to their place in Sussex as soon as she can leave the hospital.'

'And?'

'Well, I thought Georgie ought to have some say in it. But I wouldn't mind the chance to see how they live, and have a bit of holiday myself.' Sussex, she thought in the back of her mind, was safely away from Nick. 'My term doesn't start for another three weeks.'

'Unlike you, I'm not a member of the leisured classes. I can't just disappear for a month without prior warning.'

'Or even with it, I've noticed.' The wolves were perhaps partly her response to being married to a man who was married to his work. Which didn't stop him resenting them, and her career. In his heart, like every man maybe, he wanted her to be at home waiting for him. 'But I can't just dash back to Toronto at the earliest opportunity, not after having vanished for eighteen years.'

Tom gave her an odd look. 'Time the great healer, eh? Everything forgiven or forgotten?'

She looked down at her plate. 'That's not relevant any more.'

'Not relevant to who? Even if you're willing to forget it, I'm not.'

Since she had left London all those years ago, this was the first time he had referred to the events that had prompted her self-exile. She had never told him any more about that, than about how Georgie had come to be born. And she didn't know what he assumed.

She pushed her chair back and walked away from the table. 'I lost my mother on account of that. When I came back, it was too late. She was dead.'

He said coldly, 'But the loss of your father wouldn't be much loss.'

She stared back at him in stunned astonishment. 'My father?'

'Did you think I didn't know? I can add up two and two as well as anyone.' He left the remains of his dinner and came after her. 'It had to be him, there wasn't anyone else you would have had to leave home for. Anybody else, you could have avoided or confronted. But you told me you were living with him. Did you really think I hadn't worked it out?'

Olivia shook her head. She couldn't speak. His logic was faulty, but to tell him so would be the same as telling him who the villain really was. By his own reasoning there was only one other man it could have been, and Tom would see that at once.

She couldn't make up her mind which was worse, for Tom to

257

think that of her father, or for her own secret to be revealed. Because it wasn't just Georgie . . .

Tom had worked that out too. He came up close behind her and put his hands on her arms. 'Who is Georgie's father, Lia?'

'No!' She jerked away from him. 'That's disgusting. It's not what you think. Wash your mind out with soap.'

'If it's not what I think, what is it?'

But he wasn't expecting an answer to that question, because he didn't believe her answer to his first question. He wasn't going to discover the truth because he thought he already knew it.

Olivia couldn't cope with either the truth or the lie. Especially not after what had happened that afternoon. On the table where they had just eaten dinner.

She thought she was going to throw her dinner back up. She put her hands to her mouth and swallowed strenuously. 'I'm going to see Georgie,' she announced, and ran out of the flat.

She didn't go right to the hospital. She went down to St Paul's and sat on a bench in the churchyard, where there were no tourists or souvenir hawkers. She was in no state to see anyone, not even Georgie asleep and undemanding. She hadn't only betrayed Tom that afternoon, she had betrayed Georgie. Tom was right; what Nick had done to Georgie was a monstrous thing. Even if Georgie had liked it. Olivia knew all about that, how he did what you liked and made you like what he did. He was a moral monster. How could she, how *could* she have let him make love to her again, after all that?

And why should she let her father take the rap for what Nick had done, even in Tom's head? Her mother was dead, there was no need to protect her any more. Why shouldn't she just tell Tom it had been Nick, both times? Why shouldn't Nick be obliged to face the consequences of his own sins?

She had no answer to any of those questions. All she knew was her instinct to let sleeping rottweilers lie. It didn't matter what Tom thought. If he had been mentally slandering her father for nearly twenty years, he might as well carry on doing it for another twenty.

Because it wasn't just that Nick was her daughter's father. It was that she had loved him. That was the real secret she didn't want Tom to know.

So as not to make a total liar of herself, she did eventually go to see Georgie.

They had already moved her from the intensive care unit to an ordinary ward, Olivia discovered. A good sign. But one of the consequences was that visiting hours were no longer round the clock. They ended at nine in the evening, five minutes from the time Olivia arrived.

258

Another consequence was that the nurses weren't vetting visitors for their family credentials, and so Luke was no longer barred from entry. He was already there when Olivia came in.

Georgie was awake, her head unswathed. Olivia had another shock: they had shaved Georgie's head. She recalled some talk of an operation, which Tom had said was to relieve pressure on the bruised and swollen brain.

Already, in less than a week, the shape of Georgie's skull was softened by fluffy blonde fuzz. She lay back on a mound of pillows, looking pale and interesting, not remotely self-conscious about her nearly naked scalp. And holding hands with Luke.

Olivia wondered whether Georgie yet knew, and if she didn't whether Olivia ought to tell her, that the solicitous uncle holding her hand so sympathetically had tried to kill her. She didn't care about the business of evidence, because unlike Tom she wasn't anxious to see her brother appear in court, not even to answer for what he had done to Georgie.

Luke got up as soon as he saw her, dropping Georgie's hand. 'I'm just going,' he said hastily.

'We'll both have to be going in about five minutes,' Olivia pointed out, 'so don't dash off on my account.' She sat down on the spot on the bed that he had vacated and said to Georgie, 'I just came by to see how you're doing. You must be okay, since they've unhooked the machinery.'

Georgie agreed. 'I'm not allowed to get up yet, but they're pretty well persuaded that I'm not going to die. They even gave me dinner tonight.'

She said it cheerfully, casually. Only that morning Olivia had wept and prayed that it might be so. So much had changed so quickly, some for better, some for worse. Olivia bent down to hug her daughter as well as she could, and Georgie hugged her back. She had embraced Georgie many times in the past few days, but this was the first time that Georgie had been able to return the gesture.

'We weren't so sure for quite a while.'

'That's what Daddy said.'

Olivia wanted to ask what she remembered of the past week, but the tall brooding presence of Luke at the foot of the bed made it impossible. And anyway a nurse was coming through the ward, shooing all the visitors out. She said good-night to Georgie, promising to come back first thing in the morning, and went out with Luke in train.

On the way down she turned to confront him bluntly. Why, after all, should he be spared? 'Does she remember that you hit her?'

He scowled and reddened. A fitting reaction, she thought, for a boy who looked like a thuggish angel. Nick must have looked like that before he had hardened. Years before she met him, that would have been. 'I don't know. I didn't ask,' he admitted. 'I told her I was sorry about the row we had.'

'Does she remember what the row was about?'

'If she doesn't, I'm not going to tell her.'

'Or me either, I take it.'

'None of your business,' he said bluntly. 'Georgie can tell you if she wants to.'

'If she can remember.'

When they went out the front door Matthew was there, waiting in the street. Waiting for Luke, evidently. Though much shorter and slighter than Luke, he appeared to have taken on the role of his brother's keeper. Except, of course, that Olivia's brothers were no relation to each other.

Matthew greeted her gracefully. 'Is Georgie okay? She was remarkably perky when I came by earlier. They were just about to move her out of death row.'

Olivia supposed that was an example of gallows humour, and was not amused. Perhaps at twenty-one it was hard to believe in death. Though Luke at twenty-one had already been introduced to mortality through his mother. 'She seems much better,' she allowed repressively.

Matthew refused to be repressed. 'Are you going back to the flat? We'll walk with you. Bodyguards.'

She started briskly down the street and they followed, one on either side, like hired heavies. It gave her a strange sense of luxury, walking between two beautiful young men. No one seeing them need know that they were her brothers. Not that they met many people to impress, at this time of night in the City.

Matthew asked questions, while Luke stalked silently, intent as it seemed on other things. 'What happened when she woke up? You were there, weren't you?'

'Yes, I . . .' She hesitated, not knowing what Georgie had told him, not knowing whether to acknowledge Nick's presence, since she didn't want that getting back to Tom. On the other hand . . . on the other hand she had already lied enough for several lifetimes. She turned to Luke. 'Didn't your father tell you?'

Luke said sullenly, 'He told me she was awake.'

'He was there when she came to.'

Luke muttered something profanely abusive. Ironically, in view of his feelings about Nick, he was so plainly his father's son. Almost as if, as Aristotle had maintained, her mother had only acted as the incubator of her husband's child.

260

'He woke her up,' Olivia told him. 'If it weren't for him, she might be still unconscious.'

That actually made Luke break his stride. 'He didn't tell me that. Is it really true?'

'Why would I be telling you stories?' Olivia demanded in exasperation. 'I'm just pointing out that you have good reason to be grateful to your father. If it weren't for him you might be facing more serious charges.'

'Bully for him,' Luke said ungraciously. But he looked at least slightly uncertain of himself, which gave Olivia an obscure sense of satisfaction.

They had reached the western outpost of the Barbican by now. Olivia gave up on Luke and said to Matthew, 'I feel really badly about turning you out of your own flat. You really are welcome to sleep on the sofa if you want to, as pathetic as that offer might seem.'

'That's all right, Luke and I are dossing down with a friend.'

She looked at Luke. Despite saying almost nothing, he seemed to keep intruding himself into the conversation. 'I thought you were both staying at Nick's house.'

'We were,' Matthew agreed. 'But now Himself is there.'

'Don't tell me he won't let you stay.'

'He hasn't expressed an opinion one way or another. Luke has enough opinions for all of us.'

Luke ignored this snipe. He leaped up the stairs from street to highwalk level with an athletic spring that Tom would have envied. Olivia watched his denim backside disappearing up the steps. She said to Matthew, 'What do you think, shall I shut up now?'

Matthew came up right behind her and put his arm around her. Megan, she thought, would have called him an old soul. 'Dear Lia, these mysteries shall be revealed in time. Luke can be amazingly articulate when he wants to be. Georgie may well be dying for a word in your ear. I can't speak for the famous Mr Winter because I've never had the pleasure of his acquaintance.'

It was her fault somehow, Olivia felt. She had let Georgie come over here and walk into a minefield. There were maybe more mysteries to be unravelled than even Matthew dreamed of. But she let him escort her up the stairs and deliver her to the door of the flat, with Luke as unwilling outrider.

Having sent her escort away, she let herself in with the keys in her handbag. Tom had already gone to bed. He must have been as exhausted as she was. She followed him within half an hour.

Early in the morning, when the light was just showing in the sky, he wakened and rolled over on top of her. Olivia, three-quarters asleep and reliving old Italian dreams, responded with unusual

261

enthusiasm. But she was ashamed when she realized what she had done, drowsily confusing her husband with an incorrigible adulterer and child abuser.

28

To the hungry soul every bitter thing is sweet.

Indoors looking out, the winter world appears inviting: bright sunny day, clear pale sky, no breath of wind. A glimpse of sunlight striking the snow aslant, shining with a golden-red glow on the pale huddled clumps of aspen trunks. Only the sun-dogs, bracketing the sun like broken shards of rainbow, give a clue to the awful truth.

Outdoors, as Olivia already knew and now discovers once more, the finest January days are the coldest. Today is just about as cold as the cold ever comes, down where the scales of Fahrenheit and Celsius meet and freeze the mercury. Her breath hangs in the still air like a speech balloon in a cartoon. It freezes upon her balaclava, and on the fringe of fur that trims her hood. Soon it fixes and freezes on her eyelashes. She has to cover her eyes with her mittens to melt the encrusted ice. By the time she gets back to the cabin, she'll look like a snow-ghoul.

Booboo doesn't mind the cold. Booboo never minds anything. He's not a stupid creature, but his heedless doggy enthusiasm generally overwhelms any ancestral wolfish caution. He trots ahead of his mistress, a handsome sight with his winter pelt all puffed up against the cold, like a small wolf parading in a film star's fur coat.

Olivia keeps to the path she had made on previous excursions, up the middle of the frozen stream. The snow in the woods is too deep to wade through without snowshoes. Booboo makes frequent forays into the woods, to see (or smell) what's happened since his previous passage. He flounders cheerfully through drifts as high as himself, in order to lift his leg against specially selected tree trunks. The stream of urine freezes as soon as it hits the snow, making vivid yellow patterns in the virginal snowbank.

Under the pressure of her moccasins the snow squeaks with cold. That's almost the only sound to be heard, aside from Booboo crashing about in the midwinter wood, and an occasional bird chirping from a birch tree, or the soft sudden flump of snowfall when a pine branch bends too far under its built-up burden of snow.

Animal trails cross the stream here and there. Booboo investigates every one, quite fruitlessly. Deep under the snow, small mammals are sleeping out the winter, knowing nothing of forty below. The snow itself keeps them safely warm.

Olivia's nose is beginning to feel the cold, in spite of the balaclava. The inside of the woollen mask is clammy from her breath. The outside has grown a sort of frost-beard, as every drop of vapour from her lungs condenses and freezes on top of the previous exhalation. There are icicles hanging from the fur trim of the hood. Not even Toronto is as bad as this, she thinks. The mice have the right idea: go to bed in October and don't get up till April.

She calls to Booboo to come back. He comes at top speed, leaping in and out of the drifts like a dolphin at play in the ocean, sending a spray of fine snow every time he springs. As his maniacally eager face flashes up with each bound, he looks ridiculous, and she laughs at him. He's a good boy, Boo. He never takes it badly when she laughs.

She's developed an itch on her left wrist. If she takes off her mittens to scratch it, her right hand will be in agony all the way home. It's far too cold for gloves, even for a glove under a mitten. Nothing less than two pairs of mittens will do. The fingers need each other's natural warmth, and even at that she has to keep curling them into fists within the mitts to keep the tips from freezing, and the thumbs regularly migrate to the main body of the mitten to thaw themselves out inside the fist.

Her nose has gone numb. She lays her mittened hand across her face to try to revive it, but that sends all the vapour from her breath up over her eyes, so that her lashes freeze together and she can't see. She can't move with her eyes frozen shut. She has to stop, to cover her face with both mittens, in order to melt the optical icicles with her warm breath. Then she pulls the balaclava free of her mouth to keep the eyelashes from freezing up again. Without the wool to warm it, the icy air stabs half-way down to her lungs. She tucks the balaclava down under her chin and begins to walk as quickly as she can, to get back before the cold has done too much damage to her face.

She sees herself reflected in one dark frosty pane of the cabin window: a small-scale version of a Scandinavian frost giant, hoary all over. The old Norsemen used to tell tales of the end of the world: that some day winter would never end, that a long midwinter's night would slip somehow into eternity, that the world would perish in ice. Too easy to believe that right now, with the sun already gone down and the pale sky going dark.

263

Booboo pushes the door open as soon as she has unlatched it. He shakes himself vigorously in front of the stove, to fling all the snowflakes from his fur.

Olivia checks her nose in the mirror. The tip has gone white. Frost-bitten.

Booboo is the cure for frost-bite. She puts her arms around him and buries her face in his fur, until her nose begins to itch and tingle, signalling that it will survive intact after all.

The cabin windows are all frosted up. She goes to the door and opens it, just for the space of a long breath. Just enough time to catch a glimpse of Orion standing in the south, and the echo of his starlight shining from the snow.

Georgie revived rapidly, with what Tom described as the healing powers of idiot youth. Olivia was half dreading the day of her release, not knowing what to do about Althea's invitation and Tom's accusation. She hadn't even got round to asking Georgie what she wanted to do. Tom was making more and more frequent noises about having to get back. Maybe if he went home and Olivia took Georgie down to Sussex, maybe that would be the best thing. If only he didn't make a fuss about her father.

She felt so guilty about the accusations Tom had made that she arranged to have lunch with her father, when he came up to London to see Georgie. She kissed and hugged him with extra fervour when they met, but that had quite the wrong effect. Any display of overt affection, especially public displays, simply embarrassed him and made him retreat into stiff and distant formality.

Olivia bought him a drink to make up for her gaucherie. 'Have you been round to see Georgie yet?'

'I've just come from the hospital. She seems to be in fine spirits.' He added acidly, 'I bumped into the culprit coming out as I went in. He seemed in fine spirits too.'

'Luke, you mean?'

'If that's his name.'

'I didn't think you knew him.'

'He has his father's face, doesn't he? Not to mention that unmistakable air of insolence. Even the walk is the same damned swagger.' He paused, brooding. 'You know, Lia, if I'd known it was so easy and inconsequential to attempt murder, I might have done it myself before now.'

'I think it's not so simple if you actually succeed. Who would you like to murder?'

Her father looked directly at her. His eyes were startlingly blue beneath his faded hair. 'For starters, the irresponsible fool who got you pregnant.'

The bitter vehemence in his voice took her aback. 'But Daddy, that's ancient history.'

'It wasn't at the time.'

'But you wouldn't want to unmake Georgie, would you?'

'I think your friend Megan would say that Georgie could have been born another time,' he said drily. 'But I didn't mention Georgie, I only said I would have liked to kill her father.'

Just as well, then, that he didn't know who Georgie's father was. But the thought of her father hating Charlie all these years was almost as disturbing as the idea of Tom hating her father, for equally misguided reasons. What an amazing mess she had made of everything.

She changed the subject. 'It's very good of Althea to keep going round to see Georgie.'

Althea had popped in (her own expression) at lunch time every day that week. Her office was only ten minutes' walk from the hospital, but even so Olivia was surprised by such faithful attention from her stepmother, whom she had always regarded as a regrettable sort of person. Maybe Althea really had taken to Georgie. Olivia thought it only just and right that everyone should love her delightful daughter, but she hadn't thought Althea capable of loving anyone, let alone her husband's grandchild.

Her father cleared up that little mystery. 'I asked her to do it, since she's so close anyway. Are you going to come down and stay with us? It's a good time to come. My term won't be starting for a few weeks yet.'

'Same here.'

'I'd almost forgotten.'

She glanced at him, puzzled. 'Forgotten what?'

He raised his glass, his austere features lit up with rare pleasure and real pride. 'I think from what Georgie said that I'm about three years too late, but better late than never. Congratulations, Dr Payne.'

'Thank you, Dr Beckett.' She lifted her glass to acknowledge his toast, with the unworthy thought that he hadn't offered her any congratulations when Georgie was born. Maybe he valued her Ph.D. more than her daughter. Whereas she valued Georgie above anything else in the world, and had proved it once by giving up everything for her daughter's sake. She was only now discovering how much everything was.

'Do you still play the violin, Lia?'

'Funnily enough, I do. I hadn't done for years, because I just didn't have time to practise. But when I started going up North I

265

took the violin along as a way of entertaining myself, and it turned out to be a useful tool of scientific research.' She smiled at the recollection. 'I discovered that wolves are very responsive to music. To violin music, at any rate. Booboo is a big nuisance when I'm trying to tune up, because he wants to sing along and I can't hear the note. But then I noticed that the wolves were joining in with him. So I tried playing something, and they thought it was a community singsong – or else they were trying to tell me to shut up. But they do sound enthusiastic.'

It was her father's turn to smile. 'What sort of taste do they have?'

'Well, none, obviously, since they seem to be cheering my playing, which is frankly terrible. But I've tried different sorts of music on them, everything from strathspeys to Bach, and the volume of the response appears to be a vote for Stravinsky. I think they like all the jarring double stops and spiky dissonance. A very sophisticated preference, when you think of it.'

'Indeed. I'm impressed. Have you written it up in a paper?'

'Heavens, Daddy, that's not proper scientific research. It's just a funny story.' Olivia changed the subject hastily. 'I don't know what to tell you about your invitation. Tom probably won't be able to stay over here much longer, and I haven't mentioned it to Georgie yet.'

'I know. I asked her myself this morning.'

'What did she say?'

'She said she wanted to talk to you.'

'A week down there might be nice,' Georgie agreed.

She seemed listless today, only half there when Olivia was speaking, and distant in her replies. In the classic maternal manner, Olivia worried that she might be suffering some sort of relapse. Especially since her surgically-designed skinhead haircut reminded Olivia of a survivor from a concentration camp. 'Did the consultant come round this morning?'

'Yeah, he said I might be able to leave on Monday. That's my birthday, isn't it? I've lost track of the days. Anyway, he said Da – Tom was to phone him.'

Olivia brushed aside this welcome news to pounce on the anomaly. 'What's this Tom thing? Two months abroad and you're too grown up to have a daddy? I've still got one at thirty-seven.'

Georgie gave her a scornful glance. 'Yeah, I know. You just mislaid him for eighteen years. Why did you do that?'

Olivia had known all summer that this question was going to come up, yet she still hadn't thought of an answer. She gazed at her hands in her lap and said nothing, not knowing what to say, hoping it was only a passing dig.

Georgie persisted. 'I used to think my grandfather must be a monster. Or else my grandmother was some kind of psychopathic dragon. Well, maybe she was, I wouldn't know, but Luke seems to have loved her.'

'So did I, for what it was worth.' Olivia began to feel an irrational anger, at being accused of emotional crimes when she was the victim rather than the perpetrator. She got up and walked to the end of the bed, aware of Georgie's stare full of its own anger. 'It's a funny thing, but children do tend to love their parents and it's very hard to put them off.'

'I might love my parents too, if I knew who they are.'

That was the question Olivia had been dreading, not all summer but all of Georgie's life. She pretended to misunderstand, pointlessly playing for time. 'What does that mean?'

'It means I've seen my birth certificate. According to which I was born fatherless.'

'Well, I can assure you that I'm your mother. I was there when it happened.'

'What about my father?'

Georgie had raised her voice. Olivia wasn't going to play this scene for the entertainment of all the other patients and visitors in the ward. She came back and sat down by the bed and said with quiet tension, 'Tom is your father, in any way that counts.'

'Biology doesn't count? The truth doesn't count?' Georgie spat out contempt in place of pain. '*Father unknown*, Jesus Christ. Matty said you must have been the town bike. Charlie Cahill thought my father must have been a football team. What kind of mother are you? Why did you and Tom lie to me all those years?'

Olivia listened with a curiously calm resignation. Not even the shock of hearing Georgie mention Charlie Cahill moved her much. The settlement day had only been postponed, not avoided – but then she had known that all along. And at least Georgie was making her accusations in hissed undertones rather than hysterical shrieks.

To her own surprise Olivia answered quite briskly. 'Strictly speaking, we didn't lie. I just didn't know what to tell you. I didn't even know what to tell Tom. But I don't think we ought to be discussing this in a public place.'

'How very genteel you are, for a trollop,' Georgie sneered.

'Stop that,' Olivia ordered, hoping she sounded calm and firm, in spite of wanting to strangle her daughter. Absurd clichés trembled on her lips: after all I've done for you, sacrificed and given up . . .

'You must be feeling better, sugar, if you're fit enough for a fight.'

They both turned to stare at Nick, who had appeared on the other side of the bed.

He looked from one to the other with the cool impenetrable gaze that Olivia remembered so well. He sat down opposite Olivia, facing her as she was facing Georgie, his knee touching the outline of Georgie's thigh under the sheets. Taking over the bloody bed, Olivia thought with dull fury.

He picked up Georgie's hand, unclenched the fist and interlaced her fingers with his. 'What's the fight about?'

'What do you think?' Georgie was still sullen. 'I asked her and she won't tell me.'

'I wouldn't tell you either, if I was her and you called me names.'

'Let go.' Georgie tried without effect to reclaim her hand. 'I hate you too. You're all in some kind of conspiracy.' She flashed a glare at her mother. 'I don't believe you that Tom doesn't know.'

'Well, ask him, why don't you?' Nick suggested reasonably.

'He'll just lie.' Anger and pain were wearing her out, setting her on the verge of tears.

Olivia could hardly deal with her own emotions – terror perhaps the foremost now, dread of giving herself away, of Nick betraying her – so she was perversely grateful when Nick took the liberty of answering for her.

'Why should he? It's easy to tell the truth when you've got no secrets, sweetheart.' He turned Georgie's hand over, stroked the palm with his thumb. 'You're too young to have secrets, aren't you, Georgie?'

Georgie was glaring at him now. But she subsided obediently, a horse brought to heel by means of some invisible bit and bridle. Olivia thought she must be too tired to argue any more.

Having squelched the hostilities, Nick went on to change the subject. 'Listen, sugar, I've lined up a couple of flats to view this afternoon. I'd take you along, but I don't think the quacks will let you out. Maybe you'd like to send your mama instead, if you can tell her what you want.'

Olivia had been watching his hand caress Georgie's. The sight took away all the dreadful emotions that had been threatening to overwhelm her, and replaced them with quite different but no less unbearable feelings. She sat up primly and squeezed her own hands together in her lap. 'What's all this about flats?'

'Nick's going to buy a flat,' Georgie explained unhelpfully. 'He's moving to Monte Carlo or Mars or some such place, and Luke's going to live in the flat when Nick's not here.'

'Then why doesn't he take Luke along to look at the flats?'

Nick appeared to take no offence at not being addressed directly. 'Because the bolshie bugger isn't speaking to me right now.'

Olivia sympathized entirely with Luke. 'Yet you're buying the bolshie bugger a flat?'

'Georgie twisted my arm. That's why I need you to come along, to make sure she's going to be happy with my decision.'

'I don't think – '

'Oh, come on, Mama.' Georgie touched her mother's clasped hands with her own free hand. An oddly charged connection, as if the girl in the bed were a conduit between two poles, transmitting some mysterious electrical force from Nick to Olivia. 'You told me D – Tom was meeting some of his old Ormond Street pals for dinner, so you don't have to dash back to the Barbican to cook for him.'

'But I do have to go back to press a clean shirt for him to wear tonight.'

'No problem,' Nick assured her breezily. 'I'm not meeting the bloke from the agency till six o'clock. I can pick you up, or – '

'I'll meet you wherever you're meeting him,' Olivia said hastily, bowing to the apparently inevitable. A perfectly innocent errand, but she didn't want Tom knowing about it if she could help. Oh God, the deception had already started again, as soon as Nick walked back into her life. No wonder the Devil is called the Father of Lies.

'. . . overlooks the park, handy for public transport, the tube station only five minutes away . . .' The estate agent was in full professional flow.

Nick cut him short. 'I never use the fucking tube.' He stood smoking by the window, surprisingly respectable in a jacket and tie, directing his attention to the street below. 'What's the crime rate like?'

'There's an active Neighbourhood Watch scheme,' the agent countered with admirably quick wit. Or maybe he had been asked that question too many times before. 'What do you feel, Mrs Winter? It's very light and airy, don't you think?'

Olivia joined Nick at the window, staring out fixedly in case she had happened to blush. Nick nudged her with his elbow. 'Speak up, Lia. The man asked you a question.'

She glared at him, which increased his amusement. Telling the agent that she wasn't Nick's wife would only make matters worse. If she wasn't his wife she must obviously be his mistress, about to be set up in a *pied-à-terre* where he could exercise visiting rights. There

269

was no point rabbiting on about stepfathers and half-brothers, a lame and unconvincing tale. Stuck with being either Mrs Winter or Mistress Winter, she left it at the former.

'Well, it looks all right to me,' she allowed, then said to Nick, 'But what do I know about it? It's your money, and Luke who's going to be living here, and Georgie's opinion you were so keen to get.'

The agent leaped to conclusions with professional speed. 'It's for your son, is it? If he wants to give me a ring, I can let him and his girlfriend have a look round for themselves. No trouble to arrange it.'

Olivia couldn't take any more of this. 'Excuse me, I'm going to have another look at the loo.'

She locked herself in the bathroom and leaned against the door. Why on earth had Georgie conned her into this? It was only beginning to dawn on her that over the summer her daughter had established relationships with all the long-lost members of her family, and that she knew nothing of these relationships. Georgie appeared to be amazingly matey with all of them, even Althea.

That shouldn't have surprised her, not by now. At some point while Georgie was growing up, Olivia had realized that the little girl who looked so much like her was actually quite a different sort of person: much more lively and outgoing, much less cautious and inclined to worry, more ready to trust other people with her affections. More likely, perhaps, to attract love.

In one respect that was a danger. She could recall vividly the handsome, immaculately dressed, but obviously mad young man who had turned up on their doorstep two years ago, to announce to a bewildered Tom that he was in love with Georgie. He turned out to be a boy from one of Georgie's university classes, with whom she had once had a five-minute conversation. She was like that, Olivia knew instinctively, and Tom had joked about it more than once: the kind of person that people fell in love with. A kind kind of girl. Too kind maybe, too ready to sympathize and console, and smile in dangerous places. This was the innocent who had gone abroad.

Olivia discovered that she didn't even want to speculate on Georgie's relations with her family. Her father had obviously been charmed; well, why shouldn't he be? Althea's interest in Georgie aroused resentment, even jealousy, in Georgie's mother. Matthew and Luke she didn't want to know about. Luke in particular reminded her of the mad young man. And Nick . . . she remembered him stroking Georgie's hand on the hospital bed. Perhaps he too had been charmed.

It was a good thing she was in the loo, because she felt like throwing up.

Someone banged on the door. Nick, obviously, even before she heard him say in a heavily sarcastic tone, 'You can come out now, Mrs Winter. The nasty man has gone away.'

Oh no he hasn't, Olivia said under her breath, but she unlocked the door anyway. The only alternative was starving to death in the bathroom. 'What do you mean, he's gone away?'

'He said he had to dash off to meet another client. He could trust us here on our own, you see, because we're obviously a respectable married couple. And because there's nothing left here to steal.'

Olivia brushed past him, into the barren sitting-room with its views of exuberant shrubbery in the park. 'I thought he was going to show us another flat.'

'That fell through. The vendor was throwing a party or a fit or something.'

'Where does Georgie come into this?' she demanded bluntly. 'Why would she be so keen to have you buy a flat for Luke?'

'What d'you think? She's going to live in it.'

Olivia felt warning prickles up and down her spine. She had been looking out the window in self-defence. Now she turned to look at him. 'What do you mean?'

He was leaning on the mantel of the boarded-up fireplace, his elbow on the mantelpiece, his hand in his short fair hair, looking down at her with that familiar, infuriating, sardonic stare. As if no time at all had passed since she left for Canada. 'Haven't you worked that out yet? They're going to live together. Luke's been knocking her off all summer.'

'But they . . . he . . .' She stopped to get her words together. 'But he's my brother.'

'Worse than that, kitten. He's her brother.'

She knew that. If she knew any one particular thing, it was that her mother's son was her daughter's brother. But she had to work it out in detail, all ways round. Georgie was her mother's granddaughter, Luke was her mother's son. Luke was Nick's son and Georgie was Nick's daughter. No halves or steps involved if you put it like that, just absolute full-blown incest.

She slid down the window pane to sit on the narrow sill. 'My God, Nick, why didn't you try to stop them?'

'They'd have taken a fucking lot of notice, wouldn't they? Especially since I didn't want to give away your secrets.'

'*Your* secrets, you mean.' But right now they were definitely hers. Georgie was in love with a man she could never marry. Olivia couldn't tell Tom what the matter was. She couldn't tell Georgie what the matter was. 'My father told me today he wished he'd

271

murdered you, only he didn't know it was you he was talking about. I wish I'd told him long ago. Maybe he would have done it.'

Nick looked faintly contemptuous. His opinion of her father was scarcely more flattering than her father's opinion of him. 'You reckon?'

'I just wish, that's all.' She took a deep breath. 'Georgie wants to know who her father is.'

'I'm not surprised. Are you?'

'You tell her, then.'

'I will, if you want me to,' he agreed to her surprise. He picked up the cigarette he had set down to smoulder on the edge of the mantel and took a drag. Probably left a burn mark, she noted automatically. It was a wonder he hadn't burned himself to death long ago, he was so careless with those things. 'But not just Georgie. What's she supposed to do, tell Luke the whole thing's off but not tell him why? And what about your old man? He's been hating Charlie Cahill all these years. Or Charlie, for that matter. You pulled the rug out from under him and the poor bugger still doesn't know why. And why should your doctor be kept in the dark? Don't you think he'd like to know who Georgie's daddy really is?'

Olivia spoke slowly, as if she had only just come in from a Canadian winter's night and still had to thaw properly. 'You make it sound like it's all my fault. Like I've ruined everybody's life. But it wasn't me. It was you.'

'Well, I haven't got a Ph.D. in biology,' he said sarcastically, 'but I do have an idea it takes a man and a woman to produce a child. Fifty per cent of the genes from each side, isn't it? And it wasn't my idea to write *Father unknown* on her birth certificate.'

'But if I'd put your name . . .'

Even now, she couldn't begin to imagine the chaos that would have resulted. What would her mother or her father have done? What, for that matter, would Nick himself have done? She hauled herself upright to face him, like a boxer who has just hit the canvas, now desperate to make some mark on her opponent. 'You're only saying that because my mother is dead. If she were still alive you wouldn't want anyone to know.'

He straightened his arm, pushing himself away from the fireplace to confront her more bluntly. 'I didn't want Em to get hurt,' he growled. 'What's wrong with that? But I never said her feelings were the only important thing. And I never leaned on you. I left it up to you to do what you wanted.'

Left it up to her to take the blame.

But that was not the beginning or the end of it. He was right in a way. What she had never been able to handle was the thought of

272

everyone knowing that her mother's husband had put his cock into her, and that she had let him do it. If he had been almost anyone else in the world she might not have cared, but her stepfather . . . She had feared appearing to others as something like a slave in his harem, a ewe buggered by the shepherd, taken not for herself but because she was around to be had. It made her seem in her own mind something slighter than unwilling, a will-less object of his random desire. A she-thing.

Was it possible her major motivation for secrecy had all along been a sort of sexual snobbery?

Nick dropped the fag end of his cigarette on the hearth and ground it out with his heel. Watching him, she thought, He's never been housebroken, never been safe to trust. Her mother had married a wolf rather than a dog: not necessarily untrustworthy in the usual sense, but moved by another, alien, set of instincts.

'Well, what the fuck, it doesn't matter now,' he observed. 'That's all history, and history is a crock of shit as far as I can tell.' An earthier version of Henry Ford's dictum, and not one that Olivia's father would have approved for either style or sense.

Nick shrugged out of his jacket and tossed it aside, not even glancing to see where it landed. On the floor, of course, since there wasn't any furniture. When he tugged off his tie and sent it to join the jacket she became alarmed. 'Nick, what are you doing?'

'What does it look like I'm doing?' He kicked off his shoes, and peeled off his socks by hooking a finger in the top at the back and jerking down, a time-saving procedure if you didn't have to do the laundry and turn them all right-side-out again. When he started to unbutton his shirt she backed away.

'What's the matter, kitten? Have you forgotten what chest hair looks like?'

'Nick, you can't carry on like this.'

'Why not? An opportunity missed is an opportunity lost, as your old gran might have said.'

The shirt followed the jacket and tie on to the carpet. When he came towards her she stepped back again, and found herself literally cornered. *Very* small rooms in this flat.

'Stop it, Nick.'

'You stop it, baby. What does the doctor of biology think about it – did she inherit her hypocrisy from her mother's side of the family or her father's?'

'I'm not talking about hypocrisy, I'm talking about adultery.'

'That didn't bother you last time.'

'I didn't have time to think about it last time.'

'Maybe you should just stop thinking, then. Feeling's what it's all about.' He had undone three buttons on her dress and she hadn't tried to prevent him. Now he stopped and stared at her, challenging her with a blunt blue gaze, like a wolf demanding submission or retreat. 'Make up your goddamned mind, Lia. D'you want me or not?'

Put like that, there wasn't any question to answer. She stared back into his familiar face, lost so long, missed so much, in spite of all the opprobrium she had heaped on him in her mind. No question but that she wanted him.

What she was going to do about that was a different problem. For now she had to answer honestly, in an unwilling whisper. 'You know I do.'

Submission rather than retreat. He softened his challenge enough to show amusement, but even that was a demand. 'Now how the fuck would I know that?'

She had lived so long without desire. To be able to feel it stirring inside her once more was like a resurrection from the dead. She threw caution to the winds, along with history, fidelity, common sense, and everything she knew about him. She undid the rest of the buttons on her dress.

The female wolf coming into season is first solicited by the male, then driven to make her own advances to him. Olivia had seen it happen every year. Now she was doing it herself, nuzzling up to Nick, inviting him to couple with her.

'How would you like it, Mrs Winter?' His voice had gone the husky blue of wood smoke. 'Standing up or lying down, on your back or on your knees, up your cunt or down your throat? Or else I could eat you out, or we could split the difference and go for sixty-nine.'

She leaned against him, wanting to laugh, wanting to lie down for him. 'You make it sould like a restaurant menu.'

'Dinner's later. First things first.' He held her in one arm, unfastening his trousers with the other. 'What the hell, why don't we try the lot?'

274

29

Think you this to be right,
That you said, My righteousness is more than God's?

Dinner was much later.

Not for a very long time had Olivia devoted a whole hour to sexual activity. By the time the obsequious owner of a very small, highly exclusive and vastly expensive restaurant was holding a chair out for her, she felt shattered and sated and screwed half to death. She also thought she must be glowing like a crossing beacon. They had done everything Nick had proposed and some other things as well, and she had come more times in that hour than in her entire married life. She was mortally ashamed of herself and idiotically happy.

She was also acutely conscious that she had nothing on under her dress. She had had an argument with Nick about that, which he had won by simple brute force. He took possession of her bra and knickers before she could put them on again, and refused to give them back to her. He said she had done it before and she said never in public, and he said who's to know and she said she would feel like a slut, and he said he thought she made a terrific slut, which she understood was intended to be more of a compliment than it sounded.

So she put her dress on over nothing but what her grandmother used to call her birthday suit. It was an old dress but one of her favourites, a soft sleeveless floral cotton with a V neck, and buttons all the way down the front. The bodice ended in gathers right under the bust, providing a sort of shelf for her breasts to rest on in lieu of a bra. Nick undid the top two buttons, which gave the neckline a dramatic plunge and exposed her cleavage. When she protested, he said he wasn't having dinner with Little Miss Muffet. And anyway the buttons could probably use a rest, he said; it must be quite a strain, trying to hold in a pair of knockers that size.

She had almost forgotten the way he talked. She was appalled and excited by it. As they went into the restaurant, she declined to admit even to herself how absurdly sexy it made her feel, to be walking about naked beneath her dress. Tom would never have dreamed of putting her into such a state, and would have been shocked if she did it herself. But it was such a simple thing; the absence of underwear had no intrinsic connection with adultery. For all she knew, Nick had been in the habit of persuading her mother to go out of an evening wearing nothing but a frock.

For the first time, she was cheered rather than dismayed by the thought of her mother's relationship with Nick. If her mother, just about the most determinedly proper and respectable woman on earth, had been willing to accommodate her husband's sexual idiosyncrasies and depravities, then it must be okay for Olivia to do it too.

Except that Olivia's husband was Tom.

The restaurateur instructed a waiter to bring them a drink. He seemed disposed to hang about and chat, but when the drinks arrived Nick told him to fuck off. Literally. And the man didn't appear to take offence. Maybe all his clientèle talked to him like that.

'I see your manners haven't improved in all this time,' Olivia said reproachfully.

'Who said they needed improving? I've always been a nice guy.' Nick touched his whisky to her sherry. 'Here's to your cunt, kitten. That's always been beyond improvement too.'

Olivia might have gone red if she hadn't still been flushed from what he had just been doing to that particular bit of her body. 'Don't say things like that. Someone might hear you.'

Right away she wished she hadn't said that. Telling him not to be outrageous was only inviting him to further provocation. 'So what? Anyone who looks at you could make a fair guess that you've got one.'

'You know what I mean. I'll leave if you don't stop. Or at least I'll button up my dress.'

By way of changing the subject, she took a sip of sherry and surveyed her surroundings. It wasn't a glitzy place, more like eccentrically posh. Run perhaps by a Frenchman who had lived long enough in London to develop a personal style, or an Englishman who had lived long enough in Paris to develop any sense of style. She didn't get to eat out much at home. Tom was too busy, she was too busy, and the wolves with whom she spent her time preferred not to live in the urban centres where most *haute cuisine* catering is to be found.

'This is nice,' she allowed. 'Is that fellow a friend of yours? He certainly seems to know you.'

'It's his business to know people, I suppose. Since Em died I've spent too much time in these bloody places. But a man has to eat, doesn't he? The only time I've had a proper dinner at home was when Georgie came over and cooked it.'

'Oh. That was sweet of her,' said Georgie's mother.

'It was Luke she was being sweet to, not me. I was only a lucky bystander.'

'All the same, you seem to be quite matey with her,' Olivia observed, recalling the conversation on the hospital ward that afternoon.

'Is it against the rules to be matey with my daughter?'

That brought up so many images and emotions so suddenly, it was like running into a tree. It reminded her of what he was. The man she had just spent an intimate hour with, letting him perform obscure and adulterous acts on her body, was the same man who had performed an obscene and abusive act on Georgie's three-year-old body.

Nick was watching her face. He must have seen her expression alter abruptly. 'Now what have I done? I haven't mentioned your cunt for at least three minutes, so it can't be that.'

'It's Georgie's I was thinking of,' Olivia said freezingly. 'And the last time you got matey with her, eighteen years ago.'

'Still worked up about that, are you?' Unbelievably, he sounded as contemptuous as she was cold. 'You can't have had much to occupy your mind for eighteen years.'

'It seems to me you've only ever had one thing occupying your mind, the whole time I've known you.'

'Yeah, well, not having a fucking doctorate in biology, I guess I've had to make do with practice rather than theory.'

She gripped the edge of the table and suffered a longing to do something dramatically physical, such as pouring her drink over his head. But since it was only sherry and she had already drunk most of it, that would have been a token gesture at best. 'You had no business practising on Georgie.'

'Who d'you think was doing the practising, for Christ's sake? I don't need any anatomy lessons. I've known how a twat works as long as I can remember. I had five sisters.'

This irrelevant assertion took Olivia by surprise. 'What have your sisters got to do with it?'

'Well, you know. Kids fool around.'

'I don't know. I didn't have any brothers.'

'Maybe that's your trouble.'

The owner returned to their table. Opportune or the opposite, depending on point of view. He produced menus and described in mouth-watering detail the savoury virtues of each item. There was not a lot of choice, Olivia noticed. He had presumably opted for quality rather than quantity, and expected his customers to trust his taste. She took the coward's way out by saying she would have whatever he particularly recommended. When he had taken their orders and gone to greet some new arrivals, Nick accused her of being a crawler.

'I was just being polite. A concept beyond your comprehension, I imagine.'

'No, I get it all right. It's a posh excuse for telling lies.' He lit a cigarette and blew smoke at the ceiling. 'Why don't you tell me about these wolves?'

'What about wolves?'

'Georgie said that's what you do. A sort of Mowgli of the North, she made you out to be.'

'Georgie romanticizes everything,' Olivia said irritably. 'Though I suppose they are more romantic than nematodes or terrapins.'

'Whatever the hell they might be,' Nick added drily. 'How did you get into wolves?'

'It was an accident, really. We were up in Algonquin Park one weekend and Tom and the kids had gone fishing. I walked into the woods and sat on a fallen tree to enjoy the silence.' Resting her chin on her fist, she looked down at Nick's hands, at the cigarette glowing between his fingers. 'You can't imagine what it's like, it's so different from here. There's nothing but wilderness, all the way up to the top of the world. And at night the stars . . . an impossible abundance of them. They take your breath away. My grandfather would have loved to see the stars like that. You can't do it over here. The English sky is too full of earthly light.'

She paused, remembering her father's father, who had taught her the names of the stars. He was dead now, and her grandmother too, her father had said. Seven years ago her grandmother had died, and her grandfather three years later. Gran died of cancer. Grandad's heart had killed him. Pieces of her life gone for ever, and she hadn't known till now.

'The wolves,' Nick reminded her gently. 'Where do the wolves come in?'

Olivia brought her mind back to the present and went on with the story. 'Well, as I was sitting there entirely peaceably, a couple of wolves came along. They stopped when they saw me, and one of them backed off, but the other one came a little closer. It was as if he was as curious about me as I was about him. He walked all the way around me, keeping a sensible distance I suppose, and then after staring for a bit longer he went away. So I thought . . . well, I thought it would be only fair to study a species that could be studying me at the same time.'

'Maybe your wolves are biologists too, specializing in people. Humanology.'

'Anthropology,' she amended automatically, and was herself taken aback by the idea of a non-human anthropologist. 'But they haven't much material for study, with only me to observe.'

'You mean you're all alone up there in that wilderness?'

'Except for Booboo, and he's half a wolf himself. Not that you'd know it, he's such a little coward. But he's good company, and he does his share of work. He catches the mice that get into the cabin, and he's terrific at maintaining our territorial fences.'

'How does he do that?'

'He pees in the right places, so the wolves know what land belongs to me. It saves a lot of aggro. What are you laughing at?'

'The thought of what you'd have to do, if you didn't have the dog.'

Olivia went a little more rosy at the thought. The thought, that was, of Nick having in his head a picture of her squatting to urinate. For all his familiarity with her body, he had never seen her like that. It would have required on the one hand a non-urban environment, and on the other hand a different kind of intimacy, absolute and all-accepting. She had never been that close to him. Never been Mrs Winter.

Come to think of it, she didn't even have that kind of intimacy with Tom. He always locked the bathroom door.

'Well, it would be easier if I were a man,' she conceded rather primly.

'So if you didn't have a dog, you'd have to take your doctor along for the fence-mending.'

'Oh, Tom would never go up North with me. For one thing, he hates flying. Being at the mercy of a bush pilot would just reduce him to jelly. He'd kill to avoid it.'

'You have to fly in one of those crates to get wherever it is you go?'

'How else would I get up there? There are no roads, except a few logging trails. It's a huge empty country. You can't farm because the soil is hopeless, and the climate's far worse than Toronto. But the wolves are used to me and Boo by now. That's one reason why it's easier for me to work on my own. And cheaper, since I don't get much in the way of research grants. I can't afford to do anything high-tech like using collars with radio transmitters for keeping track of the wolves.'

'Just as well for the wolves, I'd say. So how do you keep track of them?'

'The same way they keep track of each other. I howl and they answer.'

That amused him. 'They think you're a wolf?'

'They know perfectly well what I am. And they know Boo's voice, but they answer him too. Why not? You wouldn't refuse to speak to a foreigner, would you, just because his English was garbled and he had a terrible accent?'

Nick looked sceptical. 'Dogs bark when they hear another dog barking. What makes you so sure the wolves aren't just joining in the bloody racket, like a dog?'

'Oh no, they have a fairly sophisticated vocal language. That's what the old Native people say, and I'd agree with them. But I'm not allowed to say so officially, because I have no proper scientific proof. There are all sorts of things to do with wolves that I can't write about, because I can't prove anything.'

'Such as?'

Since Nick appeared, to Olivia's amazement, to be genuinely interested in her wolves, she didn't mind staying on that safe subject while they ate dinner. It was a rare pleasure, in any case; Tom was sick of wolves, resented them, and refused to listen to her talk about them. So she took full advantage of Nick's attention.

'Well, basically, what determines whether a science is considered hard or soft is how measurable, repeatable, and predictable the events are that you're studying. The harder the science, the more respectably scientific it is. Physics is really macho, biology is a bit iffy, and sociology is in the same league as astrology. So to move a soft science upmarket, they try to concentrate on the measurable, repeatable and predictable bits. Things like how many wolves in an average pack, how many deer they eat in an average year, population movements and dynamics – pretty well anything that can be put into a graph. Graphing something has to involve hard numbers, so everybody likes graphs because they prove you're dealing with something concrete.

'But as soon as you start speculating about what goes on inside a wolf's head, or describing your own observations about social relationships between the wolves in a pack, you're in effect moving out of biology into psychology or sociology, and people start accusing you of sentimentalization and anthropomorphism.'

Nick had paused with his wineglass half-way to his mouth during that last sentence. 'Not me, baby, I wouldn't dream of doing that,' he assured her when she paused. 'Do you have to learn to rattle off words like anthropomorphism to get a Ph.D.? It sounds like a fatal disease.'

Olivia took a mouthful of her own wine to cover her confusion. Maybe he thought she was trying to put him in his uneducated place, or maybe he was just needling her for his own unguessable reasons. Whatever the motivation, his remark had tripped her up, made her feel foolish and resentful, and she hardly knew how to respond. 'Sorry,' she mumbled. 'I just meant, it's a cardinal sin to suppose that animals think and act like human beings.'

'Why? We're animals too, aren't we?'

That took her aback again. She had been trained to play god among the brute beasts, but Nick was right. In a biological context, she was at best merely one of the seraphim observing life among the common or garden angels, and at worst a chimpanzee studying baboons. 'Well, we are, of course. I hadn't thought of it that way.'

'Maybe you should be learning that wolf-language you mentioned. It might be a real eye-opener to hear what they're saying about you.'

'They'd have a very odd idea of human society if they theorize from what they can see of my behaviour. They'd think we're obsessed with wolves, for starters.'

'And have no sex life.'

That wouldn't have been a million miles from the truth, Olivia admitted to herself. But it reminded her of the most recent episode in what sex life she did have, namely the hour she had spent with Nick before dinner. Which in turn stirred up adulterous images and longings. All that screwing hadn't slaked her desire for him at all. Strengthened it, rather. The appetite that grows by what it feeds upon.

She resolutely returned her mind, and the conversation, to the scientific study of wolves. 'That actually illustrates just what I was getting at. Most of the studies of wolf behaviour have been done with wolves that were brought up in captivity, because the people doing the studies can control everything more easily. I can't really control anything at all, by myself in the middle of the wilderness. I can only watch the wolves going about their daily business. But because wolves are supposed to live their lives largely by instinct, those experiments conducted in captivity are considered valid scientific studies of the wolfish psyche and society.'

'I can tell you don't agree.'

'No, I don't.' This time she ignored his gently mocking tone. 'What they're creating is a *Lord of the Flies* situation. Infants, even wolf cubs, learn what to do and not to do from their parents. The family group, parents and children, is the basis of every animal society. It has to be, doesn't it? That's what society is *for*. It's designed to ensure the preservation and perpetuation of the species. In any sentient species, the parents love their children and look after them, and the children love their parents in return.

'If you take the children away from their parents, you're removing the essential glue that holds a society together and makes it more than just a group of individuals. When the orphaned cubs grow up and have their own children, they still don't behave the way wolves do in a natural state. The males and females don't behave the way wolves do in a natural state. The males and females don't bond properly when they mate. All the social relationships are in constant turmoil, with everyone involved in a struggle for dominance and the losers being killed or ostracized.

'And since they get fed automatically, they don't have to go hunting. Because the wild wolves have to rely on each other's co-operation in the hunt, they have to keep on friendly terms with each other, or else they'd all starve. And they learn to share out the results of the hunt. In captivity the wolves don't have that sort of life-and-death basic economic motivation to behave decently towards their pack-mates.'

'They're wolves in a welfare state, you mean,' Nick commented.

'We're talking biology here, not politics,' Olivia reproved him. 'Don't complicate things.'

'I thought I was simplifying them. I'm all for simplicity, myself.'

Again he had flustered her. She couldn't quite tell if he was making fun of her or not. 'Well, the point I'm making is that, compared to the wolves I watch, I'd say the captive wolves live in a state of relative anarchy: social, sexual and emotional. They're deprived and depraved. It's like studying human beings on the basis of people who grew up in council care. But the behaviour of those wolves is measured and graphed and described and cited as if it was normal.'

'And – let me guess – if you try to tell your biologist mates all that, they'll tell you you're coming down with a bad case of – what was that word?'

'Anthropomorphism.' Olivia giggled in a very unscientific manner. 'You're right, it must be a sort of mental disorder.'

After the dinner had been consumed – and very good it was, Olivia had to allow, though whether it was good enough to warrant the price the anglicized Frenchman or gallicized Englishman had put on it was a different matter, and not one that really concerned her much, since Nick was picking up the tab – when the dinner had disappeared and they were finishing off the last of the wine, awaiting coffee and cognac, Olivia returned to an earlier topic, this time more in the spirit of scientific enquiry. 'Did you really play doctor with your sisters?'

'Play doctor?' Nick leaned on his hand and looked at her, amused. 'Is that what you call it? Or is that what your doctor calls it when he does it to you?'

'Stop calling him my doctor.'

He ignored the protest. 'What a great line. I wish I was a doctor.' He placed his hands together and leaned towards her, lowering his voice and producing a passable imitation of Tom's accent. 'Now this won't take a minute, Mrs Winter, and it won't hurt at all. Just close your eyes and try to relax.'

Olivia buried her nose in her wine glass to keep from laughing. He had no right to make fun of her husband, especially not after having cuckolded him so comprehensively. The worst thing was that Nick's joke had unwittingly described her marital sex life with appalling accuracy. But that was her own fault, not Tom's.

No, it was Nick's fault, because for eighteen years she couldn't bear to think of him.

'I'm Mrs Payne, not Mrs Winter,' she said repressively, 'and don't you forget it.'

'It's not me that's in danger of forgetting who you're married to, kitten.'

The waiter arrived just then with the coffee and the brandy, a merciful distraction. By the time he had removed himself Olivia was able to speak again, in what she hoped was a normal tone. 'I thought playing doctor just involved looking. I don't know the rules because I never played it myself.'

'A deprived childhood, I see.' Nick produced an after-dinner cigarette and lit up. 'Didn't you even get to touch?'

Olivia was faintly shocked. 'You didn't feel up your own sisters, did you?'

'Sure I did.'

'That's disgusting.'

'They didn't think so. They didn't have the advantages of your refined upbringing, of course. And it taught me how the female body works, because they didn't mind telling me if I wasn't doing just what they wanted.'

'But your sisters – how could you possibly want to do that to your sisters?'

'Well, I didn't happen to be that matey with anyone else's sister, not till later on anyway. I guess they had to make do with me for the same reason. Jesus, Lia, what planet do you come from? It's nothing to do with fucking romance. Kids are just little animals, they do whatever feels good. And it's more fun to have someone else do it for you than to do it yourself. Even you must have worked that out by now.'

Olivia stared at him. Nor for the first time, she wondered seriously how anyone so profoundly depraved could go about looking like an ordinary person. Well, not ordinary, he was much too attractive to be ordinary. But if God were looking out for the rest of the world, surely someone like Nick should have come with a moral health warning: *This man is just an animal, he does whatever feels good.*

'Is that your excuse for what you did to Georgie?'

His blue eyes flickered, not with guilt but with anger and impatience. 'I don't reckon I need to make any excuses there,' he growled. 'Not to you, at any rate.'

That was the last straw. She didn't care if he was the greatest lover who had ever lived, there were more important things than that and Georgie was one of them. 'Then I'll make mine and leave,' she said, pushing back her chair and rising.

He rose at the same time, grabbing her wrist. He leaned towards her and spoke very softly across the table. 'Sit down, you stupid little bitch. You walked out on me eighteen years ago and you're fucking well not going to do it again. Georgie's my daughter too, remember? The only one I've got. There's no way I'd ever do anything to hurt her. What d'you think I am?'

She looked at him steadily, controlling her anger, considering what he had just said. 'I don't know what you are.'

'Sit down and maybe you'll find out.'

He was still holding her wrist in an uncomfortably harsh grip. He jerked it downwards, to add physical inducement to his invitation. She took her seat again, from what motives she couldn't tell. Not fear, this time; if she screamed, everyone would come running. Maybe it was the same sense of even-handed curiosity that had led her to study wolves.

When she was seated again she said calmly and primly, 'Now tell me why any normal man would molest his baby daughter.'

Nick didn't respond quite so calmly. 'What kind of word is that, *molest?*'

'You know perfectly well what it means.'

'Sure I do. It means you don't approve of what I did, so you're trying to make it out to be something else.'

'I'm calling it by its real name.'

'You're giving it a name. Just like you're trying to pin one on me.'

By now he was calm and she was flustered. 'Calling you a pervert, you mean?'

'Yeah. Handy word, that. And fair enough, if I was the sort of guy who gets off on *molesting* little kids.' He weighed the word with sarcasm. 'But you don't really believe that. You just mean you don't like whatever it was you think I did to Georgie.'

'I know what you did. She told me. You told me.' Anticipating his answer, she added, 'Not in those terms, of course. But that's what it was.'

'You're writing the dictionary, are you? I thought you wanted to learn something.'

Olivia was as disconcerted as if one of her wolves had suddenly spoken to her. She swallowed her instinctive reaction, tried hard to be fair. 'Okay, tell me why a normal man would . . . deliberately touch his daughter *there*.'

'First you have to tell me why any normal person would decide it's okay to touch their own kid anywhere except there.'

'Because that's private,' Olivia explained patiently. She spoke slowly and carefully so that even an idiot or a Martian could understand her. After all, she was apparently talking to a moral idiot. And a Martian. 'It's invasive and threatening to their sense of self.'

'So is a clip around the ear, but nobody's tried to claim that's a uniquely horrible and perverted thing to do. And while Georgie was in nappies you must have touched her there every day.'

'But that's just functional, something that has to be done.'

'You mean it's okay as long as she doesn't enjoy it. Sounds kind of backwards to me.'

Olivia thought about that. She was reminded of St Augustine's view of sexual pleasure, allowable only as long as it was incidental to the act of procreation. 'Well,' she said carefully, picking her way, 'maybe the thing to watch out for is that *you're* not enjoying it. Otherwise you could be saying you were doing it to give the baby pleasure, when it's your own pleasure you're after.'

'Lia, I swear to you, I haven't been turned on by little girls for more than forty years, not since I discovered big girls. But all you're saying there seems to amount to the old line about how this'll hurt me more than it hurts you.'

'You're deliberately twisting everything I say,' she said sharply. 'You can't compare adults and children like that. Adults automatically have power over children, by their greater size and strength if not by superior knowledge and authority. And when it comes to sex it's even more complicated, because adults have sexual urges and children don't.'

Nick had been sitting hunched forward over the table, his head down close to hers, listening attentively. Now he leaned back and laughed. 'Jesus, Lia, not even Em could have produced you. It must have been the Virgin Mary herself. Are you going to sit there with a straight face and tell me you never felt an itch between your legs till I turned up?'

He could hardly have put it in more humiliating terms as far as she was concerned. She squashed a strong desire to get up and stalk

285

out; she was determined not to let him even think he had won. 'Listen, Nick, it doesn't matter whether children have sexual impulses or not. It doesn't matter whether they might or might not derive pleasure from what some adult does to them. That's all irrelevant. The only thing that matters is that they're not capable of consenting to it as an equal. They can't understand what it involves.'

'So who the hell does? I reckon most people don't understand most of the things that happen to them. Nobody asks you if you know the rules. You just have to get on with it.'

'But parents have a duty to protect their children from harm, as much as they can. And you're Georgie's father.' She said with a passion that surprised even herself, 'You should have been protecting her instead of corrupting her. Do you want her to remember you as someone who was willing to take advantage of her? Who had more regard for his – his own *amusement* than for her vulnerability? She'd be really proud of you, wouldn't she, if she ever finds out who her father is.'

Nick shrugged sulkily, as if he couldn't be bothered to argue any more. 'Why don't you finish off your brandy, and I'll sort out the bill.'

Olivia sipped at the brandy to cool her emotions, while he called the waiter over and settled the bill. She didn't suppose she had actually converted him, but at least she had managed to silence him.

She wondered if he had any real understanding of what she had meant by *corruption*. He struck her as not so much a wicked man, who knowingly did wrong, as a man who had no notion of right and wrong. She used to imagine that before Adam and Eve discovered fashion, they had led a blameless life, doing no wrong; but now it seemed to her more likely that, like Nick, they simply hadn't grasped the concept. All the apple had done was to make them see their own behaviour in a different, guilty light.

She wished she had one of those apples around right now.

On the way out of the restaurant, Olivia discovered that Nick hadn't exactly given her the last word after all. The owner came over to wish them good night. Seeing Olivia's grim expression, he said to Nick, 'Is your friend displeased about something? The food was not prepared to her satisfaction?'

'Everything's fine,' Nick assured him brusquely. 'The lady's just being a pain in the arse.' He put his hand on the backside in question and propelled her towards the door.

'Stop that,' Olivia hissed at him as soon as they were outside. 'What motivates you to be so deliberately crude in public?'

'The look on your face, sweetheart. And also, in this case, the feel of your arse.' He stroked her bottom, reminding her that she had no knickers underneath, which in turn made her feel sexy in spite of her anger. Which was undoubtedly what he had had in mind when he did it.

They walked down towards Piccadilly, his arm less controversially placed around her shoulders. The arm felt wonderfully protective and comforting. His body at the other end of the arm was both reassuring and exciting. She wondered if modern medicine could come up with a way to remove his brain, leaving her with just the arm and the body.

When they found a taxi, Olivia took care to sit well away from both the arm and the body. That lasted till the first traffic light, at which the body – no, alas and dammit, *Nick* kissed her, putting his tongue inside her mouth in an intimate and arousing fashion. Half-way down her throat, in other words. At the same time he unbuttoned the bodice of her dress to stroke her breast.

Over eighteen years she seemed to have forgotten how erotically responsive the female breast can be, or at least how much response Nick could get out of hers. Quite quickly she forgot her anger, forgot the cabby in the front, forgot about anything but Nick, and the pleasure he was giving her.

'Hey, Lia,' he said in her ear, 'what would your wolves be doing now?'

Olivia whispered back. 'He'd be licking her.'

To make her meaning clear – not that he was likely to misunderstand – she wriggled her bottom along the seat with something between a sigh and a giggle, until her head was in his lap and her skirt up around her hips. He twisted sideways, leaning over her. He brought his mouth to her crotch, pushing his head between her thighs, licking like the wolf she had described, giving her little nips in tender places, making her yelp. Love bites, not hard enough to hurt, just enough to startle and torment her. She made pleading importunate moans that even to her own ears sounded like the lovesick whining of a bitch in heat – her own little bitch at the cabin door, pining for the wolf outside.

When the taxi arrived at the Barbican, Olivia had to pull her shattered self together enough to get out. Nick was already standing on the pavement, taking out his wallet. She crept out after him, too ashamed to meet the cabby's eye, and fled up the nearest staircase towards the highwalk.

Her body was still on fire. On the second landing, overlooking the gardens and St Giles Church, she stopped and leaned back against the broad concrete parapet. As she heard Nick's footsteps on the stairs below her, she unbuttoned her dress from top to bottom.

He came up to her and ran his hands over her revealed nakedness.

287

She unzipped his cock and put it between her thighs and impaled herself upon it. He picked her up and perched her on the balustrade and thrust into her with thrilling intensity. She clung to him as he bent her back out over dangerously empty air. He addressed her by a variety of insulting obscenities as if they were endearments, and she begged him to do a variety of obscene and even illegal things to her, but all they actually did was copulate as simply as two wolves mating, until they were both satisfactorily exhausted.

She said against his hair, 'I thought old men couldn't do it more than once a night.'

'I wouldn't know what old men get up to. I mean don't get up to.' But he was short enough of breath to have some trouble getting his response out.

She slid down off the balustrade, scraping her bottom on the concrete, and buried her face against him. She wriggled to enjoy the rough feel of his clothes against her bare flesh. He was turning her into a nymphomaniac as well as a wolf.

'You're an unspeakable brute,' she whispered. She must be drunker than she had thought, to be saying such stupid things. Or maybe that was just the sort of thing lupine lovers said to each other. 'I've got bruises all over.'

'That's your own fault, you insatiable little tart. Your doctor doesn't look after you properly. I don't think you've had a decent fuck for eighteen years.'

The mention of Tom dissolved her euphoria. She pulled away from Nick and began to button up. 'There's more to life than sex.'

'Like what?'

'Well . . .' She thought frantically. She must have been doing something of interest or value, all those years away from him.

Her brain wouldn't work. Her fingers wouldn't work either. She fumbled with the buttons until he finished the job for her.

'Go away, Nick. I've got to get inside before Tom comes home.'

'Aren't you going to invite me in for coffee?'

'No, absolutely not. Go away.'

They argued as she started up the stairs. They were still arguing about it when he followed her into the flat.

Tom wasn't there. Couldn't have been, now that she thought of it, because she had the keys. He would have had to wait outside, and he hadn't been there. 'Thank God,' said Olivia aloud. 'I'm going to have a cup of tea.'

'That sounds good to me.'

'You're not staying. Go away at once.' She kicked off her shoes and unbuttoned the dress again to examine herself. She really did have bruises on her breasts and thighs, some of them suspiciously like teeth marks. Also scratches on her backside, presumably from the concrete balustrade – which added a whole new dimension to the idea of architectural brutalism. 'Good heavens, Nick, look what you've done. What am I going to tell Tom? Give me back my underwear, I've got to put it on before he gets in.'

'Can't. I left it at the flat.'

She stared at him. 'What's that little man going to think, when he goes back and finds a pair of knickers and a bra lying around?'

'Very exciting thoughts, I expect. Your kettle's boiling.'

She did up one button to hold the front of the dress together while she made the tea. She should have been horrified by her own behaviour, and by the prospect of Tom walking in and finding Nick on the premises, but she was still nicely tipsy, and moving, mentally and physically, in a pleasant rosy glow. She headed for the bedroom.

'Lia, where're you going?'

'What do you think? I'm going to get dressed.'

'Don't bother with that. Just button yourself up and you'll be all right.'

She stopped at the bedroom door and looked back at him. 'Don't be silly. What would Tom think?'

Nick came over to lean his arm against the door jamb between the sitting-room and the tiny inner hall, the inevitable cigarette dangling from his fingers. 'He's a man, isn't he? He'll think it's fucking sexy.'

'But how would I explain it?'

'Why shouldn't he assume you've done it for his benefit?' He dragged on the cigarette and smiled sourly. 'You do actually screw this guy, don't you?'

'Of course.' She tried to sort things out in her mind, which wasn't working very well on account of the sherry and wine and cognac. 'But Nick, I can't – '

'You'd do it for me but not for your doctor, is that it?'

She was going to explain that she didn't have that sort of relationship with Tom, and then she began to wonder what sort of relationship she did have with Tom, and what sort of relationship she had with Nick, if any – though how you could do with somebody what she had done with him tonight, and then maintain you didn't have a relationship of any description, took a bit of explaining in itself . . . While she was sorting all this out in her head, the doorphone buzzer sounded.

She stared at Nick, open-mouthed. She had meant to get him out of here before Tom arrived.

He came over to her and did up her dress for the second time and pushed her back out into the sitting-room. 'Go let him in, kitten.'

After she had pressed the button to release the entry door, she caught sight of herself in the little mirror on the stand by the door. 'Oh, God, look at my hair! It's all come undone. On acccount of all that messing in the taxi. Why didn't you tell me?'

'Don't panic, baby. Here, hold still.' He unpinned the leather grip, smoothed her hair back with his hands and refastened it all in a knot at the nape of her neck with a casual deftness that astonished her. 'That must be a bloody pain,' he observed. 'Why don't you cut it off?'

'I think about it from time to time, but then I lose my nerve.'

She went into the kitchen and occupied herself with cups and saucers. The rosy warmth had gone. Now she felt sick at the thought of having to face Tom. It wasn't just what she had done that was so dreadful, it was that she had so desperately wanted Nick to do it to her, had begged him to do it, had invited him to do it in a public place because she couldn't even wait the three minutes it would have taken to get up to the privacy of the flat. What if Tom had come up the stairs while Nick was screwing her on the balustrade? She was mad. She was shameless and depraved. She was the tart that Nick had called her.

Tom knocked on the door of the flat and she opened it. But he wasn't Tom, he was Matthew.

Olivia felt unutterably grateful. Not only was he not Tom, but his presence in the flat when Tom did arrive would make Nick's less suspicious. 'Oh, Matty, come in, we're just about to have a cup of tea.'

'That sounds great.' Matthew walked past her into the flat. It was his flat, actually, of course, in a way.

Olivia followed him, suddenly much more cheerful. She wasn't obliged to explain Nick's presence to Matthew, but she found herself doing it anyway. 'I've been helping Luke's father look for a flat for Luke. Georgie made me do it.'

'Yeah, she told me when I went round to see her tonight. Hello, Luke's father.'

Nick nodded from the seat he had taken at the far end of the sofa. Olivia glanced from him to Matthew. 'You two haven't met before?'

'Not so I noticed. This is a historic occasion.' Matthew drifted towards the kitchen. 'Where's this tea you promised me?'

Nick said to Olivia, 'He's got your old man's mouth, hasn't he?'

'He's been very good to Luke,' she told him in a flustered undertone, hoping Matthew hadn't heard any of that.

'Just like your old man, then. Another sodding saint.' He eyed Matthew, who was returning with his cup of tea and a generous handful of biscuits. 'Lia says you're Luke's minder. Christ knows, he needs one.'

'Tell me about it,' Matthew invited sardonically. 'Feeble-minded, the Victorians used to call it.'

Olivia had started for the kitchen to pour tea for Nick and herself, but she paused to defend her younger brother. 'I think he must be quite talented,' she said over her shoulder. 'Georgie showed me some drawings he did, of her and some of the other people on the ward. They were really clever.'

To her surprise Nick agreed. 'Of course he's got the bloody talent. He's never done anything but doodle and draw since he was old enough to hold a pencil. But when he landed at this so-called art college, they pretty well told him not to bother with all that. Élitist, they called it.'

He lit himself another cigarette. Olivia wondered what on earth he had done with the fag end of the last one. She would have to remember to look for it later. 'Y'know, I've always had an idea that most teachers really don't want anybody to use their brains. They don't want to actually teach you anything, they don't want anybody asking questions, they just want you to do what they tell you. This lot at Luke's college were just the same as the bunch of wankers I had to put up with at school.'

Olivia knew that Nick's education had been irregular and illegally brief, and guessed that his teachers, however incompetent, must have had quite a lot to put up with from their point of view.

'Knowledge is supposed to be valuable,' Matthew pointed out. 'Why should they give it away?'

'That's what they're paid to do, isn't it? But I reckon part of the problem is that they don't know sod-all themselves. And they don't have to, do they? They're the buggers who decide what the right answers are.' Nick took the cup of tea Olivia offered him, tasting cautiously. 'Good girl, you didn't forget the sugar.'

Eighteen years and she hadn't forgotten. 'I couldn't forget your sugar, Nick. You're the only one I know who takes it.' She sat down at the opposite end of the sofa with her own cup. 'Matty, what have you done with all the biscuits? There are none left in the tin.'

'I ate them, of course. What else would one do with biscuits?' He swallowed the last of his stolen handful. 'Where's Tom? Still out on the town?'

Georgie must have told him about that too, Olivia deduced. 'It's not all that late,' she defended her absent husband. 'Just gone eleven.'

'He'll be home soon, then. Not much fun to be found after the pubs have closed. Are you going down to stay with my parents next week, when Georgie gets sprung?'

'Well, I'd like to, and it would be good for Georgie to be able to sit out in the garden. On the other hand, Tom says he's got to get back, and Alex is starting school again on Tuesday . . . Don't do that, Nick, I'll get you an ashtray.' She set down her teacup, leaped up and dashed into the kitchen to dig out the unmatched saucer she had given him last time. Then she watched him transfer his cup to the odd saucer and carry on flicking his ashes into Althea's good china. 'You are disgusting,' she told him. 'Why are smokers such slobs?'

He waved her back to her seat with the hand that held the cigarette, dropping more ash on the carpet in the process. 'Sit down, for Christ's sake. You're turning into Em.'

Turning into Mrs Winter, Olivia thought with a shiver.

Just as Matthew had predicted, Tom came home not long after. He was in the same mellow state that Olivia had been in half an hour before. He greeted Nick and Matthew cheerfully, apparently not surprised to find the flat full of people so late at night.

Olivia made coffee this time, while Tom made enquiries about the rules of cricket, and Nick and Matthew got into an argument over the answers. They carried on until after midnight, when Olivia announced that anyone who didn't belong there would have to leave, because she was about to go to bed. She shooed her visitors out the door, still disputing.

'I thought they'd never go,' she said to Tom with perfect truthfulness.

'I thought they were both pretty funny,' Tom replied, tipsily genial. 'That Matt's inclined to be a brat, but he's sharp all the same. So is your stepfather, in a kind of cross-grained way, don't you think?'

'Oh, he's hilarious,' said Olivia with a sigh. 'Let's go to bed.'

'Good idea.' But Tom didn't necessarily have sleep in mind. He came up behind her, and ran his hand down her back and over her bottom. 'Hey, you haven't got anything on under there.'

He didn't sound too shocked. Pleasantly surprised, more like. And she was shocked to realize it. 'Do you mind?'

He was already hauling up her skirt to confirm his discovery. 'What do you think?'

The sex life of the porcupine, Olivia happened to know, has a number of unusual features for obvious anatomical reasons, but one extraordinary behaviour with no bearing on anatomy is that just as the male porcupine marks his ownership of territory by urinating on the boundaries, so he marks his ownership of a female by urinating in her face, the theory being that the smell of him on her will warn off any rivals.

If any proof more than the evidence of appearance were needed that humans are not closely related to porcupines, Olivia had it provided now. It had seemed to her that she positively reeked of sex, and of Nick in particular. She had – irrationally, perhaps – been terrified that Tom would be able to smell his rival on her. But Tom hadn't a procupine's nose, or even a wolf's for that matter. 'Christ, you smell sexy.'

Not just her smell. She was shocked yet again, this time to discover how arousing it could be, to have sex with her husband when her lover was, in a sense, still in her.

Afterwards Tom said, 'You should take off your underwear more often, if it has that effect on you.'

30

Ever learning, and never able to come to the knowledge of the truth.

Georgie was definitely coming home, in time for her birthday on Monday. Tom had discussed it at length with the consultant in charge of her. She was well out of danger and could recuperate just as well if not better at home. And besides, the consultant didn't add, somebody else needed her bed. So a week after being on the verge of death, or at least living death, she was being sent home.

Not home home, not to Toronto. The consultant had unwittingly assisted Olivia here by strongly advising against putting a patient who had suffered head injuries on to a transatlantic aeroplane, unless it was absolutely essential. Not much room for argument there, but Tom and Olivia had one anyway.

First they argued about Tom's announcement that he was going home even if no one else was. Olivia was terrified by the idea of being left alone in England, with only her wedding ring between her and Nick. It was herself she was afraid of, she admitted in the darkest watches of the night. Nick was a constant, Tom or no Tom; he would do anything that occurred to him by way of getting her into bed. Bed being in this case euphemism rather than metonymy, since they hadn't been anywhere near one yet.

She was ashamed of herself for craving him. It wasn't as if she had no one else to love her. It wasn't even as if he loved her. Or ever had.

Maybe she had more in common with wolves than her science would allow. Maybe, because he had screwed her for so long when she was young, she had bonded to him in some mysterious biological way. But the bond had only worked one way in this case. Nick was like the orphaned wolves she had described to him. Incapable of love.

Whatever, the fact was that she didn't want to want him. She wanted to want Tom. She did everything she could think of to convince herself she wanted Tom.

Over the weekend Dr Payne MD and Dr Payne Ph.D. copulated like a couple of demented mink, in bed, on the sofa, in the bath, even over the kitchen sink. Tom clearly couldn't believe his luck. He wouldn't have considered it luck, she thought guiltily, if he could have seen inside her head while he was shoving his prick into her, if he had caught her adulterous thoughts, imagining the prick inside her was another man's. She tried not to think those thoughts but they kept putting themselves into her brain, every time Tom put himself into her body.

But it wasn't Nick that caused the argument. Olivia was indignant about Tom's openly expressed view that it was her duty as a mother to care for and comfort her convalescent daughter, but that he had no such duty as a father. Furthermore, that his duties as a doctor automatically took precedence over her own professional duties, whether of teaching or research. He seemed incredulous that she would even dispute this point with him.

'Be serious, Lia. Nobody's going to die if you don't turn up in time to teach them.'

'Is life-or-death the big criterion, then? I might half believe you, if I didn't know very well you'd pull the same arguments if you were a lawyer or an accountant. Anyway, your patients won't drop dead if you're not around. They're more likely to come down with chicken-pox than the plague, and even the ones who do get into difficulties will be rescued by some other doctor.'

He played his trump card. 'Well, you knew I was a doctor when you married me. You know how I feel about my work. What's the point of complaining about it, twenty years later?'

'For one thing, I'm not complaining on my own behalf. I think Georgie's going to feel that you're shirking your paternal duties.'

'What about your maternal duties to Alex? He's supposed to be starting school on Tuesday, and you're not even going to be there.'

'If a boy of seventeen can't get himself to school in the morning without the assistance of his mother, he's got real problems. He can even drive a car now without help, remember? And he won't starve, your mother will make sure he gets fed properly.' Properly in Alex's case was about three times the normal human ration.

'The same goes for Georgie,' Tom pointed out triumphantly. 'She'll be twenty-one on Monday, for Christ's sake. And it was her idea to

294

come over here in the first place. Would she expect me to hang around in some tropical hellhole, for instance, just to keep her company while she recovered from dysentery?'

'Well, she might, actually. But, Tom, that's not the problem this time,' Olivia said wearily. 'The problem is that she's seen her original birth certificate. She knows you're not her biological father.'

That did give him pause for a moment. Just for a moment. 'When did she spring this revelation on you?'

'Yesterday. I meant to tell you, but there wasn't time.' And intervening events – Nick, that was – had driven it out of her mind.

'Well, it wasn't my idea not to tell her. Anyway, most adopted children go through a phase of resentment, no matter what or when they've been told about it. Come to think of it, plenty of children living with their natural parents become convinced they've been adopted.'

'In the first place, Tom, she's not a child. She'll be twenty-one on Monday, as you just pointed out. In the second place, she hasn't been adopted.'

'Not my fault,' Tom said resolutely. 'It can't be done without the consent of the natural father, and I don't have a clue who that is.' He gave her a sternly meaningful look. 'Do I?'

'He was a football team,' Olivia asserted defiantly, recalling Georgie's, or rather Charlie Cahill's, gibe. 'How was I supposed to get the signed agreement of eleven guys whose names I don't even know?'

Her husband looked at her in a rather alarming way. He looked inscrutable, and Tom had never been a mystery to her. 'Lia, I really cannot believe that even as a feckless fifteen-year-old, you would have accommodated eleven strangers at one go, without any form of contraception, and not aborted the consequence. One thing you definitely are, and that's ruthless when you want something enough. Why did you want Georgie so much?'

Olivia's defiance had deflated to sullenness, not yet desperation. She had, ironically, brought this on herself. 'I just wanted her. Young girls do, when they've got no one else.'

'Your devotion to your daughter is not in question, but she wasn't the result of an immaculate conception. She still had to have a father. And you know very well who he is.'

'Since I didn't even know you existed then, what I might know is, frankly, none of your business. Or Georgie's either, unless you believe biology is destiny. But I wasn't referring to the question of who Georgie's father might be. Where you come in, and need to do your stuff, is the problem of who her father isn't. She was elaborately referring to you as Tom rather than Daddy. I don't think she really

295

cares which stranger is her father. What she cares about is that you're not. And what are you going to do about that, Dr Payne?'

Tom slouched out on to the balcony, obviously feeling hounded.

Olivia followed him. There was no way it was Tom's fault, what she had got up to at fifteen. And not telling Georgie the truth about Tom hadn't been a policy decision. It was just that Georgie had been so young that she forgot quite quickly about the time when Tom hadn't been there. And when Alex was born he was Tom's child unquestionably, so telling would have made distinctions. These were not reasons, they were only explanations. Tom was guilty only in that he had never at any point said, Hey, we really have got to tell Georgie the truth, that she's not really my daughter. But by the time Georgie was old enough to understand what that meant, he had almost forgotten himself, and had no reason to want to remember.

Olivia put her arms around him from behind. If only they could have dealt with this in Canada, with none of her family to arouse Tom's suspicion and hostility, no Nick to make her feel vulnerable. She rested her cheek between Tom's shoulder blades. 'I didn't mean that the way it sounded. I wasn't trying to be aggressive about it. I've no grounds for complaint, and neither does Georgie. I don't know what we'd have done without you.'

'I'm sure you'd be coping somehow.'

'Well, of course.' Olivia drew back, faintly affronted by his flat tone. 'It wasn't a – a life-threatening situation. But it could have been dreadfully damaging to Georgie.'

'I know that. I told you so. You knew it anyway, or you wouldn't have come to see me in the first place. You were so aware of the possibility. Most mothers wouldn't have noticed, or would have dismissed it somehow, but you picked up on it right away. So I knew you must have had some experience yourself, to make you suspicious. A middle-class girl with a baby at sixteen – they're not very common.'

Now she understood, after eighteen years, what guesses he had made about her then, and why. What had led him to suppose that her father was not only guilty of another man's sins, but that he had committed even worse ones. Ones that had never happened. Obliquely she tried to defend herself and her father. 'Tom, I remember perfectly well what you resuced me from. Georgie and me, I mean.'

'What do you mean, rescue?' Tom growled. 'That makes me sound like some kind of Sir Lancelot. And you didn't marry me out of gratitude, did you?'

That was a rhetorical question, so she didn't answer. After a pause he repeated it without the rhetoric. 'Did you?'

Olivia shook her head. There had been other reasons, though not necessarily the ones he would have hoped for. Alex, for instance. And Georgie, for that matter.

'Well, why did you?'

'I've forgotten now. Why did you?'

'I guess it seemed like a good idea at the time.' It must have, she thought, since he had deliberately made her pregnant, to add the force of nature and social pressure to his proposal of marriage. 'What exactly did you have in mind I should say to Georgie? "Sorry I'm not your father, I would have been but I didn't meet your mother in time"?'

'I didn't ask for a speech. I just said this is no time for you to disappear.'

'I'm not disappearing. I'm going home. To Alex. For perfectly proper reasons. I presume you'll both be along in a week or two.'

After what Nick had told her about Luke and the flat, Olivia was not at all sure about that. But Georgie hadn't said anything yet (aside from the postcard) about not going home, so Olivia wasn't going to either. Maybe Nick had got it wrong. Or maybe Georgie had gone off Luke, after he put her in hospital. She wasn't going to think about it right now.

All she said to Tom was, 'I've got to be back by the first day of term. And even then I'll have missed the departmental meeting. They won't be pleased about that.'

'Bugger them. The whole department could miss that meeting and the earth wouldn't alter in its course. But what about your wolves? They'll think you don't love them any more.'

'First time you've ever worried about them.'

'Well, somebody has to, if you don't. Aren't you afraid they'll be pining for you, poor critters?'

'Not only them, I hope.'

That truce lasted till Monday morning. One o'clock on Monday morning, to be precise. That was the point at which they were wakened from deep sleep by the sound of the door buzzer.

Tom got up to deal with it, as befitted the man of the house, or at least of the flat. Olivia's curiosity was not keen enough to keep her awake. It was probably some drunk pressing the wrong button on the entry panel downstairs.

She was roused again, not very gently, by Tom. 'It's for you.'

'For me? What do you mean, it's for me?'

Her brain was trying not to have to wake up, and she asked her pointless question partly to play for time, partly because she couldn't think of any possibilities. But by the time she had finished asking, at least one ghastly idea had entered her head. What if the drunk in question was her stepfather?

'It's for you means it's for you, what do you think it means? A member of your family, I believe, and he sounded either drunk or deranged.'

Olivia rolled out of bed, suddenly almost awake. She peered around with half-functioning eyes for Tom's dressing-gown and failed to find it. After another minute of searching she realized he was wearing it. She had to pull on her emergency night-gown instead. 'Which one is it?'

'One of the weird brothers, I think. If it's Luke, tell him to piss off. Or better still, invite him out on to the balcony and I'll shove him into the lake.'

If push came literally to shove, it was more likely to be Tom who ended up in the lake, Olivia reflected as she went barefoot into the sitting-room. Luke was taller than Tom, and broader in a helpfully athletic way, and of course he was half Tom's age. Tom's university career as a quarterback and his usual hour of hard-played handball twice a week were not going to make up for those disadvantages.

She found her way to the entry-phone and pressed the voice button. 'Who's there?'

'Lia?'

A great weight of anxiety lifted from her sleep-fuddled heart. A young man's voice. Not Nick. 'Who's that?'

''S Matt. Lemme in.'

He did sound drunk, even in those few words. 'What's the matter? It's one o'clock in the morning.'

'You're telling me. I want to crash on the sofa.'

She pressed the buzzer to let him in. She hadn't seen either of her brothers for eighteen years, and as soon as they came back into her life they started causing mayhem – trying to kill Georgie, turning up drunk in the middle of the night. Had they always behaved like that, she wondered, or were they just trying to make her feel at home?

Tom appeared in the doorway of the little hall. 'You didn't let him in, did you?'

'I had to. It's his flat as much as mine.'

Tom snorted. 'Well, he can have it all to himself tomorrow.'

He meant tonight, because it was already Monday. 'I think's he's going to be down in Sussex, same as us.'

'Wonderful. What for?'

'It's Georgie's twenty-first birthday, remember? Althea seemed to think a family party was in order.'

He rolled his eyes. 'Even better. She's invited the psychopath too, I suppose?'

'If you mean Luke, absolutely not. Althea and my mother were never even on speaking terms. What else would you expect with my father's first and second wives?'

'That makes him sound like the Sheikh of Araby. To look at him, you wouldn't think he had the stuff of two wives in him.'

'Don't be horrible. He's not as old as all that. When I left home he was the same age you are, and a wonderfully handsome man.'

'I guess he still is, in a desiccated way,' Tom allowed grudgingly. 'He just doesn't look like the two-wife type.'

Or the incestuous type, Olivia wanted to add. She couldn't really believe that Tom could really believe anything so bizarre about her father. 'Who is the two-wife type? You?'

'I couldn't cope with more than one. Especially not if she carries on the way you've been doing this weekend.' He put his arms around her and began to stroke her bottom through the cotton night-gown.

They were interrupted by the door bell.

'There's Matty.'

'You deal with him, he's your brother. I'm going back to bed.'

Tom disappeared into the bedroom, closing all doors behind him. Olivia opened the front door for Matthew, who more or less tumbled into the flat. He must have been leaning on the door to hold himself up, because he didn't look as if he could stand up by himself. He regained his feet laboriously, with the assistance of the doorknob. The rucksack he had slung over one shoulder slid down his arm and thudded to the floor.

'Sorry.' He started to bend down, to pick it up.

Olivia intervened. She could see that this manoeuvre was likely to end with him on the floor again as well as the rucksack. She hauled him and his luggage inside, closed the door, and deposited him on the handiest chair, beside the table.

'Sorry what?'

He slumped against the table like a propped-up rag doll, gesturing vaguely in the direction of the door. 'Sorry for this performance.'

'So you should be,' Olivia said sternly, standing in for absent Althea. 'What on earth are you doing, wandering about in that condition at this time of night?'

'She threw us out.'

'Who's she? Who's us? And why?'

'Sophie. She's just a girl I know. We've been dossing with her because her parents are away and Luke refuses to go home while his father's there. She chucked us out because we had a fight.'

Olivia sat down carefully in the chair around the corner of the table from him. 'You had a fight with this girl?'

'No, with Luke.' He glanced up towards her as he spoke, leaning on his hand. It didn't help to make his mumble more intelligible, but the state of his face told a tale in itself, which she hadn't really taken in till now. His left eye was swollen nearly shut, and the right side of his mouth and jaw had met with some similar misfortune.

'My God, Matty, did Luke do that to you?'

He tried to smile, but only the left side of his mouth was capable of expressing amusement, or whatever it was that had prompted the smile. 'That bad, is it? He told me once that he was naturally left-handed, but he'd learned to use his right for most things because it was easier.'

'From the evidence, I'd say it was a tie.' She stood over him and took his face in her hands, tilting it towards the light to inspect his injuries. 'I seem to recall that the only time you and Luke got together when I still lived here, he managed to give you a poke in the eye. Daddy was furious. He said it was evidence of congenital depravity.'

That had been the time when she had brought Georgie and Luke back from Italy, while her mother was in hospital. She had argued with her father, saying it was unscientific to suggest there could be any such thing as a moral element to heredity, and besides, her father, who had always called himself a socialist, was the last person who should be making such claims. But he had refused to retract his heresy, preferring to be unscientific and unsocialist rather than allow that Nick's child could be as blameless as his own.

Current events would appear to have proved him right.

'Anyway,' she added, 'you should know better than to get into an argument with Luke. He seems to prefer body language to closely-reasoned debate. After what happened to Georgie, I'd say you're lucky to be alive.'

'Georgie was a misunderstanding. Ouch, that hurts.'

'You want a cold tea-bag for your eye and an ice pack for your mouth,' Olivia announced, straightening. 'And an egg nog for the hangover you're going to have tomorrow.'

'What's a neg nog?'

'Egg nog,' she corrected. 'It's just raw eggs beaten into milk. Tom says it's the simplest and fastest way to deliver protein to the body, and that's what you need to sustain your blood sugar level. Alcohol plays hell with the blood sugar. But protein converts to glycogen, which the liver stores and releases into the bloodstream as it's needed, in a gradual way so as not to panic the mechanism for insulin production in the pancreas.'

300

'Whatever you say,' Matthew mumbled. 'It sounds too gruesomely technical for me. That egg nog also sounds disgusting.'

'It's not, actually. With a little rum or brandy it's quite good. But you're not getting brandy in yours. You'll have to settle for vanilla essence.'

She strapped the tea-bag in place with one of Tom's handkerchiefs, which gave him the look of a drunken pirate suffering from a scalp wound. She was in the habit of taking a couple of Tom's handkerchiefs with her whenever she left home, since they were so useful for so many purposes. The ice pack (an ice-cube bag) Matthew had to cradle in the hand that was holding up his head.

When he had dutifully downed the raw egg concoction, she poured them both a cup of tea and sat down at the table again. 'What did you mean when you said Georgie was a misunderstanding?'

He touched his piratical eye patch gingerly, adjusting the arrangement of the tea-bag inside. 'Did I say that? I don't remember.'

'Yes, you did, and yes, you do. Stop trying to distract me. Luke's refused to say anything about that little incident, even to the police, and Georgie says she doesn't remember anything. What was the misunderstanding about?'

He leaned on the ice bag and tried to concentrate his drunken thoughts, focusing his one good eye on the cup of tea. 'Well, I don't think misunderstanding is the right word. It was a misjudgement on Luke's part because he didn't mean to bounce her off that post, or at least not so hard, and he certainly didn't mean to kill her, whatever he might have said. On the other hand, he was pretty much right about what they were rowing about. But he did misunderstand what had happened, and anyway it wasn't Georgie's fault, not really.'

'And now you've told me everything, and I'm none the wiser. How come you know all about it?'

He shrugged. 'They told me.'

'How could Georgie tell you? She said she doesn't remember.'

'She told me before. And Luke told me after. He was going to do himself in, but I persuaded him to turn himself in instead, on the off chance that Georgie might survive and be sorry if he wasn't around any more. Anyway, the whole business seems to have been forgiven and forgotten by both parties, so I wouldn't worry about it if I were you.'

Olivia glanced over her shoulder at the door to the bedroom. It was still firmly shut, of course. She lowered her voice and leaned towards Matthew. 'Nick said that Georgie and Luke are . . .'

She didn't dare say it, just in case Tom happened to hear through a wall and two closed doors. Flimsy construction in these modern flats, she knew. She tried to think of a suitable gesture to convey the idea of a sexual relationship. The only ones that came to mind were too gross to use in any context that included her own daughter, so she settled for two twined fingers.

Matthew had another go at smiling, with no more success than the first time. 'You mean . . .' And he made one of the gestures that Olivia had rejected as far too crude, involving both hands, two fingers and a thumb. As a result he dropped the ice pack on the floor, and then fell off the chair trying to retrieve it, so that Olivia had to pick up both him and the ice bag. When he was seated again, she discovered he had managed to jar the table on his way down and both mugs were now surrounded by a puddle of tea. What with lager and tea, Matthew and Nick, Althea's table was never going to be the same again.

'Sorry.'

'Never mind. You were saying . . .?'

He looked blank. 'Was I?'

'About Georgie and Luke.'

'Oh, yeah, didn't she tell you? She was all nervous at the prospect of breaking the news, so I might as well do it for her. She says they're in love.'

So Nick hadn't been mistaken. He hardly ever was. It was one of his most irritating characteristics, albeit one in a long list of contenders. 'What does Luke say?'

'Well, he hasn't said that. He wouldn't, would he? Not to me anyway. Chaps like Luke don't go about telling other chaps they're in love. But he has been going round behaving like a lunatic, which I understand is one of the signs. On the other hand, I didn't know him before, so maybe he's always behaved like that.'

'I hope not. It would have been very tiresome for my mother.' She finished her tea and stood up again. 'I'm going to bed now, so you'd better go to bed too. I'll dig you out some bedding.'

'That's okay, I don't need anything. I'll just flop.'

All the same Olivia took the precaution of metamorphosing the sofa into its bed shape, getting out a blanket and pillow, and making sure that Matthew actually made it back from the bathroom and over to the sofa.

'This is really good of you, Lia. Sorry to be such a bore.' He sat down on the sofa-bed and surprised her by remembering to take off his shoes. Well, he had grown up in Althea's house, after all; things like that must be second nature to him by now.

'Where did Luke go, after you were thrown out of your friend's place?'

'Dunno. Home, if he had any sense, which I doubt. I'd have gone home myself, but the trains don't run this time of night.'

'Was he as drunk as you?'

'I guess he must have been, since Soph called us a couple of drunken boors when she showed us the door. But he didn't tell me where he was going because he wasn't speaking to me by then.'

'Why not?'

'Because of the fight we had.'

'What was that about?'

'Can't remember now. Georgie, I expect. He's touchy on that subject. Morbidly jealous, to put it another way.' He stretched out on top of the blanket, tried a yawn but gave it up because it hurt too much. 'Weren't you going to bed?'

Olivia had begun to worry about Luke by now. She felt obliged to, not only because he was her brother just as much as Matthew, but also because their mutual mother was no longer around to worry about him, and his father didn't give a damn. Whereas Matthew at least had her father and Althea to worry about him. 'You shouldn't have let him go off like that. He's only out on bail. If he does anything at all and the police pick him up, he'll get stuck back in jail.'

Matthew closed his only visible eye. 'Safest place for him, I should think.'

31

His words were softer than oil, yet were they drawn swords.

Monday was an eventful day. Georgie came out of hospital and celebrated her twenty-first birthday *en famille*. Olivia saw her father's house for the first time. And Matthew nearly got thrown out of his own home.

For Olivia events started early. She woke up still fretting about the thing that had been bothering her last night. It was seven thirty. The sun was well up, of course, but Tom and Matthew were not. She got up and dressed and went into the kitchen to phone Nick.

He took ages to answer, as usual, but the answering tape didn't cut in, so she knew he must be around somewhere. She also didn't believe he would have had to go all the way downstairs to pick up the telephone.

Someone finally lifted the receiver and hung it up again right away. Undeterred but annoyed, she dialled again. This time he didn't hang up right away. He just said nothing.

Waiting for the password, she supposed. Just think, the telephone was supposed to be a means of communicating. 'Nick?'

'Yeah?'

Well, he hadn't hung up again, that was encouraging. It was also enraging, because it was his son she was calling him about. 'Did Luke come home last night?'

'How the hell would I know? I haven't seen him since I got back from New York.'

'Could you go and look, please? It's important.'

Silence, not aggressive this time but disbelieving.

'Really important,' she added sharply.

A clunk, and then more silence. A lot of it. Then another clunk.

'He's not in his bed. Anywhere else you'd like me to look?'

'I don't suppose you'd like to phone the police, to see if they've picked him up?'

'For what?'

'For anything. He's on bail, remember.'

'Yeah, I do remember. I guess I should thank you for that.' But he pointedly didn't. 'What's he been getting up to now?'

'Nothing that I know of,' Olivia said hastily and untruthfully. 'But Matty turned up here in the middle of the night. He said that he and Luke had been thrown out by the girl they were staying with. He was very drunk and I assume Luke was too. So I just wondered if he might be sitting in a police cell somewhere, refusing to ring you.'

'Well, if he is, he can go on sitting there as far as I'm concerned. Are they letting Georgie out today?'

'We won't know for sure till the consultant does his rounds this morning.'

'And then what?'

She didn't want to tell him that, she just wanted to disappear. But of course if he rang the flat, Matthew would be here to tell him where they had gone. 'We're going down to my father's house in Sussex. Near Glyndebourne.'

'Where's that?'

He must have heard of Glyndebourne, even if he wouldn't dream of being caught dead there. She wanted to say, What do you care? But she didn't, she said quite politely, 'It's near Brighton. My father teaches at the university in Brighton.'

'How handy. Wish Georgie happy birthday for me.'

He didn't wait for a response to that, he just hung up. Olivia swore aloud at him and hung up too. Then she put the kettle on to boil, and opened the drapes that covered the entire western wall of the flat, to reveal the morning, the lake, and the rest of the world.

Also, when she turned to face the room again, also to reveal

Matthew on the sofa with one eye open. Now he looked like a hung-over pirate with a scalp wound. He dragged off the handkerchief and tea-bag, transforming himself into a hung-over choirboy. She still couldn't quite believe that these people, the viking angel and the streetwise choirboy, were her brothers. Especially when she recalled the babies she had left behind.

'Are you still alive?'

'Just. Was that Luke's da you were giving orders to?'

Giving orders? Not bloody likely. 'Yes.'

'But Luke wasn't there.'

'No.'

'I expect he'll turn up, one way or another.' Matthew rolled over to hide from the morning light, then changed his mind upon discovering that both sides of his face hurt when pressed into the pillow. 'If you're going down to Sussex, can I hitch a ride with you?'

'That's fine with me, but I have no say in the matter. Today is a holiday, which you might not know, since you haven't got a job and every day appears to be a holiday to you. Althea is coming up to collect us this afternoon.'

'That's okay, then. Just wake me up when you're ready to go.'

He closed his eyes and went off to sleep again almost at once, assured of his mother's acceptance even unasked.

As the mother of a baby, Althea had distinguished herself chiefly by her absence. But perhaps that had mattered less, the older Matthew got. Or perhaps, as with Olivia's father, the older the child grew, the more interest his mother had taken in him.

Olivia thought about that. There was some evidence that Matthew loved Althea and Althea loved Matthew. As to loving Matthew, she could understand that; she had loved him herself once. And more than Althea ever did, she thought resentfully.

Mother-love was a powerful thing, in both directions – as powerful by its absence as in its presence. It seemed to be as necessary to human beings as sunlight was to plants.

Plants were green because of the chlorophyll in their leaves, which they needed to transform sunlight into food. But there were plants with purple leaves: the copper beech, for example, or the polka-dot plant. The colour of the leaves, striking and attractive as it was, meant that only a small portion of the leaf contained chloroplasts, which alone are capable of that vital magic upon which all earthly life depends, the transformation of sunlight into starch and sugar. As long as sunlight was plentiful, a small part of the leaf was enough. But the copper beech only grew as an ornamental tree, never in the dense shade of a natural beech wood. The polka-dot plant, liberally splashed with pink in a sunny window, lost its spots and turned boring green when set in a darker corner of the room where life was real and earnest.

If you knew your mother loved you, you could afford to shrug off all sorts of appalling and otherwise unendurable things. If your mother didn't love you, or you had no mother to love, it was hard to cope with the world at all. Even, as she had explained to Nick, if you were a wolf.

She didn't know what metaphor to use for the love of a father, until she saw the trees at Underhill, twisted and shorn by the sea wind. Without the south-west wind, the rain would not come and the trees could not thrive. But where it blew too insistently . . .

Sunlight, like rain, came down from heaven to earth to bless the just and the unjust alike. But the wind had a will of its own, and the wish to make all bend to it.

Georgie had been given the all-clear, along with strict instructions to take it easy. An injury of the sort she had suffered was like a cracked rib or a sprained ankle, Tom had explained: not a lot anyone could do about it, except leave it alone to heal itself and don't aggravate it.

Althea seemed to think a paraplegic comparison offered a better guide. As hostess and commander-in-chief she issued instructions for Georgie to be installed in one of the large garden chairs with a high back to provide a head-rest, and a footstool to support her legs. 'After all, you haven't used them much for a fortnight,' she commented, as if in two weeks Georgie might have forgotten how they worked.

With Georgie settled and forbidden to move, the others were given orders, either entertaining Georgie or assisting with the party preparations. Olivia's father was to be Georgie's minder. Matthew and Tom were sent off to search for birthday candles, on the grounds that Tom wouldn't know where to find candles, and Matthew, if sent alone, couldn't be relied upon to return before midnight.

Olivia herself was put to work peeling potatoes and icing the cake. As she listened to Althea describe the menu for the feast they were about to be presented with, she reflected that at least in eighteen years Althea must have learned to cook.

But Althea had more than cakes and potatoes in mind when she brought Olivia into the kitchen. 'Where did Matty get beaten up, do you know?'

Olivia shrugged. If Althea couldn't get the truth out of her son, she wasn't going to get it out of her stepdaughter. 'He said something about a door, didn't he?'

'It must have been two doors then, a left-handed door and a right-handed door.' Althea tossed a handful of something into the skillet, making it sizzle satisfactorily. 'I've managed to keep him out of Ross's way so far, but at some point even Ross will have to notice and then we'll have a row on our hands.'

It was true, what she implied about Olivia's father. He could spot a sheila-na-gig at fifty paces in a gloomy Italian church, yet take all day to notice that his son had the mother of all shiners.

Olivia remembered that sheila-na-gig. Her father had gone on to explain to his bemused eleven-year-old daughter that the part of Italy they were touring had in ancient times been known as Cisalpine Gaul because it was full of Celts, who had once spread their language and culture over all of Europe from Czechoslovakia to Spain and the Hebrides, which explained why a carving of this grotesque split-tailed mermaid was to be found here in Italy, as well as in its more familiar haunts of the Highlands and Ireland.

At the time these remarks had made small sense to her, without a context to put them in, but even now she could recall vividly the sense of obscure excitement that had risen in her when she touched the mermaid's leering face. A first feeling for the depth and continuity of history, a childish intimation of how the past, even when unknown, surrounds and shapes our lives: a great ghostly river, in which we live and move and have our being.

How long ago were these Celts, she had asked her father. Two, three thousand years, he had answered vaguely, his attention having been caught by something else. As long ago as that, she had murmured, feeling a thrill without a clue.

What Olivia's father had not told her, though of course he must have known, was that the sheila-na-gig was a representation of some prehistoric fertility goddess, and she was holding the ends of her split tail in her hands in order to reveal her vulva, which was the point of her existence, here in the Italian church and also in Ireland. Two or three thousand years of peasant women had come, surreptitiously perhaps under the reign of Christianity, to touch the place between her tails and pray for pregnancy.

Althea was still going on about Matthew. 'When he was sent down from Oxford, Ross went absolutely ape. It was positively Victorian – blots on the family escutcheon, all that sort of thing. He was seriously threatening not to let Matty come home.'

'What, just because he got thrown out of university?'

'Well, it was partly because of the drugs, I suppose, though they all do that now, don't they? But Ross had big plans for him.' Althea gave Olivia a sidelong look, brutally sharp and meant to be cutting. 'You should know. If it had been eighteen days or eighteen weeks instead of eighteen years, I don't think he would have let you back through the door either. And what you did made it a whole lot worse for Matty. He was supposed to make good twice over.'

Olivia wondered if she was meant to fall down on her knees and beg forgiveness of Althea for her sins against her father. 'I didn't realize I was being used as an instrument of torture.'

'I thought you were trying to do some torturing yourself.'

Althea came over to lean across the wooden table, above the half-iced cake. She hissed at Olivia with eighteen, no, twenty-five years of pent resentment. 'What did you think you were doing, swanning off like that? You knew what you were doing to Ross. You knew how important it was to him that you should get your life in order and turn out a credit to him, especially after having been stupid enough to have a baby at sixteen. That was so stupid I still can't believe you did it. I thought you must have done it just to get at him, because you resented his marrying me. So you decided to cut off your nose to spite your face, and had that baby, which was just about the worst thing you could have done as far as Ross was concerned – wrecking your education and making yourself look like a stupid slag without the brains to buy a condom. And then when he stood by you, and gave you all the help you needed to get on with your life in spite of the baby, after all that you go off to Canada, saying you'd rather be a nanny. How could you be so stupid and selfish? How can you come waltzing in here now as if nothing had happened?'

Throughout this diatribe Olivia had concentrated on icing her daughter's birthday cake. At the end of it she said with a calmness that astonished her, 'Sorry, but Harrods was all out of sackcloth and ashes.'

She set down the knife and licked the stray splashes of icing off her fingers. 'Would you like me to take Tom and Georgie and go away now? Or is it just me you want to go away and get lost again?'

'You can't go away now, that would be worse,' Althea admitted. She went back to her station at the Aga, summoned by the needs of the dinner. 'Besides, you haven't done the potatoes yet.'

That was meant to be an offer of truce, not an insult, and Olivia took it in the right spirit. She hadn't really expected any of her abandoned family to greet her with open arms, Althea least of all. From their point of view she deserved every insulting word that Althea had just thrown at her. There was nothing she could say in her own defence, so she didn't say anything at all, she just set to work on the potatoes.

'It was dreadful when you left,' Althea continued in a more conversational tone. But she dropped her usual sharply confident head-girl's voice several decibels to the quieter level that women automatically use when talking seriously about men: like servants discussing employers, prisoners exchanging information about their jailers, or maybe adults concerned about the children. 'I honestly thought he was going to have a nervous breakdown. First he was furious, then he was seriously depressed, and after that he just froze over. He even kind of turned against Matty. You nearly ruined your father's life,' Althea said in that conversationally conspiratorial voice. 'Did you even think about that?'

Thank God for those potatoes. They were little new potatoes, needing to be scrubbed rather than peeled, and then the dubious spots had to be dug out with a knife. It took a lot of time and all of Olivia's concentration.

The idea that it might be within her power to ruin her father's life by her presence or absence, was not one that would have occurred to her when she left home. She wouldn't have dared to imagine such a thing. She had never been at all sure how much her father loved her, or sometimes even if he loved her at all. Now Althea, of all people, was telling her the answer when it was too late. Well, there was no use weeping into the potato-water over events eighteen years gone by.

'Nothing I can do about it now,' she said flatly.

'An explanation might help.'

Olivia shrugged. 'It doesn't matter any more. And it was nothing to do with you or Daddy anyway.'

'If you just wanted to chase after Tom, you could have said so at the time.'

If that was the explanation Althea had invented, Olivia wasn't going to contradict her. 'Daddy would have sympathized with that, wouldn't he? But what's wrong with Tom? Why shouldn't I have chased after him, as you so flatteringly put it?'

'Nothing's wrong with him, as far as I can tell. He seems a charming man and a respectable sort of person.' By this Althea meant a respectably middle-class and affluent sort of person. 'He's obviously been a good father to Georgie, from the way she's talked about him. Which reminds me, I couldn't believe it when I found out you hadn't told her the real situation there.'

Olivia shrugged again. It was getting to be an automatic response. 'Just another example of my uncanny ability to ruin other people's lives.'

Matthew's talents seemed to run more towards ruining his own life. He didn't return with Tom and the birthday candles until the dinner was about to be served, by which time Althea had begun to worry that Matthew had decided to show Tom how Beachy Head worked, and Olivia's father unkindly expressed more concern for the fate of his Land Rover than the fate of his son.

Matthew explained that they had had to go all the way into Brighton to find a supermarket open on the holiday. Althea said they hadn't needed a bloody supermarket, any little newsagent would carry birthday candles for heaven's sake, they were all open on the holiday in order to sell rubbish to tourists, and would he bloody well get poor Tom a drink to make up for having taken him on a wild-goose chase.

They finally sat down to dinner, Olivia's father and Althea at opposite ends of the table, Olivia on her father's left and Georgie on his right, Tom on Althea's left, next to Georgie, and Matthew between his mother and Olivia.

They were through the starters and well into the main course when Olivia's father noticed Matthew's black eye. 'Matthew, what's happened to your face?'

Matthew mumbled something to his plate. The mumbling was perhaps excusable, since his mouth wasn't working properly.

His father said to Althea, 'What did he say?'

'Something about a door.'

'You walked into a door,' his father repeated with heavy sarcasm. 'Were you drunk at the time?'

Matthew mumbled again. Once more his father turned to Althea for enlightenment.

'He says probably.'

'I should think it more than likely. Was the door drunk too?'

Matthew shrugged. He shovelled potatoes into his injured mouth to excuse himself from answering.

'I can think of no good reason,' his father announced, 'why I should be expected to subsidize piss-ups and punch-ups. If you can't come up quite quickly with a more sensible and productive way of spending your time, I shall forbid you the use of that flat. Where have you been living for the past week, by the way, since we haven't had the pleasure of your company down here?'

After a pause to work his way through the mouthful of potatoes, Matthew answered more audibly. 'Staying with friends.'

'Sponging off them, you mean. Was the awkward door by any chance one of these friends?'

Matthew spoke very clearly this time. 'What's it to you? Do you want to congratulate him or what?'

'I'm sure he's an ex-friend by now,' Althea interceded briskly. Olivia guessed she was used to doing that. 'Can we talk about something more pleasant, seeing its Georgie's birthday? How are you feeling, Georgie?'

Georgie thought she wasn't feeling too badly. 'I haven't taken any painkillers since this morning and I haven't got a headache, so I guess that's good.'

Matthew was not prepared to let things ride. 'Did you walk into a door too?'

Georgie looked at him, faintly puzzled. Olivia stuck her elbow firmly in his ribs, but he ignored her.

'The same door, by any chance?' he persisted. 'My door's name was Luke.'

The name of Luke was a stray dog in a kennel of hounds. Everybody bristled, except Olivia, who cringed, and Georgie, who looked confused. Althea said to Matthew, 'It was *Luke* who beat you up?'

Matthew renewed his interest in his dinner. Althea's maternal instincts obliged her to tell him, 'Don't fill your mouth so full, for goodness sake,' and impatience added, 'Why?'

'I'm hungry.'

'No, why did Luke hit you?'

Matthew chewed reflectively. 'Well, I think he thought he was acting in defence of Georgie's honour, but he was mistaken. Luke is often mistaken, I've noticed, and seldom aware of it.' He ate another potato and gazed around the table. 'Why are you all watching me eat?'

Olivia as a child had often been the victim of her father's sarcasm, and up to now had been inclined to feel sorry for Matthew, but bringing Georgie into this had finished off her sympathy. She was thinking seriously about causing a dramatic distraction by, for example, tipping over her wineglass or developing a leg cramp, when her father said, 'What in God's name were you doing with him?'

'Nothing of any importance.'

'That goes without saying,' his father said icily. 'But I'd prefer you to do nothing in other company, out of consideration for Georgie's feelings at the very least.'

Matthew had cleared his plate by this time. He set down his knife and fork and picked up his wineglass and smiled at Georgie in a dark alarming way. 'Oh yes, Georgie's feelings. I agree entirely that we should consider them. What are they, Georgie? Why not lay them on the table so we can all discuss them?'

Georgie had gone quite white while he was speaking. On account of her injuries, Olivia was afraid her daughter was going to faint, and was torn between rescuing her and shutting Matthew up. She did both, by accident, reaching for Georgie across the table and knocking over the open bottle of claret.

Georgie didn't faint after all. She stood up and ran out of the room instead.

32

I sought him, but I could not find him;
I called him, but he gave me no answer.

Olivia dreams of Esau.

Jacob and Esau. Twin brothers, the only survivors of their litter. Mortality among wolf cubs is high even by Third World standards. Higher even than in the days of the Old Testament. Hard to imagine, in modern Western times, when millions are invited to mourn the death of almost any child, how women could come to bear that level of grief and bereavement. Did it cripple them, or make them more compassionate? No question of withholding the heart, she knows that at least. A woman as much as a wolf is bound by nature to love her babies, even if half of them are doomed to die in infancy.

Jacob and Esau at any rate didn't die. Jacob was the runt of the litter, Esau the pick of it, and when they grew to maturity things were still not so much different between them. Esau had a faint reddish tinge to his tawny ruff, a colour Olivia had never seen in any other wolf. He rose to be the alpha male of the pack, and mated with the alpha female, Rachel.

Jacob, smaller and darker, was his right-hand man. Leader and lieutenant, that's how it goes in wolf packs: Macbeth with his Banquo, Othello and Iago. Then Esau suffered some injury. Broken ribs, from the way he was walking. An elk's hoof could do that readily.

And Jacob in ascendancy drove his brother from the pack.

Esau might well have lived to recover – it was summer time, easy living even for wolves – but he never returned to the pack and she never saw him again, so his fate remains a mystery. Next spring the father of Rachel's cubs was Jacob.

It is Esau alone she dreams of tonight. Dreams that Rachel follows him into the woods, and helps him survive and grow strong again. The real-life Rachel would never, could never do that, because it would mean leaving her cubs.

Love, as Olivia knows, is an expensive commodity: sometimes worth the price, sometimes more than you can afford. But dreams are sometimes free.

Something woke her.

Whatever it was had gone away or stopped by the time she came to consciousness. She slid back into sleep and was wakened again, but once more the sound had stopped. She peered at the clock. Ten past one. This was getting to be a habit.

While she was awake she decided to check on Georgie. Despite what the consultant had said, and despite having her very own doctor on the premises, she was irrationally convinced that Georgie might suddenly stop breathing. Cot death at the age of twenty-one.

She pulled on her night-gown and crept into the room next door, and waited in the dark for the sound of Georgie's breathing. It came, very soft, very even, the sound of dreamless sleep.

Another sound came. The one that had awakened her. She knew it immediately, though she had only heard it in her sleep. A sound like hail, if hail could rustle as well as crack; rain and hail falling at once, maybe.

And a third sound, more familiar. A footstep on gravel.

She shut the door of Georgie's room and went into her own room, where Tom was still sleeping. She shook him awake. 'Tom, there's someone outside. Right outside the house.'

As she said it, all the stories she had ever come across of entire families being slaughtered in remote country cottages came into her head in gloriously gory detail. She clutched at Tom more urgently. 'Do get up, Tom. It can't be anything legitimate at this time of night. They'd have rung up first or knocked on the door.'

'Probably kids,' Tom muttered with his knuckles in his eyes.

'What kids? There are no kids around here. This house is in the middle of the countryside.'

'Drunks, then.'

But he hadn't convinced even himself. He was fully awake by now, an easy trick for a doctor. He pulled on his trousers and shirt and went barefoot into the hall.

'Don't turn on the light,' Olivia whispered after him. 'It'll warn them.'

'It'll scare them away, more likely.' But he whispered back, and left the light switch alone. 'Where the hell do we find a flashlight?'

'How do I know? In the kitchen, maybe.' Olivia followed him out into the dark hallway.

There was one other person in the household guaranteed to be a light sleeper, the only other mother in the place, and sure enough Althea appeared on the opposite side of the stairwell. She switched on the light. Everybody blinked several times, including her.

'What's the matter?' She too was whispering, but being Althea it was more of a stage whisper. 'Are you hungry?'

Tom gallantly chose to blame everything on his wife. 'Lia claims there's someone outside.'

'Only one?'

'I don't know,' Olivia admitted. 'I heard a noise that woke me up, and then the sound of someone walking on gravel.'

'Well, let's go downstairs and see,' Althea suggested with surprising enthusiasm.

The noise, however supposedly subdued, of the search party assembling in the upper hall wakened Matthew. He had yielded his own room to Tom and Olivia and was sleeping in his father's study, at the top of the stairs and right alongside the congregation in the hall. He stuck his head out of the study door. 'Is this a geriatrics' rave?'

'Keep a civil tongue in your head,' his mother told him sternly. 'There's a burglar downstairs.'

'A brave man,' Matthew remarked, surveying the company. 'Why do we think he might be there?'

'Lia heard someone.'

'Where?'

'In the drive, I guess,' Olivia explained. 'I was in Georgie's room just now and I heard him crunching on gravel.'

'Careless as well as brave. Excuse me a moment.'

He disappeared into Georgie's room and returned almost immediately. 'I thought so.'

'You thought what?' Olivia added accusingly, 'You didn't wake Georgie up, did you?'

'No, no, of course not. What kind of brute do you think I am? But I have to report that the trespasser is not a burglar but a door.'

They had all had more than enough of Matthew that evening. When Georgie fled her birthday party, her grandfather had sent his son after her with strict instructions to apologize for whatever it was he had said that had upset her. Olivia had invited herself along as chaperone, on two grounds: one, she was Georgie's mother, and two, she was the only one besides Matthew and Georgie who knew exactly how he had offended.

On the way upstairs, she had a stern word with Matthew about his behaviour on several fronts, with the result that he had apologized abjectly to Georgie and behaved almost impeccably thereafter. He was obviously in the habit of driving people to the brink of

314

homicide, and then pleading innocence behind his choirboy's face. One day, Olivia thought darkly, he was going to go too far. Perhaps he had nearly gone too far with Luke the night before.

Their mutual father came out of his bedroom. With his grey hair disarranged and an expression of profound moral disapproval on his thin handsome ascetic features, Olivia thought he looked rather like an Old Testament prophet, emerging from his cave in the desert to denounce the wickedness of his people. And well he might have done, if only he had known wherein their wickedness lay. 'What's going on? A plague of insomnia?'

'No, Daddy.' Olivia at least had taken the meaning of Matthew's remark. 'We thought it was a burglar but it's only Luke.'

'Only Luke?' Her father glared at her. 'Surely you mean only a burglar.'

'Oh, Daddy.' She was already running down the stairs. 'You can all go back to bed. I'll scream if I need any help.'

She heard Tom say 'Lia – ' and Matthew say 'Leave her,' and then she was unbolting the kitchen door.

She stepped out into the night. Not into darkness, because the moon was just past the full and the clouds had scarpered away suddenly and dramatically. By the light of the moon she could see them fleeing towards the horizon, a flock of giddy celestial sheep startled by a wolf on the prowl.

She didn't know where Luke was now, or even if he was still around. She went down the garden and called his name quite softly.

No answer. No human response, at least. What she did hear was a distinctly conversational meow, coming from the darkness at her left hand. The moonbeams caught cat's eyes – real ones – peering sleepily over the edge of a hammock.

'You go back to sleep,' she told the cat. 'This fuss has nothing to do with you.'

The cat blinked and disappeared, apparently taking her at her word.

She walked barefoot across the grass, all the way down to the bottom of the garden, and stood by the hedge looking back towards the house. This time she spoke in a conversational tone. 'Luke, it's Lia. Where are you?'

'Where's Georgie?'

It came like a growl from behind her and she nearly jumped. When she turned he was there in the moonlight, his shaggy hair shining like spun silver.

She had been worried about him all along, in the back of her mind. There was no one else to worry about him. Georgie, of course, but that was only Juliet fussing helplessly over the absent Romeo. And

315

Matthew, but his concern was ambivalent at best, as she had seen tonight. Her mother, his mother, was dead. And Nick refused to take any responsibility whatever. God damn them all. She, Olivia, was the last line of defence, not her brother's keeper but her brother's mother.

She faced him, her hands covering the bodice of her night-gown. She had done some daft things in her life, but standing in her father's garden in her night-clothes at one o'clock in the morning, calling her mother's son as if he were a stray cat, struck her as one of the daftest. 'Georgie's asleep, of course. She's still recovering from what you did to her.'

He advanced across the lawn. The moonlight made him more angelic, less thuggish. 'You mean she doesn't know I'm here?'

'I told you, she's asleep. The only one in the house who is. What did you think you were doing, throwing gravel at a window in the middle of the night in the middle of the countryside? Why are you down here anyway?'

'I thought . . . Matt said she was going home. And I didn't have a chance to talk to her this morning, before she left hospital.'

'How did you find your way here?'

'Well, you weren't in the flat, and it was the only other place I knew of where she might be, if you hadn't taken her back to Toronto.' Which was what he had feared, of course.

He was scowling down at her. He should have been a ridiculous figure, in the wrong place at the wrong time, or an evil figure, lusting after his sister's daughter. At least an unwelcome figure, come to make her daughter unhappy.

But all that Olivia could think of was the difference it would have made to her if Luke's father had ever come to her house in the middle of the night and thrown stones at her window. Even if he only wanted to talk to her. Even if – the bourgeois majority of her soul shuddered at the thought – even if the entire household had been awakened, like tonight. If he had come to her, it would have meant something. Maybe that he loved her.

But he never came.

So she hardened her heart to Luke, his father's son. 'You were mad to come here. What did you think would happen? Georgie's still ill, she has to get better. Go away and let her recuperate without having to worry about you. Go home to your father's house.'

'I'm not going near that bastard.'

'All you've got to do is sleep in your own bed. Don't speak to him if you don't want to. But at least then I won't be worrying about you, and Georgie will know where to find you if she wants you. Okay?'

He shrugged sulkily.

Olivia let that pass for assent. 'What are you going to do now? Tonight, I mean?' She hoped he didn't have a car, because he was clearly over the limit.

He shrugged again. 'Dunno. I was in the pub till it closed. I didn't think about after that.'

Or before that, for that matter, she thought. 'Well, I'd let you come inside, but the rest of them won't and it's not my house. There's a hammock between those two trees,' she pointed, 'which should keep you quite cosy and out of the dew, if you don't mind sharing it with the cat.' She thought of offering to sneak down a blanket, but decided it would serve him right to suffer for his idiocy. And anyway it was a clear mild night.

When she came back into the house, they were all in the sitting-room, quite chatty and companionable. She had the impression they had almost forgotten about her, when no blood-curdling screams had rent the night air. She said truthfully, 'Everything's okay,' and added untruthfully. 'He's gone away now.'

'What on earth did he want?' Althea wanted to know.

'He wants his head examined,' Tom growled.

33

There is no hope, no; for I have loved strangers, and after them will I go.

Matthew managed to make a nuisance of himself the following night too, this time by announcing as soon as dinner was over that he wanted to catch the next train up to London, which would be leaving in a quarter of an hour.

'Why don't you just go up with me in the morning?' Althea asked.

'And get up at six o'clock? Don't mock. Anyway, I'm supposed to be going to a party tonight, and the next train is the last one going up.'

'Why didn't you say something earlier? You are a pain sometimes, Matty.'

'He'll just have to walk,' his father said briskly. 'I'm not going to risk getting booked for being under the influence. It only takes a couple of drinks to do it nowadays.'

'Oh, come on, live dangerously,' Matthew invited him ironically. 'Think what it could do for your public image. Transformed in an instant from stick-in-the-mud to Jack-the-lad.'

'I'll drive you,' Olivia offered hastily, to prevent another row.

'That's if you'll trust me with your car, Daddy. I've only had one glass of wine.'

'Don't bother, Lia. Let him walk.'

'He'll miss the train,' Althea pointed out.

'And learn a lesson.'

'I really don't mind doing it.' Olivia got up decisively. 'Come on, Matty, get your kit. Althea, where do you keep the car keys?'

In the car she took the opportunity to make it clear to Matthew that she hadn't acted entirely out of an irresistible desire to do him a favour. 'Really, Matty, you don't seem to have grown up at all since I left. You're behaving like a naughty three-year-old who needs a spanking.'

Matthew smiled at her, totally unrepentant. 'Is that a proposition?'

'A naughty three-year-old with a dirty mind,' Olivia amended. 'And it's very tiresome for everyone, believe me.'

'Oh, I do believe you,' he assured her cheerfully. 'I find your remarks most encouraging. But you haven't been such a good girl yourself, have you?'

'What do you mean?'

'I mean Luke's old man.'

Olivia was negotiating a sharpish bend in the road just at that point. She nearly drove into the hedge. 'Oh, Christ,' she exclaimed, apparently in response to the near-disaster.

Matthew looked on indifferently, as if his fate was not in her hands at the wheel. 'I thought you said you'd only had one glass of wine.'

'I'm stone cold sober. Stop distracting me.'

'Sorry.'

He fell silent, leaving her to dither over whether she should leave it at that, or deny everything. She had nothing particular to deny, since he hadn't accused her of anything specific. She drove through the village and down to the highway without having reached any conclusion.

At the main road she glanced at him. 'Which way now?'

'Go along to the left and turn right at the petrol station.'

She waited for a break in the traffic, then pulled out quickly before the next convoy of cars arrived. He chose that moment to say casually, 'It didn't take him long to get your knickers off again. Or was he the only one you didn't leave behind?'

This time she almost collided with a car coming in the opposite direction. 'Matthew, you're a menace. Keep your mouth shut, for heaven's sake.' After a moment's reflection she added coldly, 'I haven't seen him for eighteen years. Just like the rest of you.'

'Here's the turn off,' Matthew pointed out. 'Put your signal on and mind that car coming up.'

'I don't need any advice from you,' she said between her teeth.

'You seem to need it from somebody, and I'm the only one around.'

She made the turn and accelerated down the lane towards the station. That leg of the journey was not without incident either. First, in her haste, she nearly ran over an old man on a bicycle, and then barely avoided smacking into a tree when she swerved to go round the bike. By the time she drew up at the station, she was a complete nervous wreck.

Olivia turned off the motor and leaned back against the head-rest to compose herself. Matthew didn't move.

'Aren't you getting out here?'

'I thought I'd enjoy the pleasure of your company until the train arrives. Or have you some more pressing engagement?'

'You do need spanking, don't you?'

'You're just talking dirty to entice me.' He leaned his arm along the back of the seat and looked at her. 'He is Georgie's father, isn't he?'

Olivia licked her lips. Like a cornered animal. 'Matty, where did you get these ideas?'

'From you, actually. The way you were with him the other night, and on the phone next morning.'

'How was I?'

'Hard to describe. You just struck me as being together somehow. That odd sort of social intimacy that couples have. Feeling free to be rude to each other, for instance. You're much more matey with him than you are with my father. And there was a certain smell of sexual chemistry – though I wouldn't be surprised if he takes that with him wherever he goes. He's very attractive to women, I should think, on a basic bull-and-cow sort of level. But I don't have to tell you that, do I?' He gave her a small pointed smile. 'If it makes you feel any better, I'd already pretty well worked it out, about Georgie.'

'That was clever of you,' she said as sarcastically as she could, considering she was shaking. 'You were a clever little kid, I recall.'

'You know my methods, Watson. What reason could there be, I said to myself, to conceal the name of the father? Not to spare poor Charlie's feelings, because you gave him the bad news anyway. And I wasn't really rooting for Charlie's football team. So what sort of man would be unmentionable in the context? Only two candidates, really. And when you eliminate the impossible, by which I mean our own dear dad – a natural troglodyte, despite having had two wives;

he was obviously seduced by the lady each time – then whatever remains, however improbable, must be the answer. Except in this case it's not at all improbable. Just what one would expect, in fact, in light of the stories Luke has regaled me with. He doesn't approve of his daddy's adventures. A bit of a puritan, our Luke.'

Olivia closed her eyes while he was speaking. It made her ashamed all over again, the idea of being just another notch on Nick's belt. Two notches, actually; the second time around must surely count as a new score. She wanted to deny what Matthew was saying, or at least refuse to acknowledge it, but there was something more important, something she needed to know. 'Okay, Matty, you can stop showing off now. Have you discussed your theory with Georgie?'

'Heavens, no. It's my theory which belongs to me. Let her work it out for herself. But she won't.'

'Why not?'

'The last thing she wants to hear is that Luke is her brother as well as her uncle. Ditto Luke. I mean vice versa. You know what I mean. Luke doesn't want to be related to his own father, let alone have Georgie related to the old sod.' He raised his voice over the approaching din of the train. 'And don't worry about my father's famously logical mind. He couldn't work it out even if he wanted to, because he doesn't know that Charlie's no longer a contender for the title.'

He opened the door and slid out, reached back in for his knapsack, and added with a wide wicked grin, 'If I were you, the only thing I'd be worrying about is what your devoted husband makes of it all.'

Olivia drove back to her father's house as cautiously as if she had been over the limit. Her nerves had been shattered by Matthew's revelations. Of course it was all, as he had said, only logical. Tom, starting with a rather different set of clues, had got as far as the second last step. Then, because he didn't know her father, he had plumped for the wrong man at the end. But there were only two possibilities, once Charlie had been scratched. No uncles, no handy grandfather. If Tom came to know her father and her stepfather better, he would sooner or later correct his original mistake.

She had to get away from here, get back to Toronto. Get Tom away, Georgie away.

Get herself away from Nick.

That was the other thing that had destroyed her ability to drive, or to interact at all with the world of events. That bit hadn't been logic

320

on Matthew's part, it was sheer intuition. She had given herself away when she was with Nick. If not completely at the time, at least completely now. Matthew might have only been making a shot in the dark with the first remark, but her response had told him everything he wanted to know. She had been right not to come back before. She would have to be mad not to leave as soon as possible. It wasn't only the past that was dangerous, but the present as well.

When she got back to Underhill, Tom was watching the news on television with her father and Althea. Georgie had gone upstairs to bed. Olivia badly needed a stiff drink, but first she went up after Georgie, to make sure she was all right, and to reassure herself, if possible, that Matthew hadn't been dropping any hints.

She knocked on Georgie's bedroom door. Georgie invited her in. She was sitting on the bed, still fully dressed, when Olivia entered. The black cat was also sitting on the bed, comfortably curled up, watching Georgie. He didn't turn his head, but his ears swivelled towards Olivia to let her know her presence had been detected.

'I thought that cat wasn't allowed in the house.'

'I didn't let him in. He was here when I came up, and looking so cosy that I didn't have the heart to throw him out. Don't tell Althea, will you?'

'I wouldn't dream of it.'

Olivia watched her daughter bring up her right foot and lay it across her left knee to unfasten her shoe, then do the same thing the other way round with the left shoe. 'It makes me dizzy if I bend over,' Georgie explained.

'How is your head otherwise?'

'Okay. No headaches today.'

'You should be able to come home with me next week, then.'

'I'm not going home.' Georgie stood up to step out of her jeans, and concentrated on unbuttoning her shirt without looking at her mother. 'I like it here. I've got no particular reason to go back right now, do I?'

'It's not fair, if you're not well. It puts all the burden of looking after you on my father and Althea. And I'd be worrying about you.'

'You don't have to worry and neither do they. I'll be okay. The doctor said I should be right as rain in a few weeks.'

Georgie shrugged out of her shirt, took off her underwear, picked up her night-gown from the bed. She paused at that point to survey her naked body. She was shorter and slighter than her mother, but with the same full breasts that had once caused Olivia such anguish. Remembering her own adolescent embarrassment, Olivia had always envied Georgie for her apparently natural confidence in her physical appearance. Of course, it must help if you resembled your mother. That was the way you would expect to look. No cause for surprise or resentment there.

'Mama.' Georgie was still holding her night-gown, still staring down at herself. 'Mama, I'm going to have a baby.'

She had spoken so quietly that Olivia took a moment to absorb what she had said. And then, just at first, she refused to believe it. 'What?'

'A baby,' Georgie repeated with more assurance. 'I'm pregnant.'

'Oh, Georgie.' Olivia came closer, leaned on the nearest bedpost. 'Are you sure?'

'Yes, absolutely.' Her next words were muffled by the night-gown on its way over her head. 'Test positive. Morning sickness. Tender tits.' She emerged from her struggle with the night-gown to glare at her mother, defying her to say the wrong thing.

Almost anything would be the wrong thing, Olivia realized. 'This is all just getting started, is it?' she ventured. It seemed a neutral sort of response, keeping the conversation going while she gathered the wits that had been scattered to the winds by Georgie's bombshell.

'Just,' Georgie agreed. 'Five and a half weeks, I make it. But there's no such thing as being slightly pregnant, is there?'

Olivia was still clutching the bedpost, to keep from wringing her hands, or possibly falling down. 'How did all this happen?'

'Well, I forgot to bring my pills down here one weekend, so I missed one then, and a day or two later I got blotto and didn't take my pill, and then I missed the last few days of the cycle, on account of the . . . my accident, so the pill failed to do its stuff. Not surprising, under the circumstances.'

'And is this good or bad?'

Georgie sat down on the bed. She ran her hands impatiently through her stubbly hair. 'Oh, Mama, do stop being so restrained and polite. Just go berserk and get it over with, I can't stand the suspense.'

'Whether or not I go berserk depends on what you want to do.'

'Well, I want it, of course. I'd have said so straight away if I didn't.' She pulled the covers aside, lowered herself carefully into bed, and drew the sheet up to her neck, perhaps as a first line of defence against her mother's opposition. 'I'm twenty-one, after all. Not like you.'

That was a fairly crippling shaft. Olivia was in no position to protest about unmarried young girls having babies too soon, et cetera, and Georgie was well aware of it. She sat down at the foot of the bed and asked the question she didn't want to hear the answer to. 'Whose baby?'

Georgie's face on the pillow stared up at her, pale and defiant, looking suddenly much younger than twenty-one, and much more vulnerable than a moment ago. The cat uncurled himself, stalked up to the top of the bed, and sat upright by the pillow like a bodyguard. A slightly deranged bodyguard, by the look in his huge round eyes.

'It's Luke's baby.'

'Oh, God.'

Inevitably she sounded more resigned than surprised or outraged. Georgie picked up on that right away. 'You knew,' she accused.

'Nick told me.' Olivia added vaguely, 'He was explaining the business about the flat.'

'Well, if he doesn't mind, why should you?'

'I can't think of anything, offhand, that *would* give him moral offence,' Olivia pointed out. That thought itself gave her moral offence. 'He's not so much tolerant as totally unprincipled.'

She had spoken unwisely, unguardedly, with too much heat. Georgie was staring at her with wide blue eyes. 'Do you really hate him?'

'No, of course not.' Olivia didn't know herself if she was lying. She got up and retreated behind the foot of the bed. 'Georgie, you can't have Luke's baby. He's my brother. It's incest.'

'Half-brother. Half-uncle. Hardly counts. Like second cousins. I worked it out. And it's not a crime, so it's not officially incest.' Georgie's hands betrayed her agitation, plucking at the bedclothes. 'Besides, I only met him this summer. How can it be incest when he was a complete stranger to me? I never even knew he existed. Calling that incest is just superstition.'

'Then you should . . . Whatever, you should wait. Even if he weren't my brother. You hardly know him.'

'How well did you know my father?'

Olivia flinched and looked away. There wasn't any answer to that. If she had known him well, Georgie would demand to know his name. If he'd been a stranger, the argument was lost. She changed tactics. 'Does Luke know about the baby?'

'Of course. I told him first.'

A bit of a puritan, Matthew had said. Though the Lord only knew what Matthew might regard as evidence of puritanical leanings. 'Doesn't it bother him, being my brother?'

'I told you, it's just like second cousins. You're the biologist, work it out for yourself.'

Olivia already had. But she was working from rather more alarming premises: my brother, your brother. And she couldn't even contemplate telling Georgie about the missing premise.

'And the baby doesn't bother him?'

Georgie frowned. 'Well, he was . . . surprised. Just at first. Because he knew I was on the pill. But now he's really keen on it.'

'Was that what the midnight visit was about? To tell you he'd changed his mind?'

'Sort of.' Georgie giggled. 'That must have been hilarious, and I missed the whole thing. Matt described it all to me this morning.'

Olivia said drily, 'I take it you've forgiven Matty for his behaviour last night.'

'What? Oh, yeah. He does things like that from time to time, and I could kick him for it.' But Georgie didn't sound seriously offended. She added emphatically, 'Not a happy person, our Matty.'

'Why not?'

'Most likely because his father doesn't love him and his mother doesn't know how to.' She levered herself up, half sitting, braced by the pillow and the headboard. 'Mama, come here.'

Olivia went. She sat beside her daughter, facing her. Georgie took her mother's hand and stroked it abstractedly.

'Listen, don't be mad at me. Don't be mad about the baby or Luke, it's going to be okay. We can't get married because it's illegal, but no one can stop us living together. That's not illegal, they can't burn us at the stake or anything. He's lovely, my Luke. He didn't mean to hurt me. It was my fault. I made him jealous and he just – got mad. And scared. Because his . . .' Georgie trailed off with an odd look on her face, as if she had just remembered something. 'Well, never mind, that doesn't matter.'

'Don't tell me. His father doesn't love him and his mother didn't know how to.'

'I don't know about his mother. But you should. She was your mother too. And I'm not sure about Nick. He's such a funny guy. He seems . . .' She paused, searching for a word, a nuance. 'Discontented. Disappointed. Like he really wanted something once and didn't get it, and now he refuses to want anything any more. Maybe Luke is just an innocent bystander caught in the fall-out.'

Olivia pulled her hand out of Georgie's grasp, withdrawing not from Georgie but from her remarks. 'Don't romanticize that man,' she said sharply. 'He never wanted anything badly in his life. He's not capable of really wanting something. He just takes whatever comes along.' A mature woman, an adolescent girl, a small child. His lover's daughter, his own daughter. Whatever came to hand.

'You do hate him,' Georgie declared triumphantly.

'Maybe he's not a lovable person.'

'Well, he's no teddy bear, that's for sure.' After a slight pause Georgie asked with elaborate casualness, 'Did you know the police have dropped the charges against Luke?'

'Why?'

'Well, I told them it was an accident, and so did he, so I guess there didn't seem much point. I also told them I wouldn't testify against him, even if they sent me to prison for contempt of court or whatever, and that inspector said he thought they had enough else to worry about.'

'I suppose he's right.' Olivia was greatly relieved by this news, but she wasn't going to admit it to Georgie. Tom wouldn't be pleased, nor her father.

Georgie inched forward down the bed to embrace her. She did it with the same unselfconscious affection as she had shown at the age of three. Olivia hugged her in return with extra intensity, as if to make up in some way for the eighteen missing years of family.

'Listen, Mama, never mind about all that. I just want to live with Luke and the baby and be happy. Genetically we're only second cousins, remember? Don't be mad, Mama, be happy for me. Please say you're happy for me.'

Olivia had to swallow several times before she could say it, and it wasn't because she was about to tell a lie. More because of what she wasn't telling, maybe. Though she would have to tell, sometime very soon. 'Georgie, I want you to be happy.'

'I will be. Really.' Georgie drew back to look into her mother's face. 'You've got to promise me.'

'Promise what?'

'Don't tell Daddy till you're back home again.'

Daddy. That was something to be grateful for. Apparently Tom had been reinstated in his parental role. As for Georgie's request, she wouldn't have dreamed of doing anything else. The longer she put it off, the more chance that she would have nothing to tell. She couldn't let this baby be born.

34

Who did sin, this man or his parents, that he was born blind?

He was only a quarter of an hour late. Not bad for a man who regarded punctuality as evidence of anal-retentive obsessions, or would have if he had ever heard of such a concept.

It was terrible how well she knew him, Olivia thought, watching Nick come down the high street of Alfriston with his unmistakable, casually confident, wide-boy stride. Eighteen years in opposite hemispheres of the world had not destroyed that familiarity, nor the forbidden lurch within when he caught sight of her and smiled. Unless that was only relief, that he had turned up at all.

Deliberately she didn't return the smile. 'You're late.'

'Traffic problems. Fucking lorry drivers.' He glanced at the door of the pub, their agreed meeting place. There were only two pubs in Alfriston and they were right across the street from each other, so he couldn't have failed to find her. 'Why didn't you go inside and have a drink while you were waiting?'

'They closed at three.' And I want to be totally sober when I'm in your company, she added silently.

'So what exactly are we doing here, if we can't even have a drink?'

'We're looking for somewhere to go and talk.'

She started down the street and he fell into step beside her. 'I'd rather look for somewhere to go and fuck.'

Olivia winced mentally and hoped that no one had been near enough to hear that. Nick was obviously impervious to such considerations, but she preferred not to discuss in public any plans for committing adultery. Not that she had any such intentions. 'Is that why you agreed to come down? Sorry to disappoint you, but I have something more serious in mind.'

'What could be more serious than sex?'

'I'll tell you when we're clear of all this.' Olivia didn't want anyone, even passing strangers, to overheard what she had to say. She needed help, and unfortunately Nick was the only one who could offer it.

She had been frantic with worry and desperation ever since Georgie dropped her bombshell about being pregnant. Georgie didn't know what she was doing. Didn't know that the man she was meaning to live with was her brother, that the baby she carried was her brother's child. And Olivia couldn't bring herself to tell her the truth.

But how, without telling, was she going to persuade Georgie to give up Luke and terminate her pregnancy? There was only one place she could go for help, because only one person knew the truth. Aside from Matthew, of course, but she was not going to admit to her troublesome little brother that his guess had scored.

So here she was, secretly meeting her sometime lover in Alfriston, of all places. She would rather have made the meeting place somewhere further afield, but her father had taken the Land Rover to Brighton and Tom had borrowed Althea's car to visit an old friend in Winchester, which left only Georgie's bicycle as a means of transport. And anyway she couldn't be gone long; she had left Georgie napping, with the cat for company.

The village street was surprisingly crowded for a weekend in September. Maybe these were all the people with no children, or grown-up children, who had waited until the parents of school-age children had gone home with their families to start school. The holiday equivalent of a second sitting.

Nick glanced around at the half-timbered façades, adorned everywhere with hanging baskets, window boxes, flowering vines and climbing roses, all designed to achieve the maximum number of blooms per square foot of wall space. 'I didn't think places like this existed outside of *Country Life*. Who the hell would be crazy enough to actually live here?'

'I imagine it's quite attractive in the off-season.'

'You mean you can only poke your nose outside when it's freezing or raining. They should get a couple of farmers to drive their livestock through the village. A whiff of cowshit would clear out the trippers in two minutes flat.' He followed her down a side passage. 'Am I allowed to ask where we're going?'

'Just for a walk. It's quieter down here.'

The passage led to Alfriston church and its ancient rectory, which constituted the main tourist attraction, aside from the village itself. The churchyard was full of trippers, and Olivia had no intention of entering it. By going left instead of right, she set herself on a path leading down to the river – an unpopular option, to judge by the empty footpath.

Once across the little bridge over the little winding river, the path offered three choices: north upriver, south downriver, or straight ahead to the eastern side of the valley.

Olivia hesitated, looking up and down the treeless path. To be in full sight without being overheard was the safest arrangement.

Nick had his own ideas and barely even paused. He grabbed her hand and pulled her forward, along the path that crossed the valley. 'Let's skip the fucking swans, all right? If it decides to rain we can lurk under those trees.'

She tagged after him, half beside and half behind him along the narrow path, craning her neck at the sky. The sun was still shining, but he was right; the westernmost part of the sky was infested with clouds, and not the fluffy bright floating pillows that add enjoyment to a fine summer day.

'If it's going to rain, maybe we should go back.'

'I thought you wanted to talk. That's what you got me down here for, isn't it?'

327

'Well, yes. Don't walk so fast.' She tugged her hand free of his. 'Nick, Georgie's pregnant.'

'Georgie?' He stopped so suddenly she bumped into him. 'Are you having me on?'

'Would I joke about that?' But his scowl obliged her to add some sort of explanation. 'She said she was on the pill, but she forgot it one night and got drunk the next night, and then she was in hospital, and so . . . well, it didn't work.'

'And while she was telling you all that, did she get round to fingering the father?'

'You know very well who the father is,' she said impatiently. 'That's why she mustn't be allowed to have the baby.'

'Remind me.'

'Of what? That he's your son and she's your daughter? That that's a definition of incest?'

Nick said slowly, 'Does Luke know she's in the club?'

'She says he does. Did you know he turned up in the middle of the night and threw stones at her window? Don't laugh, it's not funny.'

'Sure it is,' he said, laughing in spite of her instructions to the contrary. 'That's pretty fucking daft, even for him.'

'I told him to go home and stay there. Has he moved back into your house?'

'He's been about, I think. He's not actually speaking to me.'

They came to a second bridge, passing over a stray tentacle of the meandering Cuckmere. The arched wooden span beneath a trailing willow was quite charming, in a rustic orientalized way. Or as Nick put it, 'More bloody twee.'

The bridge was wide enough to allow a herd of cows to cross in single file, but just too narrow for two people to walk abreast. Olivia watched Nick's broad shoulders rise and fall against the sky as she followed him over the hump of the bridge. 'Why isn't Luke speaking to you?'

The shoulders lifted in a shrug. 'How do I know? He won't speak to me to tell me.'

'Well, you're going to have to speak to him. And Georgie.'

'Yeah?' He glanced at her as she came alongside, where the footpath widened. 'Why is that?'

'Look, they can't . . . you know . . . they really can't. You'll have to tell them something.'

'Changed your mind about that, have you?'

'This baby has changed my mind. I thought everything would blow over when she went back home. Now she says she's not going back. She wants to stay here and live with Luke and have his baby. And she can't.'

328

'Why not? It's not a crime, is it?'

'Well, that's the funny thing.' Olivia, like a proper academic, had done her research on this point. 'Anything they've done so far isn't a crime, because they don't know the truth. But if we tell them, and they . . . carry on, then they're committing a crime.'

'What's the stretch?'

She almost laughed aloud at his blunt practicality. 'Seven years.'

That checked his stride. 'Christ almighty.' She watched him consider her news for a few paces. 'So if you keep your mouth shut, it's no crime. If you blab, you could be sending your daughter down for seven years.'

She didn't care at all for the slant he had put on the situation. 'But she doesn't understand. She doesn't know what she's doing. She thinks he's just a sort of semi-uncle. A second cousin, she kept saying, and genetically she's quite right, as far as that goes. But she can't have a baby by her brother.'

'So you keep saying.'

'Well, they wouldn't have done it if they knew, would they? It's disgusting. It's sinful.'

'Spoken like a true scientist,' Nick said drily. 'I thought it was all to do with inbreeding and imbecility.'

'That's only a problem if you're carrying recessive genes for serious congenital disorders,' explained Olivia Payne Ph.D. in a distracted voice. 'Within a larger breeding population, it probably doesn't matter. It's only if the gene pool becomes isolated over several generations that inbreeding really weakens the potential for survival. Remote mountain villages and suchlike. You know, all those stories about congenital idiocy in the Appalachians.'

They stepped out from a belt of trees into a narrow lane. The path beyond the lane rose steeply, marshalled between ditch and hedge.

As Olivia crossed the lane, she looked back over the valley, no longer sunlit. The church and churchyard were surprisingly close, as if she had gone no distance at all; the trippers milling about over there were clearly visible.

She felt a fleck of rain: the west wind rising. She looked up to survey the sky. Someone in heaven spat on her again.

'It's going to rain. We should go back.'

'Where's your sense of adventure? Anyway, we're already most of the way to somewhere else.' Nick pointed to a sign directing them up the hill, with ¼ *mile* written alongside some vandalized and indecipherable destination.

After half a lifetime abroad, Olivia was amused. Nowhere in Canada would you encounter a sign saying *Someplace* ¼ *mile*. A quarter of a mile didn't count as any distance at all. That was partly because nobody walked anywhere, except in the middle of the city, or in the wilderness where there were no destinations to be a quarter-mile away from.

This time Olivia went ahead, addressing Nick over her shoulder. 'Listen, Nick, don't be so obtuse. Immorality is one thing and moral illiteracy is another. Even you have to admit that some things are just plain wrong.'

'Maybe they are, but that doesn't mean Georgie and Luke is one of them. They're just a couple of kids dead keen on each other. What's wrong with that? There must be lots of people in their situation, lots of people who could meet their half-brother or half-sister without knowing it. Think of all the people who have kids and break up, or even break up before the baby's born. Or married women who get knocked up by some other bloke. Happens all the time, doesn't it? And what do the kids know, when they grow up? What they don't know won't bother them, but what they might know would make them criminals. It seems to me that makes the law some kind of pervert, turning an ordinary relationship into a kinky one, depending on what they know about each other's parents. Or about their own parents, for that matter.'

Olivia had to delay her reply, and pause in her progress at that point, to allow an elderly couple and a dog to pass, on their way down the hill. She stepped back into the hedge and responded politely to the old man's greeting as he went by. 'Going to rain,' he predicted cheerfully. He could afford to be cheerful about the prospect because his wife was carrying a large umbrella, big enough for both of them and probably the dog as well.

The path broadened after that. The hedge vanished to reveal an open field of stubble, littered with enormous round bales of straw like the millstones of the gods. Olivia waited for Nick to get alongside her before she resumed her denunciation.

'Look here, is there anything you would definitely say is absolutely not on? If it's okay for a man to seduce his adolescent stepdaughter, and molest – sorry, *tickle* – his own three-year-old daughter, and okay for a young boy to have a sexual relationship with his sisters, and for a brother and sister to live together and have a baby . . .' She caught her breath here, partly because the hill was steep, and partly to consider this astonishing catalogue of sins, to see if she had left out anything relevant. 'Tell me something that's *not* okay.'

Nick shrugged. 'None of that stuff involves pushing other people around, does it? Why shouldn't you be allowed to do what you like, as long as you don't hurt anyone? I mean, who cares? But what I'd call really shitty behaviour is where you make someone do something against their will, knowing that they can't do anything about it.'

'Like what did you have in mind?'

'Like, for instance, my old man.'

He had mentioned his father once to her, a long time ago. 'Beating you up, you mean?'

He made a dismissive gesture with his hand. 'That wasn't the worst.'

'What was the worst?'

'He used to fuck my sisters.'

The answer took her breath away again, this time so comprehensively that she had to stop. She stared at him, ignoring the first timid irregular raindrops, scouts for the storm. Stared at Nick's familiar face as if it were a stranger's. 'Your *father* did that?'

'I said so, didn't I?' He spoke flatly, returning her stare with a challenge. He was daring her to say . . . what? Something he didn't want her to guess?

She asked something safer. 'How do you know?'

'He put one of them in the club. At thirteen. I had to take her down to get rid of it. She was too scared to go on her own, but I made her go. I made her say it was some kid who'd done it. Otherwise . . .' He paused to choose his words. 'Otherwise we'd all have ended up in care.'

'Wouldn't that have been better than your father . . .?'

'Are you kidding? Those places are crawling with pimps and perverts.'

'How old were you, when – when this happened with your sister?'

'I guess I must have been fourteen. She was a year younger than me.' He paused. 'Eleven months. We had a standing joke about being one-twelfth twins.'

'What did . . . what about your mother? Didn't she . . .'

'She didn't want to know, did she? Maybe she just wanted him to leave her alone. Some women are like that, aren't they? Maybe she thought it was better than him going with other women. How the fuck would I know what was in her head?'

'Didn't you try to tell her?'

'I did once. And she was bloody furious. At me.'

Nick looked past her, towards the church spire away across the valley. From here it appeared to be very far away, an outpost of another world.

'That's still not the worst.' He was speaking softly, without any expression in his voice or on his face. She had to come close to hear him. 'He started on the youngest when she was seven.'

'Seven!' Olivia put her hands to her mouth. She would rather have put them over her ears. '*Seven?*'

'You heard me.' The distant stare became challenging again,

returned to Olivia's face. He went on in that terrible dead-pan voice. 'She didn't understand what he was doing to her, but she knew it bloody hurt. We were all shit-scared of him. He was a big bastard, the size of Luke. He looked a lot like Luke, come to think of it. But when I found out about the little one . . . The next time he lit into me I returned the favour. I might have killed him, if my mother hadn't come after me with a kitchen knife.'

'Your mother? After all that?'

He shrugged. 'Defending her man, wasn't she? Bloody stupid cow. So I thought, fuck the lot of them, and I left.' He lifted his head to stare at the sky. He smiled suddenly. 'Hey, it's raining. We're going to get wet.'

We're already wet, Olivia realized with astonishment. 'There's supposed to be a church up here,' she recalled. 'It must be in those trees.'

The rain came down in earnest as they reached the semi-shelter of the trees. Another indecipherable signpost pointed off to the left, past an old orchard littered with fallen apples rotting on the grass. Still no sign of a church, and they were drenched. Nick caught her hand and hauled her up the hill at a run, across the slippery grass, through a broken gate, between tilting gravestones like ancient teeth, up to the weathered door of a small flint building capped by a low square steeple.

'It'll be locked on account of vandals,' Olivia warned.

The doorknob was an iron ring. Nick wrenched the ring. The heavy door creaked open. They stumbled inside, still blinded by rain.

He shut the door and leaned back on it. He was laughing. They were both soaked to the skin, dripping on the flagstone floor. It was horribly uncomfortable. Olivia began to laugh too.

After a minute to catch her breath, she pushed away the wet strands of hair that had blown into her face, and turned to see where they had fetched up.

It was a very tiny church, with scarcely room for more worshippers than the apostles and their wives. There were no pews, no organ, not even an altar. Only a stone lectern in the north-east corner, an incongruously ornate stone font in the opposite, south-west corner, and a bell rope hanging by the door. Nick gave the bell rope a tug. Nothing happened, no peal, no bell on the upper end. Nothing here for anyone to steal.

Or maybe it was just that everything had already been stolen. Vandals had certainly left their spoor, breaking several small panes in the leaded windows as a mark of their passage. One of them had sprayed a crude black cross on the eastern wall where the altar must have been. At least it was a Latin cross, not a swastika.

332

Nick walked up to the front of the church and turned to face the door. 'Not much of a church, is it? More like a bus shelter.'

'Shelter for us, anyway, even if we were a bit late getting here.'

Being inside the church wasn't all that much of an improvement on standing in the rain. The air in here was stone cold, bone cold, with a medieval mustiness. Olivia hugged herself. She drifted towards Nick, perhaps drawn to the only source of warmth in that dead and desecrated place.

He reached out to unbutton her shirt.

At his touch she began to shiver uncontrollably. He stopped in mid-button. She was shuddering violently, visibly, helpless to hold herself still. It wasn't just the cold and the wet. It was what Nick had told her, down the hill. Told her about the goings-on in hell.

'D-d-don't . . .' The only word she could get out.

He put his arms around her and held her against him.

They were small comfort to each other at first, sodden and shivering from the downpour, like fish-flesh under sea. Only gradually the shudders turned to trembling, then to occasional involuntary shakes. She was definitely warmer where her body touched his.

He caressed her. He was warmer too; she could feel the heat in his hands, even through her damp shirt. She stroked his shoulders, by way of returning the favour. He kissed her. That warmed her up a lot, and not just her lips.

Him too, evidently. 'Changed your mind about a screw?'

'We can't do that here.' The idea shocked her. She drew away, looked around. 'It's a church.'

'Was a church.'

'Once a church, always a church.'

'Not true. They can de – decon – what's that word? – deconstruct them?'

'Deconsecrate.'

'Yeah, that's it.' From the corner of her eye she caught his dry, slanting glance. 'Does your doctor appreciate being married to a dictionary? Anyway, they do that to churches all the time. They turn them into bingo halls or whatever.'

'Well, nobody's been playing bingo here. This church just looks abandoned.' She touched the carving on the font. There would once have been a lid as ornate as the basin, but that must have proved much easier to steal. 'Funny sort of place to put a church, in the middle of nowhere. It was probably built on a pagan shrine. A holy place from prehistoric times. Maybe there used to be a spring here.'

Nick sat down at the eastern end of the building, on the step that once had led to the altar; it was bowed into a smooth hollow curve in the middle, worn away by centuries of devout knees. He pulled out a packet of cigarettes, inspected them for water damage, succeeded in lighting one. The idea of smoking in a church appalled Olivia almost as much as the idea of having sex in a church.

Nick was looking around the tiny church with detached interest, as if it were his first visit to a Shinto temple. 'Now how the hell would they decide which places were holy? Did they walk around with one of those dowsing rods? Or maybe somebody saw a ghost up here. And what do they do to make them unholy?'

Olivia indicated the black cross on the wall behind him. 'Aerosol paint seems to be a popular method.'

And effective too, it seemed. There was no breath or hint or sign that God had ever entered here. Whatever divinity had dwelt in this place, maybe since men first came to the Downs, had been driven out at last by unbelievers. Perhaps the Christian God had met the fate of all the other gods before Him, a victim of human indifference.

Maybe only the Devil was around to listen to prayers nowadays. She had prayed in St Paul's and been answered . . . with Nick.

He was watching her, she realized when she glanced in his direction. Watching her intently enough to make her feel uncomfortable. 'What's the matter?'

'Nothing. I'm just admiring you.'

Olivia turned away, refusing to meet his look. Not wanting to think about him, or about how much she still wanted him to . . . admire her. 'I'm not very . . . admirable.'

'Sure you are. You're sexier than any of the scarecrows I make my living off of.'

She wanted to stop up her ears. 'That's right, lay it on with a trowel, why don't you? When I was a silly little girl I used to believe you when you said things like that, but I've got wise since then. It's so much easier to tell some credulous woman she's gorgeous than to tell her . . .'

She stopped, appalled by what she had so nearly inadvertently revealed. Nick was still watching her with that unnerving intensity. 'What d'you want me to tell you?'

'Nothing.' Her fingers caressed the font again, caressed an angel's face at the centre of a Celtic cross. 'You weren't faithful to my mother, were you?'

He didn't answer. Maybe he took it for a rhetorical question.

'Did you give her this crap about being sexier than the scarecrows? And what did you tell your floozies about her?'

That stung him into response. 'What d'you think, I brought them home to dinner? She didn't need to know, did she?'

'Luke knew.'

'Luke has an artistic imagination. And I don't have to justify

334

myself to my idiot son.' He went on smoking and watching her without speaking for a while. Then he said abruptly, 'Anyway, it's all your fault. I didn't do that sort of thing when you were around.'

'You kept it in the family like your father, you mean?'

Olivia didn't seriously imagine he was going to hit her, but he did look for a second as if the idea was crossing his mind. Oh yes, go ahead, she thought, give me something to take back to Tom. And don't think I wouldn't tell him where it came from: Matthew's door's daddy.

Tom might even spot the family resemblance for himself, and correct his mistake about Georgie's father. And speaking of Georgie . . .

'How could you do a thing like that to Georgie, after what your father did to your sisters?' she demanded. 'Aged three! Even *he* wasn't that depraved.'

Nick went quite still, staring at her. Everything was suddenly very quiet. Even the sound of the rain had stopped. 'Was that why you left? You really thought I'd fucked her?'

'If I'd thought that, I certainly wouldn't be here now. I wouldn't even consent to be in the same room with you.' Olivia turned away, pressing her cheek against the angel in the cross, embarrassed for no reason that she knew of. In dealing with Nick it was a fatal handicap to feel embarrassment, because he never did. 'I did wonder at first just what . . . But Tom examined her and said no. And that wasn't how she talked about it. She didn't say you'd hurt her, she didn't sound scared.'

'Fucking right she didn't. It was just a game to her, and it felt good. You were the one that was scared.'

Olivia left the safety of the font, approached him in a roundabout way. 'I thought maybe you were . . . like your father. With little girls. Only I didn't know about him then.'

'He didn't care what age they were, as long as they had a serviceable cunt,' he said in an astonishingly matter-of-fact tone. He was still sitting on the worn step, his arms resting on his knees to bear the weight of his hunched shoulders. He spoke to the empty church rather than to her. 'Didn't even have to be a cunt, come to that. Any old hole would do.'

She dropped to her knees beside him, where the altar rail would have been if either the altar or the rail had still been extant. 'What do you mean? What did he . . .?'

'And you a doctor of biology? I thought you said you'd got wise.' He turned his head a fraction, just enough to fix her with a look of bleak amusement. 'You want me to show you?'

She couldn't answer, not even to say no. She just stared at his face, a foot from hers, as if she had never seen that face before. And maybe she hadn't, not like she was seeing it now. With hidden patterns burning through the opaque surface, patterns made from the memories in his head.

Nick turned away, dropped his cigarette stub on the flagstone floor, ground it under his shoe in a very deliberate fashion. She watched his hands ball into fists. 'After Joey told me what he'd done to her, I took to sleeping with a knife under my pillow. Just in case he got too drunk to tell which bed he was getting into.' He struck his fists together, end to end. Slowly he uncurled them, gazing down at his hands. 'If you waste all your nasty words on me, Lia, what'll you do when you meet someone like that?'

Olivia couldn't breathe. She didn't dare to touch him. She edged away, still on her knees, as if he might detonate at any moment. 'Nick, I didn't really . . . I knew you hadn't done . . . anything like that. But don't you see, I thought if I stayed – when Georgie got older, you might . . .' She swallowed hard. 'Well, you did it to me, didn't you?'

'Are you going to try to tell me you didn't want me to?'

'But I . . . does that make everything okay? Maybe Georgie liked what you did to her at three. Maybe she'd have liked a little more of you at thirteen.' Her voice came thin and flat, exhausted of emotion, or at least of the capacity to express it. 'I didn't go because of what you'd done, I left because I was afraid of what you might do. I didn't trust you any more. And I didn't want you . . . fucking my daughter.'

She half expected that to trigger some sort of explosion, of anger or denial. His head swung round slowly. He looked at her, impassive. After a silence he shrugged. 'Too bad you didn't get around to telling me all this at the time, instead of running away from home for eighteen years.'

Olivia said scornfully, 'You thought I wouldn't mind, did you?'

'Well, yeah, like I told you, it didn't occur to me.' He produced another cigarette and went through the routine of lighting it while he was speaking. 'It's like when you're a kid and you go to someone else's house where they do everything differently, and you don't know what the rules are. You can pick up the obvious ones, or the ones they talk about, but you never know what kind of rules they have for the things you never see them do.'

Once she would have retorted that some rules were surely universal, but she knew better now. She also knew that even if you didn't approve of the rules you had grown up with, that didn't mean you knew of any better ones to put in their place. That sometimes you even failed to notice that you were still carrying the old rules inside you, unwitting and unwillingly, like a secret virus ready to infect the new order with the plagues of the old one.

But understanding all of that didn't mean she was ready to forgive him for anything. 'So maybe I was right to worry about what might have happened later. Seeing they had such funny rules about it in your house.'

'They only had one rule.'

'Only one?'

'Yeah. The usual one.'

'What's that?'

'You can do what you like, if you're strong enough to do it.'

He flicked aside his cigarette, and rose and came towards her. She was still on her knees, for some reason. When she went to stand up he pushed her back down, taking her one-handed by the throat, his fingers bruising her skin: forcing her backwards, down to the floor, which on this spot was somebody's gravestone. She caught his wrist with both hands to pull his hand away, or at least to hold herself upright, but he kept up a steady, painful, irresistible pressure – not throttling her, just forcing her down and back.

'Nick, you're hurting me.'

'So why don't you stop me?'

'I'm trying to.' Without any success whatsoever.

He gave her a shake, like a dog with a rat.

'Ow, that really does hurt. Nick, don't!' Her protest this time was on account of his other hand starting to unbutton her shirt again.

He was looking down at her with icy, raging eyes. 'What's the matter, don't you want it? You wanted it last time. And the time before that. You used to want it any time you could get it.'

He was terrifying her. She thought he must have gone mad; she was choked with fear and cold. 'But I told you – not here, not now –'

He shook her again, more violently. 'What's the difference? A fuck is a fuck, isn't it, whether you want it or not?'

In her anger she tried to shout, but the hand clamped across her throat reduced it to a croak. 'If I don't want it, it's rape!'

'So you do know the difference, after all.'

He gave her one last shove, releasing her to collapse on the cold tombstone, and walked away.

Olivia tried to pull herself together, physically and figuratively. In practical terms that meant doing her blouse up and soothing her bruised throat.

Nick had his back to her, apparently devoting all his attention to applying his lighter to the tip of another cigarette, a replacement for the one he had flung aside in his fury. She stared at that broad back, with the muscles still tensed, to judge by the set of the shoulders. She had forgotten how frighteningly powerful he was. Most of the time he didn't need to use his strength to get what he wanted.

When she thought she could trust her voice again, she said, 'All right, I'm sorry. You're not . . . quite . . . as bad as your father.'

Nick glanced back over his shoulder. 'Spoken like a gentleman,' he said drily.

She had managed to get to her feet by now, regaining the confidence and composure that his attack had cowed out of her. 'And now that you've made your point, perhaps you'll acknowledge mine.'

'About screwing Georgie? No, I don't think I would've done that.' Astonishingly, he spoke without emotion, without any sign of shame or embarrassment, just as if she had presented him with an abstract philosophical problem. 'Not if she'd been around all the time, not if I'd known her for ever. She'd have been my daughter, wouldn't she? Like a real daughter, I mean. I knew a guy who grew up in a kibbutz, where all the kids lived together in some kind of crèche, and he said all the girls were like sisters to him, he just couldn't get interested, y'know? A couple of them were real stunners, he said, but they didn't do a fucking thing for him.'

After a pause he added, 'Besides, you'd have been around.'

Olivia couldn't guess what her presence or absence had to do with anything, but she knew that something was making her angry again. Maybe it was his casual tone, dismissing the dreadful possibility that had driven her away. Driven her to throw away a huge part of her life. 'All a misunderstanding, was it, then? Some kind of culture clash?'

'I'd say so.' He turned then, and his look and tone were as cool as hers were heated. 'Lia, do you think I'd've deliberately done anything, anything at all, that would make you bugger off for twenty years?'

Somewhere in his words she caught a glimpse of an alternative universe. She considered the prospect, slightly breathless. 'What did *you* think? That I'd continue to make myself available as your bit on the side for the next twenty years?'

He shrugged again. 'Well, it's better than being married to the wrong person for twenty years, isn't it?'

'You've no right to make assumptions like that,' Olivia protested. 'I've been happily married for nearly eighteen years, and what would you know about it anyway?'

He exhaled, smiling in an infuriating way. 'It does you credit, kitten, the way you leap to the defence of your doctor. Who said I was talking about you?'

More than one alternative universe, then. All these hypothetical

338

doors opening must have let in some cosmic cold; she could hardly speak for the chattering of her teeth. 'If you – if you mean my mother was married to the wrong man, I knew that from the beginning. If you mean yourself . . . well, you married her for security and domesticity and respectability and all that sort of thing, and that's exactly what she gave you, so you've no cause for complaint. Everything happened the way you made it happen. You chose, you decided, you did what you wanted, and to hell with everyone else. So if you're not happy about the consequences, you've no one but yourself to blame.'

Nick was not abashed, only amused. He pointed to the lectern. 'That's the place to deliver a sermon, isn't it?'

He turned his hand over, idly watching the smoke from his cigarette curl upwards through sunlight. 'Hey, the sun's come out again. You'd better be getting back to Georgie.'

Georgie. He had remembered, and she had forgotten. 'Nick, will you speak to her? About the baby?'

She asked again because she had no one else, not because she expected him to agree. When he didn't answer right away she found herself gazing at him, clasping her hands together at her waist like some anxious little wife. And was all the more astonished when he said, still without looking at her, 'Yeah, okay.'

They went down the long hill in close formation, the marching method of lovers. Side by side, hand in hand, arm in arm, even intertwined where the path permitted, never losing touch but without a word between them.

Perhaps Olivia had not only caught sight of but fallen into another universe. It certainly seemed a different world. This one was filled with sunlight rather than threatening rain.

Going back the same way they had gone up, she noticed many things that the cloud must have obscured before: scarlet poppies in the stubble at the edge of the field, thorn trees bright with crimson haws, blackberries blooming and ripening all at once, jack-in-the-pulpit thrusting up its bold orange fruit, plump red rose-hips dotting the hedge, elderberries deepening to purple. Things once familiar and taken for granted, now seen again with grateful pleasure after a long absence.

There was warmth in this world. She could feel the heat of a September sun, even through her rain-sodden clothes. She could feel the warmth of Nick's hand in hers, of his arm around her. She was even aware of her own internal heat, like the fire at the heart of the earth.

Maybe the old Norsemen had been wrong. Maybe the world wasn't going to end in ice.

35

The harvest is past, the summer is ended,
and we are not saved.

At the twilight time, when the sun goes down and the moon comes up, when the creatures of the day retire to their dreams and the creatures of the night rouse to their work, at this fulcrum point of the turning world, a wolf comes down to the sunset shore of a northern lake.

It is the coldest time of the year and the lake is frozen thick. Snow has fallen, snow on snow, but not for at least a week now, so that the crust on the lake is marked with all manner of trails from creatures taking a shortcut as they go about their affairs. Only those who have nothing to fear would have ventured on to the open ice. Those who are large and strong, or fleet-footed, or possessed of wings, or with other defensive weapons in their armoury such as sharp quills or vile smells. Or else those, like the wolf, who have nothing to fear because they are themselves the source of terror.

The wolf steps out on to the ice. She investigates the messages left involuntarily in the windswept snow. The most interesting, since she is not hungry just now, is the track of another wolf.

The long narrow lake, product of ancient glacial gouging, marks a boundary between two hunting territories. The western territory belongs to her own family. The track in the snow has the scent of a stranger from the east.

She turns her head to look westward, over her shoulder, where the sunset stains the snow at the edge of the wood. Her family is somewhere there, miles away by now. She has been driven out, exiled till spring; not from the territory, but from the company of the family. Only one female in every family can mate and bear cubs. When the winter breeding season starts, the alpha she-wolf drives away any rivals who show signs of coming into heat. Only one mating, one birthing, in each family, to ensure healthy cubs and good hunting. An old-fashioned idea to the human mind, but wolves, unlike men, have never managed to repeal the laws of nature.

Now she looks east, to a winter moon rising. The strange wolf must have come from the eastern shore. She remembers last summer, a wolf-meet at the southernmost point of this lake. Her family and the stranger's kin, neighbours meeting and greeting. Their territories are large, the borders not everywhere so well-defined as here by the lake. Misunderstandings could happen, or accidental trespass in hot pursuit of game. It's just as well to know your neighbours and keep your fences mended.

She is young and strong and healthy, this watching wolf. She is two years old, has just reached sexual maturity. But maybe, like a Victorian housemaid, she is doomed never to have a family of her own, for want of a way to feed them. When the lake ice begins to melt she will be able to return to her pack, all rivalry forgotten, to hunt and to help with the raising of her elder sister's cubs.

Eastward there is no sign of the sunset's blushes in the snow. There the world is blue and silver, the snow like diamonds in the moonlight. The colder the night, the brighter the sparkle of snow. Tonight will be a deep and bitter frost in which a man out of doors might well perish, but the wolf will stay quite comfortable. Her winter coat was made for just such weather. In the old days a trapper would have earned twice as much for a wolf pelt in winter, and twice as much again for the coat of an Arctic wolf. Nowadays there are no trappers, no bounties, no market for the fur. There are laws forbidding the killing of wolves. But also there are planes and snowmobiles, and still there are men of a hunting disposition.

This wolf does not have men on her mind tonight. Or rather, she does: the east wind has brought her a scent which she recognizes. The stranger on the lake is coming back. She knows him for a neighbour, and waits with a great deal of curiosity and little fear.

He appears on the opposite shore, standing on a rocky promontory at the edge of the ice, in the best tradition of alpha he-wolves. He has a silver coat, or maybe the moonlight makes silver of him the way it makes diamonds of snow. The lake is narrow here, not a hundred yards across. The stranger is upwind of her, but he has the moon behind him and she knows he has seen her. He jumps down from the point of rock, down to the ice.

He trots forward quickly, easily. The lake is no man's land. In summer each family fishes from its own shore; in winter anyone may venture upon the ice. The wolf from the western shore decides to go and meet her neighbour, to see what he has to say. They meet in the middle of the lake.

As they approach, each wolf is holding up its tail like a truce flag, giving small formal wags to indicate non-hostile intentions. At first

341

they circle warily, not wanting to be first to make open overtures. Then they sniff cautiously to confirm the other's identity. The strange wolf, being older, larger, and male, holds his head down and to one side to let the younger, smaller, female wolf inspect him without shyness.

They have each been living alone for some time. When the introductions are over, they both feel so pleased to have company that they sing to each other, an impromptu wolves' opera. An ignorant human listening might have said they were howling at the moon.

In high spirits, fresh after a day's drowse, they nudge each other playfully and begin a very cubbish game of tag. When they have tired of this they stop to gaze at each other, tongues out, breathless but still excited. The strange wolf nudges the she-wolf, butting her in the ribs with his shoulder. She promptly rolls over in the snow, feet in the air, like a young cub. She has never been on heat before.

Perhaps the stranger is more experienced, or perhaps he has paid more attention to the goings-on in his own family in previous winters. Wolves do their courting in the open; the whole family knows who is doing what to whom. And why should they not, since it concerns them all closely, their inheritance, their livelihood, their survival.

But these two are lone wolves, in the middle of a frozen lake, and nobody is watching the start of their courtship. Unless you count a snowy owl passing overhead, who is keeping a keen eye out for creatures very much smaller than wolves, and who would not in any case dream of licking his mate between the legs, even if he had a tongue to do it with.

It had been settled somehow that Tom would go back on Sunday and Olivia would follow a week later. Something else that had been settled was that Georgie would not be coming home with her mother, but Tom didn't know that yet.

Georgie wanted Olivia to break the news.

'Aren't you talking to your father any more?'

Georgie waggled her fingers to indicate an iffy situation. 'Well, that's the problem. I had a chat with him about, you know, about how he isn't really my father. Not even my adoptive father. In other words, not my father at all, only my stepfather. He was very gallant about you' – Olivia winced – 'but it was a tad strained. He seemed to think it shouldn't matter at all to me. He kept saying it didn't matter to him. He said that's why he hadn't said anything about it. He said as far as he was concerned I was his daughter just like Alex was his son. He got quite shirty when I said it wasn't his feelings I was bothered about.'

Olivia had already heard the other side of this story from Tom, who had expressed the view that Georgie was being absurdly romantic, unrealistic, and (only hinted at) damned ungrateful. All of which was true, of course, but Olivia was in no position to say so, since she was the source of the whole dilemma. It seemed a particularly unpropitious time to have to tell Tom that his romantic, unrealistic, ungrateful stepdaughter was not coming home after all. As for telling him the reason why, there was no moment in eternity propitious enough for that.

On the other hand, Olivia as the guilty party, so to speak, was in no position to tell Georgie that she was being absurdly romantic et cetera. 'Does my father know you're not going back to Canada?'

'Well, I did mention it, before . . . before all this.'

'You'd better tell him and Althea that you're still determined to stay, and see if they're still willing to have you. Why don't you break the news to everyone tonight?'

'Couldn't you just turn up back home without me next Sunday, and explain to Daddy then? You can tell him everything all at once – the baby and Luke and all, I mean.'

'Thank you for the suggestion, but I don't reckon to be a widow for a while yet. Just tell everyone all at one go. But not about Luke and the baby,' Olivia added hastily. It was her fixed intention that by the time she went home there would be no Luke and no baby in Georgie's life. So perhaps – it occurred to her for the first time – with nothing to keep her here, perhaps Georgie would be coming home after all.

The point of making the announcement in public was to prevent Tom from making a fuss. He would almost certainly make a fuss later, of course, but by that time he would have already had a chance to get used to the idea, and his objections would hopefully be less intemperate. And coloured by the knowledge that persuasion was the only weapon he had. Georgie was free to come and go as she pleased. She was already two years older than Olivia had been when she left her home and family as it might have been for ever.

In the event, that evening, Tom's dismay and Olivia's father's delight just about cancelled each other out. Olivia thought of her father's reaction as delight when she saw his face light up, but all he actually expressed was mild pleasure, as if someone had offered him a glass of whisky. He was much better at articulating downs than ups, as she knew too well. 'I thought you'd have been put off England for ever by your recent experiences.'

Georgie waved aside her brush with death. 'That was just an accident. I wouldn't dream of holding it against the whole country.'

'Accident or not,' Tom said in a tone that made it clear which interpretation he favoured, 'you shouldn't be traipsing around on your own in a foreign country while you're recovering from a serious concussion.'

Olivia's father looked faintly affronted at this description of England as a foreign country. Georgie gave a more practical response. 'In the first place, Daddy, they're going to check me out on Thursday to make sure everything's okay, and if it isn't, Mama will still be here. In the second place, if Althea and Ross don't mind,' she gave her grandfather her best blue-eyed gaze, 'I'd like to stay in their flat for a little while, till I've found a job and a place to live. And Matt will be there, in case I go into convulsions.'

'Matthew's presence offers no reassurance whatsoever,' Olivia's father observed tartly. 'But yes, you're welcome to use the flat for as long as you like.'

Althea had no objection either, which was just as well because she hadn't been consulted. Perhaps she was thinking more of Georgie keeping an eye on Matthew than the other way round. At any rate, everyone else's approval left Tom with no serious leg to stand on.

Which didn't prevent his protesting to Olivia later that night, in the privacy of the bedroom.

'It was supposed to be a holiday. Now she's talking about living here.'

'Lots of young people do that sort of thing, go abroad for a year or two before they settle down.'

'Well, I don't like the idea of her hanging around with that crazy.'

'What crazy?'

He smiled sardonically. 'I was going to say, your brother, but they're both crazy, aren't they? But the Beckett boy seems to run more to self-destruction, whereas young Mr Winter is a danger to anyone who crosses his path. I don't want Georgie mixed up with either of them, and particularly not Luke.'

'Neither do I,' agreed Olivia, more earnestly than Tom could tell. 'But it's no good issuing dire threats and warnings, because there's nothing we can do about it. She's in a really bolshie mood right now, on account of this business of, you know, the birth certificate. If you tell her not to do something, it'll just make her more determined. I'll have a go at her next week, but I don't suppose it'll be any use. We'll just have to wait for her to get over this phase or whatever it is.'

'Goddamned kids,' muttered Tom, unbuttoning his shirt with the vigour of irritation. 'Just one damn phase after another. You'd think they had no rational mind at all.'

'Is it any different with adults? It seems to me that growing up is simply coming to terms with the fact that you're never going to mature much beyond fifteen.'

'Speaking of fifteen . . .' He leaned across the bed to stroke her nearest breast. 'Is it the English air or what? You don't look any older than Georgie these days.'

'It's all right, I'm your wife. You don't have to chat me up to get me into bed.'

'No, I mean it, you're absolutely blooming.' She let him lay her down and lean over her, admiring her and displaying his admiration with appropriate kisses and caresses. 'Listen, Lia, why don't you just forget about those goddamn wolves?'

Olivia stiffened. 'What do you mean, forget about them?'

'You know, give up on them and study something else. Spiders or something, that you can keep in the lab, that'll let you get home sharp on six every night.'

'And would you be home sharp on six as well?'

He ignored that. 'No, listen, I'm serious. Alex is going off to McGill next year, remember? If Georgie stays over here, and you disappear up North while he's away, I'll be batching it all by myself. It wasn't too bad while Georgie and Alex were around, but I'm damn well not going to live like a student at my age. You're supposed to be my wife, remember?'

She had continually been reminding herself of that fact over the last two weeks. 'I remember.'

'Well, it's high time you started to act like it. I thought all this wolf-chasing would die down once you'd gotten your Ph.D. You don't need to work full time.'

'I should treat it like a hobby, you mean?'

He didn't even notice the sarcasm. 'Well, why not, eh? It's not as if you were working on a cure for cancer. Nobody gives a damn about those stupid wolves and what they do all day long. I make enough money for both of us. I'm fed up with everybody saying, Oh, poor Tom, has she gone off and left you alone again? It makes me feel like a real sap, playing second fiddle to those fucking wolves. I'm fed up with it, do you understand me?'

By now he had forgotten about love-making and was gesturing vehemently. Olivia tried to calm him down, while trying to keep calm herself. 'Don't shout, Tom, I'm not in the next room. But several other people are. Why not leave all this until I get home?'

'I'm just warning you, that's all. I've had it up to here with wolves.' He glared at her. 'And with not having you around when I want you.'

'I'm here right now,' she pointed out, 'and all you're doing is shouting at me.'

36

All the foundations of the earth are out of course.

Despite her promise to Tom, and her own resolution, by Wednesday Olivia had still not worked her way round to breaking the news to Georgie. Nick had said he would talk to her, but Olivia wasn't convinced that he would really do it, and time was passing. She was due to go home next weekend.

She told herself it would be easier somehow when she and Georgie were on their own in the flat. Because Georgie had a hospital appointment on Thursday morning, and Olivia wanted to do some shopping, they had arranged to go up to London on Wednesday evening and come back down to Sussex on Saturday.

Matthew was not in the flat when they arrived. Olivia assumed that he had decided to stay clear of it while she was there.

Her assumption proved incorrect when she was wakened in the middle of the night by someone thumping around in the sitting-room. She was already wearing her night-gown, but she pulled on Tom's dressing-gown as well; she had asked him to leave it behind, since it had so frequently proved so useful. Doubly armoured, and armed with one of Althea's stiletto shoes in her hand, she crept out to see what was happening, quietly shutting the bedroom door behind her. Georgie hadn't wakened, and Olivia didn't disturb her. It was a mother's duty to defend her child, wasn't it? Even if the child was now quite grown up, and physically fitter than the mother.

Thinking to take the intruder by surprise, she switched on the light. Matthew stood swaying in the middle of the room, blinking in bewilderment.

It wasn't just the sudden light that had confused him, Olivia realized. His dark eyes were slightly unfocused, his expression more than slightly half-witted. After staring at her in this intellectually inefficient manner for some time, he straightened slowly and appeared to be pulling himself together. 'Oh. You're here.'

'Daddy said he'd warned you we were coming up to London.'

'I forgot.' He bent over, clutching his stomach and covering his mouth, and staggered towards the bathroom. 'Sorry to be rude, but I think I'm about to heave.'

Olivia waited, containing her indignation until he re-emerged. He shambled over to the sofa and collapsed full length on it. Evidently his body wasn't working any better than his head. Hence all the noise that had wakened her.

She stood over him, still clutching the shoe, like an irate wife confronting her drunken husband in some old-fashioned cartoon. 'Matty, do you do this every night?'

'Do what?'

'Get wrecked. What have you been taking?'

'How the hell do I know? Whatever was going round. It didn't seem neighbourly to ask.' He propped one arm behind his head and flung the other across his eyes in a dismissive gesture. 'Do me a favour and turn out the light, will you?'

'In a minute. You can't carry on like this for ever, you know.'

'Like what? I'm only trying to sleep.'

'I mean this idiotic attempt at some sort of *fin de siècle* decadence. It's so bourgeois.'

Matthew giggled. 'You're really cute, Lia. Is Georgie here?'

'Of course. Daddy said he told you all about it.'

'Maybe he did. I tend to turn off my ears as soon as he opens his mouth.'

'You turn off your brain, you mean.'

He flapped his fingers at her without moving his arm. 'Why don't you just turn off the light and save the lecture for the morning? It won't sink in now anyway. My brain is not only turned off but totally out of commission.'

He was right on that point. She switched out the light and went back to bed. Georgie hadn't stirred.

Georgie was due at the hospital at nine o'clock the next morning. They had ways of looking inside her head to see what was happening there. Physically, that was. Olivia thought she could have done with a machine that let her see inside someone's mind, rather than just their brain. There were several heads she would have liked to see inside, starting with Matthew and moving on to Luke and his father.

Matthew was still sprawled on the sofa, showing no sign of intelligent life, when they got up.

'Where did Matty come from?' Georgie wanted to know.

'He wandered in in the middle of the night. Claimed he'd forgotten we were coming.'

Olivia didn't believe he had forgotten. Much more likely that he just didn't care, or that this was one more shot in the unending war he appeared to be waging against the world and more particularly

347

against his parents. People talked about someone going off the rails, but Matthew seemed to be hijacking the tracks and using them to lay down his own private railway to some obscure infernal destination.

Georgie stared down at Matthew for a little while longer. 'Why don't you take him back home with you?'

'What, to Toronto?'

'Sure, why not? A straight swap. Me here, him there.'

'I can't imagine why I'd want to do that.'

'He's sort of at a dead end here. Keeps hitting his head against the wall because he can't get himself turned round. If he were somewhere else he'd have to worry about different things.'

'Well, I'm not, in the famous phrase, my brother's keeper. And I don't suppose he'd want to come, anyway.'

'He might. I could maybe talk him into it.'

'Please don't bother, my darling. I've enough else to worry about. Come on, we've got to be going soon.'

Anticipating a long wait at the hospital, Olivia popped into the bathroom before departure. The toilet refused to flush. Pulling the handle produced no results but a gurgle and a trickle. It *would* have to wait till Tom's gone, she thought irritably. She might be able to work out for herself what the problem was, but she wouldn't know how to describe it to a plumber.

But when she lifted off the lid of the tank, the trouble was immediately apparent, even to her unmechanical intelligence: a plastic bag had got wedged against the outflow valve. She removed it, replaced the lid, and reflushed with satisfactory results.

The next mystery was the bag. It was two bags, actually, one knotted inside the other to keep the contents from getting wet. Within the inner bag were several handfuls of gelatine capsules, the standard sort used for any kind of medicinal powder, and appropriately filled with a white powder. Whoever put them in the tank either suffered from migraine on a truly hellish scale, or was not using the capsules for therapeutic purposes. Unless getting bombed out of your skull was now considered a therapeutic experience.

She had no need to say *whoever* in that hypothetical way. She knew very well the *who* had to be Matthew. He must have cached it there last night when he first came in, meaning to retrieve it later when Olivia and Georgie were out of the way, and then been too zonked to get up and rescue it. The ploy was simple to the point of idiocy, but then as he had said himself, his brain had switched off.

She set the dripping bag in the sink and stared at it. There must have been five hundred capsules inside. Again there were two possibilities. Either he was addicted to this whatever-it-was to a degree that called for immediate intervention, or he had bought the stuff in order to resell it. Which also called for intervention, but perhaps not immediately.

Her first reaction had been to flush it down the toilet, but maybe that wasn't such a good idea. If the water was recycled, half of London might end up stoned. Or it might do serious damage to the tiny brains and primitive nervous systems of the fish downriver. On the other hand, if she didn't dispose of it somehow, there was no telling what it might do to the even tinier brains and cruder nervous systems of Matthew's customers.

The bag was too big to flush just as it was. There wasn't anywhere in the room to hide it. This was a neat, modern, Althea sort of bathroom, with a fitted bath and a minimal medicine cabinet. *Faute de mieux*, she took it with her into the kitchen.

'What's that?' Georgie demanded.

Olivia held up her discovery. 'You tell me. I found it in the lavatory tank. It was blocking the outflow.'

Georgie tutted, seemingly more in dismay than disapproval. 'What a twit that child is. Because he didn't have his knapsack with him, I suppose.'

Olivia dropped the bag into the rubbish bin. 'You don't sound surprised.'

'Well, no, I'm not. Don't look like that, Mama,' she added impatiently. 'He's not some kind of drug baron or dope fiend. And it won't be anything hard, heroin or that kind of thing, that's all too down-market for Matt's friends. They're just looking for little social trips.'

'Well, whatever he's up to, he's not getting up to it here. My father would have a fit if he knew.' Olivia tied up the bin liner and handed it to Georgie. 'Get rid of that, will you? And then we've got to go.'

The expectation of a long wait at the hospital proved well-founded. But after several hours, mostly spent sitting about in one room or another, Georgie received absolution from the consultant. 'She's recovering beautifully, Mrs Payne,' he announced briskly to Olivia. 'Is your husband not here?'

'He's gone back to Canada. I presume he could see for himself she was healing well.'

The consultant looked disappointed, perhaps at the prospect of having to explain himself to a mere layperson. He addressed himself to Olivia, who though merely the mother of the patient and without medical qualification, was at least one step up from Georgie, who was only the patient.

'Well, in a healthy young adult like your daughter, not long finished her growth, the body tissues are usually remarkably resilient. They'll restore themselves very quickly, even without medical intervention. The affected brain cells suffered some considerable trauma – that's why she was in a coma for so long – but there's evidently been no permanent harm done.'

He looked very pleased with himself as he said this, though according to his own testimony the happy outcome hadn't been his doing because there was nothing he could have done. He even ventured a very small joke as he ushered them out, warning Georgie not to try any headstands for a few weeks yet.

Georgie was offended. 'Does he think I'm a kid?'

'I shouldn't think so, not after you announced that you're pregnant.'

'Well, I had to, didn't I? Those machines throw off all sorts of gamma rays and things like that, and the foetus is extremely vulnerable to chromosomal damage in the first trimester.'

She was perfectly correct, of course. What had dismayed Olivia was the obvious pride with which Georgie had made her announcement to the doctor and technicians.

I've made a great mess of this, Olivia realized. Even if I tell her the whole story today and she agrees to terminate the pregnancy, there won't be time to do it before I go home. A moment later she consoled herself with the corollary – in that case, Georgie would have to go home with her.

They did some grocery shopping on the way back to the flat, and enjoyed a late but leisurely and well-earned lunch. Matthew had disappeared, no doubt to avoid a confrontation over the vanished bag of drugs.

After lunch Georgie went into the bedroom for a nap. All those brain cells busily repairing themselves, Olivia supposed. And then corrected herself: no, it's because she's pregnant.

It was amazingly easy to keep forgetting that. As if she really didn't want to know, and only recalled it when something obliged her to remember. Tonight, she told herself, tonight I really will talk to her. We'll have a nice cosy meal and everything will get sorted out.

At seven o'clock she was just starting to work on preparations for the cosy meal, when the buzzer went. Matthew, she supposed. Unlike last night, he couldn't let himself in because he had forgotten his keys; she had noticed them on the table earlier. Well, if he planned to go out and get stoned tonight, he was welcome to do it. Olivia wanted Georgie to herself.

It was Matthew, but he was not alone. When he came up he had Luke with him.

'I thought you two weren't on speaking terms.'

'I'm not one to hold a grudge,' Matthew announced airily. 'Where's Georgie?'

'In the bath.'

'Well, Luke here wants a word with her. I'm not staying, I just came back to get my keys.'

'They're on the table,' Olivia told him. 'Can you be a little quieter when you come in tonight?'

Matthew said to Luke, 'Isn't she wonderful? I always wanted two mothers.'

He collected his keys and went out. Definitely avoiding me, Olivia thought. Luke remained, hovering by the door, eyeing her uneasily.

Maybe it was the way she was looking at him that made him uneasy. She was wondering whether it might not be easier to tell Luke rather than Georgie. She decided not. Telling Georgie would be awkward and embarrassing, but telling Luke might be downright dangerous, given his attitude towards Nick and his propensity for expressing himself physically. There was no guessing how he might react to the news that before he himself had even been born, his father had deprived him of the possibility of legitimately loving Georgie.

On the other hand, without his father's sins, there would have been no Georgie at all.

Olivia left off staring at Luke, and moved into the kitchen area. 'How good of you to come at a civilized hour. I've found an unbroken night's sleep hard to come by in this country.'

Luke went faintly red. It made him look appealingly vulnerable, quite a trick for someone the size of Luke. He edged towards the kitchen after her. 'Listen I – I'm not such a lunatic as you think.'

'How much of a lunatic are you, then?'

'When I turned up down there . . . I thought you were going to take Georgie back home with you. Matt said that's the way her father was talking.'

'So you thought you'd come round to put the wind up Tom, and make sure we took her home with us.'

'All right, I know it was moronic. I just couldn't stand not seeing her.' He mooched around at the far end of the counter, picking up and putting down anything available. 'She says she told you about the baby.'

'How do you feel about that?' This was a tangential, side-by-side conversation, Luke prodding at innocent objects, Olivia briskly denuding innocent vegetables.

'At first I felt like I'd been punched in the gut, if you really want to know. Because I hadn't considered it at all. And then I thought,

351

hey, yeah, why not? Seeing I haven't got a family any more.' He added half to himself, 'It doesn't feel right not to be sort of anchored. Like there's not much point getting out of bed in the morning.'

'A baby would certainly get you out of bed, and not just in the morning,' Olivia told him drily. 'Why did you hit Matty?'

Luke went distinctly red. Not so much vulnerable as definitely needing someone to look after him. The combination of this unlikely insecurity with the natural physical confidence of a tall, athletic, good-looking young man, made him doubly attractive, and inevitably irresistible to a girl like Georgie. Funny that he could look so much like Nick, yet be so different.

Also a great relief, come to think of it.

'He was winding me up,' he mumbled.

'Was Georgie winding you up when you hit her?'

Olivia couldn't tell what colour he was now, because he walked away from her. 'I didn't hit her. I didn't mean . . . I told you, it was an accident. But I didn't hit her, I just gave her a shove.'

Olivia set down the knife and folded her arms, leaning back against the counter. 'What will you do next time she makes you angry?'

'Okay, okay, I deserve that.' He stuck his hands in his pockets, to stop them from waving around or picking things up, and returned to the far end of the kitchen. 'Honestly, Lia, I've never done anything like that before, not to any woman, and I won't ever do it again.' He added in an intense undertone, 'I'm not like *him*, if that's what you're thinking. I really will be good to Georgie.'

He lacked his father's cynicism, at any rate, if he could say something like that with sincerity. Olivia saw very well who would be taking care of whom where Luke and Georgie were concerned. 'What's your father like that you're not like?'

'Well, he's a bloody animal, isn't he? Completely antisocial, no idea how to behave. He does what he wants and everyone else can lump it. He made my mother dance attendance. She was scared of him.'

'Scared of what? Did he hit her?' Olivia paused fractionally. 'Or even give her a shove?'

Luke scowled this time instead of blushing. She had pushed him as far as he was willing to go. 'Look, what the hell do you want me to do? You can't believe how sorry I am about all of that.'

'Did he hit her?' Olivia persisted.

'Not that I ever knew,' Luke admitted, 'though I wouldn't put it past him. No, I think she just never knew what he was going to do or say. She didn't have a clue what was going on in his head. And she was always afraid he might leave her – small loss, I say – on account of all those women forever throwing themselves at him. For their own career reasons, of course.'

'Of course.' But Olivia needed more answers. There was still the mysterious business of how Georgie had ended up in hospital. She spoke sternly, in her best maternal grown-up voice. 'Now listen to me, Luke. If I don't get a proper answer out of you about this, I'll do everything I can to keep you away from Georgie. Everything, do you understand me?'

Everything was quite a lot, and he knew it. He wasn't blushing now. He looked at her coolly, levelly, adult to adult. 'An answer to what?'

'About whatever made you hit . . . sorry, shove her.'

'You want to know why I hit her?'

'No, I want to know why you decided to forget about whatever it was that made you hit her. Either it was a trivial thing, in which case you have a serious problem with your temper, or it was a serious thing, in which case I want to know what made you change your mind about it.'

He was even cooler now. He was really grown-up – meaning he wasn't striking any adolescent poses. She had known from the beginning that he had his father's devastating honesty somewhere in his soul, and now he gave it to her. 'I haven't forgotten about it. It's not a question of forgetting.'

He took a deep breath and made what was for him a long speech. 'When Georgie – when I – you know, when it happened – I was so stunned I didn't know what to do. All these people ran up to her and . . . I don't know what was the matter with me, it was like my head had closed right down. I don't even know what I did for the next twelve hours. I just remember wanting to kill myself, I felt so godalmighty shitty. Well, I was a shit, I know it. I still don't know how I could have done something like that. I ended up at Matty's flat and told him what I'd done, and he talked me into going to the police instead of killing myself.'

Olivia tried to visualize Matthew's ironic detachment confronting a distraught and demented Luke. 'The voice of reason, was he?'

'No, he was mad as hell. He said I'd messed up everything and who the bloody hell did I think I was to treat Georgie like that. I'd never seen him actually – um – emoting before. But he didn't call me a shit, he called me a bloody fool. He said I was letting my father ruin my life, instead of just getting on with it. He said I was throwing Georgie away. Which I had done, hadn't I? Literally. Jesus.'

Luke looked nothing like Matthew, and as he quoted Matthew the resemblance did not grow. But by this time Luke himself looked as Matthew might have wished to, like an angel in the original sense, a messenger from God. He caught Olivia's arm and stared down at her.

'Are you listening to me, Lia? Just so you'll know that's all blown over. He said to me, Make up your pathetic little mind, is it love or hate you want, the past or the future? Are you going to nurse your grudges, or are you going to get a life?'

'How very . . . eloquent of him.' But she thought that maybe the eloquence was Luke's; Matthew wouldn't have put the case in quite those words. 'So what did you decide?'

'Well, I thought . . .' He hesitated, suddenly self-consciously shy. 'I decided I wanted Georgie and the rest didn't matter.'

At that point Olivia heard the bathroom door open.

The left side of Georgie's pink and naked body appeared around the corner. 'Hey, Mama, where did you . . .' She saw Luke and went a much deeper shade of pink, before disappearing altogether. Her disembodied voice floated back to them. 'I'll be right back. Don't go away, Luke.'

Luke wasn't going anywhere. He was rooted to the spot, transfixed by a demi-glimpse of Georgie.

Olivia knew her duty when it stared her in the face. 'Can I fix you a drink, Luke?'

Eventually it sank in, not the words but the fact that she was talking to him. 'What?'

'A drink. Would you like one?'

He would. She went to the hall door and called to Georgie, 'Do you want me to make you a drink?'

'Just apple juice on ice. I'm pregnant, remember.'

'I keep forgetting,' Olivia muttered, mostly to herself. Georgie obviously didn't forget, even for a minute.

The offer of a drink was the thin edge of a wedge that Georgie widened when she reappeared. She hooked her arm through Luke's and asked her mother if Luke could stay for dinner. To which there could be only one polite answer.

Several hours later, Olivia thought perhaps it hadn't been altogether a bad thing. She had lost a chance of telling Georgie the truth about Luke, in return for a chance to find out the truth about Luke for herself. So far she had met him only in extraordinary circumstances, when it would have been charitably said that he was not at his best. But now she could see that his physical resemblance to Nick was a misleading guide to his character. He was rather sweet and slightly unworldly, adjectives which no one would have dreamed of applying to Nick, and he was utterly besotted with Georgie. Olivia couldn't help feeling a secret liking for any young man who was so clearly and deeply appreciative of the many virtues

354

of her beautiful daughter. And by now she was truly persuaded, just as Matthew had told her, that the nearly-fatal argument was history.

I could tell them both now, she thought. I should just say, You can't do this, you're brother and sister. But it was only a fantasy. She hadn't the heart to shatter their tangible happiness when it was displayed right in front of her.

The telephone rang at the end of dinner, as Olivia was going into the kitchen to make coffee. She had just picked it up and said hello when Georgie called, 'I'll have tea, please, Mama. Coffee's supposed to be bad for the baby's chromosomes.'

'Just a moment,' she said to whoever was on the phone, not having caught whatever they had said, on account of Georgie. 'What did you say, Georgie?'

Georgie repeated her instructions about tea and her observation about coffee and chromosomes.

'Tea, okay. Sorry, what did you say?'

That was meant for the telephone, but Georgie thought she had been asked for another repetition of her request. 'Tea, tea, for heaven's sake. Are you deaf?'

'No, not you, I heard you all right. Sorry, I didn't hear you.'

'She's deaf,' Georgie told Luke.

'Shut up, Georgie. No, not you,' to the telephone. 'Hello? Is anyone there?'

Apparently not. The line had gone dead. Olivia replaced the receiver and put her head around the partition wall. 'Thanks for all that. They've hung up on me.'

'They probably thought you were crazy,' Georgie giggled. 'Why didn't you put your hand over the phone when you were talking to me?'

'I was carrying the kettle, I had no spare hand.'

'My mother is a brilliant scholar,' Georgie said to Luke. She was the same becoming shade of pink as when she had emerged from the bath. Not tipsy, because she had had only a small glass of wine. It was Luke who was intoxicating her, making her act like a giddy little girl.

As her mother, Olivia found it very slightly wearing, but she could see that Luke would have disagreed, so she ignored her. Children seemed to think it their privilege to be rude about their parents, possibly in revenge for the way their parents used to talk about them when they were supposedly too young to understand. She boiled the kettle and made tea and coffee and carried them back to the table, and the door bell rang.

'Must be one of our neighbours,' Georgie guessed. 'Or else Matty. The buzzer didn't go.'

Olivia voted for Matthew. But Georgie was wrong both times: it was Nick.

'How did you get up here?' Olivia demanded, too surprised to be polite. 'We didn't hear the buzzer.'

'One of your neighbours opened the door downstairs.' He didn't wait for an invitation at this door either, but walked into the flat, leaving her to shut the door after him. 'You've been feeding the motherless child, I see.'

Georgie and Luke responded to his entrance with a smile and a scowl respectively. He pulled out the untenanted chair at the table and sat down, again without invitation.

'Do take a seat,' Olivia said sarcastically, following him back to the table. 'Some kind soul has been feeding the poor widower, I presume.'

She presumed because he was wearing a dinner jacket. In the old days he had never possessed or worn such a grand item of apparel. He must truly have gone up in the world, or else her mother had semi-civilized him.

She hoped her mother had had a chance to enjoy that. Her mother's egalitarianism had never gone further than a vague desire for everyone to be nice to everyone else; it emphatically had not included any hankering after the abolition of evening dress and the opportunity to wear it. And quite right too. Why should a fondness for dressing up be equated with putting on airs or oppressing the poor?

Nick allowed that he had had dinner. 'I even came back early for it.'

'Came back from where?' Georgie demanded. 'Have you been away?'

'All week.' His pale eyes flickered to his son. 'I don't suppose Luke noticed.'

Luke pretended not to notice that his name had been mentioned. But Georgie wanted more details. 'Where've you been?'

'Morocco.'

'Oh, wonderful. Was it good?'

'It might have been, if I hadn't had to work.'

'You call that work? I'd like to have your job.'

Nick lit up and leaned back. 'Actually, I came to offer you a job.'

'Doing what?'

'Well, I'm buying a flat and I want you to keep the home fires burning when I'm not around. And when I am, of course.'

Georgie looked at Luke and her mother and then at Nick again. 'You're going to pay me to live in your flat?'

'That's the idea.'

356

'What about Luke?'

'I don't give a fuck who sleeps in your bed, sugar, as long as they don't write on the walls or smash up the furniture.'

Georgie peeped at Luke again, at the thunder threatening in his fair face. She turned back to Luke's father. 'Did Mama tell you I'm pregnant?'

Nick blew smoke at his disapproving son, but kept his eyes on Georgie. 'Why d'you think I'm offering you a job?'

'Oh.' Georgie stared back at him. Her cheeks went pink, then pale. Her glance slid sideways, to assess Luke's response to this statement. Luke put his head into his hands and stared at the table. 'That's . . . ah . . .' Georgie struggled for the right word and found it. 'That's very thoughtful of you, Nick.'

Olivia escaped into the kitchen, on the pretext of fetching milk and sugar for the tea and coffee.

The phone rang again as she opened the fridge.

'Hi,' said Tom.

'Oh, hi. Did you call before?'

'I tried a few minutes ago, but it must have been a crossed line. All I could hear was some people bellowing at each other. Is everything okay?'

'Absolutely fine. Georgie's been given the all-clear. How is everything there?'

She listened with half an ear to Tom's lengthy response. The other half of her attention was being distracted by Nick, who had paused at the entrance to the kitchen, on his way back from the bathroom.

She deliberately turned away from him and murmured Uh-huh, yeah, at appropriate points in Tom's report of events at his clinic.

Nick came up behind her. Someone had given him a very good dinner indeed. She could smell his wine-and-whisky breath as well as his cigarette. The hair at the nape of her neck was prickling. Or maybe it was her thumbs.

He kissed the side of her neck, the right side that didn't have the protection of the telephone receiver. Bit it, actually. Ditto her ear lobe. She had to bite her own lip to keep from making a sound. He unbuttoned the top of her blouse and did the same thing to the exposed shoulder. Then he pushed her bra strap down and freed her breast from its protection. All this with a cigarette jammed between his fingers. Olivia didn't dare to resist either verbally or physically, for fear that Tom would hear, or Georgie and Luke would overhear, or that in any struggle, something – most likely her clothing – might catch fire.

The presence of the cigarette didn't prevent his hand from doing some quite breathtaking things to her bare breast, things that in other circumstances would have made her want to hang up the phone and remove the rest of her clothing. With Tom chattering earnestly into her left ear, and Nick whispering obscene proposals into her right ear, and the danger of Georgie and Luke in the very next room, she was torn between squirming and screaming.

'Just a minute, Tom.' She put her right hand over the phone and held it well away from her. 'Stop it,' she hissed at Nick. 'I'm trying to talk to Tom.'

'I know that, kitten.'

Well, of course. That was what it was all about. She hauled his head down to speak right into his ear: 'Go away, Nick, I'll talk to you later. Go back and entertain Georgie.'

She didn't know what sort of euphemism he took *talk to you* to mean, but at least it persuaded him to go away. She restored her clothing to respectability and put the phone back to her ear.

'Lia, are you there?'

'Yes. Sorry. I was trying to do two things at once.'

'You sound out of breath.'

'I'm okay. Is Alex there?'

'He's just come in. Is Georgie there?'

By the time she had spoken to Alex, and Tom had reassured himself first-hand that Georgie was alive and well, Olivia had dampened down the improper desires that Nick had so abruptly aroused in her by his outrageous assault. The whole episode made her furious, his behaviour and her response to it, especially since the outrage and the assault were directed at Tom rather than her. She was only the territory being fought over, and Tom didn't even know he was involved in a fight.

Olivia returned to the table, recalled why she had gone into the kitchen in the first place, went back to the kitchen to fetch the milk and sugar, and finally got to sit down and pour herself a cup of tea. She felt quite shattered.

Georgie wasn't going to let her rest. 'Have you got time to go and see this flat with me tomorrow?'

'I suppose so. Is Luke coming?' The more the merrier, Olivia thought, after her previous experience of flat-hunting with Nick.

Georgie glanced enquiringly at Luke, who shrugged. 'Yeah, he is,' she translated. 'We can do our shopping in the morning, and go around there after lunch. Is that okay?'

Olivia said that it was, though it wasn't at all. She didn't want Georgie staying in England or living with Luke or having his baby, and she didn't want to see Nick again. She hadn't forgiven him for the goings-on in the kitchen, and he hadn't yet kept his promise to speak to Georgie about Luke. Worse than that: he was giving them a place to live. He was encouraging them.

So she did, come to think of it, want to see him tomorrow, in order to tell him not to do it. He would do exactly what he wanted anyway, of course, but she had an obligation to tell him.

Luke went home with his father, not at all pleased to be doing it, but conceding to common sense and practicality when Olivia threw them both out at midnight. After that, for a change, she slept undisturbed until morning.

37

What must I do to be saved?

'How's that, then, love? Do we like it?'

Love didn't know. She stared at her new self in the mirror, trying to square it with her old self-image. The new Olivia looked glamorous, fashionable, confident – how could a haircut make you look confident? – while the old Olivia wondered how she was going to confront the world in what seemed to her essentially a lying guise. For twenty-five years she had worn her hair long, for fifteen years had tucked it into a knot at the nape of her neck. Not really a hairstyle in any meaningful sense of the word. She felt naked without all that hair, even though she had only let it down when she went to bed at night.

But the hair-do did look good, no question, and that was really what the chatty little man wanted to know. So she meekly said it looked very nice.

The man who had done all the work didn't seem to be dismayed by her lack of enthusiasm. Maybe he was used to dumbfounded clients, or maybe they were all blasé about his miracles because they had got used to looking like that.

Olivia thanked him politely and wandered off, still dazed, to find Nick. It was Nick who had arranged and paid for her transformation at the hands of the trendiest and most expensive hair-stylist in London. Which meant possibly in the whole world.

A surprise, he had said.

She had good reason to be wary of his surprises. In the past they had usually been arranged at least as much for his benefit as for hers. But he had told her this was something she could take home,

359

which automatically excluded everything that had first sprung to her mind.

A couple of hours ago, Olivia had been dutifully inspecting the flat in South Kensington in which Georgie had been invited to live. And a very nice place it was too: at least twice as nice and twice the price of the first one she had seen, Olivia reckoned. She wondered what had prompted Nick to move the scale of his generosity so sharply upmarket.

Georgie seemed a little stunned, if not actually intimidated. She wandered through the flat in a vague daze, admiring everything aloud: the big bright rooms, the floor-to-ceiling windows, the well-designed kitchen, the period details of decoration. 'And there's a park. Look, Luke, right in the middle of the square. I can take the baby there.'

Luke for his own reasons refused to admire anything. 'Oh, a park, bloody good,' he muttered. Georgie gave him a wary, rather nervous glance which her mother caught. Was she afraid of his temper, Olivia wondered? He had certainly given her grounds for that.

'Residents only,' the agent pointed out. Unlike the last agent, this one mostly spoke only when spoken to, having perhaps grasped the principle that sales patter never sold a property. 'The park gates are kept locked. Every house or flat in the square comes with a key.'

Georgie was in a mood to marvel even at this. 'What a great idea. I guess it keeps out the vandals and muggers.' She gave Luke a nudge. 'Hey, don't you like the idea of a private park?'

'Smashing,' Luke said gloomily.

Olivia shared his lack of enthusiasm, though presumably from different motives. She imagined that Luke resented having to accept his father's charity, and also, perversely, the fact that he was a beneficiary only by proxy, since Nick had pointedly made his offer to Georgie rather than Luke. Maybe he had done it that way because he thought Luke might feel obliged to refuse, or because it had been Georgie's idea in the first place.

Olivia's own unease rose partly from disapproval of Nick's deliberately abetting that relationship. The other part was just plain mistrust of his generosity. When Georgie dragged Luke into the kitchen to show him its wonders, Olivia took the opportunity to have a word with Nick.

'You said you'd talk to Georgie about the baby.'

'Yeah, and I did. I told her she didn't need the baby in order to get the flat.'

'What did she say?'

'She said Luke wants it, and she's in love with Luke. End of story.'

'What about Luke? Did you speak to him?'

'What's the use? He's in love too. With rather more reason, I'd say.'

'What's reason got to do with it?' Olivia brooded on the situation. 'Nick, this is a very expensive flat. Much dearer than the last one we looked at. Why are you being so generous all of a sudden?'

He was amused by her suspicion, she could tell by the look he gave her. 'It's child maintenance, kitten.'

'Child maintenance?'

'Better late than never, wouldn't you say?'

Afterwards, when Olivia was on the brink of returning to the Barbican with Georgie and her morning's purchases, that was when Nick announced he had a surprise for her to take home. So Georgie had gone off with the shopping and Luke, and Olivia went with Nick.

He was waiting now at the door of the salon. He smiled when he saw her, a slowly widening smile which meant he really was pleased.

Olivia stood in front of him, clutching her handbag in both hands like an ill-at-ease schoolgirl. 'Do you like it?'

'You look terrific.'

She suddenly felt terrific. Felt glamorous, fashionable, confident, all the good things that this new appearance implied about her. She felt so good she even let him put his arm around her as they went out into the street.

'I knew he'd do a good job,' Nick was saying. 'He does all my girls.'

Olivia stiffened. 'All your girls?'

'Yeah. You know, the ones I get paid to shoot.'

She tried to pull away. He wouldn't let her, but the attempt amused him. 'Hey, Lia, you're not jealous, are you?'

'I'm not one of your girls,' she said coldly, holding herself rigid within his restraining arm. 'Why are they yours?'

'Because I pick them. I only shoot the ones I like.'

He was still walking, taking her with him, and she went along rather than make a scene. 'Don't your clients want you to use the most famous models?'

'If I shoot them, then they're famous. It works that way round.'

'Is that what the models think?'

'They're not paid to think, even if they had any brains to do it with. They get paid to do what I tell them.'

'How nice for you,' Olivia said sarcastically. 'Where are we going?'

'More surprises.'

361

'But I have to get back to Georgie.'

'She's all right. Luke's looking after her.'

'That's what I'm afraid of.'

'My son isn't good enough for your daughter?'

'*Your* daughter,' she echoed with a different emphasis. But she wasn't going to argue in the street about the undesirability of incest.

And didn't have time to. He steered her into the second surprise. A shop full of beautiful and breathtakingly expensive clothing.

After peeking at a few price tags, Olivia retreated to hover nervously by the door, feeling like a virgin at an orgy. Several people were browsing through the racks. Some of them were actually buying things. Without fainting when the total popped up on the till.

Nick was doing something more organized than browsing. He must have had very firm ideas about what he was looking for, or else he had done some reconnaissance on what was available here, because he was pulling garments off the racks, looking them over and replacing them in a briskly decisive way. Olivia felt sorry for the rejected clothing that had failed in some manner to meet his exacting criteria. Fancy being the designer of such clothing, having to watch your creations dismissed off-hand by a man who made models famous when he turned his camera on them.

He came back to her and bundled half a dozen items into her arms. 'Try these on, why don't you?'

'Don't I get to choose for myself? Don't you trust my taste?'

'No problem with your taste. It's your judgement that's not going to operate here.'

'What's wrong with my judgement?' She glanced at the tag on the topmost garment. It was a blouse, and about five times as expensive as any blouse she had ever bought in her life. 'Nick, you're not allowed to spend that kind of money on me. I would never spend it on myself.'

'That's what's wrong with your judgement,' he said drily. 'That, and the way you think you ought to look. Just go and try them on and look at yourself.'

'Don't you want to see them too?'

'That's up to you, kitten.' He gave her a push towards the dressing-room. 'Now get in there, for Christ's sake.'

She went in, if only to postpone the inevitable argument. The simplest way to avoid a scene might be to pay for them herself.

Tom would go berserk. She wasn't even going to have the nerve to tell him how much her haircut had cost, let alone who had paid for it – or why. Which was worse, to be a spendthrift wife or a whore?

To Olivia's surprise, the clothes Nick had chosen were not the sort of pointless frippery he must have to spend most of his time photographing. They were simple but sophisticated, plain and glamorous, just like her new hair-style. A skirt and a blouse, a jacket, another blouse (more of a shirt) with a pair of trousers, a dress for casual wear and a little black number for evenings out. Designed for everyday life – if one had the nerve to put on hundreds and hundreds of pounds' worth of clothing just to go out and do everyday things. On the other hand . . . she could hardly imagine a greater luxury.

Everything fitted her beautifully. He hadn't even had to ask her size. The colours were attractive in themselves and becoming to her. They didn't make her look trendy or overdressed, or – as she had secretly, perhaps absurdly, feared – as if she had got herself up in someone else's clothing. Her other fear had been of mutton dressed as lamb. Most high-fashion clothing was aimed at young women, whereas she was nearly forty, about to become a grandmother. But the clothes Nick had chosen just made her look, well, really good.

The way she remembered her mother looking.

Her mother had always had an innate sense of style, and taken pleasure in dressing well, but it was only her marriage to Nick that had allowed her the financial freedom to indulge her taste for good taste. Unlike Olivia's father, Nick had never seemed to mind the money her mother spent on clothes. He liked her to look good, she used to tell Olivia with incredulous pride. Olivia reckoned she herself would have to turn out naked in order to get Tom to notice what she was wearing – or not wearing, as the case might be.

She put her own skirt and blouse back on, and emerged from the dressing-room with a fortune in her arms.

'Well?'

'They look great. They fit perfectly. You have unimpeachable taste.' She began to hang them back on the nearest rack.

He retrieved each garment from the rail as soon as she had replaced it, and deposited the lot in a heap on the counter by the cash register.

Olivia dithered. Should she try to snatch them back? Stick her credit card in first?

The girl at the till looked like a model herself, that unmistakable and unearthly breed of supremely self-conscious creatures, constructed and made up to resemble ordinary women as little as possible. 'Will that be all, sir?'

'Isn't that enough?'

He smiled encouragingly. The girl smiled back at him, and suddenly looked very young. Maybe she would like to be a real model.

Did she know that the man she was smiling at could make her famous, if he took a fancy to her face? She could become one of his girls.

Olivia was appalled by how angry that thought made her. Nick could throw away his money if he wanted, but she wasn't going to accept the clothes. Let him find someone else to wear them. They wouldn't fit any of his girls at any rate, skinny little wraiths that they were.

She took her busty, hippy, thirty-seven-year-old body out of the shop.

In Sloane Street she had to pause for a moment to work out which way went towards the nearest tube station. After eighteen years' absence her sense of direction in London was a bit rusty. Eventually she decided to go right, towards Knightsbridge.

As it happened, it didn't really matter which direction she chose, because she soon discovered that she wasn't going to get anywhere. Nick came up behind her and grabbed her arm.

'In a hurry all of a sudden, are we?'

'I didn't see much point in hanging around.' She tried to shake off his hand on her elbow, but of course she needn't have bothered. She did keep walking, though. 'I've got to get back to the Barbican.'

'Georgie said you're going home on Sunday.'

'That's right. So what?'

'So what if you didn't go?'

'I've got to. I'm already late getting back. I have to start teaching next Tuesday.'

Nick stopped moving. Since he was still holding her arm in an unshakeable grip, Olivia was obliged to stop too. 'You don't have to do that shit. You can chuck the lot if you want.'

'Don't be silly, it's my job,' she snapped, pushing an impatient hand through her new hair. 'Some of us have to do real work for a living, not just flying off to New York or Morocco for a few days' photography.'

'Fuck Morocco,' he said roughly. 'I'll take you anywhere you fancy.'

His face shifted out of focus for a moment. Or maybe it was something inside her that had shifted. She pushed at her hair again, this time with tentative fingertips, as if she wasn't sure it was there, or if she had the right to touch it. 'What are you talking about?'

The impatience was on his side now. 'What d'you think? I don't want you to go back.'

'I've got to,' she repeated, reminding herself. 'I have a job there. My son's there. My husband. Everything.'

'Not bloody everything. Georgie's over here. Your son's already seventeen. Your doctor doesn't even know how to fuck you.'

'Stop that,' Olivia hissed, throwing an embarrassed glance at two old ladies approaching. 'Anyway, there's more to life than sex.'

'Maybe, but it's way ahead of whatever's in second place.'

'That should be money,' she corrected automatically.

'Yeah, okay, sex first, money second, that sounds about right to me. Listen, Lia, I'll give you whatever you want.' To make it clear that he didn't just mean material or physical desires, he added, 'You name it, I'll do it for you.'

He took her by the shoulders as he said it. Trying to bully her and bribe her at once, she thought. She knew him far too well. Whatever he was offering her, it wasn't what it seemed. 'I don't want anything from you. And you have no right to give me anything. You never had a right.'

'Why not?'

'Because you married my mother. And now I'm married to Tom. You're right out of luck, Nick.'

That seemed a good line on which to exit. She pulled free, or he let her go. She dodged past him, heading, she hoped, for the tube station.

But Nick hadn't let her go after all. He was right behind her. Talking to her.

'What d'you mean, you don't want anything from me? You were begging for it in that taxi. You went down on your hands and knees for it the time before. How about putting your life where your cunt is, you hypocritical little bitch?'

He wasn't exactly yelling, but he hadn't bothered to lower his voice or soften his vehemence, even though the pavement was quite crowded. She saw passers-by with shocked faces, eyes averted in English embarrassment or staring with open amusement. There was no use running, he would just keep on after her. She knew him too dreadfully well. She was mortified, but he didn't know the meaning of shame.

She turned to confront him, nearly in tears. And saw that he thought it was funny, having humiliated her like that. Just the sort of gallant, sensitive gentleman every woman dreams of running off with.

'I'm only doing what you did, aren't I?' She went up close to him, speaking as softly as the intensity of her feelings would allow. 'You opted for the safe respectable life. You married my mother. You thought you could have your cake and eat it too, and now you've got nothing. The choice was yours and you made it, and you can't go back and change your mind about everything, just because you don't like the consequences twenty years down the line.'

Nick manoeuvred her out of the flow of shoppers, into the shelter of a doorway. The gawkers had moved on, to Olivia's relief. 'That's all fucking history,' he said impatiently. 'And it's no reason to make the same mistake twice.'

She stared at him stonily, in no danger of crying now. 'Not my mistake. Yours.'

'This time it'll be yours.' He put his hands on her arms, to shake her or caress her, or maybe just to add force to his argument. 'Anyway, you were too young before.'

'Don't make excuses. You could have waited.' She pulled away from him. He dropped his hands. 'Nick, you know perfectly well I can't go anywhere with you. I can't just step on everyone else. You didn't do it and I won't either.'

He didn't look terribly broken-hearted, which made her feel a tiny niggle of disappointment. 'Okay, kitten, we'll scrap Morocco and New York. How about a drink at my house instead? It's only five minutes from here, your family won't have time to miss you.'

The house where he had lived with her mother. She was curious, if nothing else. 'Just a cup of tea, then. I've got to get back to Georgie.'

It all seemed remarkably grand when she got there, especially when she recalled the house in West Hampstead-cum-Cricklewood-by-Kilburn where she had lived all her childhood, where her mother and Nick had still been living when she left England. It must have given her mother great pleasure to decorate and furnish a beautiful Georgian town house. Nick wouldn't have minded spending money on that either. He liked things to look good.

The paintings and drawings on the walls were obviously his taste, not her mother's. The paintings were abstract, the drawings spare and dry. They reminded her of . . .

'Do you still do real photography? I mean . . .' She paused to rephrase that while he watched, plainly not offended but enjoying her discomfiture. 'You used to do subjects that interested you, just for your own satisfaction. Pictures with no people in them.' She remembered those photographs, of real objects obviously, but as abstract in effect as the paintings he had chosen to decorate this house.

'No people?' he echoed sardonically. 'That sounds too good to be true. Life would be perfect if it weren't for other people. But no, I

366

don't bother to keep up pretensions any more. Luke keeps telling me that photography isn't art, so there didn't seem much point. Photography posing as art doesn't make much money.'

'Surely you're already making enough money to be able to afford to do what you want.'

'Lia, are *you* telling *me* that money can buy what I want?'

She turned away, discomfited again. He was so good at throwing her off-balance. She wandered through the doorway into the hall. 'Is it okay if I explore?'

'Be my guest. That's what you came for, isn't it?'

He followed her, as she moved from room to room. Each one was exquisitely decorated and furnished; it looked like a house in a magazine, not a place where anyone actually lived. And in a sense no one did live here now. Her mother was dead, her mother's husband and son already departed in spirit and intention.

'Did you say you'd sold it?'

'Some Armenian offered a million, so I thought I'd take him up on it.'

Olivia stared. 'A million pounds?'

Nick smiled. 'You want to change your mind about Morocco?'

She shook her head irritably. 'What are you going to do with the furniture?'

'Georgie can take some of it for the flat, if she wants, and flog the rest for me.'

'What about Luke? Doesn't he get a say in all this? It was his home, after all.'

Nick shrugged. 'If he wants a say, he'll have to talk to me about it. At the moment he's not talking to me about anything.'

'I expect that's because every time he opens his mouth you sneer at him.'

'Every time he opens his mouth, he's denouncing me for some crime against humanity, meaning himself and Em.'

Olivia felt like shaking him, but she knew that if she lost patience with him, he would refuse to hear what she was saying. 'Nick, listen to me. You lost your daughter because you were too pig-headed to say sorry. Are you going to lose your son the same way?'

He stared at her for a long time. She had never been able to guess what he was thinking behind those pale blue eyes. Never been sure what he really thought about anything. Not even herself.

He reached over her shoulder to stub out his cigarette in the ashtray on the mantelpiece behind her. He was concentrating on that, not looking at her, when he said it. 'Sorry.'

'Tell it to Luke, not to me.'

'Luke can work it out for himself, if he's half as smart as he thinks he is. You're the one who doesn't seem to understand anything if I don't spell it out in four-letter words.'

'There are five letters in sorry.'

'That wasn't the word I had in mind.' He gave her an assessing sort of look. 'If I said I was sorry about Georgie, would you stay with me? I mean, go with me?'

Olivia didn't give herself a chance to even think about that. 'I wouldn't believe you. I think you'd say anything to get what you want.'

He showed no sign of taking offence. 'Maybe you're right, maybe I would. But that doesn't mean I don't want to take it all back anyway, for other reasons.'

'Take all what back? What else have you got on your conscience?'

'How do I know what the hell is going to get up your nose?' Nick growled. 'All I can say is, maybe I did some things you wouldn't like, and I wouldn't have done them if I'd known.'

'Known what?'

He shrugged. 'Known you were coming back, I suppose. I might even have been faithful to Em, if that would've made you happy.'

Olivia said coldly, 'Was it such a chore to be faithful to my mother?'

'I didn't mean that. Jesus Christ, Lia, stop twisting my words. Listen, I want to make you understand something.' He took her by the shoulders to confront her. 'I'd never knowingly have done anything, *anything at all*, have you got that? anything that would have driven you away, or kept you from coming back. If I'd known you were coming, I'd never have . . .' He stopped in uncharacteristic confusion.

Olivia was definitely intrigued by now. This was the first time she had ever seen him show any sign of something like real regret. But people could be sorry for all sorts of reasons: sorry for the consequences rather than the sin itself. 'What's got under your skin, Nick?'

'Nothing.'

That was proved untrue by the way he said it, irritably, glancing aside. He leaned his arm on the mantel shelf, looking as sulky as Luke.

She said, 'You seem to be wanting me to absolve you for unspecified offences. To sign a blank cheque, in other words.'

He did look at her then, with a hint of amusement. 'So what? Georgie tells me that's what love means. And it's all your fault anyway. I wouldn't have done any of those things if you'd been around.'

What things? There was no point even asking. 'Don't you go

blaming your bad behaviour on me. Do you mean to say that Georgie has been lecturing you about love?'

'Explaining my paternal responsibilities towards Luke.' His tone had flattened. 'Apparently I'm a total fucking failure as a human being.'

'I'd say that was about right. Though I don't imagine she put it quite like that.'

'No, no, of course not. You brought her up to be a lady like yourself, didn't you?' He added in a warmer voice, 'It gave me the hell of a shock when she first walked into this room. Like seeing a ghost.'

'Mummy, you mean?'

'No, you. She does so many things just like you. Gestures and mannerisms. It really made me feel . . .' He trailed off with a shrug.

Olivia was totally taken aback to hear him speak of love in any context whatsoever. He had used to regard it as a nonsense or a mere obscenity. Was it because of Georgie that he had apparently added it to his vocabulary?

She had been so obsessed, even now, with what had happened long ago between him and Georgie, that she had given very little consideration to what sort of relationship they might have developed this time round. She didn't know what Georgie thought of Nick, much less what Nick thought of Georgie. It wasn't the sort of question she could get answered for the asking.

Maybe Georgie coming back had changed him somehow. He must have changed at least a little, to have uttered those two forbidden words, *sorry* and the other one.

He had turned away from her, perhaps contemplating his failure as a human being. No, he was lighting a cigarette.

'Nick?'

'Yeah?'

'That four-letter word you had in mind,' she said rather breathlessly. 'It wasn't love, was it?'

He looked at her a long moment, expressionless. 'Does your doctor love you?'

'Yes. Of course.'

'Then that wasn't the word.'

'You mean you don't love me?'

'Not if that's what it means.'

Olivia was indignant on Tom's behalf. 'What's wrong with the way he loves me? He married me. *Me*, not my mother. He's been faithful to me. He's a good father to Georgie. He's a proper human being.'

'Another bleeding saint,' Nick said drily. 'But Jesus, Lia, if you were married to me I'd bloody well know if some other bugger was

369

knocking you off. I'd know if you were even looking around. How can you say he loves you, if he can't even tell when another man's prick has been up your cunt? Christ, if you were my wife I'd keep you too sore to have time for anyone else.'

Olivia was dismayed to discover what a thrill that idea gave her. She wondered briefly if it was intended to be some sort of sideways Nick-like proposal of marriage. 'But you wouldn't be faithful.'

'Why not?'

He said it blankly, naïvely, as if it went without saying. That made her furious. 'How can you stand there and say that? I don't believe you've ever been faithful to anyone longer than it took you to find the next lay. You were unfaithful to my mother long before you'd married her.'

'Just with you.'

'And that doesn't count? Anyway, I don't want to be one of two. I want to be the only.'

'Well, I might be able to cope with that, seeing it's you.'

She looked at him with suspicion, trying to guess how serious he might be. 'You don't sound too sure.'

'I've never tried it before.' He returned her look with amusement. 'D'you want to have a look upstairs?'

The stairs was as far as they got. He kissed her on the bottom stair, unfastened her blouse and bra over the next few steps, paused half-way up to devote his whole attention to her breasts. In the process of having her knickers removed she ended up sprawled just below the hall landing, naked to the waist, knees drawn up, skirt out of sight, thighs wide apart, while Nick knelt a couple of steps further down with his head between her legs – or as he chose to put it, with his face in her cunt.

When he raised his head to kiss her, she could taste her own body, salt and must, in his mouth. He stroked her between her legs, then caressed her breasts, her thighs, her back, with sticky fingers, till she smelt and felt of her own desire all over. It was grossly physical, like some beastly mating ritual which repels the human onlooker but works like sexual magic on the animals involved. A sow, for instance, doing the swinish equivalent of spreading her legs when the boar drools on her. Nick was unquestionably a species all of his own – the rarest in the world, and a good thing too – but Olivia must have been the female of it, because everything he did to her was unendurably exciting.

He brought his mouth back to her crotch, focusing her frenzy, bringing it to a peak. She came with a carnal intensity that left no space or breath for the higher functions of the heart.

Not love, he had said. Maybe this was what he meant. Whatever this meant.

Without giving her time to catch her breath he unzipped the front of his trousers. A surreal sight, Olivia thought: a man immaculately dressed in a suit and tie – well, he had loosened the collar and tie – anyway, fully and formally dressed, with a stiff naked cock. 'Here, come on,' he said urgently, 'get down here.'

There's no creature on earth less sentimental than a man with an erection, she thought. This time she went down below him, between his thighs, and used her mouth and hands on him. But he had a different idea of what he wanted, and made it clear.

What he wanted was to use her cleavage to rub his cock. She had never tried that before, but it seemed to work when he squeezed her breasts together. It must have been exciting for him, because he climaxed very quickly.

Maybe it was the thought of the consequences that had excited him most: semen splashed all over her throat and breasts, spattered in her face and her new hair-do. Her eyelashes, even. Not so much a boar as a porcupine.

Olivia was amazed, amused, appalled. Instinctively she put her hands to her bosom, and brought them away slick and slimy. 'You've got it on my skirt! How am I going to explain semen stains to Georgie when I get back?'

'They come out in the wash.' He didn't sound terribly concerned. What he did sound was shattered and satisfied. 'Christ, Lia, I always said you had fabulous tits. Hey, where are you going?'

'To clean myself up.' She paused only to step out of her skirt, to prevent further damage, before heading up to the bathroom.

'No, don't do that. Come here.'

He caught her as she tried to edge past him. He pulled her down to straddle his thighs. She was naked and sticky all over, and he was still fully clothed. 'Don't Nick, you'll ruin your suit.'

'Fuck the suit.' He began to kiss her all over, using his mouth and tongue to remove the evidence of his pleasure. He must have noticed her eyelashes too, because first of all he kissed her eyes. Then he moved downwards.

It felt good, especially on her breasts, but she didn't say so. 'Nick, that's disgusting.'

'Is it?' He took her nipple between his teeth quite gently and flicked it with the tip of his tongue. 'How about that, is that disgusting?'

'No, that's nice. Do it again.'

He did it again. He put his hands under her bottom and hoisted her up to trace with his tongue the drops that had slid down her belly. She put her hands in his hair and held him while he did it.

'Is it disgusting to suck your pussy?'

She moved her hips in response to the pleasure of his mouth. 'No, no, that's wonderful.'

'How about coming in your mouth?'

'That's okay too.'

He carried on this catechism while arousing her all over again, doing or describing to her various acts that sounded depraved in theory but which she had either enjoyed with him or was responding to right now. When her responses had disarticulated into murmurs and moans, he changed the form of the question: did she want him to . . .

She was too sunk in swinish or porcupinish pleasure by now to argue with whatever he wanted to do. She just wanted him, in any way at all. She took off his clothes, as far as she could reach.

'Come on to bed, baby,' he said in his husky voice.

By the time they had stumbled the short distance across the hall to the bedroom and the bed, she had managed to remove all the rest of his clothing. They made love to each other, exhaustively, comprehensively, neglecting no orifice or potential erogenous zone, however theoretically off-putting Olivia might once have thought it. Nothing about his body, or her own, disgusted her now; nothing he did to her repelled her. She loved him, all of him, whatever he was or did. Loved him in that primitive, point-blank, non-negotiable, soul-devouring way that fuels half the misery and three-quarters of the happiness in the world.

In the end she said it, and so did he. I love you.

And after all that, they did something they had never done before. They fell asleep together on the bed.

38

Cannot my taste discern perverse things?

'Mama, where on earth did you get to? We'd just about given up on you.'

Georgie, calling from the kitchen, sounded more curious than indignant. It was only bad conscience that made Olivia feel like a cat creeping home at daybreak after a night on the tiles. She hoped she didn't look as guilty and furtive as she felt.

'It's eight o'clock, not midnight,' she pointed out defensively. 'Can't I go for a drink without your calling the police?'

'Well, you'd have been worried if it was me.' Georgie emerged from the kitchen, stared at her mother and flung up her hands in exaggerated amazement. 'What have you done to your hair?'

'I've had it cut.' Olivia felt even more defensive. The cut was all that remained of the world's most expensive cut-and-blow-dry; she had had to wash Nick out of her hair before coming back to the flat. This blow-dry job was Nick's own amateur effort, and not bad at that. 'Don't you like it?'

'I love it.' Georgie walked around her, inspecting from all angles. 'I can't believe you're my boring old mother. You look like some glamorous celebrity. Luke, come and see this gorgeous stranger.'

Luke. Of course. He was the other half of the 'we' that had supposedly just about given up on Olivia's coming home. He followed Georgie out of the kitchen and smiled broadly when he saw Olivia. 'You do look great. You look like Georgie's sister, not her mother.'

He looked great too, Olivia thought. She had never seen him look so genuinely, almost naïvely pleased. The smile gave him an ingenuous charm that suited his appearance as a post-adolescent angel. A darker afterthought suggested the likely reason he was feeling so much more pleased with the world. This was the first time he had been completely alone with Georgie since the day he had so nearly killed her. Olivia didn't need more than one guess as to how Nick's son would have spent that time. Probably the same way as Luke's father had done.

'Your stuff arrived,' Georgie was saying. 'I was very good and didn't peek.'

'What stuff?'

'It's in the bedroom.'

Olivia followed her into the bedroom. The bed was littered with boxes and bags, all bearing the name of the shop Nick had taken her into. She had assumed, when he came after her so quickly, that he had abandoned the transaction, but no such luck.

'Aren't you going to model them for us? Luke says this is a top-class emporium. He says everyone who's anyone goes there. Apparently the owner is a friend of Nick's.' Georgie started to unbundle the packages. 'Hey, this is amazing. You must have spent a fortune. You never go shopping like this at home.'

'I never have time,' Olivia entered her automatic plea. It was true, but not the whole truth. For so long she had had neither an interest in displaying herself, nor any confidence in her own beauty. Georgie must have grown up thinking her mother a frump. Olivia would have had to agree with her.

'You never have time for yourself,' Georgie remarked. 'You should take some time. Alex and I are grown up now, you can't use us as an excuse any more. And you've got your Ph.D., so that pressure's gone as well. Why shouldn't you spend some time and money on yourself, eh?'

She was chattering, not lecturing, laying out the clothes on the bed while she chattered. 'Luke and I are going to get on with the dinner now. Why don't you put on a fashion show to entertain us while we're slaving away in the kitchen? Oh, I love this blouse. You wouldn't like to leave it behind when you go back, would you? I'd give it a good home.'

'You can have it.'

Georgie stared at her. 'Do you really mean that?'

'Why shouldn't I mean it?'

'Well, you know. It's a lot of money.'

'Not my money. This was all Nick's idea.'

Georgie looked at the clothes again, then at her mother. 'Well, good for him. I think it was a brilliant idea. You've never had anything this nice before. Anyway, I was only joking about keeping it,' she added heroically. 'You put it on, and come out and show us.'

When Georgie had gone out and shut the door, Olivia sat down among the clothes on the bed. She would have given them all to Georgie, if they, or she, had been the right size. They were a beautiful, expensive, carefully considered bribe.

The message that came with them was nothing so crude as Stick with me, baby, and this is the life you'll lead, nothing but the best that money can buy. It did say that, of course, but that was only part of what Nick had meant to convey. He also wanted that shopping trip to say something like this: Although I am a busy man, I am taking all this time and trouble to please you. I know you are a beautiful woman and I want everyone else to know it too. I am not a crude boor, I have taste and sensitivity (at least when I feel like going to the trouble). I appreciate you in ways that your boring husband does not.

Did it also mean Sorry? Or maybe even I love you?

Those were not the only messages his actions had communicated to her that afternoon. When she stripped to put on the new clothes for Georgie, she was acutely aware of what else Nick had done. She felt sumptuously tender all over; there didn't seem to be a square inch of her body that he had not paid some particular erotic attention to. Before leaving his house she had shared the shower with him, not the sort of brisk scrub-up she underwent each morning but a long-

374

drawn-out affair, demonstrating, among other things, the sensual possibilities of soap on skin, and the use of the shower spray as a sex aid. Thinking about it now made her feel beautiful and sexy and desirable all over again, remembering the things he had said and persuaded her to believe, in despite of her own eyes and the bathroom scales. Even, for about half an hour, that he loved her.

Well, she wasn't going to ruin her life for the sake of a first-class fuck. Not to mention the lives of her entire family. She grabbed the little black bribal dress and pulled it on and went out to show Georgie and Luke.

They were engaged in the time-honoured practice of snogging in the kitchen, but they broke off and politely pretended interest in Olivia's clothes. On her second entrance they were more prepared and less distracted.

'I do love that blouse,' Georgie sighed. 'If you weren't going back to Toronto I could at least borrow it from time to time.'

'So you could if you were coming home with me,' Olivia pointed out.

'Well, I won't fit anything in a few months' time anyway.'

'My mother had a dressing-room full of this sort of stuff,' Luke remarked suddenly. 'Fashionable but not relentlessly trendy. Some of it might have done for you, Georgie. Only it's too late now.'

That was the first time Olivia had heard him mention her mother in the way of casual conversation. 'What happened to her clothes? She used to have just about the most extensive wardrobe I've ever seen.'

'Well, it didn't get any smaller after you left. But my father gave the whole lot to Oxfam. First and last act of charity he's ever performed in his life. Still, they must have made a fortune flogging it.'

'It was the shoes that really got up my father's nose,' Olivia recalled. 'I suppose he noticed them most. I remember a really colossal row they had once, when he opened the door of the wardrobe and elaborately counted all her shoes. Twenty-two pairs she had. He said it was sinful and frivolous for any woman to have twenty-two pairs of shoes when other people were obliged to go barefoot.'

She remembered the rest of the argument. Her mother had said that nobody went barefoot in this country in this day and age, and anyway shoes were her only luxury. Her father had said she had shoes that had only been worn once or twice, which was decadent however you looked at it, he said, and it wasn't a question of luxury but of vanity. That was probably true, because Olivia's mother's feet had been small for her height and slender like the rest of her body, and they had looked wonderfully neat and elegant in a smart pair of shoes.

Olivia remembered other times. Her mother taking a brand new suit to the cleaners, so as to pretend when she brought it home that it wasn't new at all. Or even hiding a new dress in the back of Olivia's wardrobe, in order to haul it out three months later and claim with some approximation to the truth that she had had it for ages. These subterfuges had probably been unnecessary, since Olivia's father never took any notice of clothes unless something was specifically brought to his attention, usually by her mother wanting him to admire her. It was hiding the bills that had been the really tricky bit.

Olivia was surprised and dismayed to find that even now, twenty-five years after the break-up of her parents' marriage, herself long since married and a mother twice over, she could feel a painful echo of her childish grief and loss. Stronger now, perhaps, because her mother was dead. She must have lost some core of security when her home had broken up. Something somewhere too deep inside her to be rebuilt by anything that happened afterwards.

Luke, whose parents' marriage had been broken by his mother's death, observed sardonically, 'Well, she married the right man the second time round, as far as clothes were concerned. I never heard a bad word between them on the subject of her expanding wardrobe. Or about money, for that matter. I guess in his line of work, it's not a bad idea to have a clothes-horse on your arm when you go out in public. Some of the couturiers he works with would even give her outfits. Free advertising, I suppose.'

Georgie, whose parents had never been married at all, said he made his father sound like every woman's dream husband.

'Now that's giving the game away,' Luke told her. 'Never mind changing nappies and helping with the washing up, what women really want is a man who gives them loads of money to go shopping and doesn't hang about the house. The bread-winner reduced to basics, is that what you're looking for?'

Georgie made a face at him. 'If I were, I wouldn't have picked you, buddy.'

Olivia retreated to the bedroom and changed into a pair of jeans and an old sweater.

On her emergence this time, Georgie had some news for her. 'Guess what? Luke has a commission.'

Olivia glanced at Luke, who looked more embarrassed than elated. 'A commission for what?'

'Someone's hired him to do a mural for their dining-room.'

Olivia offered congratulations to Luke. He seemed to feel he was accepting them under false pretences. 'It's just one of my father's clients. He's obviously twisted their arm.'

'He might have done,' Olivia allowed, 'but you know very well that he'd never have recommended you if he didn't think you'd do a good job.'

'And if you do do a terrific job,' Georgie chipped in, 'all their friends will see it, and maybe want you to do something for them too. Do you know what they have in mind?'

'I've got to go round and see them tomorrow. A sort of site survey.' Luke was determined to make the worst of his good fortune, if only because his father had engineered it. 'They'll probably want something really naff.'

'No chimney pots, you mean,' Georgie said pertly. 'Well, whatever they want, you can't blame them. They're the ones who'll have to look at it. And at any rate it'll give you a chance to actually do some drawing and painting. And you like to draw, Luke, you know you do. That's all you ever did when you came to visit me in hospital.'

'Well, it might be kind of fun,' Luke admitted.

Olivia was amused but not surprised to hear that Georgie had more practical concerns. 'Make sure you really sting them for it. You said Nick said they were loaded. And the more they pay, the more they'll brag about it.'

She had wolf dreams again. A story from the far North, tundra rather than taiga, the bleak barrens where there's no shelter from the freezing wind.

A wolf chasing a caribou. One wolf, not a pack. One caribou, not a herd. Her heart is with the caribou. When the wolves go hunting they leave her behind, physically and empathetically. Perhaps she lacks the ruthlessly practical instincts of a natural predator.

Snow has fallen, or not yet melted. Early spring rather than late autumn, she thinks. The tail end of winter is the leanest time of the year, for caribou and wolves alike.

Wolf trails caribou for miles. Always the wolf keeps the same distance behind her. Always she is aware of its steady relentless presence and intent. They pass through miles of deep snow, in which they both flounder. More miles of light powdery snow, where they go at a slow but steady pace, kept warm by the work of their muscles. She can feel herself flagging, her lungs labouring hard, her heart crashing against her breastbone.

At last she comes to the top of a sheltered southern slope. The snow barely covers the ground here, protected as it is from the north wind. She takes her chance, last chance for escape.

377

Summoning up all her reserves of strength, she pounds down the frozen slope. The wolf comes racing behind her, fresher than her; she had set the pace in the snow, as fast as she could go, and he had only to keep up. Now she's running as fast as she can, and so, at last, is he.

Her fastest is no longer fast enough. Her flagging strength has failed her. A hundred yards and he's upon her.

She falls in the shallow snow, brought down by the force of his leap and the weight of his body. Lethal teeth snap at her throat, at her belly.

She is flooded with warmth rather than pain – the heat of her own heart's blood, maybe, spilling into the snow. An unexpected consequence of dying. She is too astonished at feeling no pain to consider the cause. The wolf is devouring her from the inside out, all the organs in turn: kidneys, liver, lungs, heart. Those organs are vital in death as much as in life; they hold all the hard-come-by but necessary nutrients that all creatures need to live. Even wolves.

Who is the Lord, that I should obey his voice?

The phone rang in the middle of the night.

It's a curse, thought Olivia. I'm doomed never to sleep without an interruption as long as I'm in this country. She stumbled out in the darkness, leaving the light off so as not to disturb Georgie more than was unavoidable.

'Lia, is that you?'

It was Althea's voice, almost unrecognizable. Althea was in tears. Olivia listened in amazement to her stepmother's incoherent tale. 'Lia, you've got to get Matty. They've locked him up.'

'Who?'

'The police. They've just spoken to Ross. Ross is raving, he can't cope. I'm worried about his blood pressure. He's been having trouble with it, you know. Please, Lia, go and get Matty. It's right near you – you know where they put Emma's dippy kid? Oh God, this is terrible.'

'What did they arrest him for?'

'I don't know, Ross won't tell me. He's apoplectic, I tell you, Lia. I'm terrified he'll have a heart attack or a stroke or something. Please, can you just go and get Matty, so I can tell Ross you're sorting everything out? Please, Lia.'

By the sound of it, her father wasn't the only one who couldn't cope, Olivia thought. She herself was still too stupefied by sleep to

378

register much more than annoyance. She would have preferred to leave Matthew to stew overnight in a police cell, but she had a suspicion that Althea would be ringing up regularly until she was satisfied that her son had been rescued from the brutal arm of the law. 'Okay, tell Daddy it's okay. I'll take care of everything at this end.'

Georgie turned on the kitchen light, just as her mother replaced the receiver. 'What's going on?'

'Matty's managed to get himself picked up by the police, I don't know for what. On past performance I'd vote for drunk and disorderly. My father and Althea are having fits. They've both gone all to pieces. They want me to go round and sort it out.'

'I'll come with you.'

'Oh no you won't. You stay here and make some tea, and answer the phone if Althea rings again. I hope Tom never hears about this. A month ago I'd never been inside a police station in my life and now I've had to arrange bail for both of my brothers. Where's the number of that solicitor, the one who's an old mate of Althea's?'

As it turned out, Olivia had only his office number, so she had to ring Althea back to get his home phone. Althea hesitated, torn between saving her son and the embarrassment of a family friend knowing about the episode. She also sounded vaguely miffed that Olivia hadn't already set out on her mercy mission.

In the end Olivia got the number out of her and rang the solicitor, who was of course sound asleep and not best pleased to be wakened. But he rose to his professional duty and promised to do what he could. Olivia was to wait there at the flat until he rang back, which he did with commendable speed, perhaps eager to get back to bed.

'Okay, it's all been fixed up. They'll hold him until you get there.'

'Oh, that's wonderful. Thank you so much.' She added as an afterthought, 'What have they charged him with, by the way?' Some drug offence, she supposed.

'Gross indecency.'

He hung up before she could recover from her surprise enough to ask any more questions. Just as well, she thought.

Georgie had been dozing in an armchair, but she roused herself when the phone rang. She repeated Olivia's own question: 'What's the charge?'

'Nothing that makes any sense to me. I expect we'll hear all about it when I get him back here, if I don't wring his neck on the way.'

Olivia was seriously tempted to do just that, when she saw Matthew. If he had been about to run an Olympic race, one glance would have had him banned. At two o'clock in the morning he looked as if he hadn't slept for forty-eight hours and wasn't likely to come down from whatever chemical cloud he was on for another couple of days.

Olivia hauled him out of the police station and into the waiting taxi. 'Matty, when it comes to keeping people awake at night, you're a worse menace now than you ever were as a baby. What on earth have you been up to?'

He waved a hand airily. 'Gross indecency is the technical term, it seems.'

'What does that mean?'

He gave her a sly look. 'You want anatomical details?'

'No!'

He clucked his tongue. 'Such prudery, in this day and age. Do you expect me to believe you're not familiar with the practice of shoving one's prick down someone else's throat?'

'For that they arrested you?'

'Well, they don't like one doing it in the street. At least,' he added reflectively, 'not when the throat in use belongs to a chap.'

Olivia stared at him. He was unperturbed by her stare. Perhaps he was high enough on whatever it was to be unperturbed by anything, even public sex and arrest for same. 'Why would you do a thing like that?'

'Because I like it. Why shouldn't I do whatever turns me on? I've only got one life, I'd like to live it in the most pleasurable way. Of course you,' he rolled an ironic eye towards her, ' wouldn't dream of doing anything improper merely because it gave you a thrill, would you, Lia? Shagging your mother's hunky blond husband, for instance. You wouldn't ever *ever* do an evil and disgusting thing like that.'

That was the point at which she came closest to strangling him. Instead, when she spoke, it sounded like someone was strangling her. 'Leave me out of it, Matty. I've never been arrested for anything in my life. You should be thinking of what you've done to your parents, with this idiotic stunt. Althea said Daddy was absolutely apoplectic, and she was in tears herself.'

'Oh, I am thinking about that, believe me. It gives me almost as much pleasure as what I was doing when the police so rudely interrupted.'

This time Olivia stared not at Matthew but at the night scene passing on the other side of her. 'You're a pervert, you know, Matty.'

'Don't be so absurdly old-fashioned. Homosex is too common to be a perversion.'

She gave him a cool glance. 'The perversion I had in mind was sadism.'

His dark face split in a grin. 'That's even more common than the other.'

'I wish now I'd turned you in this morning.'

'What for?'

'That stash of illegal substances I found in the loo.'

'Oh, that. I did wonder what happened to that. To spare your regrets, I should point out that there's absolutely no evidence the tooth fairy didn't put it there. Also that those substances aren't necessarily illegal.'

'So just because legislation can't keep up with all these designer drugs, you think it's okay to flog them to your friends?'

'Why not? They're not addictive. I'm not dealing in, what's that wonderful phrase, death, degradation and misery, I'm selling ecstasy. They want it, they buy it, why shouldn't I sell it? We're all consenting adults.'

They had arrived at the Barbican, and Olivia was too tired to argue any more. Or maybe she had run out of arguments. 'Matty, you're so sharp you'll cut yourself one day.'

39

Bless me, even me also, O my father.

Going down to Sussex the next day, Olivia had a depressing feeling that she was functioning as Matthew's bodyguard. If her father had got through the night without suffering the cardiovascular crisis that Althea had feared, he was bound to be in danger of disablement all over again when confronted by the object of his outrage. What with one thing and another, Olivia felt more like killing Matthew than defending him, but when it came down to the wire she had not the heart of a wolf. Her instincts were to protect rather than attack.

She had briefly discussed tactics with Georgie, who was not at all surprised to learn the precise nature of Matthew's offence. 'Oh, I knew about that,' Georgie admitted. 'It really was dumb of him to be so careless, though. I guess it's like any addiction, you have to keep upping the dose to get the same effect.'

They were finally back in bed again, talking quietly after the disruption to their sleep. Matthew had been left to roam the rest of the flat, apparently too hyper to think of sleep. Olivia had given him several cups of tea and advised him to take a hot bath. By the sounds of active plumbing he was taking her advice.

'What exactly is it he's addicted to?' Olivia wanted to know. 'Drugs? Strange men? Bad behaviour?'

Georgie dismissed the drugs hypothesis. 'What he's on is just something to keep you going all night. They say it's better than speed because it's supposed to enhance your sexual response.'

Olivia noted the careful use of the distancing phrase *they say*. There were limits to the frankness of a conversation with one's mother. 'And does it encourage you to go and find some sex to respond to?'

'No, that's a different sort of thing. You know what men are really like: they want it, they have it, they forget it, like eating when they're hungry. I mean, that's what they're like when they don't want someone particular. But women don't like it when men behave like that. For women sex is the beginning, not the end, isn't it? So if a guy feels like some action when he's not in a relationship, he wants it right away and he doesn't want a hassle. Even taking somebody out to dinner is too much trouble for some guys sometimes. So maybe they go to a prostitute, who'll take the cash instead of the dinner, or maybe they go and find another guy, who also doesn't want a hassle.'

Olivia was very glad they were lying in the dark, so that Georgie couldn't see her stupefaction at hearing this casual analysis of male sexuality coming from the lips of her own daughter. Or maybe if they hadn't been in darkness Georgie wouldn't have been saying such things to her. 'How do you know all this?'

'Mama, you can't study anthropology without discussing sexual behaviour. And you don't have to have much experience of men to know that it's true, do you? It sticks out a mile, the way they talk and behave. Biologically, they're programmed to try to impregnate anything that moves. Human culture tries to override that for all sorts of reasons, including biological ones, such as making sure your children survive to reproduce themselves, but I guess some men acculturate more readily than others.'

'Some of them actually grow up, you mean,' Olivia said tartly. But she couldn't really argue with Georgie's assessment of the situation. She had said it herself, hadn't she: *He takes whatever comes along*. 'So you think Matty does this because he can't be bothered to find a girl and take her out to dinner?'

'Well, it's a lot more complicated than that. He does take girls out to dinner or whatever, and also to bed afterwards. But sometimes he just wants to go out and get laid. And he . . .' Georgie hesitated while Olivia waited in the darkness. 'Well, he thinks it's exciting, that's all. And I guess it is exciting, in a funny way, doing something that would horrify the people you know.'

Olivia didn't want to hear any more about that aspect of it. She knew all about horrifying the people you know. Not that she had ever done it deliberately.

They discussed ways and means of dealing with maternal hysteria and paternal fury at Underhill. Georgie's assessment was that Matthew could probably cope with Althea, but that Olivia ought to divert and if possible defuse her father, while Matthew was squaring his mother.

Olivia observed to herself that this strategy neatly absolved Georgie of any responsibilities. But by now she was getting quite used to smoothing things over for all the badly-behaved members of her family – just about everybody, in other words. She could hardly wait to get home to Toronto and have nobody to mediate between but Tom and Alex. 'What do you suggest I say to him?'

'How do I know? He's your father, isn't he?' Georgie yawned noisily and rolled over, and was asleep before Olivia could think of an answer to that.

She still hadn't thought of an answer to her own question by the time they arrived at Glynde station in mid-afternoon. She couldn't even think of an answer to Matthew's late-night defence of his drug dealing. She began to long for the loneliness and moral simplicity of life and death in the sub-arctic forests.

Althea turned up to collect them, looking flustered and unhappy, not at all her usual sleek unflappable self. After the distraction of getting the luggage stowed away, Matthew invited Olivia to sit in the front passenger seat, while he himself got into the back seat with Georgie and continued the conversation the two of them had been having on the train, to do with events in a film which they had both seen but Olivia had not.

Althea visibly steeled herself to do her duty as a hostess. 'You've had your hair cut, Lia. It looks really good. Who did it?'

Olivia had to think for a minute to remember the man's name, but Althea recognized it at once. 'How did you manage that? I heard you had to wait for weeks to get an appointment, and even then be related to a celebrity.'

'Well, I am, I suppose. Nick pulled all the strings for me.'

'Lucky you.' Althea was openly envious. 'Do you think you could get him to do the same for me?'

Olivia wanted to point out that asking someone you had always openly despised to do you a favour was frankly a bit thick. But on the other hand she was Althea's guest for the night, and Althea was her father's wife, and already in a tizz on account of Matthew. 'I don't know.'

'Would you ask him for me?'

The prospect of having her hair snipped by the same scissors that had been applied to so many famous heads seemed to have distracted Althea from her misery over Matthew. Olivia was surprised to find herself sympathizing with her stepmother. The nine years' difference that had provoked so much antagonism twenty years before, had by now dwindled to insignificance. They were both married and mothers and no longer young, separately struggling in similar circumstances. If a haircut was going to improve Althea's spirits, then who was Olivia to deny her? 'Yes, if I can get hold of him before I leave.'

Olivia's father was not so easily deflected. When Olivia and Georgie came into the house, laden with luggage, he forbade Georgie to carry anything anywhere. Georgie protested that she wasn't carrying things on her head, but he collected the bags from both of them and took them all upstairs.

When he came down again, Georgie had discreetly disappeared and Olivia was putting the kettle on for tea.

'Where's that fool Matthew?'

'He came down with us, but then he went off to the supermarket with Althea, to get something she'd forgotten for dinner.' When he looked frosty, Olivia added, 'You'll have to wait your turn to yell at him.'

'You make him sound like a naughty child. He's an adult and he's committed a serious criminal offence.' And a disgusting one as well, his tone of voice clearly said.

Evidently he had decided to yell at her instead, since she was here and Matthew was not. 'Well, he didn't mug or maim anybody, or cook the books, or abscond with someone's savings,' she pointed out coolly, 'so it's not as serious as all that.'

'You're making excuses for him.'

'No, Daddy, I'm not. I'm just putting it into perspective for you.'

'What perspective would that be? The one that says anything goes, as long as no one gets hurt?'

'No, I don't believe that. It sounds all right in principle, but the trouble is that we don't seem to notice when we're hurting someone. Ignorant armies clashing by night.'

'Quite so. I would imagine that's why we have moral rules, not to mention laws. To prevent sexual anarchy, among other things.'

For Matthew's sake Olivia had to say it. Once upon a time her father had been her mother's husband, and Althea had been not his wife but his mistress. 'There are rules against adultery too, Daddy. Laws, even, in some times and places.'

Her father, half turned away from her, went as stiff as stone.

384

When she reached out to touch him, thinking to take the sting out of her words, he drew away just enough to warn her off.

He spoke as stiffly as he stood. 'Do you think it would have been better to have gone on suffering the consequences of a mistake for the rest of my life?'

'When you say *mistake*, Daddy, do you mean me?'

'No – I . . .' He sat down suddenly, quite pale.

Olivia recalled Althea's panic the night before. His blood pressure, Althea had said. Maybe he really was ill. And after all, what was the use of confronting an old man with his old sins? Or even stirring up an old ache in her own heart?

'Are you all right, Daddy?'

'Yes.' He didn't sound completely confident of it. He wiped his face with a shaky hand. 'Lia, do you . . . would you mind pouring me a glass of whisky?'

She poured it and set it on the table in front of him. He did look unwell. But the whisky going down brought a little colour back to his face, even if the hand on the glass still trembled. 'Are you sure you're all right?'

'Yes. Sorry.' He passed his hand over his face again and stared at the empty glass. 'Listen, Lia – I . . .' He paused and swallowed, and looked away. 'This has been terribly hard on Althea, this business with Matthew. What's distressing her most . . .'

When the pause had gone on for some time, Olivia prompted him gently. 'What is it, Daddy?'

'She's afraid that he . . . Lia, do you know, is Matthew *gay*?'

Olivia was shocked to hear her father, always so determinedly liberal, utter that word as he might have said, Is Matthew a pervert? Or even, Does Matthew have Aids? And what about Althea, the cosmopolitan capitalist? Maybe sophistication stopped at your own front door.

But it was neither funny nor cause for jeers. Her father had spoken for once without the defence even of irony. Straight from the heart. And what it revealed was not a homophobic hypocrite but a man aware of his own mortality, who loved his only son and wanted him to be happy, in the only way he himself understood human happiness; a normal man, a married man, who looked to his family for the invisible support of his soul. Olivia knew all about men like that. Most of the men in the world. Maybe even including the ones who didn't acculturate readily.

She tried to imagine how Nick might have reacted, if Luke were the one to be arrested for Matthew's offence. She didn't need to stretch her imagination very far. Any man who relied so heavily upon a macho sexual persona for his own self-image and his confidence to deal with the world, would inevitably feel diminished by his son's shirt-lifting propensities. As appalling as Nick's father's behaviour had been, at least it was safely heterosexual.

Or so . . . the possibility occurred to Olivia for the first time . . . so it had been described. By Nick. She recalled his remark about the knife under the pillow. What if that had been a defence rather than merely a precaution?

Well, at least her father didn't have to deal with baggage like that. Or even worry about Matthew's sexual orientation, according to Georgie. 'I don't think going with a man necessarily means you can't stand women, Daddy, if that's what you're wondering.'

'I wasn't referring to misogyny,' he said stiffly. 'I meant homosexuality.'

Olivia wanted to laugh and hug him at the same time. Tom was right, her father was a bolshie old bastard. 'That's what I meant too. Georgie says he has a girlfriend. She assures me he's entirely normal. She thinks this whole business is just a way to . . .' She searched for a phrase and recalled what she had said of Nick. '*Épater les bourgeois.*'

'Maybe she's right. I hope she's right.' Her father cleared his throat. 'She's a sweet girl, your Georgie.'

Olivia could hardly believe her ears: her father offering an unsolicited compliment. Not that she didn't agree with him. She said as much.

Her father didn't appear to hear her. His thoughts had moved on.

'Lia.'

'Yes, Daddy.'

Her father sat hunched and silent for some time. Brooding before he broached the subject, she realized when he spoke again. 'Why did you never write?'

'I did.'

'One postcard.'

'Well, you never wrote back, did you? And you'd made it very clear you were totally fed up and disillusioned with me when I left. You said you didn't give a damn if I ever came back or not.' She paused, recollecting the scene after so many years. 'A bloody goddamn, you said.'

Her father waved an impatient hand. 'Naturally I was profoundly disappointed to see you throwing away your educational opportunities – for the second time, I might add. I didn't mean I never wanted to see you again.'

'What was I supposed to do, read your mind?' She stared severely at his bowed head, silver-grey now instead of black. Whatever the colour, she couldn't see through it into his thoughts, then or now.

'Are you going to tell Matty you're totally fed up and disillusioned with him, and you don't care if you never see him again?'

He lifted his head to return her look, almost defiantly. 'I *am* bloody well fed up with him. He's done everything he could to make sure of that.'

'So you don't love him or care about him or what happens to him, is that right?'

He was bristling now. 'Don't be absurd. He's my son. Of course I care about him.'

'He thinks you don't.'

'Then he's a fool.'

'He may be a fool, but he's not a mind reader. How is he supposed to know you love him, if you never do anything but tell him he's an idiot and you're fed up with him? That just makes him more determined to show you what an idiot he can be when he's really trying.'

'That's exactly what he's like,' her father agreed, perversely triumphant. 'He has the brains to do anything he wants, but he devotes himself to making a mess of his life just to annoy me. He's always been bloody-minded.'

'He can't help it, he's your son.' Olivia perched herself on the table top, moved the whisky glass aside, laid her hand on his. This time he didn't pull away. 'Daddy, Daddy, you really will drive him away if you carry on like this. Do you want to lose your son the way you lost your daughter?'

Indeed she is my sister;
She is the daughter of my father, but not the daughter of my mother;
and she became my wife.

'What did you say to Ross?' Georgie demanded, as soon as she had shut the bedroom door to ensure privacy. 'He didn't say boo to Matt all evening. He was even being nice to him. Matt couldn't work it out. He'd been expecting to be killed.'

'Hoping to be killed, I think,' Olivia amended.

'Maybe it's better to be murdered than to freeze or starve. I mean, at least someone has to go to some trouble to murder you. And I'm so glad you changed your mind about inviting Matt to come and live in Toronto for a while. He needs a chance to get his head together, and it's hard for him to do that with Ross and Althea leaning on him all the time.'

'He can have Tom and me to lean on him for a change,' Olivia agreed. 'Maybe we'll push in more responsive places. I've already told him, if I catch him taking anything stronger than aspirin I'll send him back home. But he can't go anywhere till he's settled this criminal charge, and if he gets a record they might not want to let him into Canada. For that matter, if Tom gets to hear about it, he might not want to let Matty into our house. He'll probably worry about Matty corrupting Alex or some such thing.'

'Alex is incorruptible. Anyone who devotes his life to hockey and spends his holidays paddling around the Yukon has got to have a soul made of steel. On the contrary, I should think a couple of months backpacking in the Rockies with Alex and his pals would make a wholesome kind of guy out of the Marquis de Sade.'

Hearing Georgie talk so cheerfully and truthfully about Alex made Olivia suddenly homesick for her son. She had not seen him since July, when he went out West and she went up North. Her longing was for something more than Alex, for her life as it had been as recently as June, with Alex and Georgie at home and no man but Tom in her head. Or anywhere else in her.

'Are you sure you won't come home with me?'

'No, Mama, I explained all that. I can stay here, but Luke can't stay there.'

Olivia sat down on the bed and put her hands up to her cheeks. This was her last chance to put everything right, to tell Georgie the truth about her situation. She had ducked it until now, but it was now or never. She wasn't going to put something like that into a letter.

'Georgie, listen to me. You can't go and live with Luke. You can't have his baby. It's worse than you think. He's . . .'

Her courage failed her at the crunch.

Georgie finished the sentence for her. 'He's my brother. I know.'

For a moment Olivia thought she had said, He's your brother, and she opened her mouth to make the crucial correction. Then she shut it again. 'What did you say?'

'I said he's my brother,' Georgie repeated patiently, sitting down beside her mother. 'I figured it out for myself eventually. But I wasn't really sure of it until last night, when you were so funny about those beautiful clothes that Nick had bought for you.

'I'd already worked out that it couldn't have been anything really bad, like a rape or a one-night stand, because Ross said you'd really wanted me. And if it was some other boy like Charlie, why not say so? I thought maybe it was somebody unacceptable to your parents, an older man, a married man . . . well, yeah, all that and more, wasn't it? I should have cottoned on to it long ago. The way you talked about him, the way he looks at you – '

'What do you mean, the way he looks at me?' Olivia interrupted sharply. 'He always looks at women like that.'

'No, he doesn't. I know what you mean, but he doesn't look at you like that.' Georgie gazed at her hands, folded in her lap. 'He's not sizing you up, he knows what size you are. He wants you to fit him, and he knows you don't.'

After a moment she added, 'I heard him call you something, yesterday. Some kind of pet name.' A curiously painful pause. 'Does he call you *kitten*?'

Olivia jumped up. She began to behave like an animated imitation of her father that afternoon. She went pale; she could see herself in the mirror looking like a ghost. She wiped her pale damp face with her hands, and when she held her hands up in front of her they were shaking. Only the whisky bottle was downstairs, and Georgie didn't ask if she was all right. Georgie just watched her.

'Never mind his penchant for pet names, for heaven's sake. How can you sit there like that? Doesn't it bother you, knowing Luke is your brother?'

'I know it should, but it doesn't. Believe it or not. And I don't think that's because I'm morally depraved. If I think about Alex, for instance, the idea of living with him and having his baby is absolutely revolting. That's because I've grown up with him, and had a chance to develop all the appropriate sisterly feelings towards him. But Luke was a stranger till this summer. And I fell in love with him as soon as I saw him, before I even knew he was Emma's son. It's no good your telling me now that he's my brother, same as Alex, and expecting me to change all my feelings for him into the ones I have for Alex, and telling me I'm sinful and wicked, because I can't wave a magic wand to make myself feel the way you think I ought to. What does *sinful and wicked* mean, anyway, if nobody believes in God any more?

'And it's not even a biological sin. He's like a second cousin on my mother's side and a first cousin on my father's side. That's about standard for any royal marriage, isn't it? So why can't we just live the way we want to? We're not hurting anyone.

'It's your fault anyway,' she added accusingly. 'If you hadn't taken me away like that, I'd have grown up with Luke, just like I grew up with Alex, and I'd have felt properly sisterly about him and none of this would have happened.'

'But Georgie, it's a crime. You could both go to prison.'

'Yeah, well, if it's such a revolting thing, how come it's not a crime in Scotland? Nothing that happens on the wrong side of the blanket is considered incest in Edinburgh. A man can screw his own daughter, as long as he isn't married to her mother. They have

389

different ideas of what's disgusting up there. And in France,' Georgie went on relentlessly, 'nothing is legally incestuous. Luke and I can go to Paris and do what we please.'

And never come back, was the unspoken part of the sentence. It wasn't yet a threat, but it would be, if Olivia persisted in her objection. She could either accept Luke and the baby, or take the risk of losing Georgie altogether, and her grandchild as well. In that light, the nature of her dilemma was clearer. She wasn't being asked to condone an incestuous relationship. She was being asked if she loved her daughter, unconditionally.

Georgie was still watching her, still wary. 'What are you going to do, turn me in? You're the only one who knows. You and . . . and Nick.' Her hands twisted together. 'Actually, that bothered me more than – than Luke.

'I really had a hard time coping with . . . with the idea of you and Nick. And him being my f-father.' She was trembling now, with some internal chill. 'The thing is, Mama, I re-remembered some-thing. I remembered what h-happened.'

'What do you mean, what happened?'

'Why you took me away.'

Olivia froze. 'You remembered?'

'Yeah. It all came back to me this summer. Something . . .' Georgie hesitated. 'Something happened that made me remember it all.'

'But how could you know? You didn't understand at the time. You kept asking . . .'

'Asking for Nick. Yeah, I know. And Matty. I really missed him. I missed everybody: Grandma, Grandpa, Althea, even Luke. I remem-bered missing them. I remembered everything so vividly it hurt.' It was Georgie's turn to jump up and walk around, under the pressure of deep emotion. 'I knew you'd taken me away because of what had happened with Nick. I thought I must be really wicked if you wouldn't let me see my family any more. That it must be a really bad thing to feel like that, to do anything like that. And I guess I didn't really shake that off until this summer, when I remembered what had happened, and could look at it in a different light.'

Olivia knew an accusation when she heard one. 'What should I have done? Let him abuse you?'

'I think – well, I don't know what I think. I don't approve of what he did, but it didn't, you know, scar me for life. Mama, I was really shocked when I first remembered. But now I think that's only because I had it in my head so firmly that it was wrong, that he must have done wrong to me. We've all been conditioned to think that, I guess. I mean, child abuse is a very emotive term, and the sort of emotions . . . well, abuse says it all, doesn't it? But that isn't how I felt at the time.'

'How did you feel?'

'Well, I guess I was in love with him. Can a three-year-old fall in love? Even very little children get crushes on other people, don't they? I think that sort of infatuation works at any age. And everybody knows that even babies enjoy masturbation.' Georgie stopped suddenly and blushed.

Olivia felt like her father again: her father being told that gross indecency, even of the homosexual variety, was not a sin that necessarily deserved hell-fire. 'But it's not right for adults to do that sort of thing to children. A child isn't in a position to refuse.'

'Well, of course it's not right. But I don't suppose it's the worst thing he's ever done, and it certainly wasn't the worst thing that's ever happened to me. It might have been, if he'd done – s-something different.' Georgie was shaking again. 'Or m-made me do it when I didn't want to. W-what it was like, was more like something between two kids.'

Maybe I've grown up since then. Olivia could only hope so. He had learned two new words, at any rate.

'He was good at hugging and kissing. I really liked that. Grandpa was hopeless at that sort of thing, but Nick didn't mind. Gosh, I loved him.' Georgie gave a small strangled sound of laughter. 'I w-wished so hard that he could be my daddy.'

The next moment her fragile laughter had turned into tears. Olivia headed for her with a homing instinct and put her arms around her daughter. Georgie clung to her like a drowning kitten.

'Oh, Georgie, I'm sorry. I didn't know. I didn't know what to do.'

'It's not that.' Between her sobs Georgie managed to get out a few comprehensible words. 'He told me to get – get rid of it.'

'Who did? Luke?'

'Nick.'

So Nick really had spoken to Georgie. Olivia hadn't been terribly confident about that. 'But that's more or less what I told you.'

'But you didn't put it like that. And you're not . . .' She couldn't go on.

Whatever Olivia wasn't, she was definitely her daughter's mother. She sat Georgie down on the bed and provided tissues. 'Georgie, why do you want this baby so much?'

'I just do. And Luke does too. I can't just . . . get rid of it.'

The words Georgie had quoted – *get rid of it* – revived memories in Olivia, at least as painful as Georgie's remembrances. So painful that they even made her think heretical thoughts. Maybe it really would be better for Georgie to have her brother's baby, rather than suffer the loss of it.

Eventually Georgie was composed enough to hug her mother in affection rather than desperation. 'Never mind, Mama,' she said, not quite without tears. 'It doesn't matter now. You don't know, but it doesn't matter. And I'm sorry I said all those horrible things to you when I was in hospital.'

Olivia wasn't sure what it was she didn't know, and Georgie obviously wasn't going to tell her. So Olivia did the only thing she could do: she hugged her daughter back. The girl she had given up everything for. A beautiful, generous, loving girl. How could she tell what might have happened to Georgie if they had stayed? Even now she wasn't sure how far she would have trusted Nick. At least, as it was, she had seen her daughter grow up safely and happily.

She took a deep breath. 'Well, now you know what you were so anxious to know. About who your father is.'

Georgie drew back and looked at her mother in a thoughtful way, as if the thoughts were new to her. 'Yeah, I do,' she said, slowly, significantly. 'Tom is my father, and don't you forget it.'

40

Beloved, be not ignorant of this one thing,
that the Lord is not willing that any should perish,
but that all should come to repentance.

Before vanishing through the infernal gate of Passport Control, Olivia remembered to turn and wave to those still in the land of the living: her father, her daughter, her brother.

She waved to her father to make it different from the last time she had gone this way, without his consent and almost for ever. She waved to Georgie because Georgie was waving to her. She waved to Matthew because he was there. Her father and Matthew were not waving, at least not so that you'd notice. They were not very good at saying goodbye, the men in her family.

She wasn't much good at it either, she realized when she had got to the other side of the anti-bomb bureaucracy. Was she going home or leaving home? Or only repeating the flight she had made last time?

When she came back again the danger would be over. Nick would have moved to some tropical tax haven, and London would be free of temptation for her. In a few hours she would be safe, with Satan behind her. In all probability she would have no occasion ever to see him again.

That knowledge depressed her. This improper sadness itself made her angry. For eighteen years she had buried, squashed, smothered, suppressed in one or another ruthless way, all her feelings about Nick and her loss of him. Now she had it all to do again, ten times worse. Now he was free, and she was not. The danger and revulsion that had driven her abroad were now old and irrelevant. Georgie had apparently forgiven him; why not Olivia?

But now, too, she had other reasons for leaving him in limbo. New reasons, new names: not her mother and father and Georgie, but Georgie, Alex and Tom.

Was that all that was keeping her from Nick, a reluctance to cause distress to her children and grief to Tom? Not moral fibre but emotional squeamishness? She wasn't a damaged and desperate adolescent now but a woman at least nominally mature, in charge of her own destiny. She had had thirty-seven years to work out a way to tell right from wrong, but when it came to a crisis she had less moral confidence than the wolves she watched. Georgie and Luke, Matthew and drugs, Nick and absolutely everything: she had lost every moral battle, every one of her arguments countered.

Which suggested that logic and rationality were not the best basis for morality.

Only it was all she had, all anyone had left. You couldn't make yourself believe what you didn't believe. In an agnostic, atomized society, everyone had to make it up as they went along. And they all seemed to come to the same unsatisfactory conclusion, the moral mantra of the modern West: you can do what you like, as long as no one gets hurt.

Yet somehow people did get hurt, all the time. Hurt by other people who believed they had done nothing wrong. Who believed they had a perfect right to do whatever it was they had done.

She moved across the vast departure lounge with heavy dragging dreamlike steps. She found an island of unoccupied seats and sat down to wait until her flight and gate number appeared on the screen. She told herself she would be glad to get back to real life again. Her teaching, Tom and Alex, comforting routines. Even sleeping in her own bed.

Thinking of bed put her in mind of other things, nothing to do with Toronto or Tom. She derailed that train of thought and made herself concentrate on less subversive subjects. Logic and rationality couldn't even order her actions, let alone the thoughts in her head.

Olivia was roused from her reverie by the smell of a cigarette.

393

'This is a no-smoking area,' she said sharply, even before she had looked up to locate the offender.

A tall blond man in jeans and leather jacket was the only person near her. He was turned half away from her, still in the guilty act of lighting up. She must have caught the very first whiff of tobacco.

He snapped the lighter shut and sat down unrepentant in the seat next to hers.

For the briefest moment she thought she must have fallen asleep, she was dreaming this. Dreaming him. 'Nick, what on earth are you doing here?'

'Flying to New York.' She must have looked less than delighted, because he added drily, 'That's all right with you, is it?'

'You can go where you like, I don't care. I'm surprised you hung about so long in London. The last time you went to New York, you told Georgie you were going for good.'

'Nothing to keep me in London now, is there?'

He drew on the forbidden cigarette and stared moodily at his outstretched feet. That wasn't like Nick at all. If something displeased him, he never hesitated to make his displeasure clear. His usual range of emotions did not include anything along the lines of this brooding discontent.

'Are you going to live in New York?'

'Christ, no.'

'Where, then?'

'Don't know. Haven't decided. I'm thinking of giving up this whole fucking fashion circus.'

That shocked her, for some reason. 'Why?'

'I'm bored stiff, for one thing. And it's a load of crap anyway. An ego-trip for the queers in the business, and a big bloody con for all the mugs out there.'

'You've only just noticed this?'

His face lightened up enough to allow a semi-smile. 'I have an ego same as the rest of them, don't I? And we've all got a living to make. But I've made enough now to keep me in champagne till I'm too old to drink it.'

'You mean you're going to retire?'

'I'll retire when I'm too old to drink champagne. Speaking of drinking, why don't we go and do some of that while we're waiting?'

Ten minutes later Olivia was half-way through a sample of the house red at Heathrow. It seemed decadent, at eleven thirty in the morning. 'They say you shouldn't drink when you're flying, because the altitude makes it go to your head.'

'You don't need to worry about that, kitten. I won't be around to take advantage of the state of your head. There's your flight coming up now.' He indicated the bank of screens over the bar behind her.

Olivia craned her neck to see for herself. 'How do you know what flight I'm on?'

'You told me yourself, didn't you. When you rang up about Althea's haircut.'

'Did you fix it up for her?'

'I'll get someone to take care of that when I get to New York.'

'Why didn't you tell me last night that you'd be here this morning?'

'I'm not a fortune-teller, baby.'

Olivia had to decipher that. He meant that when she had spoken to him at seven last night he hadn't been intending to leave today. Something had come up in a hurry, she supposed. 'I didn't know there were any emergencies in your line of work.'

'I guess they crop up all the time, but they're not my problem.'

She persisted, still puzzled. 'So why are you here?'

He was watching her, openly amused. 'Damned if I know. It just came over me all of a sudden, this urge to fly to New York.'

The brick wall became transparent; Olivia understood at last. This was no coincidence at all. She changed the subject immediately to hide her confusion. 'What will you do if you're giving up photography?'

'I didn't say I was giving it up. There are plenty of things to point a camera at, without involving anorexic tarts with big mouths and no brains, or greasy limp-wristed wops and frogs.'

'What sort of thing did you have in mind?'

He lit another cigarette, his third since she had encountered him. He blew the smoke aside and rolled the virgin ashes off against the edge of the ashtray. 'Well, I was thinking about wildlife.'

'New York is the place for that, surely?'

'No, I'm serious. There's a big market for material about endangered species. Especially if they're sexy.'

'Sexy wildlife? What are you talking about?'

'Jesus, Lia, you've been hanging around with those wolves too long. I don't mean, you know . . .' He made a graphically obscene gesture involving both hands to explain exactly what he didn't mean. 'Small and cutesy is okay, but big, beautiful, and romantic is even better.'

She stared at him. He was watching her, smoking patiently, waiting for her brain, befogged by his presence, to start working. Which it eventually did. 'Timber wolves, for instance.'

'Brilliant, baby, absolutely brilliant,' he congratulated her ironically. 'I was thinking maybe tigers, but they're just a touch flash and obvious. And partial to eating people. But wolves are perfect. Can you introduce me to a few?'

Olivia was still staring. 'You're not serious.'

'Sure I am. Why not? Your furry friends could use some favourable publicity to counter the likes of Little Red Riding Hood.'

'They certainly could. But you can't just book them into your studio for Wednesday morning and start ordering them about. You'd have to go where they are, and work to their whims and convenience. It might take months to get what you want, and there's no handy five-star hotel to go back to in the evening. What am I saying, evening? You'd have to work nights. The wolves do.'

Nick leaned his chin on his hand, the hand with the cigarette. 'I can cope with all that if I grit my teeth and really try, kitten. Now tell me about the fucking mosquitoes and the forty below.'

'Those too, but not both at once, thank God. Nick, is this your idea of humour, this idiotic proposal? Because if it is, I'm not amused.'

'I can see that, baby. But I'm dead serious. Why not? I haven't got a wife now to keep in the accustomed style, and my kid can stand on his own two big feet. I'm bored out of my skull with what I've been doing for thirty years. Your wolves have got to have more brains and manners than the slags I'm shooting now. So what's the problem?'

Olivia tried to work out exactly what the problem was. She tried to envisage Nick hiking through the taiga, paddling a canoe, waiting patient hours at an observation post, ignoring an invasive army of blackflies. Nick sharing the tiny cabin with her and Booboo . . .

At that point in her hypothetical vision she paused. The idea of sharing her bed with Nick instead of Booboo (probably as well as rather than instead of, since Boo was jealous of his privileges) had its obvious attractions.

And drawbacks. The prospect was not of the tropical retreat that Nick had previously proposed to her, not even of the sanitized suburban existence she led with Tom in Toronto, but of primitive grot and primeval squalor. Left to herself, as she always had been up till now, she had opted for not so much light housekeeping as no housekeeping. She could be, and was, as sluttish as she liked, with no one but Booboo to criticize. Boo had not a critical bone in his canine body when it came to standards of hygiene. But the thought of Nick seeing her in such circumstances gave her a panic attack on the spot.

'You wouldn't want to put up with the way I have to live. It's unbelievably primitive, like living in a teepee. You'd hate it. And you'd be bored.'

'Lia, I'm not signing up for a stretch in the Navy. If I don't like it I can leave. Okay?'

It was a question that demanded an answer. He wasn't going to let her evade any longer. Incredible as it seemed to her, he really was serious.

She couldn't say she didn't want him around. He wouldn't believe that, and anyway it wasn't true. She did want him. She had just been struggling with her grief over the loss of him, dreading how she would cope with it, or fail to cope. The thought of spending next summer with him consoled her magically.

She stared at her wedding ring. 'I won't be going up North again until next summer.'

Maybe, by that time, she would have stuffed the unwanted genie back into his lamp. Maybe by then Nick would have forgotten, or changed his mind. Maybe Tom would have browbeaten her into giving up the wolves.

'Okay, next summer.' He glanced at his watch, rose and gathered up his paraphernalia. 'I've got to go or I'll miss the fucking flight.'

Olivia stood up too, collecting her handbag and flight bag. 'I should go too. The screen says they're boarding now.'

'So long, sweetheart.' With his free arm Nick drew her to him, a brief unerotic embrace. 'I'll see you next summer, all right? Christ, you'll be a gran by then.'

'You too. Grandfather, I mean.' Olivia had a free arm too. She put it around his middle. Then she dropped her bags and embraced him with both arms.

He ran his hand into her hair, pulled her head down on to his shoulder. She took a deep breath. The familiar smoky smell of him, mingled with the tang of his leather jacket, went down to her lungs and up to her brain. Smell is the most evocative of the senses, as the wolves would have told her and she knew for herself. The smell of Nick evoked old pain and recent pleasure in such strength it was like a physical blow. She closed her eyes and buried her face against his neck.

'Sorry, kitten.' His voice was rough and smoky too. 'I guess I'm not much of a lover.'

She understood him. He didn't mean a lover in the sexual sense, but a lover as in one who loves. Not much good at loving.

'I've got to go,' she said, not moving, not wanting to move. 'So have you.'

'It wouldn't be the end of the world if we stayed right here.'

'Yes, it would.' Olivia lowered her arms and drew back.

He let her go.

To distract herself she dropped to her knees and rooted about in her flight bag for some unspecified but vital object. Out of the corner of her eye she watched his denim legs walking away from her. Other legs, strangers' legs, intervened. When the interlopers had gone by, Nick was gone too, legs and all.

At that point she discovered she really did need something from her bag. She found it almost at once. One of Tom's big handkerchiefs.